Born in Lancashire and educated in Yorkshire, Alexandra Connor has had a rich variety of careers, including photographic model, cinema manager and PA to a world famous heart surgeon, but it is as a novelist that she has found her real forte. As well as writing over twenty acclaimed sagas she has also written thrillers and non-fiction art books. Alexandra is a highly accomplished painter and has presented programmes on television and BBC radio. She is also a Fellow of the Royal Society of Arts.

The Jeweller's Niece

ALEXANDRA CONNOR

headline

First published in 2009
by HEADLINE PUBLISHING GROUP

First published in paperback in 2010
by HEADLINE PUBLISHING GROUP

3

Cataloguing in Publication Data is available from the British Library

ISBN 978 0 7553 4775 9

Typeset in Sabon by Avon DataSet Ltd,
Bidford-on-Avon, Warwickshire

Printed in the UK by CPI Antony Rowe, Chippenham, Wiltshire

Headline's policy is to use papers that are natural, renewable and
recyclable products and made from wood grown in sustainable forests.
The logging and manufacturing processes are expected to conform to
the environmental regulations of the country of origin.

HEADLINE PUBLISHING GROUP
An Hachette UK Company
338 Euston Road
London NW1 3BH

www.headline.co.uk
www.hachette.co.uk

The
Jeweller's Niece

PROLOGUE

I was only a girl then, and yet I had already learned discretion. I could cover my tracks well, throw suspicion off myself, make sure that there was never the slightest hint that could give me away. Because I had a terrible secret.

My father's half-brother, David Hawksworth, had taken me under his roof after my father begged him to look after me. I don't know how hard it was for my father, Frederick Coles, to ask the favour, I just know that there was no one else who could take care of me. And so my uncle took me in. He was a rigid man. A dour-faced widower of about fifty, his wife not long dead, his only son estranged and living abroad. Not that he told me that. Our neighbours did.

The Palmers were on one side of my uncle's jewellery shop, their newsagent's a cramped haven of exotic tobacco smells and newsprint, because often the evening papers arrived wet from the Burnley rain. Only the top couple of copies, but the smell of ink lingered, even after I left the warmth of the tobacconist's for the narrow gloom of David

1

Hawksworth, Jeweller, Burnley. People didn't come to my uncle's shop for his company, but for his quality jewellery and his skill, which was impressive – I knew that, even as a girl. He could mend anything. Fine jewellery, ring mounts, worn chains, even clocks, which he had a feeling for. Tenderness, which he never showed to a living thing, he showed to timepieces, working until late, hunched over his bench in the top room, under the eaves.

I would watch him then, knowing he didn't know I was there, and try to find some resemblance between him and my father. But the half-brothers seemed total opposites to me, with no obvious sharing of blood. Of course I knew from the first day I was sent to the jeweller's shop – on the day my father was arrested – that I must never mention him. The shame of having a thief in the family was corrosive, and it burned into my uncle's soul like acid. I could imagine only too easily how the local paper in the Palmers' shop next door would have taunted him when he had gone in for his smokes. Because for a while, my father's face had been on the front page.

Frederick Coles, widower, found guilty of theft. Sentencing tomorrow.

Found guilty. Of theft . . . From the day my father was sentenced, he ceased to exist for David Hawksworth. Looking back, I can see how irksome it must have been for him to have me under his roof, a constant reminder of the scandal. And besides,

2

I resembled my father very much. But David Hawksworth was an honourable man. And with his chilling, moral character he couldn't refuse me a home. But he could withhold affection. He could act as though my father was dead. He could instil guilt. And he could – and often did – remind me who I was. Never in words. But as the first months of my father's incarceration passed, there was a certain look my uncle gave me that told me that while he might try to forget Frederick Coles, might reject my father's insistence on his innocence, might pray that the scandal had been forgotten, he knew it never would be.

Because I was the living reminder of my father. The scandal breathed as I did. As Frederick Coles did, behind the walls of the prison that held him. The prison my uncle tried so hard to forget.

The prison I visited. Oh yes, even though I knew there would be terrible repercussions if my uncle discovered what he would see as my betrayal, I passed through those grim gates weekly. I heard the hostile sounds inside, felt the cold as I entered, and my stomach always turned over with fear. Because it was a hellish place, with its smells of urine, disinfectant, sweat and damp. Always damp. But hateful as it was, it became, over the years, familiar to me . . . And so I lived between the mundane, closed world of the Hawksworth jewellery shop, and the secret visits to the echoing jail. I left the normal streets behind as I waited with the other visitors outside. In all weathers. Waited for those short visits.

For the hurried exchange of news. For the weekly reassurance that Frederick Coles – whom everyone else wanted to forget – was still there.

You see, to me, my father was never dead.

PART ONE

For there are sometimes other voices
Other hearts that tie our own.
And somewhere there are destinations,
Other places, other homes.

Anon.

ONE

Burnley, 1919

'Chilly bastard, that,' Mrs Palmer said dismissively, throwing the stack of *Burnley Gazette*s on to the counter and slicing the holding string with a pen-knife. Turning to her husband, she waved the knife in his direction. 'That David Hawksworth isn't the right kind of man to bring up a girl on his own.'

'He's not that bad. He had a son of his own, after all,' Mr Palmer replied, taking the knife out of his wife's hand and clicking it closed. Florence was a loving partner, but – when provoked – she had a temper. Indeed, before he married her, there had been some talk of her breaking the nose of her intended. Not that he remained intended after that. 'I can't imagine it can be easy for him.'

'*Easy for him!*' Florence snapped back. 'Who cares about *him*, the miserable old sod? It's his niece I worry about. Pretty girl too, and quiet, so quiet. Not that she'd be encouraged to be anything else in that place.' She paused, regarding her husband thoughtfully. Harold wasn't much to look at, but their sex life was lively. 'I thought she could come over to the shop. You know, get out of that place more.'

'Best not to get on the wrong side of David Hawksworth. We've rubbed along nicely enough for years. He's not the sort of man to take kindly to someone poking their nose into his business,' Harold replied, turning to the evening papers and setting them out.

Suddenly he could feel his wife's hot breath as she blew on his neck. 'Ah, come on, Harry luv, don't go all masterful on me. I weren't thinking of adopting the girl, I just think it's important that she knows she has a bolthole.'

'You think he's mistreating her?' Harold asked, his expression anxious.

'Nah, nothing like that! Although he were hard enough on his own son.'

'Adam Hawksworth was easily led. I think his father tried to toughen him up.'

'Oh, he toughened him up all right,' Florence replied scornfully. 'Toughened him up all the way to New Zealand.'

Sighing, she began to sort the papers with her husband. At any moment the paperboy would arrive and start the long delivery trek around the inner town circle of Burnley, on an old bike he had inherited from his brother, who the Palmers had had to let go when it turned out he had thrown one evening's worth of papers into the mill-house stream. When they asked him why, he shrugged and said he was bored. Years – and several run-ins with the police – later, he ended up at the prison. *Working there.* Like

8

many said, who would have thought it? *Inside* a cell, maybe. But as a trainee warden – who would have thought it?

'We wouldn't be interfering,' Florence went on, returning to her previous thoughts. 'I just think it would be the right thing to do. And I'd like to have company sometimes. I've been watching her for a while. A girl like Emma would be nice to have around.'

Harold studied his wife's upturned face. 'I don't suppose there's many round these parts who'll want to know her, because of her father. What was the sentence? Eleven years . . . She'll be in her mid-twenties when he comes out.'

'What Frederick Coles did was down to him,' Florence replied curtly. 'You can't blame his daughter for his thieving.'

'Maybe not, but people will. I dare say Emma's getting a hard ride at school.'

Florence shook her head. 'Damn my memory! I meant to tell you and forgot. Apparently she's not at school any more. David Hawksworth might have given the girl a roof over her head, but not for nothing. She's to earn her keep from now on. Working in the jeweller's shop and keeping house.' She paused. '*Now* d'you see why I want her to spend some time over here?'

I will make the best of it. I will make the best of it . . . Endlessly Emma repeated the mantra to herself. *I will make the best of it . . .* But however many times

9

she said it, when she looked around her she always felt a crippling dread. Her uncle had given her his son's old room, and although it was reasonably sized, it was full of boy's paraphernalia. Scuffed football boots hung on a hook on the back of the door, rows of cheap books and comics were stacked under the bed. On the chipped paint of the windowsill, a hand-made sailing boat leaned rakishly against the dusty glass. Stubs of library tickets were still pushed into the edges of a chipped mirror, and a yellowing photograph of a dark-haired boy stared out morosely above the jug and bowl. Someone – probably the boy himself – had drawn a cynical halo over his head. The reminders of the lost son seemed to be everywhere. But oddly there was nothing of David Hawksworth's dead wife. Emma would have to ask her father about that.

She stopped short, taking in a breath. She did that a lot now, always shaken by the realisation that her beloved father was in jail. For eleven years. Eleven years without seeing the sun or being able to walk alone in the park. Eleven years without catching a tram, or buying a smoke. Eleven years locked in with men who weren't like him at all. The two of them had lived together since Emma's mother had died, eleven years earlier. Since poor, confused Catherine had walked out late one night and hadn't come back. They'd found her two days later, after everyone had been searching for her. Found her hanged at the back of the deserted pet shop in Lloyd Street.

The balance of her mind had been disturbed, they said . . . At four years old, Emma had been too young to understand fully, but all her life she had watched her father's kindness and his valiant attempts to lift her mother's depression, asking Frederick repeatedly what was wrong. Why was her mother like this? Later she began to doubt herself, even asking if it was *her* fault. If she had done something wrong. At such times her father would hold her tightly and tell her that she wasn't to blame. That her mother was poorly, that they had to take care of her . . . Which they did. But what hurt Emma the most was her mother's withdrawal from her family. That slow slipping away until she became little more than a spectre, remote, often mute, and yet given to bouts of intense and unexpected affection. After which she withdrew again. Until her withdrawals were constant and she took the lonely walk to Lloyd Street . . .

Emma shuddered at the memory, but in truth, her mother had left her long before she actually died. Afterwards it had been just her and her father. And after their initial, intense grief, it had been a happy time, Frederick freed from the crippling responsibility of a sick wife and Emma allowed to be a child again. She thought of that time with longing. Eleven years living alone with her father . . . Suddenly Emma wondered about that. If there was some kind of message in the timing. Eleven years with her father. And now there would be eleven years without him.

Her eyes fell on the water jug and she rinsed her hands, feeling out of place and wondering how she was going to spend one decade and one year with a stranger.

'Emma!' a voice shouted from below. 'Can you come down, please?'

The courtesy was there, but the kindness was not. No teasing in the voice, none of the lighter tone her father would have used. Or the intensity. Especially when he had protested his innocence. Over and over again, begging her to believe. *I didn't do it, Emma, believe me, I'm not a thief. I didn't do it* ... His words came back to her in that instant, along with the pleading in his voice. *I didn't do it* ... But that wasn't enough, was it? she thought, suddenly angry. If he *had* been innocent, why hadn't he made everyone see that? Why had they still put him away? And sent her here? If her father had convinced them, they would still be together, and she wouldn't be here, locked up with her hated uncle, as incarcerated as her father.

'Emma!'

Her rage subsided in that instant. Anger was no good to her. She had to suppress her feelings, manage her own life. She had to be brave and calm – just as her father was being. Because otherwise she wouldn't be able to serve her sentence either.

Moving downstairs, Emma walked from the narrow back kitchen into the dim jeweller's shop. Wedged between Palmer's newsagent's and Jack Rimmer's ironmonger's on Holland Street, Hawkworth's jeweller's glowered like a maiden aunt between two nubile nieces. The walls ticked and chimed with the dozens of clocks hanging there, the counter facing the door blocking any further movement forwards. On the door itself, heavy iron bars gridded the glass, and at night the front windows were barred also. From the outside, a passer-by might try to look in, but only a flicker of light from a half-hidden gem or the quiet chime of a clock would be apparent.

'Did you call me, Uncle?'

He turned, tall in an old-fashioned dark suit and winged collar. 'I was thinking,' he began, his Lancashire accent more pronounced than Frederick's. 'I should teach you how to look after the shop. I've been doing it since my wife died.'

'I'm sorry.'

'What?'

'About your wife dying,' Emma said, trying to keep her voice steady. 'You must miss her.'

'She was a quiet woman,' David replied, implying that he counted such reticence as a virtue, something he would like to see in his niece. 'It was hard that the influenza killed her. But that's the way life is – you have to take what blows are dealt you.'

Emma looked down, uncertain of what to say.

Clearing his throat, David continued.

'You have to clean the shop up, Emma, it'll help you earn your keep. And be careful when you dust the counter tops. They're glass.' He paused, cleared his throat again. 'Glass is expensive. No leaning too heavily on it, and no putting your hands inside the cabinets. You don't touch the clocks either.'

'All right, Uncle.'

'You're dainty enough, you should do all right,' he said curtly.

'I'll do my best.'

He paused, staring at his niece, suddenly vacant of words. Every time he looked at her, he could see Frederick. The same wide grey eyes, the same long nose, high cheekbones and jawline. Even a hint of a cleft in her chin – like her father.

David glanced away from the reminder of his half-brother, the boy he had once liked. Until David's attitude shifted when he realised that Frederick Coles outclassed him. Better-looking, wittier, a born sportsman, even tipped by some to get a try-out for Burnley Football Club. And as his younger brother became popular, David retreated into a cool snobbery. Having never been outgoing, his shyness seemed awkward next to Frederick's easy charm. A strong physique, inherited from his father's side, and his good looks marked Frederick out from childhood as someone men would admire and women would want. In another family, David's austere but quiet attractiveness would have been noteworthy – but not when pitted against Frederick's muscular sensuality. In fact, Frederick had inherited not only the physical stature of his father, Ernie Coles, but the confidence of that strength.

David's tall, angular frame was gangly by comparison; his lack of self-esteem making him diffident around girls. Whilst Frederick always had females around him – gathered like greedy birds over a newly tilled field – David settled down young and married Jenny, an insecure version of himself . . .

David coughed. 'Well, you know what to do.'

'Do you want me to tidy up now?'

As Emma asked the question, all the clocks behind her chimed. Some soft, some melodious, one running a little late, its tone impatient. One, two, three, it snapped, David checking it against his own fob watch. His attention diverted, he moved over to the wall clock and reset it. Emma watched him. No one would have thought it to look at this austere man, but he was a hero. Not in the war that had just finished – he had been too old to fight in that skirmish – but an honest-to-God domestic hero. Apparently he had rescued one of the mill workers' children from the Leeds–Liverpool Canal. The boy had wandered away from the safety of the Cameron Mill and scrambled down the bank, falling into the freezing February water. David Hawksworth, who had called to see the owner about his pocket watch (and was keen to get a good customer), noticed the body of the child in the canal and, taking off his shoes, dived in. When he brought the boy out, he was barely alive. At once, a hero was born. Unfortunately, the effect of the cold and the long immersion in the water left the child mentally retarded, and he became known as Daft Davy. It was an affectionate term, his parents grieving less for his handicap than they would have done for his loss, and as time progressed, the adult Davy became a familiar figure in the Burnley streets.

Still watching her uncle, Emma remembered what her father had told her about him. Oddly, David Hawksworth's act of bravery had not made him any more approachable. Remote as a minor god, he had remained intimidating. He had been admired, but had never possessed the common touch. Her father, Emma thought, was the opposite. If it had been Frederick who had saved the child, there would have been banners and bunting in the Burnley streets for weeks afterwards. Not that her father would have played on his heroism; it was just that he looked a natural champion.

'Strange,' David said, to no one in particular, 'that clock usually keeps perfect time . . .'

Emma felt one of her stockings begin to slide down her leg, but didn't dare to pull it up.

'As I say, don't touch the clocks.'

'No, Uncle.'

He turned back to her, wondering when he would get used to having Frederick's daughter around. Or if he ever would.

'If you go into the back, you can tidy the kitchen.'

'Yes, Uncle.'

'Then come back at five thirty and clean up the shop.'

'Yes, Uncle,' Emma repeated, then, realising she had been dismissed, moved into the shaded back room and closed the door.

Sitting down behind the counter, David wondered if he had sounded too hard. But it was difficult for him. He had never had a girl around, only his son. And everyone knew that sons were easier to bring up. Even Adam . . . David sighed, angered by the battering from his own memory. He had thought his life was sorted out, safe. He had grown used to poor Jenny being gone, and even adjusted to his son's estrangement . . . Rubbing his forehead, he felt unusually perturbed. His moral thermometer was letting him down. He was too hot, too dry, too full of fire. Tormented by his past decisions, he remembered Adam. The son he had loved so much.

Had he been too harsh with his own child? But he had only wanted to keep Adam safe. On the right path. Surely that was what a good parent was supposed to do? With reluctance, David thought back. His mother, Netty, had married Morris Hawksworth and been widowed when David was only nine. David's memory turned back the pages, looking through his own personal photograph album. Once he had been the loved child of the respectable Morris Hawksworth, Netty spoiling him. Then Morris had gone. Seemingly disappeared within a welter of tears and a hurried funeral. The loss had been enormous to the young David. Suddenly there was no father, no safety, the rudder of his life gone. In that uneasy time, David lived alone with Netty. Some nights she held on to him, and talked about his father, crying softly. At other times he would hear her weeping as the knocker-upper tapped on the neighbour's window and the rag-and-bone man turned his cart down the end of the street. In those muted, suspended months, David had relished his premier position in his mother's heart. He had known – from overhearing certain snatches of conversation – that they had very little money, and had realised from his mother's intense anxiety that Netty was desperate, unsure of how they would survive. But he had also known – by her every touch and word – that he was her life.

Of course David Hawksworth as a grown man understood what his mother had done next. Being a pretty woman, opportunity came along within twelve months – in the shape of Ernie Coles. A huge man, he had fallen in love with Netty, and treated her well. But David mistrusted him instinctively. From the first there had always been something unnerving about Ernie, something sinister. Some underlying threat of violence. He had worked on the Liverpool docks before coming to Burnley, and had once run a pub. Not at all like the respectable Morris Hawksworth . . . Surprised by his mother's choice, David had soon found himself sharing Netty's affection. Then his stepfather lost his job on the market – for fighting. His own father would never have been dismissed from any job, but Ernie had been a bull of a man, unwilling to take orders from anyone. Timid in his stepfather's company, David had begun to hate him. But worse was to follow. Three years later, Frederick had been born.

The boys had got on well, but when Ernie lost another job, money became tight. Forced to move further afield from Burnley, Ernie had spent the next decade touting for work – *any* kind of work – wherever he could find it. He had delivered coal, washed windows, done flittings, often in the early hours, moving families and their possessions on a cart before the bailiffs came at dawn. He had kept fighting, too, and gradually had got a taste for it, until he realised that he could make a living out of his fists and enjoy his work at the same time. Physically strong, he was someone people came to rely on, sometimes for work others wouldn't take on . . . Netty had never known about this increasingly suspect side of her husband. To her, Ernie was a grafter. And you needed a man who worked when times were hard. God knows how many families had been thrown out into the streets, unable to pay the rent. As for the kids . . . Netty knew of many children who had been sent off to relatives far afield, or put to work in the factories, no one asking their age. Childhood, when times were hard, was short.

Netty admitted that Ernie did have a temper, but he had never raised his hand to her, and in the rough area around Top Street, that was a novelty in itself. Besides, she didn't see that much of him during the week, and if gossip did reach her ears, she dismissed it. People, Netty observed drily, liked to talk. And anyway, Ernie had made a few enemies, people he had stood up to – unlike the milksop men who kowtowed to everyone. But if she was honest, she enjoyed Ernie's reputation for being tough – never realising that in Salford, Hanky Park and Stockport, Ernie Coles was often called upon to provide a bit of real muscle, and was developing an appetite for brutality. If she *had* known, Netty would never have been able to relate the big man who made love to her so tenderly to the threatening figure who called on people late at night. Whilst she lay next to him on Sunday mornings – the boys asleep in the cramped attic room next to theirs – she would never have suspected her man of being hired to lean on late tenants. Not Ernie, not the husband who came home with biscuits for the kids and ribbon for her. And if she *had* known the truth about him? She would have made excuses – because she loved him.

David knew that only too well. His mother would never admit to what he was beginning to realise – that his stepfather was a thug. No one put on the Coles family, because no one dared, and they were protected around the rough area where they lived. And even though David was only his stepson, Ernie's reputation extended to his protection. Growing ever more distrustful and afraid of his stepfather, David avoided Ernie Coles as much as he could, and his suspicions were finally confirmed when he was thirteen.

It had been an overcast day as David had walked towards the corner leading home, then paused to pull up his socks. But before he could move on, he heard his stepfather's name mentioned, and listened to the conversation over the wall.

'I heard Ernie Coles were working for Foster Gunnell,' the first voice had said. When he spoke again, David was amazed to realise that it was the local priest, the one Netty went to for confession. The man with long nose hairs and a heavy footfall. 'Aye, Ernie's running with a hard crew now.'

'He can handle himself. Always could.'

'Aye, but Gunnell . . .'

'Even Gunnell,' the other man had replied dismissively. 'Anyway, you shouldn't speak badly of Ernie. I saw him put money in the vestry box the other day.'

'I never said he were mean,' the old priest retorted.

'You never said he were a believer.'

'Well, it depends *what* he believes in.'

'Not God, and that's a fact.'

Amused, the old priest had chuckled. 'Keeps trouble in check round here, though, and that's no mean feat. I reckon I should be paying him – putting money in *his* vestry box.'

His companion had laughed. 'I don't suppose Ernie Coles will be rolling up for confession any time soon?'

'If he's mixing with Gunnell, no amount of Hail Marys will be enough.'

Unnerved, David had returned to the cramped flat over the butcher's, wincing at the dry smell of the sawdust, which only ever half disguised the overhanging odour of blood. In silence, he climbed up the narrow stairs to the chilly bedroom, silently re-running the conversation over in his head. So it *was* true, he thought, all the rumours about Ernie Coles were true . . . He had thought of his own father then, of how different life would have been with Morris Hawksworth. Respectable. A father he could have been proud of. A man he could have talked to and spent time with . . . In that instant, David realised that his secret ambition would never be fulfilled. He might have dreamed of further education, even of training as a teacher, but it was only too easy to imagine how Ernie would take that news. Or anyone else. How could Ernie Coles's stepson put on airs? Think of following a profession? It was a laughable thought. The teachers and tutors would find out about his stepfather and that would be it. Even if he got as far as being considered, who would take on the hard man's kid?

There and then, the first twinge of bitterness had taken shape in David's head. He had realised how his stepfather – and by extension his family – was seen. And not in the way he wanted. As Morris Hawksworth's son, he would have been respectable. But no more. Now his reputation was directly in line with that of his stepfather. No wonder his family had had an easy ride. No wonder small gifts were left on the Coles' doorstep. No wonder Netty could always find something decent to eat when so many others were struggling. Their home, their food and their security were down to the brute strength of Ernie Coles, and the likes of the notorious Foster Gunnell.

In silence, David had sat staring into space. At the age of thirteen, his first taste of the world's judgement had come from the mouth of a priest – and the words would affect him for life.

TWO

Throwing a pail of dirty water out of his shop front door, Jack Rimmer shook his head and stopped, listening. He could make out the chimes of the church clock and checked his watch, noticing that it was running slow. Bugger it, thought Jack. When he had some money, he would take it next door and get David Hawksworth to have a look at it. It would cost, mind, but the man did a good job . . . Suddenly aware that he was being watched, Jack turned to find Emma standing behind him.

'It's a penny to look.'

'What?'

'A penny to look,' Jack repeated, winking at her, his floppy grey hair a slurry on top of his narrow head. 'I were teasing yer, girl.'

'Oh, I see.'

'Did you want summat?' Jack asked, his large watery eyes peering short-sightedly at the girl.

'My uncle wondered if you . . . if you . . . if you would mind not doing that.'

'Doing what?'

'Throwing water on the pavement.'

Jack put down the bucket and folded his scrawny arms. He'd been throwing water out on to Holland Street every day for the last twenty-one years and no one had complained. So why was Hawksworth suddenly objecting and sending this lass round to do his dirty work?

'Are they wet?' he asked, his tone abrupt.

Emma blinked. 'I don't understand.'

'Yer uncle's shoes. Are they wet?'

'Well, no . . .'

'So if his shoes aren't wet, what's he complaining about?'

'Oh, I see,' she said, smiling faintly. 'My uncle said someone could slip.'

'Oh, aye, there've been dozens of accidents over the years. More than anyone could count. At one time, around Christmas, yer couldn't move for bodies.'

Amused, Emma smiled again. 'What shall I tell him?'

'Tell him I'll stop throwing water on the pavement when he stops his bloody clocks chiming through the night. Every quarter. Every half-hour. Every hour. Chime, chime, chime.' He paused, changing the subject. 'I bet you feel a bit strange.'

'What?' she asked, surprised.

'Living with yer uncle. I mean, yer weren't close before, and he's a solitary type of man. And only your half-uncle. I mean, if it were down to David Hawksworth, he'd have it that he were an only child, with no Frederick in the mix. But he can't get away

24

with it now. Oh no. Yer here and yer Frederick's daughter.' Jack sniffed loudly, picking up the bucket again. 'I were sorry about yer dad. I liked him.' Touched, Emma bit her lip, Jack watching her. 'I'm a one-off, luv, and I speak my mind. I'm not going to ignore yer father's existence, whether he nicked stuff or not—'

'*He didn't!*' Emma replied, her tone vehement. 'My father's innocent.'

'Well, be that as it may,' Jack countered, 'folk round here won't mention it. I mean, the Palmers, they're all right, but she gossips – mouth on her like a bakehouse oven, if you know what I mean. As to the rest around these parts, I know them all. They'll want to pretend all that bother with yer father never happened. Sweep it under the carpet, with all the other unpleasantness . . . but yer can't do that, can yer?'

'No.'

'No,' he agreed, swinging the bucket cheerfully. 'So if it gets right heavy with yer uncle, and he gets on yer bloody nerve ends, pop in and see me. I'm not good company, but the time might come when yer want to talk about yer dad – and I'll listen.'

Hesitating on the corner of Holland Street, Bessie Holmes stared at the forbidding entrance of Hawksworth's jeweller's. On the far side, Palmer's newsagent and tobacconist looked cheerful, the lights making the window inviting, coloured sweets in huge glass jars drawing the children in. And on the near side, Rimmer's hardware store was a beehive of colour: steel buckets tied up on the pavements, coloured brooms and cheap mats hung from strings on the awning, and all manner of spools of wire, thread and string in every hue, loaded and perched one on top of the other in the broad grinning space of the window. Reluctantly Bessie's gaze moved back to the middle shop, the jeweller's, sullen, sulky as a toad.

From inside she could see a light burning, and she cursed herself for not having the courage to approach. She was Emma's best friend, after all, and even if her parents insisted that she never speak to Emma again, Bessie was damned if she was going to obey them. They had been friends for too long, before they started school and afterwards. Whilst Emma's mother was alive, and after she died and Emma lived with her father. Besides, Bessie liked Frederick Coles, and she didn't think he was a thief.

'A disgrace,' her mother had said, only that morning. 'That man brought shame to his family. And as for that poor girl . . . Well, of course it's not Emma's fault, but you can't see her again. You know what people are like, Bessie, you'd be tarred with the same brush. Birds of a feather flock together.'

Peevishly, Bessie wanted to mention her brother Ricky, who had once worked for the Palmers. Ricky, who had thrown the newspapers into the stream; who had climbed on the roof of the theatre and made ape noises; who had stolen the wheels of the policeman's bicycle for a bet. *That* Ricky. Mad Ricky, handsome Ricky, the Ricky who was impulsive and reckless . . . How many people had said that her brother would end badly? But in fact he'd ended up at the jail as a trainee prison officer. In the same jail that housed Frederick Coles.

Bessie knew something else that her mother didn't – Emma visited her father. Ricky had told her that, swearing her to secrecy, because Emma didn't want anyone to know. She was terrified of the news reaching David Hawksworth, who had expressly forbidden her to ever visit the prison. For her own good, of course.

'What are you staring into space for?' her mother had asked suddenly as she sat down next to her daughter at the kitchen table.

'I was thinking.'

'Well, if you were thinking about Emma Coles, you can stop thinking now.' Mrs Holmes had paused, trying to be reasonable. 'I know she was a close friend, luv, but life's not fair and you don't want to make it harder on yourself by being associated with the likes of her. You're respectable, with the future to think of—'

'I work in a cobbler's, Mum,' Bessie had replied dismissively, stirring her bowl of lumpy porridge and wondering how much she could leave. 'My chances aren't exactly glowing.'

Mrs Holmes hadn't liked to agree with her daughter, but Bessie had been right there. She was pretty enough, but cursed with poor eyesight, and glasses that covered her best feature. As to her clothes – it was obvious that Bessie wasn't interested in fashion. She was neat and clean, but always seemed to wear things that were slightly too large, as though she was hiding under them. Mrs Holmes sighed as she stared at her daughter's dark serge dress and unflattering woollen stockings. Bessie was not the kind of lass boys found appealing – too smart, too much like hard work . . . But as Mrs Holmes kept watching her daughter, she consoled herself with the fact that Bessie was a hard-working, responsible girl, not the type to keep secrets. Not the type to worry her parents.

Suddenly Bessie's thoughts came back to the present as she saw the door of the jeweller's open. Tensing, she watched as Emma walked out and began to move down the street. Hurriedly Bessie ran after her, tapping her on the shoulder as she reached the corner.

Emma jumped, startled, then smiled warmly. 'Bessie! I was just thinking about you.'

'My mother will kill me if she knows I'm here, but I had to come and see you,' Bessie replied, slipping her arm through Emma's. At once she noticed the weight loss. Emma had always been slim, but now she seemed almost fragile. The change was worrying, and quick. She had only been living at the jeweller's since Frederick had been sentenced six weeks earlier.

'Are you OK?'

'I'm all right,' Emma said, nodding.

'What's he like to live with?'

'My uncle's . . . not like my father.'

'But he treats you all right?'

Emma paused, glancing at her friend with gratitude. 'He's not mistreating me. He's not friendly, but he's not cruel, just cold. He was backed into taking me in, after all. It wasn't his choice.'

And there it was, Bessie thought – Emma's natural sense of justice. Even though she might be uncomfortable, and resent where she was living, she could see the other side of the equation. See how difficult it was for David Hawksworth.

Bessie doubted that *she* would have taken it so well. 'You have your own room?'

'Of course, at the top of the shop.'

'In the attic?'

'It's nice up there next to my uncle's workshop,' Emma replied. 'If you look out of the window, you can see over the houses all the way to Market Street.'

'What a treat.'

Emma nudged her friend playfully. She was more than pleased to see Bessie after so long and knew what it cost her to disobey her mother. If Marjorie Holmes found out, there would be hell to pay.

'Does he make you work?'

'I cook and clean for him, and tidy up the shop.'

'God, he's got a bloody slave!'

Emma raised her eyebrows. 'Aw, come on, it's not that bad.'

Together they walked down the street, a tram passing and splashing through a puddle, throwing muddy water over the hem of Emma's dress. Annoyed, she stopped to wipe it off, stepping back when another tram came round the corner.

'I've missed you,' Bessie said suddenly. Emma looked up and squeezed her friend's arm.

'Me too,' she said honestly. 'It's so quiet in the shop.'

'Ricky sends his best.'

'Send mine back,' Emma replied, smiling.

She adored Ricky; who didn't? After all, she had known him for most of her life. Had listened to his exploits and seen Mrs Holmes slap him round the back of his handsome head a few times when he'd exasperated her. She had also been influenced by him, on more occasions than she would like to admit. Once, he had persuaded her to break into a deserted shop for fun, and then pretend to be the guy on Bonfire Night, dressing up and sitting in an old pram so that passers-by would give them money – until Emma had got bored after two hours and climbed out of the pram, sending several children running off, screaming.

Ricky was Emma's safety valve. The elder brother she had never had. Her reckless, dashing alter ego. The boy she knew so well, the man she cared for so much. But not as a boyfriend . . .

Walking arm in arm with Emma, Bessie knew her mother wouldn't spot them because she never ventured into this part of town. Thought it was common. Of course Bessie knew that Ricky was in love with Emma. It was obvious. In fact, she would guess that he had fallen in love with her about three years earlier, when Emma had first started to change from a weedy kid into a willowy brunette. And the reason he had thrown the Palmers' papers into the stream was not boredom, but the result of an argument with Emma. It was easy for Bessie to see why Ricky would be in love with Emma: she was fascinating. Striking and feisty, and now adorned with all the attributes of the tragic heroine. Oh, it was true that some boys would shun her, but for an unusual kind of man – like Ricky – she would be irresistible.

'Can we go for a walk?'

Emma frowned. 'I can't . . . but I wanted to talk to you.' She paused, diffident. 'I've been thinking about Dad a lot. And Mum, for some reason.'

'Your mum?'

'Yeah. She would have been thirty-six yesterday,' Emma said, shaking her head sadly. 'It was a waste of a life, wasn't it?'

Bessie nodded. 'But it was no one's fault.'

'I know that. There was nothing I could do. And there was nothing more Dad could do. He was so caring, so patient with her . . . I don't know if I could be that patient if I was married to someone like that.'

'I hope you never are,' Bessie replied, thinking of Ricky and wondering if and how she could effect a romance between her brother and her best friend.

'God,' Emma said suddenly, looking at her watch. 'I have to run an errand for my uncle and he'll expect me back soon.'

'Does he pay you for your work?'

'Why?'

'Because I was wondering, that's why . . .' Bessie went on, automatically dropping her voice, 'if you had enough money. You know, if you need some cash.'

Immediately guarded, Emma reacted cautiously. 'Money for what?'

'To get over to see your father, that's what.' Bessie hurried on, seeing Emma pale. 'Oh, don't worry! No one knows except me, and Ricky's keeping it a secret.'

'Not much of a secret, if he's told you!'

'Ricky tells me everything,' Bessie went on, 'and you know damn well that I can keep quiet.'

Dropping her voice, Emma said, 'I haven't seen Ricky at the prison.'

'No, but he's seen you. And besides, your visits are news over there. What with the court case and everything.'

'My father's innocent.'

'I believe you.'

'No one else does.'

'Well, that's because no one else knows your father well enough to know he's not that type of man.' Bessie was all briskness. 'Now, the same couldn't have been said for your grandfather.'

'It counted heavily against him, didn't it?' Emma said quietly. 'Everyone talking about Ernie Coles.'

'Well, they could hardly resist, could they? Seeing as how he's the local villain . . .'

'And my father was judged on his reputation.'

Pretty much like they are judging you now, Bessie thought, remembering how the papers had been full of lurid details about Ernie Coles. Local hard man who had worked as a bailiff for the notorious Foster

Gunnell, the worst kind of racketeer in Manchester. Then other exposés had followed – Ernie had been running a bookie's in Hanky Park and a pawn shop in Preston, his greed growing with his muscle. When everyone else was trying to recover from the war shortages, he was raking in money from black-market goods, selling on watered booze from cheap imports. And then there was the matter of the attack on Stanley Gruberman. No one could prove that it had been Ernie Coles, but Gruberman had made money during the war from selling armaments – and Ernie had always been a patriot. Loved England, and would tell anyone as much. And flatten anyone who didn't agree with him. When they found Gruberman, he needed forty stitches in his head and treatment for a burst spleen.

Bessie sighed inwardly. How easy for most people to presume that the son of a man like Ernie Coles could be a thief . . .

'I hate all the secrecy and the creeping around,' Emma said suddenly. Bessie turned to her.

'What?'

'All the secrets. Making sure my uncle never finds out about me visiting the prison . . . God, he'd go crazy if he knew.'

'You have to be careful, Emma.'

'I am! But sometimes I think if I just turn round on the tram, he'll be there, sitting behind me. Watching me.' She shivered. 'I feel such a liar, but I have to see my father. I can't just leave him there, forget all about him.'

'You'd never do that.'

'No, I know how much he needs me,' Emma replied. Rain was beginning to fall and she pulled her shawl over her head. 'Can you come again?'

'Do you have to ask?'

'Thanks.'

'What for?'

'For being a friend.'

'Oh,' Bessie replied mischievously, 'I'm only doing it to spite my mother.'

THREE

Proud of his uniform, Ricky Holmes stood in the guards' room, looking out into the prison. Before him stretched two rows of cells – one on the left and one on the right – the narrow corridor between them scrubbed clean. Because it was evening, the prison was quiet, but as Ricky looked up he could see above him the next floor, a replica of the one beneath. And suspended between the two floors was a net. There had been several deaths caused by prisoners jumping off the mezzanine – one of which had apparently been murder – and the authorities had erected the netting to prevent any further incidents.

The senior officer on watch with Ricky, Reg Spencer, had been at the prison for thirty years and knew all the old tales. Of special prisoners, internal murders, child killers and rapes. During the first week Ricky had been with Reg, he had been given a sordid and shocking history of the jail, with no details spared. He heard about men who smuggled money in their anuses to keep it safe from the other prisoners; about younger prisoners who were raped, and battered if they refused; and how overcrowding had meant mixing some prisoners who would otherwise be segregated.

'It's an old place,' Reg had told him. 'Can't break out of it, but otherwise it's bloody Dickensian in parts. Not like Preston or over in Strangeways, no, it's altogether harder here.' He complained most bitterly about the plumbing and said that in spite of the war, lack of government money, and cutbacks, they should have proper facilities. He declared bluntly that if the MPs had shit thrown at them by prisoners, or urine chucked in their eyes daily in protest, they would get the sodding plumbing fixed. At night the prisoners had to use chamber pots, but in the day . . . 'Too many arses for too few crappers.'

Ricky had been shocked at first. Even though he'd not had a sheltered childhood, the grim coldness of the prison he found intimidating. And the lack of natural light, making the prisoners lose colour, bleeding it from them. In fact, before long he could tell who the new arrivals were just from their skin. And their manner. Some came in cocky; others hung back, walking pressed against the walls, trying not to be seen. Which was impossible. Every prisoner was seen, twenty-four hours a day. Even at night there were lights on in the corridors and hallways, guards parading hourly, shining their torches into the cells to check that the beds were occupied.

What Ricky had found most oppressive was not the smell, the cold, or the threat of violence, but the hopelessness. When he had first arrived, he had some idea that he would be able to strike up relationships with the inmates if he treated them right, but apparently that was naïve. Treat the inmates too kindly and they despised you. Treat them too harshly and they loathed you. But they feared you too. And that was preferable. Very few guards – Reg being one of them – could walk the line between harshness and indulgence. Thickset, with an impressive moustache and hefty arms, he exchanged pleasantries with the old lags, but made the new arrivals work for his respect.

'See that bastard,' he said suddenly, breaking into Ricky's thoughts as he pointed to the third cell on the left. 'The man holding his hands out?'

Ricky nodded. 'What about him?'

'Got thirty years for battering his old lady to death with a hammer,' Reg said quietly. 'Never get within reach of his arms. They tried to plead insanity at his trial, but that shit's not fucking mad. If you have to get him out of his cell, you tell him to turn round and put his hands through the bars and you put on the handcuffs outside, you hear me? Then you can go in. And always have a back-up.'

'Is he the most dangerous prisoner here?'

Reg shook his head. 'Oh, I've not taken you to the North Wing yet, lad. That's where they usually keep the dangerous inmates. It's just that he's here because of the overcrowding.'

He turned to look at his charge. Ricky Holmes, just eighteen, keen as mustard and a bit cocky. But not stupid, Reg thought; no, Ricky had the makings of a fair officer, if he listened and learned. After all, he had been very eager to enter the service, having finally made his mind up about a career. He had told Reg all about himself, laughing about what a bloody nuisance he had been when he was growing up. But Reg didn't mind that. A lively lad could turn out to be a good officer. Often better than the 'by the book' sorts.

'You pay attention, you hear?'

Ricky nodded. 'Sure.'

'You learn and listen and follow advice. That way you get to keep your wages and to stay safe.'

Tempted by the reasonable wages, and the escape from the sewage works and mills that employed most of the Burnley population, Ricky had decided on his career and stuck to his choice. It was true that he had to travel out of town to work, and then walk a bit after the bus stopped ten minutes short of the prison. But he could manage that, and besides, he was used to the Moors . . . Ricky's mind wandered. There had been another reason why he had wanted a better job – to impress Emma. But it had never occurred to him that within six months of beginning work he would be guarding her father.

'And cell number 45,' Reg continued, breaking into Ricky's thoughts, 'he needs watching. A forger, nice enough little bugger, but gets het up sometimes. They do that, lad, you need to know. At times being locked up gets to them and they panic, start screaming and smashing things. You stay away, you hear, until you get help. Three guards go in when they're playing up.'

'*Three?*' Ricky countered. 'For a little fella like that?'

'Don't be fooled. When they get into a state they're all strong as madmen, and they strike out. At anyone. The worst injury I ever had was from an ex-vicar, no more than eight stone. Came at me with his shit pot and smashed it over my head. Cracked my bloody skull, and my old lady couldn't get the stink out of my uniform for a week.'

Ricky stared at him, trying not to laugh. 'What happened?'

'I had seventeen stitches in my scalp, and the ex-vicar calmed down. Died just before he was due to be released,' Reg said wistfully. 'Left me his books, like we'd been best mates.'

'What about number 78?'

Reg gazed down the hallway, towards the cell marked 78. 'You know him, don't you?'

'Yeah.'

'Someone told me that you were very interested to see who came to visit Frederick Coles,' Reg said, his tone shrewd. 'Acquainted with his daughter, are you?'

'Yes,' Ricky said, grinning. 'I know his daughter.'

'Looks like you'd like to know her better,' Reg teased, laughing and slapping Ricky on the back. 'Childhood sweethearts?'

Raising his eyebrows, Ricky tried to sound calm. 'Emma's only fifteen.'

'I heard she were a pretty girl.'

'Very . . . Who was talking about her?'

Amused, Reg laughed again. So Ricky Holmes was

in love, was he? And him being such a good-looking young man, the type who could get any woman, with his thick brown hair and long-lashed eyes. But here he was, in love with a kid. Poor sod.

'The guards in the visitors' area told me. Said Frederick Coles's daughter had some nerve, coming here on her own. There's not many grown women who'd do that, let alone a girl. I mean, most of the prisoners' women are hard cases, used to the life. But Coles's girl? She doesn't sound like that type. She must be special.'

'She is,' Ricky said seriously. 'I don't think it's right she's coming here.'

'Is that so?'

'Yeah, that's so,' he replied firmly. 'It's not a proper kind of place for her.'

'I'd agree with that, but perhaps Miss Coles has a good enough reason to come.'

'Her father.'

'Number 78.'

Ricky could feel his heart speed up. 'He didn't do it . . .'

Reg rolled his eyes. 'They're all innocent, lad. Even the ones who've been caught red-handed.'

'But Mr Coles *wasn't* caught red-handed, and he isn't that kind of man. He was respectable. He worked in the office at Oldfield Mill. People trusted him,' Ricky persisted, his tone heated, 'and he's always said he didn't do it.'

'Like I say, prisons are full to bursting with innocent men.'

'*Some might be innocent!*' Ricky snapped back.

'Frederick Coles was tried in a court of law, by twelve men, and they decided that he was guilty.'

'They were prejudiced.'

Sighing, Reg smoothed down the front of his uniform. Over the decades he had seen many young recruits begin in just this way. Wanting to see the best in the worst of people. Wanting to tilt at legal windmills, because they couldn't believe that the man they were guarding could have killed his children. Or thrown acid in his wife's face, or stolen money from a blind woman. They would insist on judging faces, voices, mannerisms. How could someone who spoke like that, looked like that, acted like that, do such things?

Because they did, Reg told the new men, over and over again. *Don't waste your breath. They've been tried and sentenced; it's our duty to guard them, not judge them.* More times than he could remember, people had been fooled. Let down, their assessments woefully off the mark. And then followed the disappointment, the bitterness of having to accept what a person truly was – which wasn't what they had wanted him to be. You couldn't get too close to any of the prisoners, Reg knew, because if you did, you couldn't guard them or do your job.

'I tell you,' Ricky continued, sticking to his theme. 'Ernie Coles's reputation all but damned his son.'

'Enough!' Reg snapped. 'That'll do now, lad. I don't want to hear another word. And neither does anyone else in this prison. Keep your mouth shut.

41

You've a job to do, so do it.' His tone softened. 'My mother told me a story when I was a kid.'

Ricky glanced at the older man. 'What story?'

'About a scorpion and a frog. Well, the frog wants to cross the river, and the scorpion says, *Jump on my back, I'm going across*. But the frog is suspicious. *You'll sting me*, he says. *Nah*, replies the scorpion, *if I sting you, I die and you die and neither of us gets across the river*. Convinced, the frog jumps on the scorpion's back. Halfway over, the scorpion stings the frog. Dying, the frog looks at the scorpion. *Why did you do that? Now we both die. Why?* says the scorpion. *Because it's what I do*.'

Ricky frowned. 'I don't understand.'

'Most prisoners are like scorpions. They kill, attack and lie automatically. It's what *they* do.'

Falling silent, Ricky watched Reg walk off and begin his check on the cells. Alone in the guards' room, he thought about the older man's words, then unexpectedly caught sight of his own reflection in the chipped mirror. God, he thought, annoyed, as he hurried to straighten his tie. But he had to admit that he liked what he saw. The uniform made him look older, his shoulders wide, even if the white collar of his shirt was too stiff. He would have to tell his mother to cut out the starch. But the short, regimental haircut was flattering and made his eyes more noticeable. In fact, Ricky decided, when Emma saw him in his uniform she would be impressed. Might finally start to see him as a man, not a chum.

Mind you, he had been a fool to speak out like that

about her father. Perhaps Reg would report him, and there would be a black mark put on his record. God, why hadn't he kept his mouth shut? Anxious, he turned back to the glass partition and watched Reg pace down the corridor. He needed this job, needed the uniform and the promise of promotion. Hadn't they told him when he came for the interview that a man could make a career out of the prison service? And get a pension when he left? Ricky had smiled at the reference to a pension – only old folk worried about something like that. But a good wage wasn't something to be taken lightly. He could help out at home, and have enough to buy a round at the pub for his mates. After all, how many mill hands and sewage workers had come back from the war to find themselves unemployed, the women working their jobs? And worse, there had been rumours of people buying from cheaper, foreign mills, and what would that mean? A further cut in jobs, that was what. All the more reason to get – and keep – a good job. Ricky kept staring at Reg's broad back. He would keep his mouth shut from now on, he told himself. Keep his opinions quiet. He would do his job, and earn his wage. But what he said *outside* the gates of the jail was his own business . . .

Ricky Holmes knew that Frederick Coles was innocent. Not just because he was Emma's father, but because he knew the man. Staring at the locked door of cell number 78, he thought back to the time he had first met Frederick Coles. The older man had been coming down the ginnel towards St Andrew's Street, passing by the church and pausing to light a cigarette. Dressed in an old but smart overcoat, he had worn a starched collar and Homburg hat, the latter perfectly setting off his refined features. Blowing out the match, he had glanced up as snow began falling and smiled . . . At that moment Ricky had been impressed. Here was someone elegant and unusual on the Burnley streets. Someone he could admire, emulate.

'That's my dad,' Emma had said, nudging Ricky. 'Go on, say hello.'

To Ricky's surprise, the idol had been friendly, welcoming and amusing, making him feel immediately comfortable. Then he had extended his hand to shake Ricky's.

'Hello, Master Richard Holmes . . .'

Master Richard Holmes. Hellfire, Ricky had thought, wait until Bessie hears about this.

'So, what are you and my daughter up to?'

And it had continued that way. From then onwards, Ricky had always been accepted at the Coles' rented flat. When her father wasn't around, Emma explained that Frederick had left home at sixteen when his mother died. Gone to Liverpool, to graft on Clyde Street as a paperboy, and then worked his way up and begun to do some filing in the office. Being smart, he had supplemented his skills by attending night school, and had taken an accountancy course. Before too long, the offspring of the rabble-rousing Ernie Coles had become a respectable accounts clerk for a small clothing company. A couple of years later he was hired as the accounts clerk at Oldfield Mill. Not bad, people thought, impressed. Not bad at all for Ernie Coles's runt.

When Frederick Coles had returned to Burnley as a respectable accounts clerk, he had made no contact with his father. Instead, both kept their distance. The son heard about the father and his jaunts in Manchester, Preston and further afield, whilst the father heard that his son had returned a smart, respected office worker. Not that Ernie cared overmuch. Netty was dead, and his affection for his son had always been erratic. As to his stepson . . . It was no loss to Ernie Coles that David had moved on too; gone to work in a jeweller's shop in Holland Street, and reverted to his father's name, Hawksworth.

Neither son wanted anything to do with Ernie, and as time passed the half-brothers also became distanced from each other. They met occasionally and kept in touch, living off the sad embers of a childhood friendship, but David never forgot that Frederick was the son of Ernie Coles. However respectable he might have turned out to be, he had some rancid blood in his veins. After all, David had grown to hate his stepfather, and although he didn't hate his half-brother, he wanted to keep his distance from Frederick. Jealousy and snobbery continued to work their magic. When the half-brothers both married, their lives split apart even further, and although they lived in the same town, they only met up once or twice a year. David could never get over his envy of Frederick, or his very real fear that somehow his respectability would be undermined again.

The thought terrified him, left him sweaty in his dreams. He would wake up still thinking he was a boy, living in the flat over the butcher's shop. Without trying, he remembered how he had been pointed out as one of Coles's brats. His family respected and reviled in equal measure . . . For a man who still grieved for his honourable, lost father, respectability became David's obsession. So when he settled down and married the unassuming Jenny – with a son and a jewellery shop of his own – he swore that no one, *no one*, would ever shame him again.

All this history Emma had explained to Ricky, telling him how Frederick had taken care of her after her mother died.

'Don't you miss her?'

She had nodded, wistful. 'Oh, yes, but I was very young at the time. And Dad was there. He took care of me. And he always will.'

And he always will . . .

'Oi, you!'

Startled, Ricky turned to face Stan Thorpe, the second in command after Reg. He had met Thorpe a couple of times before, and had automatically disliked the man. Whey-faced, with a long nose and yellowed teeth, Thorpe towered over everyone at six foot three, but although tall, he was cadaverously thin, and mean-spirited. Reg had already warned Ricky about Thorpe. *He's not an outright bully, hasn't the balls, but if he takes a dislike to you, it's not good. Thorpe's been here longer than anyone and is meaner than most of the prisoners. Watch your back.*

'I'm talking to you,' Thorpe went on, his East End voice at odds with the mostly Northern accents in the prison. 'Are you stupid, or what?'

'No.'

'No, *sir*,' Thorpe replied, moving over to Ricky and leaning down. His breath was stale. Cheap smokes, troublesome teeth and bad digestion. 'You need to get some things straight, lad, from the start.'

'Yes, sir.'

'You and I are likely to become at odds if you don't do as I say,' Thorpe went on, staring into Ricky's handsome face. 'I suppose you think you know it all?'

'No . . . sir.'

'Every kid that comes here thinks he knows it all at first. But none of them do. They know shit.' Thorpe put his long head on one side. 'Yer not bright, are yer?'

Thorpe was feeling mean. His digestion was poor, and the prison food hadn't helped it. Acid burned into his guts and made his body sour. He had come to the Moors Prison like Ricky, once upon a time. But although he had crawled high enough up the backside of the Governor and his superiors to progress, he was reviled by the inmates. And as he aged, his bad stomach ate away his bulk, and he became as parsimonious in his appearance as in his good nature. Of such beginnings bullies are made, and Thorpe was no exception.

'I've got a feeling about you, lad.'

'Yes, sir,' Ricky replied uncertainly.

'Did I ask you to speak?' Thorpe replied peevishly. 'Did I say, Mr Holmes, please reply? Please answer my words with your own? Well, fucking did I?'

'No, sir.'

'No, sir,' Thorpe agreed, turning away and looking out through the glass partition. 'You waiting for a bus, lad?'

Ricky blinked. 'I don't understand, sir.'

'Let me make it very simple for you. Because I see yer a dozy boy, a bit backwards perhaps. Yer mother a bit simple? Yer father a bit slow?' He turned back to Ricky, his face only inches from the younger man's. 'Why are you standing here like someone waiting for a bus, when you should be out on the passage, relieving Mr Spencer?'

Ricky moved hurriedly to the door, Thorpe watching him then calling him back.

'Before you go, lad,' he said, his voice quiet. 'I hear you know the daughter of one of our guests. A Miss Emma Coles?'

Ricky could feel his heart quicken. 'A little.'

'*A little*,' Thorpe repeated. 'I see. I heard different. That it weren't such a little . . . But then what would I know? Me being the smartest man in here, who knows everyone, and everything that goes on. How would I know?' He peered into Ricky's face. 'Or maybe you don't think I'm the smartest man in here? Maybe you think you are?'

'No, sir.'

'No, sir,' Thorpe repeated. 'That's right, no, sir. No, sir, you are not the smartest. I am that man. I have always been that man. And I will remain that man.' He jerked his head towards the door. 'Relieve Mr Spencer, Mr Holmes. Remember, I'm watching you. And I have to say – it pains me, but I have to say it – I don't fucking like you. Not one little bit.'

FOUR

Checking the time with the old grandfather clock by the door, David spun the sign round to CLOSED and locked the door. Business was over for the day. As always, on the chime of six. Turning off the lights in the shop, he moved upstairs to the workroom at the top of the building, calling for Emma to follow. Surprised, she did so, walking into the workshop and skirting the long table, which was scattered with clock parts. Staring at a large faded dial, David touched the hands tenderly. He did not look at his niece, but seemed to be communicating with the clock instead.

'Did you want to leave school?'

Emma was taken aback by the question, and wondered how to answer it without insulting her guardian. 'I . . . I'm grateful to be here.'

'That's not really an answer,' David replied, his voice expressionless. 'Would you have liked to stay on at school?'

'Yes, I would.'

'Why?'

Emma could feel her palms beginning to sweat,

and was grateful that her uncle's attention was still fixed on the clock face. 'It would have been nice to learn more.'

'But you're a girl; usually girls don't want much education.'

'I could have trained to be a secretary,' Emma offered timidly.

At school there had been much talk of this new business. A profession that was expanding rapidly, bringing with it new job opportunities in offices, the chance of independence for women, and freedom from the usual mill work. In fact, becoming a secretary had been a dream Emma had confessed to her father only weeks before his arrest. A dream that events had overtaken and overturned.

'A secretary . . .' David mused.

He fell silent, and Emma wondered if she was supposed to leave. Wondered if she should slip away and tidy up, make supper. A moment passed, then another, before her uncle spoke again.

'I wanted to be a teacher once.'

The words shook her. Such a confidence, so unexpectedly given. 'A teacher,' Emma repeated. 'Why . . . why didn't you become one?'

'Circumstances,' David replied, reaching for a delicate instrument and bending down over the clock face again. 'It would seem that both you and I have been prevented from following our own wishes by the force of events.' He paused, tinkering with the back of the clock face, and then turning it over gently. 'I cannot afford to pay for a secretarial course.'

She was horrified. 'Oh, no, Uncle! I didn't mean ... I wasn't asking for that. What you've done is more than enough.'

He cleared his throat, his nervous habit kicking in. 'But I could teach you some kind of profession. I could teach you about running a shop, about jewellery. My late wife used to say that every female likes jewellery.'

Surprised by the unexpected offer, Emma hesitated. 'I can do anything you want me to.'

'But would you *want* to do it?' David countered, finally glancing over to her. He held her gaze for an instant, then turned away. 'Of course not, I was expecting too much. I apologise, Emma.'

'Oh, I didn't mean—'

He cut her off. Not unkindly, but with detachment. 'I think our original plans were for the best. If you could attend to the house, I will attend to the business.'

Unnerved, Emma replayed the conversation over and over in her mind. She was still thinking about it when she boarded the cold bus that would take her out of Burnley towards the Moors. She didn't know quite how she had done it, but she had somehow managed to reject an opportunity and offend her uncle at the same time. His had been a generous offer and one she should have grasped. But she had been clumsy and missed the chance, and now she was relegated to housekeeper/dogsbody again. She wondered then if David Hawksworth would see her response as a rejection. Even ingratitude, after he had given her a home. After all, the offer had seemed genuine. He had even confided about his own lost hopes and intimated that he sympathised with her predicament. Not that his understanding had been obvious. David Hawksworth was not an obvious man, and even the remotest reference to his past would be certain to ignite memories of Frederick Coles.

Emma shuddered, uneasy. Dear God, what would her uncle do if he found out that she was visiting his half-brother? That, she knew, would be the ultimate betrayal. But how could he honestly expect her to reject her own father? Huddling further into her seat and wrapped up against the chill, Emma kept her face averted from the rest of the passengers. She hated the visits, hated the jail, but she had no choice. How could she turn her back on her father? The man who had been so kind, so endlessly loving? They had been inseparable after her mother's suicide; how could anyone think that she could reject him? Even if he was a thief.

Sighing impatiently, Emma tucked her chin down into her collar. Even the thought of Ricky Holmes working at the prison did not lighten her spirits. Ricky liked her, Emma knew that only too well, but what if he let something slip? Mrs Holmes wasn't known for her tact and had a big mouth – what if Ricky or Bessie mentioned Emma's prison visits? Dear God, Mrs Holmes would have that scandalous news spread quicker than butter on hot toast. From her own grim experience, Emma knew how quickly gossip travelled. How a salacious piece of news could flood the Burnley streets and alleyways in hours. She had learned that the hard way over the previous nine months. When people had first heard about her father being taken – handcuffed – from Oldfield Mill.

Uneasy, Emma tried to dismiss the thought, but it was lodged tight. That terrible day she had been at school, learning about the pharaohs, and the class had been disturbed by the arrival of the deputy head. Emma – along with everyone else – had watched the woman speak to the teacher, and then seen them turn: *And look at her* . . . That look would stay with Emma until the day she died. She knew that. It had been a look of layers: uncertainty, sympathy, disbelief and embarrassment. A look that had scalded her skin as she responded to her name and followed the deputy head out of the classroom.

After that day nine months ago, she had never gone back to school, and none of her school friends apart from Bessie Holmes had kept in touch. The shift in her circumstances had rocked Emma. Having been protected and sheltered by her father, she couldn't understand why she was hurriedly being taken to her uncle's shop. Shaking, she had stood, cold to the bone, in her school dress, whilst the clocks ticked sonorously around her. She was certain that her beloved father was dead. Surely he had to be; why else would they take her out of school? Why else would everyone be looking at her with such horror?

'Where's my father?' she had asked brokenly. 'Is he all right?'

'He's fine, miss, but he's been arrested.'

'What for?' she had asked, her voice faltering.

'For theft, miss.'

'Theft!' she repeated, incredulous. 'No, not my father.'

'I'm sorry, luv,' the policeman had replied. 'But they say your father stole from Oldfield Mill. The owner, Mr Gregory Walmsley, called us in and your father's been taken into custody.'

All questions had ended there, silenced by the arrival of David Hawksworth, who had walked into the shop and looked at her. She knew him from the infrequent visits with her father – but he seemed taller, thinner, colder now that she was alone. And his voice was more distant, without emotion. Emma could never remember her uncle's exact words at that time, only that she was going to have to live at the shop with him because her father had been arrested. And as David Hawksworth had said it, his tone had jammed, as though the idea was a dry crust that stuck in his throat.

Immobile, Emma had stood rigid in her school uniform, whilst Mrs Palmer – whom the policeman had called in from the tobacconist's next door – fussed over her. Then, as David walked into the back parlour, Mrs Palmer bent down to Emma, whispering.

'I was told to get your things from your flat, luv. I've brought them here for you.'

'What? But my father . . .' Confused, Emma had been silenced by the sound of David's footsteps approaching again.

'I would appreciate it,' he had said, his voice flat, 'if you could refrain from mentioning your father to me. But I want you to know that you have a home here, Emma, for as long as you need it.'

A terrible chill had run through her then, slicing into her. As David walked off, Mrs Palmer put her arm around the girl's shoulders.

'Don't mind him, luv. It's just his way. Look, I've put your things in the bedroom upstairs. It were Adam's room, Mr Hawksworth's son. I've tried to make it comfy.'

But Emma had not been able to take in any of it. She had just kept staring ahead blindly. 'When's my father coming home?'

Wrong-footed, Mrs Palmer had hesitated. She had been instructed by David Hawksworth not to tell Emma if her father was granted bail. She had to believe that Frederick Coles was already in jail, and staying there. That way, she would forget him all the quicker. Or so David Hawksworth thought.

'How long do I have to stay with my uncle?' Emma had asked, thunderstruck.

'For a while.'

'How long is a while?'

'Until things are sorted out.'

'Until they find out that they're wrong about my father, you mean!' Emma had said defiantly. 'He wouldn't steal anything, I know that. How could Mr Walmsley think otherwise? He likes my father, he always has.'

'Emma, my luv, calm down.'

'How can I calm down!' she had exploded, looking round at the dark shop. 'Why am I here? I live with my father. And if he's been taken away for a while, why can't I stay at our rooms until he comes back?'

'You're too young to be on your own.'

'But I don't want to be here!'

'You have to do as you're told,' Florence Palmer had replied, 'It's hard for you, luv, I know that. But you have to be brave.'

'Why?' Emma had replied rebelliously. 'I'm not the one in jail.'

Pushing the memory to the back of her mind, Emma stared out of the window at the falling snow. Next month it would be Christmas. And what kind of a Christmas would it be this year? Her father in jail and her living at the jeweller's. She wondered then how she would manage to get away on Christmas Eve for a prison visit. It had been easy so far. David Hawksworth believed her when she said she was seeing a school friend, and Emma imagined that he was pleased to have her out from under his feet. Besides, he wasn't a man to ask questions. Providing she was back at a reasonable time, Emma believed that she could continue her visits to the jail on the Moors. *But at Christmas?* Now that was going to be more difficult.

Still, she consoled herself, she had some weeks to think about that. No point worrying before she had to. Wiping the condensation off the window, she looked out, but could see little, as the winter day-light had virtually faded. As the journey progressed,

Emma noticed men and women leaving the bus as they moved further away from town, out towards the banking of the Moors. Before long she knew that the only people left would be prison visitors. She had learned how to spot them. Sometimes it was easy – a woman wearing make-up and cheap clothes. A man not at work in the daytime. A hard-faced type who paid his fare without blinking: 'Prison, return.' But sometimes there was an older person, diffident and embarrassed. Someone's mother or father, looking uneasy. Not liking what they had to do, not wanting to make the journey out of town. Not wanting to take that walk from the last stop to the high gates of the prison entrance.

None of them ever spoke. The prostitute, the old lag, the wide boy, the shamed parents, all made their way to the jail in silence. At first Emma had expected the women to talk to her, especially as she had been young and on her own, but there was no camaraderie. Not amongst this group. The only, early, communication had been one woman making fun of Emma, teasing her for being so obviously a newcomer and asking if she had come to see her pimp – a remark Emma didn't even understand. From then on, she did what everyone else did: she kept her gaze averted and made no eye contact. From being a beloved daughter, Emma Coles had begun the long journey into lonely segregation. The knowing looks she saw exchanged in town when she passed she brazened out. The whispering she ignored, and her heart closed against the jibes. The mottled kindness of the Palmers and Jack Rimmer, the loyalty of Bessie, and the devotion of Ricky Holmes – together with Emma's own strength of character – stopped her from becoming bitter. But the tension of living at the jeweller's – of being forced to ignore the very existence of her father whilst visiting him secretly behind David Hawksworth's back – was draining. Within weeks Emma had learned that she had to adjust to two sets of circumstances. No matter how hard it became, or how long it lasted. She had no choice.

But there was one conviction she hung on to through everything. One belief no one and nothing could shake. *Her father was innocent.* She knew it, and she would make sure that one day Burnley, and the rest of the world, knew it too. No matter how long it took. Or what she had to do to prove it.

FIVE

Whatever her mother said, however much she might encourage her, Bessie wasn't going to marry young. Not that anyone had asked her yet ... Smiling, she looked round the cobbler's shop, inhaling the smell of leather, hot irons and wax. Some women might like perfume, but to Bessie, this was the aroma of the gods. Well, the northern gods, anyway. Outside she could hear a sudden thump, followed by a crash. Old man Letski was getting on, all right. By the town's reckonings, he had to be pushing ninety already. Bessie thought of her employer, the simian-featured Igor Letski, with his broad, flat nose, his high forehead and stooped back. And his extraordinary Russian accent, the butt of neighbourhood jokes.

The local boys rang the shop bell often, then ran away, knowing that Letski would call from inside, *'Come in, come in. Bring your shoes, your boots. Come in.'*

Round the corner they would mimic him: 'Come in, bring your shoes, your boots, your Russian bears ...'

Letski was hard of hearing, with deteriorating

eyesight, and no one was sure how much he saw or heard, but when the door didn't open he would sigh and shrug and move back behind the counter to mend the shoes he was working on. Mrs Holmes told Bessie that he had been there for years; that her own late parents remembered him, and that once – in better days – he had had a shop on Market Street. Amongst much other gossiping, the rumour went round that Letski was an anarchist. A rumour intensified by the Russian Revolution in 1905, when he would bend anyone's ear about the virtues of Leon Trotsky. But by then Letski was old and considered harmless – a harmless Communist cobbler in north-west England.

Bessie thought he was fascinating, and when a note had gone up in the window six months earlier – WANTED: HELP IN SHOP – she had applied. Having never wanted to stay on at school, and knowing she needed to bring in a wage to supplement her widowed mother's outgoings, Bessie had decided that she would get a job. But not in the cotton, timber or saw mills. Not in the sewage works, and not somewhere like the local grocer's. If she had to work, she wanted to do something different. Her first impressions of the ape-like, round-shouldered Letski had fascinated her. He, in his turn, was equally intrigued to hire a feisty, intelligent girl. He had wanted a male assistant, he had told her, but no men had applied for the job. Which was hardly surprising, as Bessie had surreptitiously taken down the sign as she first entered.

From that day onwards, Bessie's mind was fixed on her future. Oh, she would marry one day, but that was a long way off, when she had a cobbler's shop of her own. Who cared if it was a damn silly ambition? Having an odd dream wasn't going to stop her – she'd get her shop and then see who was laughing. After all, Bessie was already learning the trade. Hadn't old man Letski shown her how to heel a lady's shoe only the other day? And his eyesight was too bloody bad for him to put the steel caps straight on the front of the clogs, so she had been doing that for the last month, and not been paid much for it. But then again, Bessie consoled herself, she was getting an apprenticeship for free. And anyway, she was paid for her general work in the shop, cleaning and tidying and looking after the customers.

It was lucky that old Letski had no family, no one he could leave the shop to. Apart from her. Oh yes, Bessie told herself, she would become indispensable, and then the place would be hers. One day . . .

'Bloody hell!' Ricky snapped, as he walked into the cobbler's, hitting his head on the low door jamb.

Exasperated, Bessie sighed. 'Why don't you duck?'

'Why don't you put a sign up?' Ricky countered, walking over to his sister. In the back of the shop he could make out Letski's hunched shape working at the machine. 'If he leans any closer, he'll get his face ripped off.'

'He knows what he's doing.'

'If he did, he wouldn't have hired you,' Ricky

replied smartly, pushing his prison boots over the counter. 'I need these heeling.'

'I can do it. After all, Ricky, things have changed. Women are getting power. It all began with the vote . . .'

'Oh God,' he groaned. 'Not again, Bessie.'

'And then, you'll see, we women will have our say.'

'I've never met a woman yet that *didn't* have her say.'

Miffed, Bessie leaned towards her brother. 'One day I might own this shop.'

'A cobbler's!' he said, laughing. 'Yer *talking* cobblers, our Bessie!'

'I'm not!' she retorted hotly, looking her brother up and down in his dark navy uniform. A portion of brass chain was showing, the whistle attached to it pushed deep down into the pocket. Unwilling to invite more ridicule, she changed the subject. 'I saw Emma yesterday.'

He brightened up at once. 'How was she?'

'OK. Don't tell Mum, though. And I promised Emma that we'd never tell anyone about her prison visits.'

Ricky nodded. 'I'm not going to tell anyone.'

'How often does she visit her father?'

'I've seen her a couple of times, and I know she's been when I'm not on duty.'

Bessie's expression was curious. 'What's he like?'

'Who?'

'Frederick Coles.'

'You know him, Bessie! You've known him for years.'

'I mean – what he's like *now*?'

'Quiet, no trouble, but some of the other prisoners can't make him out. He doesn't mix, but if you talk to him, he's polite.'

'What did he say when he first saw you?'

Incredulous, Ricky shook his head. 'He came out of the cell, spotted me, and said, "Master Holmes, pleased to see you again." Just like the first day I met him. He was trying to make *me* feel at ease, when it should have been the other way round. He never stole that money from Oldfield Mill.'

'I don't believe it either.'

'I'll *never* believe it,' Ricky continued. 'He isn't that kind of man. And he'd never have done anything to shame his daughter. Emma was his life.'

'I reckon they locked the wrong man up. They should have put Ernie Coles behind bars long ago, not his son. I mean, everyone knows Ernie's a villain.'

Ricky shook his head. 'Everyone at the prison has heard about the trial, of course. Not national news, but interesting around here. And Frederick being like he is – well-spoken and smart. Even in a prison uniform he stands out.'

'No more than his daughter does.'

'No,' Ricky agreed, thoughtfully. 'No more than Emma . . . People talk about her, you know. In the prison, the guards all comment on a girl coming to visit alone.'

'You mean you've got competition?'

'Not like that! I mean, there *are* other people who visit who aren't like the usual lot. Some of them look shattered being there, dragging their kids along behind them. But Emma's so calm. She looks out of place, but she acts confident. No one can believe she's only a kid.'

'Hardly!' Bessie said, leaning towards her brother. 'Old enough to get married – to the right man. Someone with a good, reliable job. Like a prison guard . . .'

'*Trainee* prison guard,' Ricky replied, smiling, but then becoming serious. 'To be honest, I've thought about it, Bessie, thought about it a lot. You know I've been in love with Emma for a while. Well, in another year I'll be nineteen and have enough of a salary to be able to rent somewhere. And support a wife, if she worked too.'

Stunned, Bessie stared at her brother. 'I was joking! Do you *really* want to marry Emma?'

He nodded his handsome head. 'Yeah, I do.'

'Have you asked her?'

'Nah, not yet. Not with all the trouble of her father and all that. I thought I'd wait until the dust had settled.'

'Mum would kill you if you married Emma Coles,' Bessie replied. 'And it might not do your career that much good either, Ricky. I mean, an up-and-coming prison guard marrying the daughter of one of the inmates.' She rolled her eyes. 'I know you care about Emma, but I didn't know you loved her.'

'I wasn't sure myself, until I saw the way she behaved during her father's trial. And now, seeing her brazen it out in the town, and coming on those prison visits, knowing how much people gossip – well, she's impressed me. She's amazing, a woman a man could admire.'

'As a wife?' Bessie countered.

'Why not? *You* didn't turn your back on her. You've stayed friends with her.'

'Yeah, but I'm not going to marry her, am I?' Bessie replied, then dropped her voice again. 'I'd think about it very carefully, Ricky. Emma's preoccupied with her father at the moment; she doesn't seem to be thinking about romance.'

'I've got time,' Ricky answered her. 'There's no rush. My feelings for Emma won't change. I can wait.'

SIX

Flinching as she heard the weighty door bang closed, Emma sat in the visitors' room, her hands folded on her lap. On either side of her were a number of other people, all seated on one side of a trestle table. Across the table were rows of benches, unoccupied, and above their heads, rudimentary electric lights threw down a grey-toned illumination. On the far wall, on either side of an enormous prison clock, old-fashioned gas lights spluttered out their blue flames, occasionally popping in the silence. And in the distance, Emma could hear the now familiar sound of a voice giving orders, then the noise of doors being slammed. One door, two doors. Then footsteps coming closer. Three doors, four.

Taking in a breath, Emma watched the large reinforced doors of the visitors' room open, craning her neck to see her father amongst the twenty other convicts. Silently they sat down, each facing their wife or family, Frederick coming to his place last. Smiling, he sat down, staring into Emma's face. Her throat constricted, and without thinking, she reached for his hand, the guard barking at her.

'No touching, keep your hands under the table.'

Awkwardly, she did so, looking back to her father. 'How are you?'

He smiled again, but the action was forced. Although he had only been imprisoned for a matter of weeks, his skin was losing its sheen.

'I'm fine,' he lied. 'Don't worry about me. How are you? Are you all right? I mean, living with David, is it all right?'

'I've told you before, Dad, it's OK.'

'Sorry . . . but there was nowhere else you could go,' Frederick said, ashamed. 'I know he can be cold, but—'

'I'm fine,' Emma replied, her manner stiff because she knew if she relaxed she would cry, and she didn't want to do that. 'I brought a cake, but the guards took it from me. Said they would give it to you later. They will, won't they?'

'Yes,' he assured her. 'They have to check it's all right, that you haven't hidden something in it.'

'Like a rope ladder?'

'Or a blowtorch,' he replied, both of them smiling. 'I'm so sorry about all of this,' Frederick said suddenly.

Emma tensed. She dreaded these moments the most. Her father's courage faltering, his anger fighting to take control. Then, after another few moments, he would compose himself again, try to become the elegant, charming Frederick Coles of old. And she wanted to say, *Don't try, don't try with me. It doesn't matter,* but she couldn't, because that would have been like telling him to give up.

'I'm happy at the jewellery shop.'

'It's a dull place.'

'But we have nice neighbours. The Palmers are quite kind, and Mr Rimmer makes me laugh. He talks about you, Dad. Sends his best, says he knows you didn't do it.'

Frederick glanced down. 'I wish he'd been on the jury.'

'They got it wrong, Dad,' Emma hurried on. 'Didn't your solicitor say you could appeal?'

'Only if they find new evidence,' Frederick replied, changing the subject hurriedly. 'I didn't want you to leave school . . .'

'I don't mind.'

'I do.'

'Honestly, Dad, I don't mind,' she repeated. 'My uncle said something about teaching me the jewellery business.'

'He did?'

She wondered fleetingly if she should have mentioned it. Especially as the offer seemed to have been taken back. But her father seemed so pleased by the idea, Emma played along. 'Well, he mentioned it. And I have to say that I was surprised. I mean, he's got a son, hasn't he? You would expect that he would want to train him up in the business. But Mrs Palmer said that his son, Adam, had fallen out with his father and gone abroad.' She paused before continuing. 'I remember that you said something about it . . . Where did he go?'

'Who?'

'Adam Hawksworth.'

'No one knows,' Frederick replied. 'Father and son fell out, that was it. No one's heard from Adam since.'

'When did it happen?'

Suddenly Frederick seemed bored with the subject and changed it. 'Are you getting plenty of good food?'

'Yes, Dad,' Emma replied, smiling. 'What about you?'

'It's not bad.'

'That isn't what Ricky says.'

Slowly, Frederick met his daughter's gaze. 'It was quite a surprise to see Ricky Holmes here. I mean, I knew he was at the prison, but to see him opening my cell door . . .' He stopped, unnerved and trying to keep his voice light. 'Strange how life turns out, isn't it? I mean, I remember meeting that lad and thinking he wasn't half good enough for my daughter.' He reached for Emma's hands, then drew back, remembering to place his own under the table. 'I've ruined your life, haven't I? The one thing I would never have done. You know that, Emma, you know I would never have let you down.'

She nodded urgently. 'I know. And in time, everyone else will know that.'

There was a long, protracted pause, Emma frowning as she watched her father. 'What is it?'

'You have to face facts,' Frederick said, trying to keep his voice even. 'I'm not going to get an appeal for a while.'

'You don't know that!'

'Emma, listen to me. I've been tried and convicted on the evidence they presented. There *is* no new evidence, and no chance of an appeal without it. I'm stuck here, and I have to get used to the idea.'

'You're innocent!' Emma retorted, dropping her voice as she continued. 'You can't give up.'

'Jesus,' Frederick said, his head bowed. 'I'm not giving up. I'm not changing my story. I didn't do it. I'm innocent . . . But I can't prove it, Emma, and I've got to find a way to survive in here. And that means I have to adjust to my sentence.' He looked up, holding her gaze. 'I've eleven years to serve. By the time I get out, you'll be in your twenties. I don't want my fate to impinge on your prospects.'

Swallowing, Emma struggled to understand. 'Why would it?'

'Oh, love,' he replied gently. 'I know people and I know how they talk. I can imagine how difficult life's been for you outside. It might be hard for me in here, but for a young woman – living with my brother – uprooted from everything she's ever known and having to bear the shame of my disgrace . . .'

'You didn't shame me.'

'The world thinks I did,' Frederick replied, looking round at the row of faces on either side of him. Quietly he continued. '*This* is how the world sees me now. As a criminal, as one of these men.'

'Dad—'

'Hear me out,' he said firmly. 'Even if I was proved innocent tomorrow, the stigma would never go away.

I'm coloured by association, Emma. That stain will never leave me.' He leaned towards her, one of the guards watching to make sure there was no contact between them. 'I want you to do something for me, something that matters a great deal.'

'Anything,' she agreed. 'You know I'd do anything you ask.'

He paused, then hurried on. 'Don't visit me again.'

'What!'

'We can write letters, keep in touch that way.' Frederick battled on, trying to disguise his feelings with a patina of calm. 'I don't want you coming here, being amongst this. Mixing with . . . Well, I don't want you here. Better that you stay at David's. Take up his offer, love, learn the business. Give yourself an education. It's what I would have wanted, if you'd been able to stay at school. You have to distance yourself from me.'

'Never!' she said hotly, her eyes filling. '*Never*.'

'You have to save your reputation. One day you'll want to marry and settle down, and I want you to make a good match. Someone respectable. Like I was, before all this. And you won't attract that kind of husband if he knows about me.'

'Then I wouldn't want him!' Emma replied firmly. 'Why are we talking about this? Nothing will stop me from visiting you, Dad, nothing. As for getting married . . . I'm still young.'

'You *are* young, and I want you to have the life a young woman should have. It would be so much easier for me to know that you're being looked after,

72

that there was a man who loved and cared for you. You've no idea how difficult it is for me to think of you at my half-brother's. David's an honourable man, but he's cold, and living there is no place for you, Emma. You need some happiness, you've had enough hardship. Your mother's suicide, this scandal – you deserve some joy.' He took in a deep breath. 'I know you would never reject me, I know that. I know you believe in my innocence – but now I want you to do what I say. *Distance yourself from me.*'

'You can't ask me to do that!' she said, close to tears.

'I don't want to hurt you, Emma. But that's what will happen, you'll be hurt more and more if you *don't* step back. You're not like the other women who come here. Knowing, down on their luck, desperate. This place will change you, and I'm not watching my beautiful daughter harden and coarsen. You're not going to serve my sentence with me. I'm doing that. And I'm doing it alone.'

Behind Emma a bell rang loudly, indicating that visiting time was over. Startled, she checked the clock on the wall, desperate for more time to talk with her father. Already rising, Frederick smiled at her, his expression tender. Around them, other people got to their feet, the man next to Emma knocking over her bag. Flustered, she leaned down to pick it up.

When she turned back, her father had gone.

No one would ever know what it had cost Frederick Coles to banish his daughter. Back in his cell, he sat down stiffly on the side of the bunk, listening to the sounds of the prisoners outside. Someone was calling for a guard, and in the distance he could just make out the noise of a lorry's engine. Memories came back like the curse of a ghost. Memories of his marriage, of the joy at the birth of his daughter, of the pride he felt training as an accounts clerk. Nothing to tip the world on its axis, but an achievement that could make a man hold his head high. And with the certificate framed and hung on the kitchen wall, Frederick Coles confirmed his ascent to respectability.

His father had been left behind. Distancing himself, Frederick slowly buried all references to Ernie Coles, and as they moved in different circles, before long he was as remote from his father as from a Russian tsar. A happy marriage continued Frederick's run of luck, and even after his wife's decline and shocking suicide, he considered himself fortunate to have a wonderful child. A daughter who loved him unconditionally. On such a sound basis, Frederick established his mature character. He was elegant and kind, because kindness became him. He was trustworthy and respected, because it was natural for him. Over the next few years, Mr Gregory Walmsley, the boss at Oldfield Mill, became a friend, inviting the newly widowed Frederick to his home one Christmas – with Emma in tow. Frederick's life was not dazzling; it was small and yet perfect. It was happy. It was safe.

Closing his eyes, Frederick could feel his stomach tighten, as it always did when he remembered the look on Gregory Walmsley's face. The expression of incredulity, then disgust. The man he had liked and trusted had been proved to be a thief . . . Oh Jesus, Frederick thought, flopping back on the bunk and staring upwards at the measured patch of ceiling. Exactly the same size as every other piece of ceiling, in every other cell. Limited, identical, bound. Row after row of ceilings and cells, bunks and slop buckets. Row after row of men, sweating and snoring, some crying in the night. And the routine of checks, and locking, of doors banging, of pots being used in the night. Of enforced closeness with men who were capable of crimes Frederick could not even imagine. His eyes fixed on the ceiling, his heart rate rising. Don't panic, he told himself, don't panic.

One, two, three, four, five . . . He began to count the tiles on the wall. Something he had taught himself, the one means by which he could slow down the anger and frustration. What was he doing here? He was innocent, he shouldn't be here. Eleven years they'd given him. *Eleven years* . . . Six, seven, eight, nine . . . Slowly his hands relaxed, the sounds of the prison and the smell of the sweating man in the bunk above him fading as other images took precedence. He was whistling, coming up the alleyway with an orange in his pocket for Emma. And she saw him, running towards him. Then he thought of the war. Unable to fight because of burst eardrums, Frederick had been excused active duty, but he had spent all his spare time doing volunteer work. He thought of Ricky Holmes then, of their first meeting. And then

75

he remembered how Ricky had stood, embarrassed, at his cell door.

Twenty-nine, thirty, thirty-one . . . Keep counting, Frederick told himself. But it wasn't working any more, and instead of remembering the old days, he thought of how a fellow inmate had challenged him the previous day.

'Oi, yer old man's Ernie Coles, ain't he?'

Ernie Coles, Frederick had thought. Of course they would talk about him here. 'What about it?'

'Are yer as hard as him?'

'No,' Frederick had replied wearily, 'I'm nothing like him. Nothing like him at all.'

But that exchange had been the decider for him. The reminder of his father, of the amoral respect Ernie Coles was held in, was enough to make up Frederick's mind. Outside, he had managed to keep himself and his daughter apart from Ernie Coles, but now that gap had been breached. Now people saw him as a criminal, the son of a criminal. But he wasn't going to let Emma be labelled . . . Covering his eyes with his arm, Frederick feigned sleep. But in reality he was saying goodbye. To his respectable name. To his freedom.

To his child.

SEVEN

Christmas Eve 1919

Uncertainly, Emma took the present David Hawksworth was offering her. She studied the little box she
was holding and felt embarrassment, having only
bought him a pair of handkerchiefs. Clearing his
throat, David sat down in the overstuffed armchair,
putting his feet on the footstool, which still bore a
faded image of roses. Emma stared mutely at the box
in her hand, but couldn't open it. Instead she thought
– as she had done repeatedly – of the prison. Of how
she had ignored her father's wishes and gone out to
see him again – only to be refused entry by the guard
on duty. Sorry, the man had said, but your father
can't see you. He said for you to write to him.

Oh, and she *had* written. Page after page, furious
words, angry words, scribbled as the tears stained the
paper. Words that burned the ink as she wrote them.
Then, exhausted, she would stop and tear up the
pages, knowing she could never send them. Knowing
that Frederick's banishment of her – terrible as it was
– had been done for her own good. Slowly, she began
writing again, this time more calmly, reaching out,

second hand, to the father she loved. Telling him news: about Bessie and how she wanted to take over the cobbler's shop one day; about Ricky and how he had asked her out. (She had refused, she reassured her father. He was, after all, only a friend. She liked him a lot, but not like that . . .) And she wrote about the jeweller's shop and David Hawksworth – who was now staring at her.

'Aren't you going to open it?' David asked, cutting into Emma's thoughts and pointing to the box in her hands.

But she didn't want to open it. Didn't want to accept a gift at Christmas when her father would have nothing. Didn't want to enjoy the holiday when he would be suffering. Because although David Hawksworth was trying to be kind, it was forced. He didn't really want Emma in his home, and she didn't want to be there. They might make the best of it, but the truth was as glaring as a crocodile in a tea cup.

'Go on,' David repeated, clearing his throat. 'Open it.'

Slowly, Emma did so, flipping back the lid and staring at a small gold cross, set with garnets. It was delicate and appealing, but instead of being pleased, she felt anger. Anger that she should be expected to believe in a deity that had imprisoned her father for a crime he didn't commit. Irritation that she should worship some god that allowed her to be plucked from her own home and put in another man's house. A narrow shop, with narrow stairs, narrow rooms and a thousand ticking clocks to remind her, end-lessly, of the eleven years that stretched out ahead . . . Holding the cross in the palm of her hand, Emma stared at it. How could she – of all people – believe in God?

And then she remembered something her father had told her, many years earlier: 'You have to be kind to people – even if you don't understand them.'

So, smiling uncertainly, Emma looked at her uncle. 'Thank you very much. It's beautiful.'

He cleared his throat, pleased.

'But I haven't got anything special for you.'

Immediately he brushed the words aside. 'Hand-kerchiefs are excellent. I don't need anything. But it's a custom to give children a present at Christmas.'

The words sounded damning. Coldly respectable. It was a custom. Adults gave children presents. Even though Emma was hardly a child, and never *his* child. Suddenly her curiosity overrode her caution.

'Where's your son?'

He reacted by flinching. Then he slid his feet off the faded pattern of roses and stood up, smoothing his black suit jacket, his tone even.

'Mr and Mrs Palmer have very kindly invited us to a Christmas lunch with them,' he began, ignoring Emma's question. 'I shall not be going, but you are welcome to accept.'

Struggling to her feet, Emma stammered, 'Won't you be lonely on your own?'

He stared at her as though the thought had never occurred to him, then took the cross from her hand.

Embarrassed, Emma thought he was taking it away from her, but instead he said:

'Would you like me to fasten this around your neck? It's what I would do for a customer.'

She turned automatically, holding her hair out of the way as he fastened the chain, without touching her skin. As she heard him step back, Emma turned and looked at her uncle. In that instant she saw the situation for what it was: difficult for both of them. A horrible, forced arrangement, born out of necessity, not choice. And she saw then something else in her uncle: a loneliness too deep to admit, a pride that forbade intimacy and a sadness that – for the first time – gave him some likeness to Frederick.

'Thank you,' Emma said again. And then, without thinking, she kissed her uncle on the cheek and hurried out.

Mrs Holmes was shaking, a tea towel wrung relentlessly in her hands. Wiry, yet well muscled, she ground her teeth and then let out a howl of suppressed rage, her friendly face suddenly transformed into a mask of fury.

'BESSIE!' she shouted, hurling herself towards the bottom of the stairs. 'Get down here, now!'

Surprised, Bessie leapt to her feet, her hair still in papers, her glasses sliding down her nose as she ran down to the kitchen, where Ricky was sitting with his head bowed, in his prison uniform. Their mother was still strangling the tea towel.

'This brother of yours. THIS BROTHER OF

YOURS,' she repeated, just in case anyone in the house, or the surrounding area, had missed it the first time, 'is in love with Emma Coles.'

Bloody hell, Bessie thought, why tell her today? On Christmas Day of all days. The turkey would be overdone, for sure. And she could already smell that the potatoes had caught.

'What?'

'What!' her mother repeated, gawping at Bessie and the papers still in her hair. 'Your brother is in love with Emma Coles.'

Bessie shrugged. 'He always has been.'

As though he had been knifed through the heart, Ricky threw her an agonised glance, as their mother hurled the tea towel across the room.

'HE ALWAYS HAS BEEN!'

'Yeah, it's just kids' stuff,' Bessie went on, acting casually, as though the matter was of no importance. Calmly she walked to the mirror over the fireplace and began to take out her paper curlers, Ricky watching her as though he expected his sister to be struck by lightning at any moment.

But the words had made their mother pause. In fact, the blasé admittance had managed to soothe her, albeit momentarily.

'*Kids' stuff?*'

'Yeah,' Bessie went on, pulling out the papers and tossing them on the fire. 'I'm always teasing our Ricky about it. Mind you, when he *really* falls in love, poor Emma will be history.' She turned to her mother, her expression surprised. 'What? You didn't think it was serious, did you?'

Relaxing, her mother took a deep breath. 'Someone said they had seen Ricky talking to Emma Coles in town.'

'Well, he could hardly ignore her, could he? I mean, they are friends.'

'I don't want either of you to be friends with that girl!' Mrs Holmes snapped back, but the fire had gone out of her. Now believing that there was no romance going on, she reached for the tea towel and flicked it playfully in the direction of her son. 'Why didn't you explain, you big daft sod?'

He rallied fast. 'You didn't give me a chance. God, Mum, you know how people talk in Burnley. They'd gossip about anything.'

'Ricky were talking to next door's cat yesterday,' Bessie said blithely. 'I bet you hear about that before morning.' She caught her brother's eye and winked. 'You working the late shift?'

Relieved, he also relaxed, both of them watching as Mrs Holmes checked the potatoes on the stove. 'Nah, I'm not working again until Wednesday.'

Careful not to be seen, Bessie mouthed, *I'm meeting Emma tomorrow in the park, want to come?*

Nodding, Ricky glanced back at their mother, who was standing with a tray of burned potatoes in her hands, her expression accusing.

'Now look what you made me do!' she said brokenly. 'I've overcooked them, getting all worked up like that. And it's our Christmas dinner.'

'Ah, Mum,' Bessie said easily, 'scrape off the

burned bits and no one will be any the wiser.'

After all, she thought to herself, a few burned potatoes were a small price to pay for avoiding disaster.

Mrs Palmer – Florence, as she insisted on being called – was tipsy on sherry, her cushiony bosom heaving in her voile top, her plump hands clasped around the cheap glass as she leaned towards Emma.

'Of course,' she confided, 'yer uncle won't talk about his son, because it was a right do . . .'

Harry sighed, watching his wife, and wondering if he could steal away and flop into the nearest armchair. Having never been much of a drinker himself, he had to admit that Florence was a good cook, even if she indulged a little too liberally with the sherry. Not that he had the guts to tell her. Florence was formidable sober. Drunk, she was terrifying.

'You could hear them arguing through the walls – couldn't you, Harold?'

He muttered something inaudible and lowered himself into his armchair carefully, as though expecting the whole of the Christmas dinner to burst through his stomach on impact.

'Men, hey?' Florence went on, raising her eyebrows and glancing back to Emma. 'You'll find a nice man, good-looking girl like you. I mean, even with your history.'

'Oh, Florence . . .'

'The truth's the truth,' she went on, her marcel-waved hair hennaed a brittle red, her focus slightly blurred as she stared at her husband. 'And the truth of the matter is that Emma's not the best catch – what with her father's trouble. Mind you, your dad's an improvement on Ernie Coles.'

Curious, Emma pressed her for more information. Although open on all other topics, Frederick had always clammed up when she asked about her grandfather.

'What's Ernie like?'

'Well, built like a brick shithouse,' Florence said, taking another sip of sherry and burping softly. 'Hands like muck shovels. I imagine he might have been handsome in a way. A while back. A long while back.'

Harold shot his wife an incredulous look. '*Ernie Coles?*'

'Oh, go to sleep!' Florence remonstrated. 'What d'you know about what a woman goes for? He were a hero in the war, you know.'

'My grandfather?'

'Nah,' Florence replied, hitching up her flesh-coloured bra strap. 'My Harold. I say,' she said loudly, as though he was sitting in the street and not a couple of feet away from her, 'yer were a hero, weren't yer?'

He waved the words aside, but Emma was keen to hear the story.

'Was he really?' she asked Florence, watching as the tobacconist's wife topped up her sherry. Behind them, the Christmas dishes were stacked in the

Belfast sink, and the stove was covered with empty pans, a ripple of gravy drying on the oven door. 'What did he do?'

'Saved a woman.'

'Really?'

'Saved her from certain death.'

Harold rolled his eyes. 'She was pregnant, not dying.'

'If you hadn't helped her . . .'

Emma thought back to the news reports during the war. 'Was she caught behind enemy lines?'

'Nah, she was caught behind the counter at the tripe shop on Grey Street,' Florence replied, then noticed the look of disappointment on Emma's face and hurried on. 'Well, she were in labour and he helped her. And it were wartime, so it counts. Harold were a war hero.'

'Oh, I see that, yes,' Emma replied, thinking of how she would enclose this gem in her next letter to her father. 'But getting back to Ernie Coles . . .'

'A drinker.'

'A drunk?'

'Nah, he could hold his drink. Some of us can,' Florence went on, not realising that she was slurring her words as she said it. 'Harold, although he's a war hero . . . I said you were a war hero, Harold,' she repeated more loudly, as though he was deaf. 'Harold can't hold his drink. I said, you can't hold your drink.'

Moaning softly, Harold closed his eyes against the onslaught, Florence leaning further towards Emma.

'But Ernie Coles, now he can drink. There were rumours about him a long time ago – my father used to talk about your grandad. But he's not stupid, Ernie Coles. Might run with a rough crowd, but he's harder than most and can handle himself.'

'But he's a criminal.'

'He's a *thug*,' Florence replied emphatically, banging her hand on the table as she uttered the word. 'Being a big man and one people found bloody frightening, well, it were easy to make a living out of all that muscle. He was a bookie's runner for a while, then a bailiff, then someone said he was called in to deal with a pub down Post Street way. He were good at that, and from then on Ernie Coles was called in to sort out pubs, clubs and people.'

'*People?*'

Behind her, Harold coughed. 'We don't know, Florence, this is only rumour.'

'Gruberman wasn't a rumour,' Florence retorted, 'and the Spencer brothers weren't a bloody rumour either.'

Emma stared at her, transfixed. 'Who were the Spencer brothers?'

'Came from over Hanky Park way, ran with the Gallagers. Well, they thought they could take over in Burnley and opened up a snooker hall by the town hall. Every no-good man in the town went there, and before long even the police wouldn't go in, it got so rough.' Florence took another sip of sherry, running her tongue over her bottom lip. 'Well, Ernie Coles went in and before long the Spencer brothers were back in Hanky Park. The younger Spencer lost an eye.'

Shocked, Emma stared at Florence. 'I can't believe it. How could he be like that?' She thought of her father, understanding why Frederick had been so reluctant to talk about Ernie Coles. And so eager to keep her away from him. 'I mean, I'd heard all kinds of things at the trial. But I thought it was gossip.'

'Nah, anything you hear about your grandfather you can believe, and probably double it.' Florence paused, suddenly reaching out for Emma's hand and patting it maternally. 'But your dad's not like his father.'

'So why is he in jail and Ernie Coles isn't?'

Behind Emma, Harold caught his wife's eye. It was a good point, one many people had made.

Hurriedly, Florence changed tack.

'Of course, your uncle won't even mention his stepfather's name. If David Hawksworth had his way, he would deny he had anything to do with Ernie Coles.'

'Or my father,' Emma added, her tone muted. 'But why didn't that make them closer?'

'Well, your dad's a reasonable kind of man, but David Hawksworth's stiff-backed, terrified of losing face. He weren't always like that, mind. When he were first married, and they had their son, your uncle was happy. I remember seeing him laughing now and again. But time moved on and he changed.'

Realising that the atmosphere was getting sombre, Emma moved back to a previous topic. 'But what about Adam, their son? When I mentioned him, my uncle clammed up. Wouldn't tell me a thing.'

'Adam,' Florence said. 'Now he was an odd boy. Very nice-looking, but a bit easily led. Mind you, that was because his mother had spoiled him. Your uncle didn't like that at all. Used to argue with her about it, make a real racket.'

'I can't imagine that,' Emma replied. 'My uncle seems very quiet.'

'Oh, he is – he was – except where his son was concerned. He were his Achilles heel, were Adam. Your uncle wanted him to make something of himself, take over the jeweller's. But Adam wasn't interested. He liked a good time, a laugh. More like his mother than his father. And I think he looked at Jenny and saw what had happened to her.'

'Florence,' Harold said warningly, 'you shouldn't be talking about people like this. It's the girl's family.'

'Which means Emma has a right to know,' Florence responded firmly. 'I'm not putting it up on a billboard; the girl asked me and I'm telling her. God, Harold, it's better she gets it from us than from half the nosy buggers in Burnley, who'd put their own slant on it and call it gospel.' Turning back to Emma, she continued. 'Jenny was very young when she married your uncle, and pretty, in a pale kind of way. Oh, you could hear her laughing with the customers and with your uncle, and I used to say to Harold, *Listen to that, they're having a good time*. But after a few years, she began to change. Got more reserved and serious, more like her husband. She spoke warmly of him, and I think she were proud of him. David Hawksworth was always a smart, well-spoken man. But over the years he became a wearer-down.'

'A what?'

'The kind of person who wears people down. Not deliberately. Not meanly. Not with violence, or unkindness. Your uncle's no more like Ernie Coles than your father is. But he's the type to think a joke's a waste of time. You can respect him, and he's honest, but not a man you'd want around a deathbed. Unless you want to go quick . . .'

Behind Emma, Harold laughed. Florence took another sip of sherry before she continued.

'Poor Jenny, but when Adam came along, she was in heaven. Clucked at that kid, nursed him, pushed him out for hours round the town, talking to everyone. And as for his layette, I remember telling Harold, *That's cost a week's wage of anyone's money*. She worshipped that boy, and when he went to school he was brilliant – to hear Jenny tell it. Although I know for a fact that Adam were no more than average, and could be a bit of a bully. But with his mother feeding him all this praise, he began to believe that he were more handsome and cleverer than anyone. So when his father tried to keep his feet on the ground, well, David Hawksworth became an ogre, didn't he? And Jenny came down on Adam's side, which were when the arguments started.'

'Did Adam learn the business?'

Florence shook her head. 'Your uncle began to

teach him, but Adam weren't interested. He'd skive off and run around with his friends, and talk about how he were going to London to paint portraits of famous people.'

'He was an artist?'

'Adam Hawksworth was an actor, an artist, a songwriter – oh, you name it, Adam could do it. Only he couldn't. He could *talk* about doing it, but that were as far as it went. And then, one day, there were this furious argument. We could hear, couldn't we, Harold? Harold!'

Harold jerked upright. 'Oh, yes, yes.'

'Adam was in the back yard and his father was out there too, and Adam was talking about how he'd bought a bike. A motorbike! With his savings. *What savings?* David asked. *You don't need to know*, Adam replied. And your uncle went mad.' Florence paused, thinking back. 'I always believe it would have blown over, but for Jenny getting involved. She came into the back yard and stood between the two of them, and somehow things got even more heated and he hit her.'

'My uncle hit his wife?'

'Nah,' Florence said shortly. 'Adam hit his mother.'

'God . . .'

'Yeah, that were a bad day,' Florence admitted. 'Your uncle threw his son out. Said he wasn't going to have him under the roof, and that he was a spoiled brat, and how could he hurt his mother? And Adam said it were an accident, and Jenny said it were too, but I'm not sure. You see, Adam *could* lose his rag

90

sometimes. He were a bit suspect at times. He had a look about him. A little edge of cruelty, slyness.'

'So Adam left?'

Florence nodded. 'In the middle of the night. No one knew he'd gone, and when I saw Jenny the next day, she was crying and saying how she didn't think he'd leave. And how he'd gone without saying goodbye. That was the beginning of the end for that marriage.'

'But my uncle was only protecting her . . .'

'Yes, but she didn't want to be protected by him. She didn't want to be grateful to him. And she didn't want your uncle to stay with her when their son had left.' Florence finished her sherry. 'They started to grow further and further apart, and within two years Jenny hated David Hawksworth. Whenever we were talking over the wall, she'd purse her lips when she heard his voice. She never went back to serve in the shop. She used to say that the shop was more important than their son, like her husband had chosen the jeweller's over Adam, and she would never help out in there again. Instead she went out. Used to go to the spiritualist church, and I heard a rumour that she'd hired someone to see if they could trace Adam. But no one heard from him – until, about three years later, a letter came. He'd gone over to New Zealand and bought himself a farm. He even said that when he'd made a fortune he'd send for his mother, but it were just another pipe dream. He were a braggart, Adam Hawksworth, a terrible liar. He'd say anything, puff himself up, lie like a rug. Trying to get a straight story out of him was like trying to plait sand.'

In silence, Emma thought about her bedroom – the one that had once belonged to Adam Hawksworth. She thought of the toy boat and the football boots, of the initials scratched in the window, and imagined the sound of a boy's footsteps running into the silence of the jeweller's shop. She could also imagine how guilty David Hawksworth must have felt, and how shocked to realise that his actions had caused the breakdown of his marriage and the hatred of his wife. As for Adam . . . Emma frowned. Why had he waited so long to write? Why torture his parents? He must have known how his mother would worry, and how his silence would damn his father. He must have waited, estimating the damage his timing would inflict.

With a further understanding of her uncle, Emma left the Palmers soon after, letting herself in by the back door of the shop. Still deep in thought, she moved upstairs to the living quarters, but, not finding her uncle there, climbed to the cramped workshop under the eaves. As she hesitated outside the door, Emma thought of everything she had been told about David Hawksworth's life. About a reserved man who had tried to be respectable. About a man with a pretty, cheerful wife. A man who had tried to keep his business running for his son to inherit. A man who had been young once, with plans and hopes. A man who had seen them all slip from his fingers, as elusive and poisonous as mercury . . .

Walking into the workroom, Emma saw her uncle bent over the table, a lens strapped around his head, so that he could see the clock's workings more easily. He hadn't heard her enter, that much was obvious, and in silence Emma watched him and felt a pity as intense as it was unexpected.

Slowly she walked over to the work table, her uncle looking up, surprised to see her.

'You're back.'

'Yes,' Emma said quietly, looking at the clock mechanism on the table. 'Is it working?'

'Not yet.'

'Can you mend it?'

He seemed surprised by her interest, and answered cautiously. 'I can try.'

Carefully, Emma picked up the fine tools her uncle used, and then, sitting down on a high stool next to him, said:

'May I watch? I'd like to.'

She thought for a moment that he would refuse. She could even sense his reluctance to accept. In those few instants she knew that their relationship hung in the balance. If he rejected her, she would be forever Frederick Coles's daughter. A burden, something to be endured, under sufferance. But if he accepted, she would become a person in her own right. She would have cracked his reserve, and risked her own vulnerability to make a connection with him . . . Downstairs, the clocks began chiming in unison, the old grandfather one beat behind.

When they finished striking the hour, David

93

Hawksworth bent down over the table and began to work again, without even glancing in his niece's direction.

The gauntlet had been thrown down. But not picked up.

PART TWO

Look in my face;
my name is Might-have-been.

Dante Gabriel Rossetti

It had been a slight chance, I knew that at the time, but it still hurt when he rejected me. In silence – I can remember it so well, even now – I walked downstairs. I didn't know what to do that Christmas evening. Whether to visit Bessie, or stay in my room. I know I was tempted to pull the cross from around my neck and throw it out of the window. But I didn't.

Did I think of visiting the prison? Of course. I had been thinking of it all day. But my father had told me what he wanted, and I had to agree. So instead I put on my coat and walked out into the silent streets. It was snowing; old Jack Rimmer waved from his front-room window as I passed. Nine months had gone by since I had come to the jeweller's shop. Nine months – not much in a lifetime, but more eventful than any other time in mine. And strangely enough, my mind felt clearer that night than it had done for many weeks.

I knew then that I could not make a life with my uncle. My time there could only be temporary. I would have to find another place to call home . . . And as I walked, I felt someone walking with me –

the ghost of Jenny Hawksworth. Her story followed me down the Burnley streets, stayed with me as I crossed Towneley Park, pausing by the memorial that had been erected to the fallen after the end of the war.

And I realised then that people didn't just fall in wartime. That events, circumstances and choices made people fall all the time. So when I finally turned away from the memorial, I made myself a promise – I would not let myself be worn down. Other people's attitudes would not break me, or change me.

There was to be no memorial to the fallen on my grave.

EIGHT

January 1921, Burnley

'I can't believe it. It's been over a year since my father went to jail,' Emma said, dropping into step with Ricky as they walked towards the bus stop to wait for the bus that would take them from the Moors Prison back home.

She had grown used to seeing him around when she visited her father, but that day she had been surprised when she left and he ran after her. Explaining that his shift had ended, he linked arms with her and they began to talk.

'A year,' he repeated, feeling the appealing warmth of Emma's arm against his own. 'God, time goes so quick. I could get a promotion soon.'

She nodded. 'You deserve it . . . Did I ever thank you? For looking out for Dad?'

'You thank me all the time. And all the time I say it's a pleasure.' He paused, took off his prison cap and smoothed back his thick hair. In the winter light he was striking, his dark eyes and hair seeming even more of a contrast with his fair skin. 'I like your dad, Emma, you know that. We chat quite a lot now, and play cards. Well, when I have the time. And I let him have the newspapers from the guards' room. He likes that, likes to know what's going on in the world. Honestly, I enjoy your father's company . . . and I'd do anything for you.'

He was determined he was going to say something. This was the perfect time. No point hesitating; he had waited long enough. He would state his case and tell Emma how much he loved her. Because he did. He loved her face, her voice, her expressions. He loved the way she walked, the tilt of her head and that slow smile that made her eyes shine. If he had been in love before, Ricky Holmes was now smitten with Emma Coles, and determined – utterly determined – that she would be his.

'My uncle made a good sale yesterday,' Emma said suddenly, hearing the snow crunching under her boots as they approached the bus stop. 'Apparently he had a ring that turned out to be French.'

Ricky's dark eyebrows rose. 'French?'

'Could have been from the French court,' she teased him, larking about with him as she had always done. 'Could have belonged to a queen.'

'In France, the men are very gallant,' Ricky said, picking up Emma's hand and kissing it. Laughing, he then pretended to spit out some imaginary fluff.

'You kiss the bare hand!' Emma said, laughing too as she slid off her glove and Ricky repeated the action.

'Madame.'

'Monsieur,' she replied archly, feeling his cool lips

on the back of her hand and smiling.

'Of course,' Ricky went on, light-headed at her closeness, 'if you were an Eskimo, you would greet a person differently.'

'But I don't know any Eskimos.'

'Well, just in case you ever meet one, I'll tell you how to behave. I mean, you wouldn't want to look ignorant, would you?'

'Not in front of an Eskimo, no.'

Grinning, Ricky leaned forwards. 'They rub noses to say hello.'

Immediately Emma burst out laughing, then tipped her head up, Ricky rubbing his nose against hers. The action tickled her, but Ricky felt a surge of attraction and drew away. Although he had been smiling, he was now serious, his eyes dark as he leaned back to her and tenderly kissed her cheek.

'Is this also what the Eskimos do?'

He could hardly speak. Just kissed her on the other cheek and then – tenderly – on the mouth.

Surprised, Emma realised in that instant that the Ricky she knew, the lad she had grown up with, was a man. He had been larking about with her, but this was attraction, an electricity she could feel coming from him, a longing that confused her, it was so unexpected.

'Ricky,' she said, drawing back, 'I don't . . .'

In that instant a couple approached the bus stop, putting paid to the conversation and any further intimacy, and leaving both of them suspended in an agonising state of confusion. Unnerved, Emma felt

Ricky's arm through hers and was suddenly embarrassed, because he wasn't her chum any more, he was a man. And he loved her. She knew that now – and knew that she hadn't understood it until then. She was fond of him, but she didn't yet love him. But maybe she could. Maybe she should . . .

In silence, they boarded the bus when it came, and in silence they watched the snow-drifted Moors fade away as they approached the town outskirts. Once or twice Emma said something light-hearted to Ricky, but he just shrugged, choked up, not trusting his voice. Confused, Emma stared out of the window. Why hadn't she realised what he felt for her? Why didn't she feel the same for him? God knows, he was good-looking enough, funny, and with a proper job. And he had been so kind to her father. Surely that was a more than good enough reason to fall in love? Baffled, she chewed the finger of her glove, close to tears and desperate to regain Ricky's friendship. They had had so much fun together, so many larks. She had been his pal, his kid sister – but not any more.

When they finally arrived back in Burnley, Ricky helped her off the bus and then smiled awkwardly.

'I . . . I love you.'

'Oh, Ricky.'

'You'll fall in love with me. If you let yourself,' he went on urgently, in a misery of confusion. 'Take your time, Emma. Just don't brush me off. Think about it, OK?'

NINE

Over a year after it was first mentioned, David Hawksworth had begun to teach Emma the jewellery business. She was pleased to have something to think about, to take her mind off her confusion about Ricky. Over the weeks that had followed, she had seen Ricky a few times, going for walks and letting him hold her hand, and feeling – what a surprise! – some simmering of excitement building up inside her. Some intimation that she might well be falling in love with Ricky Holmes. When she had confided her tentative feelings in a letter to Frederick, her father had responded encouragingly. He liked Ricky; he was a good man, and he loved her. In fact, Frederick wrote, he wouldn't mind Ricky Holmes as his son-in-law.

But there was no pressure, not from Ricky or Frederick; they both let her take time to come to her own decision. Which was exactly what Emma needed. Staring out of the window of the jeweller's shop, she watched a couple passing by, deep in conversation. The man said something and the woman laughed, and Emma laughed too, caught up in their private moment. *And knowing that she was falling in love too.* Albeit slowly and cautiously . . . As she kept staring out of the window, she noticed that the weedy tree at the end of Holland Street had started to break into leaf, and when she looked up to the sky, the clouds were making way for the first shimmer of sunshine. Over the rooftops and chimneys birds flew again, and the rain left its shiny evidence on cobbles. And across the street a boy played with a hoop, the far-off factory hooter sounding cheerfully as it straddled the morning air.

In reality, the long northern winter was over and spring was coming. Inside Emma, *her* winter was over too, the dark days of her loss and confusion, and suddenly she was longing for her own personal renaissance. She had gladly accepted her uncle's offer, and begun to learn the jewellery trade. And what a trade it had turned out to be . . . Unlocking the partially gilded steel door of the safe, her uncle would take out tray after tray of rings, followed by soft pouches stuffed with gold chains. Surprised, Emma had stood, listening to him talk, and watching his dour, cold character open, just as the door of the safe had opened.

As he touched the gold, his clean hands running over the chains, he did not express avarice, but admiration. When he held a jewel to the desk light and let the colours prism like fireflies, he was not covetous, but wondering. He spoke of the pieces as another man would talk of his family, with affection and pride, and when he returned them to the steel nest of their safekeeping, it was like watching a mother put her children down to rest.

At the same time, Emma was wondering about her uncle's life and her own; thinking that being married to Ricky Holmes was an appealing idea. She knew him, and already loved him, albeit as a surrogate older brother. Surely that love could change to become a romantic love? Ricky was handsome, and funny, and he understood her and what had happened to her father. How many men would be so understanding? So accepting and forgiving? Not many, Emma knew. God knows, she had hardly been accepted by anyone since her father's imprisonment, and there had been no boyfriends. No male interest, despite her good looks. Gossip and scandal had soured her chances.

But had it? After all, Ricky Holmes loved her. Knew her inside out. Had been around her life for years, and cared for her father. Could she – in all honesty – hope for a better match?

'We should weigh this chain,' David said suddenly, cutting into her thoughts. Emma lifted the small brass weighing scales. Carefully her uncle placed a gold chain on one side and a selection of weights on the other.

Then he sighed contentedly. 'Good. Good quality. *Gold.*'

Transfixed, Emma stared at the gold chain shining in the brass cup of the scales. She wondered how Ricky would measure up if *his* virtues were weighed. At that moment she knew his value, and made up her mind.

*

'Give it here, our Ricky!' Bessie said, snatching the book from under her brother's arm and reading the cover. Raising her eyebrows, she looked at him, feigning shock. '*Women in Love*! You mucky little bugger! I've heard all about this book, and none of it's good.'

'Give it back!' he hollered, snatching the dog-eared novel from his sister. 'It's not mine.'

'I bet you wish it was,' she replied, laughing. 'I would never have thought it of you. You wait until Mum hears about this . . .'

He winced. 'You'll not tell her, Bessie?'

'What's it worth to keep quiet?'

His demeanour changed in an instant, a sudden knowing look coming into his eyes. 'You can't afford to be gabby, little sister. What with that secret you're hiding.'

'Which is?'

'Doug Renshaw.'

Miffed, Bessie tossed *Women in Love* back to her brother. When she answered, her voice wasn't as steady as usual.

'Who's Doug Renshaw?'

'Don't try and fool me. That lad you're seeing. The one with the long neck who keeps hanging around the cobbler's.'

Hurriedly she shushed him before their mother overheard. Grabbing his arm, she then led him into the back yard. It was early spring, making its way into summer, but not hot enough to bring out the flies.

'*What* have you heard?'

'Are you courting?'

'Are you?'

His bravado deserted him immediately.

'I told Emma I loved her.'

'Blimey!'

'And what did she say?'

'She was shocked, but she didn't turn me down flat.' He paused, staring at his sister. 'I've seen her a couple of times since. Even saw her yesterday, in the park. She let me kiss her on the cheek.'

'Blimey!'

'Oh, for God's sake, is that all you can say?'

Miffed, Bessie slapped her brother on the back of his head. 'What are you worried about, you ass? Sounds to me as if Emma's coming round nicely.'

'You think it's hopeful?'

'Yeah, I do,' Bessie replied, her tone sincere. 'Give her space and time, and I think it'll work out for you two.'

'And Doug Renshaw?' her brother queried, his tone teasing. 'You going to run him to ground?'

'He's mad for me.'

'He's mad, more like, wanting you!' Ricky joked, then turned protective. 'What's Doug Renshaw like, anyway? I want all the information on this boyfriend of yours. Is he honest? Hard-working? *Is he decent?*'

'If he was,' Bessie quipped cheerfully, 'I wouldn't want him.'

TEN

Spitting on to the concrete floor of the exercise yard, Stan Thorpe watched Frederick Coles as he walked around the enclosure. Something about the man had always irritated Thorpe. With his good looks and implacable calm, he stuck out from the other inmates and grated on the guard's nerves. Thorpe couldn't place the reason for his dislike, and would never have admitted that he was jealous of Frederick Coles. Because even though he was locked up, with another nine years, seven months to serve, Coles was the better man, and Thorpe knew it. He also knew that the other inmates liked him. And that Ricky Holmes – who had been promoted too quickly for Thorpe's liking – was clearly fond of the man. And even fonder of the daughter.

Still watching Coles, Thorpe lit a cigarette and put out his foot, one of the other prisoners tripping over it.

'Mind where yer going, yer fucking idiot!' Thorpe barked, glancing over to Frederick.

But, as ever, the man remained aloof from everything that was going on. Oh, Thorpe mused, he would like to rattle that bastard's cage. But he had no reason. He might try and provoke him, but Coles never rose to the bait. He had thought to use his daughter against him, but that idea had been scuppered. Emma Coles no longer visited the jail.

'How's things?' Reg Spencer asked, walking over to Thorpe and leaning his bulk against the wall.

'I've just stopped a riot single-handed,' Thorpe replied meanly.

Unperturbed, Reg stared at the exercising prisoners. He didn't like Thorpe and knew him for the bastard he was, but that morning there had been a rumour that trouble was afoot. In the North Wing, where the murderers and rapists were kept, one of the guards had found a letter from outside containing a demand that an inmate settle a score. It wasn't unusual. If the prisoner had been part of a gang outside, he remained part of that gang. But that was obvious; some others' ties were more subtle and more deadly. Sometimes a man's legal fees had been paid by an anonymous benefactor, only for the prisoner to discover that his humanitarian ally was also a criminal. Owing money, the inmate would be compelled to do services inside the prison. Sometimes they were simple: he would merely have to report back what he heard. There was always the fear that his betrayal would be discovered and he would take a beating, but if he was careful, a man could carry on the deception for a long time and gradually pay off his debt. The guards didn't intervene. After all, it didn't affect the running of the prison.

But sometimes the favour was called in for a higher price. A killing. And then the prison did intervene, because if an inmate was killed, it affected the whole jail. Besides, unless the inmate was stopped, he would always go through with it. He was already a murderer, and if he refused, he was a marked man.

'I think there's going to be trouble,' Reg said, glancing over to Thorpe, whose thin fingers were wrapped tightly around his smoke. 'I put another couple of guards on the North Wing.'

'On a Sunday? You were lucky you could find anyone spare.'

'How long are you on for today?'

'Another hour,' Thorpe replied, 'and before you ask, no, I won't stay longer.'

Sighing, Reg tried a different approach. 'It probably won't amount to anything, I just wanted to make sure we had some extra help if anything did kick off.'

'Jesus,' Thorpe replied meanly. 'You're worried, Reg, or you wouldn't have bothered. Why don't you just lock up the fucking troublemakers?'

'I don't know who they are. I know who the victim's supposed to be, but not the attacker.'

'So lock up the victim.'

'I can't. It's Bernard Maas. Last time we segregated him, a riot broke out.'

Impatient, Thorpe dropped his cigarette butt and ground it out with his heel. Maas's family had originally come from Holland, and despite his father being a respected local councillor, Bernard had killed two women during the war. Whilst everyone else was running from the Germans, he had come home on leave and – after visiting his wife and children – stopped long enough to kill. Twice. Not only had he killed, he had raped and mutilated the bodies. A plea of insanity had been rejected, and Maas had been given the death sentence. The only reason it hadn't been carried out was that his solicitor had found reason to appeal.

'Who'd bother killing Maas? He'll be hanged soon enough.'

'That's the point,' Reg replied. 'If someone manages to kill him first, it sends out a message that they can overthrow the system. That the inmates are more powerful.'

'Why not send a fucking telegram?' Thorpe replied nastily, still watching the exercising prisoners. 'Why haven't you told the Governor?'

'I can't reach him. He's put his deputy in charge, and he's bloody useless.'

'So why don't you lock down the whole wing?' Thorpe replied. He was a bastard, but a good officer, and hard. No one pushed Thorpe, they were too afraid of him. Even on the North Wing. 'Get the prisoners in their cells and leave them there until morning.'

Reg had already thought of that. Many years of working at the prison had honed his instincts, and he could sense that something was imminent. Without alarming any of the other guards, he had counted the men available. Sundays were usually quiet. For some

111

reason, Thursdays and Saturdays were always the worst. But on Sundays, the inmates had visitors and that normally left them thoughtful. Even cheerful. Not that day, though. By the time Reg had counted the staff, he reckoned he could manage, but if there was trouble, he would have liked a couple more guards to call on. Which was why he was talking to Thorpe.

'Work the afternoon, will you?'

'Piss off.'

'Stan, come on, it's just once.'

'It's Sunday.'

'What difference does that make? You going to church or something?'

Thorpe shook his head. 'I never work after noon on Sunday. I spend the day with my wife. Lucky cow.'

'Just for a couple of hours . . .'

'No,' Thorpe replied emphatically. 'Get hold of the Deputy Governor if you're really worried.'

'You know he never makes a decision.'

'Well, if it were me, I'd lock up Maas and the rest of the North Wing.'

'Which might *cause* an incident.'

Despite himself, Thorpe paused. 'How many guards are on over there?'

'Five. We're two short. Both off sick.'

'Call a couple more in. They'll do it, for overtime.'

'If you stayed . . .'

'Nah, not me,' Thorpe replied, making a big show of looking at his watch. 'Time up, I'm off.'

Watching him leave, Reg waited for the next guard

to take Thorpe's place, and was surprised to see Ricky Holmes enter the exercise yard. Ricky was a quick learner and a good guard, but he had never been on the North Wing. God, Reg thought, on a day when I need some old hands . . .

Smiling, he walked over. 'Hello, Ricky, how's things? I thought Bert was on this shift.'

'He swapped with me. Wanted a Sunday off.'

'You should have asked permission,' Reg replied, unusually sharp.

'I didn't think it would be a problem.'

Regretting his brusque tone, Reg turned to the younger man. 'No problem, lad. But we might have a busy afternoon. Did Dave Lomond come on duty with you?'

Ricky shook his head. 'Nah, no one else came in with me, and there was no one in the guards' room. Dave said he was going to be late today. Coming on at four.'

Now troubled, Reg mused over the information. They had four hours and were down three men . . .

'Right, lad,' he said, his voice composed. 'I want you to get these prisoners back on the wing.'

'Now?'

'Yes, now!' Reg snapped, watching Ricky jump into action. Glancing at his watch, Reg looked at the time. Twelve fifteen. No point panicking, he told himself, maybe nothing would happen. But if it did, there were only two men available to help. Himself and Ricky.

Ten minutes later, Ricky had all the prisoners back

on the wing, the sky darkening and a heavy rainfall slamming against the vaulted roof. Dim already in the faltering light, the wing seemed even gloomier than usual. Some prisoners had been called to the visitors' room; Frederick was reading in his cell. Concentrating on his book, he was surprised to find Ricky standing in the doorway.

'Hello there.'

'Hello, Mr Coles,' Ricky replied, hovering on the threshold.

Smiling, Freddie beckoned for him to come further in, Ricky taking the hard chair opposite the bunk.

'You doing all right?'

'Fine,' Frederick replied. 'I heard you got promoted, well done.'

Smiling, Ricky nodded. 'Got a pay rise.'

'That's good, too.'

'Not bad,' Ricky replied. He had taken off his guard's cap and was turning it round repeatedly in his hands. 'Means I could rent a place of my own.'

'A man should have his own place,' Frederick replied, putting a marker in his book and swinging his legs over the edge of the bunk. He could sense that Ricky wanted to talk, and was curious.

'Yeah,' Ricky went on, 'a place of my own. Well, for me and . . . It could be big enough for a couple.'

Frederick smiled, teasing him. 'A couple? Are you getting married, Ricky?'

The younger man's expression seemed to veer between happiness and anxiety, his hands still turning the hat around.

'Emma . . .'

'What about her?'

'You must know, Mr Coles,' Ricky hurried on. 'You must know what I think of your daughter. I've cared for her for a long time.'

'I know that, Ricky. The way you talk about her gives it away.'

'So you don't mind?' Ricky countered.

'It's not up to me, it's up to my daughter. Have you spoken to her about how you feel?'

'I don't know what she thinks about me. I told her I loved her, but she seemed shocked. Not repelled, just amazed. As if she hadn't thought of it before. I mean, I know we were kids together—'

'And you were a very bad influence,' Frederick teased him. 'Don't think I don't know about how you two broke into that abandoned shop.'

Ricky flushed. 'I always looked out for her.'

'God help you if you hadn't.'

'But I don't think of her like that any more. Not as a friend. I love her.' He paused, shaking his head. 'I told her to think about it. I mean, she didn't brush me off; it was like she needed to get her mind round the idea.'

'Ricky,' Frederick said truthfully, 'I don't know what to say.'

'I think she'll come round to it. I think she'll fall for me.'

Frederick thought it wouldn't be such a bad thing. Ricky had been a tearaway, reckless and high-spirited, but he had changed. Still good fun, but now responsible. A reliable man, who worked hard. He had proved that by getting a job and a promotion. But he was still so young, only twenty . . . Frederick stared at the floor between their feet. He had warned Emma to keep away from the prison, desperate that she didn't ruin her chances. But here he was, the man who loved her – *his guard*. The man who locked him in at night. The man who turned the key. The man who was in charge of him. The irony was not lost on Frederick. He had hoped for Emma to make a good match, and had worried that his shame would hamper her progress. But Ricky Holmes knew everything about her – and loved her despite it.

'Talk to her,' Frederick suggested.

Ricky smiled cheekily. 'Will *you* talk to her again?'

'About what?'

'About me,' Ricky said firmly. 'You know me, Mr Coles, and I know that what you say goes a long way with Emma. If you could put in a good word, speak up for me, she might look on me more favourably.' He stopped turning his hat and held Frederick's gaze. 'You know I would look after her, and love her. You'd have no worries on that score. She thinks of me as just a friend. But you could talk to her, remind her that I've *always* loved her, and that nothing will ever change that.'

ELEVEN

'Mum! Mum!' Bessie cried, running into the kitchen and grabbing her mother's arm frantically. 'There's a riot at the prison.'

Struggling to her feet, Mrs Holmes stared into her daughter's ashen face. 'What? What are you talking about?'

'It's all over town, Mum. I've just heard about it. There's a riot at the jail – and our Ricky's on duty!'

Grabbing her coat, Mrs Holmes made for the door, Bessie following her. Together the two women ran to the corner of Noble Street, where they stood, Mrs Holmes tying a scarf around her head, waiting for the next bus. The older woman's face was grey as she looked round impatiently.

'How did you hear?'

'Annie told me,' Bessie replied, 'and then I went in her house and listened to the radio. They said that the North Wing was in an uproar.'

'Our Ricky's not on the North Wing. He doesn't go there,' Mrs Holmes said, trying to calm herself as the bus arrived and they both climbed on. Paying

117

their fares, she then slumped into a seat. 'Ricky's never worked the North Wing.'

'I know,' Bessie agreed. 'Maybe we shouldn't go up there. Maybe we should just wait at home.'

'What did the radio say?'

'That some guards had been taken hostage,' Bessie said, her voice low. 'By the prisoners on the North Wing.'

'Ricky doesn't work on the North Wing.'

'No.'

'He never has. That's where they keep the murderers, isn't it?'

Bessie took her mother's hand. She could feel it shaking in hers. 'Ricky will be all right, Mum. We should have stayed at home and waited for news. He won't half be angry we've made such a fuss.'

'He'll be fine,' her mother said distantly, 'but it's right that we're going to the prison. He'll give us hell when he sees us, though.'

She glanced at her daughter, Bessie nodding. 'He'll say you made a baby out of him.'

'But we should go, nonetheless,'

'Yeah, Mum. We should.'

In silence they made the trip out of town towards the Moors. The trip Emma had taken many times alone. As they drew closer to the prison, they watched the passengers thin out, until only a few remained. People who didn't talk and who avoided eye contact. Huddled into her coat, Mrs Holmes stared out of the window, Bessie craning her neck to see ahead. Then, from out of nowhere, the huge bulk of the prison came into view.

It struck terror into both women, Mrs Holmes reaching for her daughter's hand. Bessie got off the bus with her mother. As they walked along the hard road that led to the gates, they could see a gathering of people. One man was struggling with a camera and tripod, and another, with a notepad, was calling to one of the guards who was standing on the wall high above them.

'Bloody hell,' Bessie said, looking round. 'It's like a carnival.' Without thinking, she called up to the guard herself. 'What's happening?'

'We have everything under control.'

'How many guards are being held hostage?' a man called out, pushing past Bessie and moving closer to the wall.

'We have it all under control.'

'That's not what the radio said!' someone else shouted. 'Radio said it were *out of* control.'

Unnerved, Mrs Holmes stared up at the guard, her gaze moving over the high, forbidding walls topped with barbed wire. In the distance, the sound of a siren started up, the noise boring into the cold air. Deafening and intimidating, it hammered into the rain. And then suddenly, after all the noise, there was silence. Catching her breath, Bessie looked round. The guard looked round too, as though surprised, then disappeared from sight over the other side. A long moment passed, everyone waiting. Even the man with the notepad was quiet, the cameraman waiting along with everyone else. The atmosphere seemed transfixed, suspended, the silence even more threatening than the calls from the crowd, or the siren.

For another two minutes the stillness persisted. Two minutes, one hundred and twenty seconds, whilst the rain continued to fall on the high walls and the metal doors. And then finally the doors opened, the crowd pushing forwards as a prison van came out. It moved slowly between the people, guards blocking the gates. As Bessie watched the van's progress, it was followed out by an ambulance. Startled, she moved towards the ambulance, losing her mother's grip as she pushed towards the vehicle. Then, frantically, she began to try and wrench open the door, the driver staring straight ahead.

A moment later, Mrs Holmes caught up with her daughter and gripped Bessie's arm, her expression bewildered.

'What are you doing? *What are you doing?*'

Behind them there was the sound of movement and hurried footsteps. Both the women turned, just as the Deputy Governor came out, flanked by guards. He told the waiting crowd that there had been a serious incident at the prison, in the North Wing. He said that two guards had been taken hostage by the prisoners, and that one had been killed. It was, he said, a terrible accident. But they had everything under control again.

'What was his name?' Bessie cried out, the Deputy Governor turning at the sound of her voice. '*What was his name!*'

'He was a guard—'

'What was his name?'

'Mr Richard Holmes,' he said finally. 'A very brave officer, who had gone to help his colleagues.'

At that moment, Bessie felt her mother slump against her, half fainting to the ground as she repeated, over and over again: 'Ricky doesn't work the North Wing. He doesn't go there.'

TWELVE

Having finished her shopping, Emma rounded the corner of her street and headed for the jeweller's. As she approached Jack Rimmer's shop, she saw that it was still open, late at night, and that Mr and Mrs Palmer were talking to the old man in hurried whispers. They all stopped talking as they saw her, Emma dropping her shopping and hurrying over.

'What is it? My father?'

'No, luv,' Florence said, taking Emma's arm. 'It's news from the prison, though.'

'Emma! Come in!' David Hawksworth called out from the entrance of his shop. 'Please, come in.'

Unnerved, she obeyed, following her uncle, who closed the door after her.

In the sombre room she stood, her face urgent. 'What's happened?'

'Your friend, Richard Holmes . . .'

'What about Ricky?'

'He was killed. At the prison where—' David stopped immediately, skirting any reference to Frederick. 'At the Moors Prison.'

'Ricky, killed?' Emma replied, sitting down as

her legs gave way. 'It can't be . . .'

It couldn't be true. It couldn't! She had made up her mind, was falling in love with him. She was going to marry Ricky, going to say yes. Going to plan her life with him. The bad times were over; she was free of the dark. But now she was being told that it was all a lie. That Ricky was dead. It was over; no love, no spring. It was over.

'He can't be!'

'I'm sorry,' her uncle replied, 'I thought I should be the one to tell you.'

Slowly Emma looked up at him, her voice remote. 'He can't be dead, not Ricky . . . Oh Jesus, how was he killed?'

'There was a riot . . .'

She flinched. 'What about my father! Is he all right?'

As he heard the words, David turned away, his thin frame slightly bowed. Although Emma had made no reference to her father for two years, at that moment she couldn't hold back. Grief over the loss of Ricky had made her reckless, and she struck out.

'*Was my father involved?* Is he all right?'

Without answering, David began to walk away, towards the back of the shop and into the living room beyond. Beside herself, Emma ran after him, and without thinking caught hold of his sleeve.

'Don't ignore me! You've ignored my father for years; you could at least tell me if he's all right now!' All the anger and suppression of the preceding twenty-four months spilled over in an instant, as

Emma confronted the remote, chilling figure. 'Why do you hate him so much? Why can't you believe him? My father – your half-brother – is innocent.'

Angrily David shook off her hand, but Emma wasn't about to stop, and followed him as he moved into the parlour.

'What did he ever do to you?' she snapped, David moving up the narrow stairs to the workshop in the eaves.

Not expecting her to follow him, he was amazed to find her running up the steps after him. 'Talk to me!'

Reaching the top landing, David moved into the workroom and bent over the work bench. It was as though there was no one else in the room and he was incapable of hearing her.

'Listen to me!' Emma said vehemently. '*Look at me!*'

But he kept his face averted, concentrating on the clock face in front of him.

'My father was part of your family. You could have supported him, believed in him.'

Enraged, Emma watched her uncle work on, unperturbed, unmoved. She was maddened with losing Ricky, and now here was her uncle dismissing her, putting her in her place. Inside she was screaming.

'Why is it so easy for you to believe the worst of Frederick Coles?'

As David continued to ignore her, Emma's patience finally snapped, and moving forwards, she put out her arm and swept the broken clock off the work table.

Stunned, her uncle stepped back, Emma standing up to him. 'Why can't you believe in my father?'

And then, finally, he spoke.

'Why can't you leave my home? Why can't you leave me alone?' he said, his tone lethal. 'For two years I've tried to do my best for you. For two years I've looked after my half-brother's child. I have gone against my instincts and housed you. But you're like him—'

'*And glad of it!*' Emma hurled back, although her uncle's words had hurt her deeply. 'I love my father, and I believe in him.'

'I don't,' David replied curtly. 'And I've more than done my duty by him. You think your father is so special, do you? Well, I know differently. He's the son of Ernie Coles, that thug who's your grandfather.' All his resentment came out in a rare show of undiluted passion. 'My mother might have married Coles, but *I* didn't choose him, and I rejected him as soon as I could. By being associated with that villain, I lost the life I could have had. I lost respectability and chances that should have been mine. You ask what your father did to me? I'll tell you. It took me a long time to make a decent life for myself, and when I did, your father snatched it away from me. His shame was my shame. His crime corrupted me. When people talked about him, they talked about me. When people judged him, they judged me. *Your father dragged me back into the gutter!*'

Breathing heavily, David paused, his composure coming back to him slowly, his temper finally under control. Then, as a shaken Emma watched, he bent down and picked up the pieces of the broken clock. Patiently he placed them on the work table. Then, without looking at her, he said: 'I never want to hear your father's name again. And if you have any sense, you'll stay away from him. And from the Coles name. You have a chance to make a decent life. I suggest you take it.'

Dismissed, Emma walked downstairs, her legs shaking. She knew she had gone too far, but the shock of Ricky's death and the argument about her father had pushed both her and her uncle over some invisible emotional edge. Reaching the front door, she turned her steps towards the Holmes' house, tears running down her cheeks. Her childhood friend, her sweetheart had been killed. With horrible irony at the Moors Prison . . . Suddenly Emma realised how much she hated the place. How much she longed to put it behind her. Whatever she might believe about her father's innocence, she had a stark choice to make. To stand by Frederick Coles and be an outcast. Or to move on and leave behind for ever the shadow of the jail.

As she walked, crying helplessly, she thought of the handsome young man who had rubbed noses with her. She thought of him kissing her hand and whispering into her ear. She thought of Ricky Holmes and ached, longed for him more than she had done when he was alive. And she knew then, with a terrible realisation, how much she had loved him.

Dead, he taunted her. Dead, he was out of her reach. Dead, his loss shattered her swollen heart.

Wrapped tightly in a coat, almost as though she was swaddled in it, Bessie walked down the pathway of the cemetery, Emma beside her. Ill with the shock of her son's death, Mrs Holmes had not been able to attend the funeral, and her daughter had gone alone. In silence Emma and Bessie walked, the sky overhung with grey cloud, a solitary pigeon pecking at the gravel in front of them. There had been a number of people from the prison who had attended, including Reg Spencer, and the Governor, taking time off to pay his respects. Alongside them, the local paper had sent a journalist to report the news for that evening's paper: LOCAL HERO KILLED AT MOORS PRISON.

Bessie knew only too well that the piece would recount the details she had now memorised. That the riot had broken out just after noon that Sunday, the North Wing understaffed, Reg Spencer in charge. Locking down his own wing, Reg had gone into the notorious North Wing to help, and had been accompanied by Ricky Holmes. Who shouldn't have been there. Who should have been off duty.

The whole story had come out at the hearing. Not that Bessie or her mother had been invited. It had been held within the prison, by the prison authorities, only the briefest details escaping to the media. Apparently Ricky – confident and buoyed up with bravado – had told Reg he would help him in the North Wing. Desperate, Reg had accepted, and together they had entered. Neither of them had expected what followed, and no one would tell Bessie or her mother any more details. The implication was that Ricky's death had been horrific. Reg had escaped only by the intervention of the authorities. But it had been too late for Ricky . . .

The letters from Frederick to Emma added nothing more. Only that he was sorry about Ricky's death, and that he had liked him very much. He spoke of the dead man with warmth, and remembered first meeting him, when Ricky was little more than a kid. But he didn't – or wouldn't – say anything more about the death. He just told his daughter how much he was grieving for her loss and how much he wished he could be with her at such a time.

Slipping her arm through Bessie's, Emma walked in step with her friend. She knew how much Bessie had loved her brother, and how great the gap would now be in her life. Even with Doug Renshaw becoming a more permanent fixture. Doug Renshaw, the eternally boyish charmer who worked the markets, the last man on earth Emma would have thought Bessie would have chosen. Silly at times, always playing practical jokes, and young for his twenty-one years, Doug was as giddy as a kipper, as light as thistledown. But maybe that was what Bessie wanted, Emma realised. Especially after her brother's savage death.

'Doug wanted to come to the funeral,' Bessie said suddenly, as though she had sidled into her friend's thoughts. 'But I said no. He's not the type for funerals.'

'Who is?'

Bessie sighed, nodding. 'Thanks for being here.'

'I cared a lot about Ricky.'

A moment's silence hung between them, before Bessie spoke again.

'I'm so sorry . . .'

'It's so stupid,' Emma said dully. 'I was falling in love with him.'

'Jesus,' Bessie said softly, sitting down on a bench and huddling into her coat, then reaching for Emma's hand. 'Why did he have to die?'

'I don't know.'

'Ricky worshipped you. He always had done, from when you were kids. He talked about you all the time. He did everything for you and your future together. I can imagine what he was thinking when he went into that North Wing: *Wait until Emma hears about this, I'll be a hero. I'll impress her.* Only he *didn't* turn out to be a bleeding hero, did he?'

Breathing quickly, Bessie stopped talking, and slumped on the bench. For a moment she felt triumph, then shame. The anger she had felt about her brother's terrible death she had turned on her closest friend. She had offloaded her pain on to Emma, which wasn't fair.

'It wasn't my fault . . .' Emma said dumbly.

'I know, I'm sorry,' Bessie replied, shamefaced. 'Look, I was a cow to say all that. I just wanted someone to blame, because I miss him so much. And I know you miss him too,' she added, accepting

Emma's hand as she reached out to her friend. 'I was such a bitch to you, sorry.'

'You're upset.'

'No, I'm a cow.'

'Yeah, that too.'

Laughing sadly, Bessie turned to her friend.

'What do we do?'

'About what?'

'About Ricky. How can we fill the space he's left?'

Choked, Emma looked away. 'I keep thinking I see him, or hear him. I was looking out of the shop window and I thought I saw him walking down the street.'

'Emma, don't . . .'

'I can't face the prison, knowing he won't be there. Knowing he'll never be there again.'

Gripping her hand, Bessie took a breath. 'I don't know what to say.'

'No one ever does. When there's bad news, or a loss, no one knows what to say.' Emma closed her eyes for an instant, then opened them again and stood up.

'I suppose life goes on,' Bessie offered at last.

'Yes,' Emma agreed, her voice lost. 'Whether we like it or not.'

For the next week, Emma concentrated on her work, learning the jewellery trade, but she was distant. Preoccupied. Remote. The death of Ricky, followed by the vicious argument between her and her uncle, had all but severed their relationship. Now it was Emma's turn to withdraw.

David Hawksworth could do nothing to help her. He didn't know how, and could only castigate himself for saying so many injurious things to his niece. Exhausted by the emotional outburst, he kept to his room in the eaves, but for once he couldn't concentrate on his work and found himself thinking back, reviewing his life. From his start in the flat over the butcher's shop, to his marriage to Jenny. He had loved her, and once she had been so proud of him. Never a demonstrative man, he had been delighted to marry her, but his uncertainty had soon cast a shadow over their lives. Emotionally diffident, he had found their sex life difficult, and his intermittent impotence had embarrassed and mortified him. When they did make love, he knew it meant a great deal to his wife, but there was always the shadow of failure hanging over him, making any overtures embarrassing and infrequent. Jenny never taunted him about it, but in bed David would remember overhearing his mother making noisy love to his stepfather, and cringe. As a boy, he had covered his head with the pillow to block out the sounds, but he could still hear them, still see an image of the boorish Ernie Coles on top of his mother . . . The thought had driven a bolt into David's sexuality, and although Jenny was understanding, she did not have the experience to help her husband.

Instead, they drifted apart, only coming together to have infrequent – and often unsuccessful – sex. Jenny, warm and affectionate by nature, found it difficult. But when their son was born, nine months after one of David's few successful attempts at intercourse, her life changed. Her attention shifted from her husband to her son, and David – although at first resentful – grew to accept the change. From then onwards he spent more and more time in the room in the eaves, watching his son grow up and trying – unsuccessfully – to rein in some of Adam's spiteful quirks. But Jenny saw nothing wrong in the boy. He was perfect, as perfect as her husband was becoming imperfect. And in return for David's rejection of her, she lavished love on her child.

As David's marriage began its slow unravelling, he watched his brother's happy marriage and burned. He envied Frederick and his family, growing sullen in their presence, until it came out that Catherine was ill. But by then it was too late; David didn't have the words to comfort his half-brother or the courage to confide in him. Instead, he watched with horror the sickness develop and the tragedy of Catherine's suicide. But he *still* couldn't reach out. He had lost his confidence, and didn't know how to comfort anyone. Not his own wife and child, and not his half-brother. All in all, David thought miserably, he had failed. And even when he had tried to help, by taking in Emma, he had managed to alienate her.

He had put his respectability first. Clung to his status in life more tightly than to his family. And now he was paying the price.

*

Spring limped on. The days grew longer, but without much sun, the trees shaking out their leaves and making shadows on the streets or on the lawns in Towneley Park. People walked in the trim gardens in the evenings and at weekends, taking children to the boating lake and buying them toffee apples from the vendors. Hard times and shortage of money didn't matter, because the park was free, the sunshine was free, and for a while people could forget their slow crawl back from the war years and their harsh day-to-day life.

By the high, steep steps that led to the rose garden, Emma sat alone. She often came to this spot to think of Ricky. It was the last place they had met up, only days before he died. And it was the place Emma had let him kiss her properly, and had felt a surge of love for him that now mocked her. Back in the jeweller's shop, the atmosphere was tense, suffocating; it was only in Towneley Park that Emma felt she could breathe. But after visiting the place so often over the last sad weeks, it was no longer comforting, and as she sat beside the stone steps, she began crying without even noticing it.

'Excuse me, are you all right?'

She jumped, surprised. 'What? What did you say?'

'I asked if you were all right,' the man went on. 'Forgive me for talking to you directly, but you seem very upset.'

Embarrassed, Emma wiped her tears with her hands, then turned away.

'Is there anything I can do for you, miss?'

'I've just lost someone.'

'Oh dear,' he said simply. 'I imagine it was someone you cared for a great deal?'

Nodding, she looked back to the enquirer. He was tall, about thirty-five, and very well dressed. Not handsome, but with an attractive, open face and thick blond hair. Taking off his hat, he smiled at her kindly.

'Would talking about it help?'

'I don't know.'

Taking that as an invitation, the man sat down a little way from Emma, putting his hat on the step between them. 'I like it here. Although I'm not from these parts. I'm from Yorkshire.' He paused, then continued easily. 'A long time ago, when I was a child, I used to come here with my parents, and so, if I'm in the area, I still take a walk here and think back. It does a person good to remember happy times.'

'I suppose it does.'

'Even when they doubt they will ever be happy again.'

Surprised, Emma looked over to him, the man putting out his hand.

'I'm Leonard Hemmings.'

'Emma Coles,' she replied, shaking his hand and then staring ahead again. 'We used to come here.'

'You and your friend?'

'Ricky, he was called Ricky. Ricky Holmes,' Emma went on, suddenly wanting to talk. She would never see this kind stranger again, and so it was safe to confide. 'I was falling in love with him. He'd loved me for years, but I hadn't realised it. Then, when I did, he was killed.'

'How?'

'He was murdered.'

Leonard took in a breath. 'That must be impossible to come to terms with.'

'I still see him, hear him,' she said, looking down to the gardens. 'We were kids together, got up to all sorts. He was terribly reckless, but fun. You know how some people are? And handsome, full of life. He did mad things, taking the wheels off a policeman's bicycle and throwing onions over the bakery roof. Crazy, but it was him. It was Ricky.'

'And you loved him very much.'

'Yes, yes, I did. But I didn't know it until it was too late.' She glanced over to him. 'I'm sorry, I shouldn't have told you all this, but you were kind and I *did* need to talk.'

'I have all the time in the world,' Leonard said simply. 'Perhaps I could buy you a cup of tea?' He paused, then hurried on. 'Please don't get the wrong idea, Miss Coles. I do not usually talk to ladies on their own. But you were upset and so I thought I could chance it. And now you're not quite so upset and you look as if a cup of tea might be welcome.'

She smiled remotely. 'Thank you, but I have to get back to work.'

'On a Saturday?'

'My uncle has a jeweller's shop on Holland Street.'

'Not by any chance Hawksworth's jewellers?'

135

Surprised, she nodded. 'Yes, it is!'

'I know the place. My father has had several clocks repaired by Mr Hawksworth over the years. How strange that we should meet up like this.' Leonard smiled, amused. 'Well, if I can't be of any further assistance, may I walk you home at least?'

'You're very kind,' Emma replied, getting to her feet and falling into step with him.

Chatting easily, Leonard Hemmings walked alongside Emma, moving back into town. He was amusing and full of stories, not light-hearted like Ricky, but comfortable in his own skin. Several times he asked her about Burnley, and Emma told him what she knew, and then asked about where he lived. Encouraged, Leonard told her about Yorkshire and its history, although by that time Emma's attention was wavering.

After another few minutes they approached Holland Street, and she paused, pointing to the shop.

'I have to go now. Thank you for listening, for being kind.'

'It was a pleasure,' Leonard said, shaking her hand again. 'I hope we'll meet again sometime. When I have another clock to be mended, perhaps?'

'Until then, Mr Hemmings,' she said, turning away.

'Miss Coles?'

She turned back. 'Yes?'

'It passes. The pain, it passes. You won't believe me now, but it does.' And with that, he tipped his hat to her and walked off.

Closing the door of the jewellery shop behind her, Emma turned the sign to OPEN again. Pausing in the centre of the shop, she listened, but all she could hear were the sounds of the ticking clocks and the faint murmur and whirling of the workings of the largest grandfather clock. Sighing, she walked towards the back parlour and paused at the door. Her uncle was in there, and looked up as he heard her.

'Emma?'

'Yes, Uncle?' she said coolly, their argument a goblin between them.

'You're back.'

'Yes, Uncle.'

'Have you turned the sign around?'

'Yes, Uncle.'

'Good,' he said simply, trying to smile, but failing. Coughing to clear his throat, he moved towards the back stairs. 'I'm going to work. Mind the shop, will you?'

'Yes, Uncle,' Emma said again, listening as his footsteps climbed upwards, then turned at the top of the stairs.

Yes, Uncle, yes, Uncle, yes, Uncle – was that going to be the rest of her life? At this man's beck and call? In this chilly, suffocating atmosphere? Unnerved, Emma found herself breathing rapidly, and loosened the collar of her dress, walking over to the window and looking out into Holland Street. Soon it would be summer and the heat would come, making the workroom in the eaves stifling, her own bedroom

137

windows thrown open, but letting in little or no air from the harassed streets below. She would toss and turn in the long nights and try to sleep. She would dream, and then wake and know it was all a dream. And then sleep again, hopefully without any dreams or memories.

Was that it? she asked herself again, her hands clenched. Was she locked into this place? Shut in, shut up, her life empty and dry as a husk? Shaking, she laid her head against the window and thought of nothing. Of no one, of no plans and no hopes. She longed for a blankness of mind, but it wouldn't come, and when there was a sudden tap at the window, she jumped, startled, as Leonard Hemmings walked in.

'Would Wednesday be convenient?' he asked cheerfully.

She frowned, confused. 'For what?'

'To bring in my father's clock? Didn't I mention that we had one that needed mending?'

He called to see Emma several times after that, and on the last occasion offered to take her out to an evening concert in the park. An offer Emma accepted. After all, he was a friend, and he knew all about Ricky. This was not a man to get the wrong idea about her. She had been straight with him, and liked his company. A friend was what she needed, and Leonard Hemmings was the perfect man for the job. Another time they went on a visit to the Victoria Theatre, to see a variety show. An easy, comfortable sort of man, Leonard made sure that Emma enjoyed herself, and he found her company more and more pleasurable. He was also pleased to note that she received a number of admiring glances. Not that he was surprised; she was a handsome young woman, likely to draw attention.

But he did wonder about their difference in age. In time, might there be a possibility that she could become interested in him, and able to assimilate the eighteen-year age gap? It was obvious that she was still grieving for Ricky Holmes, but Leonard believed that after a while she would need to be loved again, and he might well be the lucky man. He was, after all, in no hurry. He had dated several women and been engaged to one for three years, but it had not worked out. To his disappointment, and his mother's distress, he had not found a wife. In fact, for the last few years he hadn't found any woman who interested him. Until he had happened to come across a young woman who was crying in a park. And suddenly Leonard was very interested.

From the first moment Leonard had seen Emma, he had been fascinated. There was something about her he found intriguing, different. The way she spoke her mind and showed her feelings. The way she was young and open. He liked that, could imagine growing to love those qualities. Because Mr Leonard Hemmings – who had been emotionally adrift for some time – had fixed his sights on Miss Emma Coles. He might be a good deal older, and from a different background, but that only added to his interest.

Mind you, he wasn't too sure how his parents

would take to his choice. For years, his mother, Elizabeth, had nagged him to settle down. As for his father, Grant was too immersed in business to care much, and left the romantic issues to Elizabeth. The pressure had started around the age of twenty-five, when Leonard was promoted in the family firm, and had increased as the years had passed. Why didn't he marry? his mother would ask. I haven't found the right woman, he would reply. Well, look harder.

Now, a decade later, his mother was distracted, something she had displayed only the previous evening.

'What about Sarah Childes?' she had asked her son, her smooth, round face turned in his direction. 'You've known her since you were children. What's wrong with her?'

'I don't love her.'

It had been the perfect time for him to tell his mother about Emma – after all, they had been seeing each other for nearly two months – but he had hesitated. Perhaps he should wait until he was sure that Emma felt something for him. After all, why rush now, when it had taken him so long to find her? One thing Leonard *did* know, however, was that his mother would be put out by his choice. She wouldn't overreact; there would be no 'drop her or get out'; she wasn't domineering and controlling. But her disappointment would be obvious. The family had made some money, but not enough to hoick themselves up into the top echelons of Leeds society. Elizabeth would not rage about his choice being beneath him, because when his parents had started, they had started from the bottom. And remembered it. No pretensions for them, no scuffed-over backgrounds. They had worked their way up, buying a faltering beer business on the outskirts of Leeds and making it into a flourishing concern.

Eager to extend the trade, Grant Hemmings had expanded his patch and begun to sell his beer in Lancashire as well as Yorkshire. Not to many pubs, but – as he said – it was a good product and worth paying a premium for. Maybe the sales would never be huge, but they paid for a house on the park and one of the first cars in the road . . . Leonard smiled to himself, still walking beside Emma. He wanted suddenly to hold her hand. He hesitated, then reached for it anyway. Her fingers seemed cool against his own, and if there was a slight resistance, it only lasted for a moment.

Hand in hand they walked on, along St James's Street, past the Golden Paddock store. Like most towns, Burnley's shops hung street furniture above their doors. A padlock for the hardware shop, a giant's boot over the cobbler's and the three circular globes above the pawnbroker's. As they reached the Bull pub, Emma pointed to the building, her voice animated.

'See that place? It's where the stagecoaches used to run from. And people held their wedding feasts and funeral wakes there. They also used it for inquests.'

He looked at her, surprised by her depth of knowledge. No lack of common interest between them; no obvious showing of the eighteen-year gap in their conversation.

'You must love your town.'

She shrugged. Falling silent, she cursed herself for talking too much. If she went on about it, Leonard would ask more about Burnley, and that was one place she didn't want to talk about. But she wanted to be an interesting companion, because he was trying so hard. She liked him for that. In fact, Emma was beginning to like a lot about Leonard Hemmings. Like the way he told her stories about the brewery, and the way he smiled when he caught her eye. A kind smile, without judgement, and without any harshness in it. It was true that he would not have been her first choice, but then Ricky was dead.

Leonard Hemmings was older and confident. Someone Emma admired, could become fond of . . . Her hand felt comfortable in his, his grip firm but not tight, and for a moment she tried to imagine what it would be like being Mrs Leonard Hemmings. It would be an escape, a way out of Burnley, away from her uncle and the jeweller's shop. Away from the memories. It would be an escape – but would it be fair?

'Are you all right?'

Emma started, surprised to find herself blushing. 'I was day-dreaming, sorry.'

He smiled. That warm smile that said that it was all right and nothing to be bothered about. 'I enjoy being with you, Emma,' he began, cheerful as ever, 'and I'd like to introduce you to my parents.'

Emma breathed in, hope and anxiety mixing in the one breath. He was getting serious about her. Everyone knew that no man took a woman home unless he was serious. But was that what she wanted? Her mouth dried as she quieted her panic. Marriage to Leonard would mean escape, a new start. *But the price was denial of her father.* She knew then what Frederick would have said. What he *had* said only the previous week, when she had written to him about Leonard Hemmings. And he – so adept at reading his daughter's thoughts – had encouraged her: *Stay quiet about me and make a new life for yourself. If he asks you to marry him, accept.*

'Well?' Leonard said, smiling. 'Would you like to meet my parents?'

'Yes,' she replied, looking at him and meeting the direct, kindly gaze. 'I'd like that very much.'

'And they will like you very much too,' he said, squeezing her hand as they moved on.

Leonard was elated by the way their relationship was going. He was also thinking that living in Leeds might be a long way away for Emma, and that perhaps they should live somewhere between Burnley and Leeds so that she could see her uncle and not feel too much uprooted from her home town . . . At the same time, Emma was thinking that she could hardly wait to leave the jeweller's shop. How every Burnley street held some bitter memory. Even though it had been two years ago and was no longer a topical subject, there were still people who saw her not as herself, but as Frederick Coles's daughter. Her father

143

might be imprisoned, but his reputation was as constant as her shadow, and as dark. She might tell Leonard about the Bull pub and other local information, but Emma remembered many of these places in a different light. The pawn shop, for instance, where she had pawned some of her father's books to pay for the fares to visit him . . .

'On Friday, then?' Leonard asked, cutting into her thoughts. 'I'll come and collect you, of course, and then we could have dinner at my parents' home. There's no reason to be nervous, you know. Just relax and be yourself.'

THIRTEEN

Elizabeth Hemmings was more than a little surprised by her son's choice of woman. Over the years, she had been surprised that no girl had captured Leonard's heart enough for him to marry her. But, she had consoled herself, one day he would find someone special. Extraordinary. Not that her son was extraordinary himself, but he had some great qualities. Not too good-looking, but with a friendly, open face, blond hair and a real, infectious smile. He was also tall and well built. Not like a hero in a book, but a decent, kind man. Elizabeth had suspected that Leonard would – given his own unflashy ways – pick a rather stable kind of woman. Someone who was nice-looking, rather than a beauty. Someone not too clever, but interested in raising a family. Certainly not a career woman, like the women they were talking about in the films and magazines. And not some down-at-heel no one either. More a well-balanced, attractive, competent type. A good mother, who would give Elizabeth the grandchildren she ached for.

So when Leonard brought Emma Coles home, Elizabeth was momentarily stunned. Of course the young woman was a beauty, that much anyone with eyes could see, but she was young. Very young. Certainly she didn't *act* too young; in fact, she was very composed. But the reality was that she was seventeen – and that wasn't what Elizabeth had expected. As for Grant Hemmings, he was delighted by the pretty young woman who came to dinner. She was certainly polite, with good manners and lively conversation, and as to her background . . . Well, not everyone was rich, and not everyone had a good start or the opportunities to get on. Besides, the girl had had a hard beginning to her life. To lose both parents and have to be taken in by a widowed relative was a cruel blow. But, decided Grant, it was a credit to David Hawksworth that Emma had turned out so well. Obviously he had been a careful and judicious guardian.

Nodding in Emma's direction, the bearded Grant sipped his wine and decided that having a daughter-in-law who had come from lowly beginnings was probably an advantage. A woman from a well-off family might demand too much, or be too critical. Grant was well aware that their own good fortune had been relatively recent and hard won; perhaps a young woman like Emma Coles would assimilate well into their family.

'Grant?'

He glanced down to his wife at the other end of the table, her narrow face piqued, her high voice rising dangerously. She was gesturing for him to do something. Something Grant didn't understand.

Finally, rolling her eyes impatiently, Elizabeth took the lead: 'Well now, shall we go into the sitting room, my dear, and let the men have a smoke?'

Taking her cue, Emma rose and followed Elizabeth out, Leonard waiting for the door to close before he turned to his father.

'So, what d'you think?'

'Very pretty, very pretty indeed,' Grant replied, his bushy eyebrows meeting as he frowned. 'But I can see from your mother's face that she thinks Emma might be a little young.'

'Did she seem young to you?'

'No . . . but she might be trying to make a good impression.'

Flopping back in his dining chair, Leonard sighed. 'Of course she's trying to make a good impression! She wants you to like her.'

'Well, *you* obviously do,' Grant replied, pouring out some more wine and gesturing for his son to drink. 'Is it serious?'

'I want to marry her.'

'Good God!' Grant said flatly. '*Marriage*. But you've only known her for a couple of months.'

'I know, but she's the one,' Leonard replied, surprising his father with his determination. 'No one has ever affected me like Emma. And I've had a few girlfriends . . .'

'And a few more your mother doesn't know about too,' Grant replied darkly.

'But Emma's the one I want.' He paused, wondering if he was pushing her too quickly. If he was catching her on the rebound after Ricky Holmes's death. Immediately he brushed the unwelcome thought aside. 'Emma is unaffected, open, intelligent. Having met her and been with her – I know it's not been for long – I couldn't imagine being *without* her. The hole in my life would be too big. I can see her now,' he went on, opening his heart, 'and I know what she will be like when she's older. I have a picture in my mind of our later years. I know I'll be old before her, but she'll keep me young. Just being married to her, with her, sharing my life with her, will make me a young man for ever.'

Impressed, his father stared at his unusually loquacious son. Leonard had always been affection- ate, but this extraordinary bond – quickly established – was poignant and incredibly touching. My God, Grant thought admiringly, you might have waited a long time to find the right woman, but it paid off in the end.

Whilst the two men were talking in the dining room, Elizabeth Hemmings was pouring coffee for herself and Emma in the sitting room. The place was stuffed with furniture and draped curtains, a flutter of tables around the sofas and chairs. Every surface shone, polished like marble, even the logs in the fire burning evenly. The maid had left the room and Elizabeth was taking a long, if discreet, look at Emma's dress. It was rather old fashioned, in the light of recent styles. Not that the hem had been raised to mid-calf, not yet at least. And as for her hair, it was tied back at the base of her neck, not cut short, which had been the mode for the last year. In fact, there was nothing flashy about Emma Coles; for all her good looks, she seemed unwilling to capitalise upon them. They were like classic pieces of jewellery, impressive, without having attention drawn to them.

But although Elizabeth could see that her son and her husband were taken with Emma, she had some niggling concerns that were not so easily dismissed. Like the age gap. Emma might find in five years – when her husband was forty and she was only twenty-two – that the distance was too big a gap to bridge. Love could be all-consuming, but so could desire. Elizabeth Coles was enough of a woman to understand that Emma was fond of her son, but not in love with him. And the thought of Leonard marrying a young woman who was in no rush to have children unnerved her. She and Grant were getting on – they had been late parents themselves – and Elizabeth was in no mood to have her dreams of being a grandmother delayed any further.

So what did the girl see in Leonard? she wondered. Security? Kindness? If so, who could blame her? She had known little happiness in her short life, and if Leonard could supply that compassion in return for the kudos of having a young and pretty wife, was that a problem? Then again, Elizabeth thought, watching Emma sip at her coffee, what if, some years ahead, this young woman caught another man's fancy? A good-looking, fascinating man, of her own age? How would Leonard's devotion stand up against that kind of passion?

'I care for Leonard,' Emma said suddenly.

Elizabeth smiled at her. 'I believe you, my dear.'

'He's a good man.'

'I think so, but then I'm his mother,' Elizabeth replied, pausing for a moment before continuing. 'He seems very serious about you.'

'I'm serious about him.'

'But at your age, how do you know? You should be having other boyfriends and going out, enjoying yourself.'

Emma thought momentarily about Ricky, and hurried on. 'I enjoy myself with Leonard.'

'But he's very steady. Not exciting,' Elizabeth continued. 'My son wants to settle down, and frankly, lovely as you are, my dear, I was hoping he would choose someone older, someone ready to have a family.' She put up her hands. 'Forgive me, I'm speaking very bluntly, but I feel that I must talk to you like this. We are women, and we can be frank. My son is a wonderful man, but why would you choose him?'

Emma's eyes widened. 'He makes me feel safe.'

'So could a father, my dear. But we don't marry our fathers.'

Emma kept her voice firm, her spirit flickering into life. She could sense that Elizabeth had a simmering doubt about her, but she wasn't going to let the older woman win.

'I'm not after your son for money.'

'We don't have *that* much, my dear,' Elizabeth replied, teasing her. 'You would be disappointed.'

Emma smiled winningly. 'I've never had much

money. Believe me, I don't want to take from Leonard – I want to give.'

Impressed, Elizabeth studied the young woman in front of her, then nodded.

'I believe you, but perhaps it would be wise to wait for a while. Let us see how this romance progresses before we rush into anything.'

It was not what Emma wanted to hear. She had been all but thrown out of the jeweller's shop, and her uncle's chilling attitude – coupled with Ricky's shocking death – had hardened her resolve. She did not fool herself; she knew she was not in love with Leonard Hemmings, but she did promise herself that she would be a good wife to him. She would love him as much as she could. He would never know it, but that would be the emotional deal she made with herself. The way she could come to terms with her decision. The way she could lessen her own guilt.

So Emma was not prepared to be held back by Elizabeth Hemmings. 'Have you spoken to Leonard?'

'About what, dear?'

'Your son proposed to me yesterday,' Emma lied rashly, without thinking, seeing Elizabeth's face pale. 'And I accepted.'

The following day Leonard Hemmings found himself back in Burnley, leaving home early in the morning, before his mother had had a chance to talk to him. Looking at the jeweller's, he had to admit that it was an unwelcoming place. The shops on either side were cheerful, not high class, but clean and in reasonable order, but the jeweller's . . . Smiling, he turned as he heard footsteps coming down the stairs, expecting to see Emma. But instead he found himself face to face with David Hawksworth. He had heard about the man from Emma, who had painted him not as an ogre, but as a distant man. Certainly the first impression Leonard had was of someone chilling, remote from the rest of the world.

Extending his hand, Leonard said cheerfully, 'Pleased to meet you, Mr Hawksworth. I was hoping we could talk.'

Shaking the stranger's hand, David led him through the shop and into the parlour beyond. The room was furnished well, but in an old-fashioned manner, a row of pipes hanging beside the fire. Lowering himself into his armchair, David put his feet on the faded footstool and stared at his visitor. Unnerved, Leonard found his usual equilibrium faltering and began to talk to ease the tension.

'I wanted to have a word – to ask for your approval to marry your niece.'

'How old are you?'

Leonard blinked his soft brown eyes. 'Thirty-five.'

'My niece is just seventeen,' David replied, glancing at his watch and then listening to the chimes coming from the shop beyond. 'I think you're too old for her.'

'I don't—'

'I dare say,' David interrupted, thinking of what he knew of Leonard Hemmings.

A visitor to the town, come from Leeds. A Yorkshireman, a stranger who would know nothing of Frederick Coles. After all, it was old news now. His half-brother had been in jail for nearly two years, and who cared about a common thief? Suddenly David could see an opportunity to find a good match for Emma. A match that would be harder in Burnley, where her background was common knowledge. A match that would see his niece settled elsewhere and satisfy his own thwarted ambition. It was something he could do for her, something good. Something he would have liked to do for his own son . . .

'What do you do for a living, Mr Hemmings?'

'I'm in my family's business.'

'Which is?'

'Beer.'

'Ah,' David said, clearing his throat.

'My family is comfortable. Not rich, but we have a small business that provides a pleasant lifestyle.' Leonard paused. 'My father told me that he knows your shop well. That he has purchased several timepieces from you.'

'Hemmings, Hemmings . . .' David measured the name against his memory, then nodded. 'Grant Hemmings?'

Leonard nodded. 'Yes, that's my father.'

'It was a long time ago,' David said dismissively, looking his guest up and down. 'Why my niece?'

'I beg your pardon?'

'Why are you interested in my niece, Mr Hemmings?' David repeated. 'You don't come from around here and your family might want you to court a better match. My niece has no money.'

'I'm not interested in a dowry!' Leonard replied, shaken. 'I'm interested in marrying her. And, not wishing to proceed on the wrong footing, I wanted to talk to you and ask your permission.'

'I see,' David replied, taking in the good clothes and pleasant manner of his visitor. No flat northern vowels; a little breeding there in the courtesy and the strong bones. He seemed to the jeweller a pleasant sort. Not someone who would make a huge impression – either by his looks or his conversation – but a thoroughly decent man. Steady, reliable. Nothing like the other men in Emma's life. Nothing like Frederick or the notorious Ernie Coles, who was lately rumoured to have moved down to London. By comparison with what Emma had known, Leonard Hemmings was the alkali to all the acid. The sop to any bitterness.

But David wasn't going to make it easy, because he was – unreasonably – annoyed that Emma hadn't mentioned the romance.

'I still think,' he said evenly, 'that you are too old for my niece.'

Leonard wasn't about to be thwarted.

'Mr Hawksworth, I have only Emma's best interests at heart, and the young lady can make up her own mind. I know how young she is, but she is also very mature for her age. More like a woman in her twenties. Perhaps that is a result of your influence?' he said, offering up a compliment, which

David did not respond to. 'Your niece tells me that you gave her a home when she needed one. I didn't want to press her for details, in case it might have caused her any distress. So may I ask, are you her only surviving relative?'

The clocks were ticking almost in time with David's heartbeat. Tick, tick, they said, *lie now, lie now*. Then again, tick, tock, *why not? why not?* Surely if he lied, David was actually protecting his niece? Making sure the truth of her background remained hidden, out of sight. Why confess the damning reality only to sour her chances? If she made this match, she would move away, live in Yorkshire. Where no one would ever know anything about Frederick or Ernie Coles . . . Hesitating, David was torn. His shame at his half-brother's disgrace was as acute as ever. And yet he felt responsible for his niece. What good would it do for Emma to be held back by Frederick's downfall? Surely a good father would want the best for his child? But if he was honest, his paternal feelings came – as they had always done – second to his desire for respectability.

'Mr Hawksworth?'

David stirred, reminded of the question, his expression even as he answered. 'Yes, I am Emma's only surviving relative. She has no one else.'

'How hard for her,' Leonard replied, touched. 'I understand your concerns, Mr Hawksworth, but I only wish your niece the best.'

Behind the door, Emma listened. She was pleased that Leonard was bringing his intentions out into the

155

open, but at what cost? Sighing, she leaned her head against the door. She had heard the question – *are you her only surviving relative?* – and had held her breath as her uncle lied. And yet she hadn't done anything to deny what he had said. Hadn't walked in and told Leonard about her father. Hadn't been outraged at the rejection of Frederick Coles. Instead, she had listened and realised that a deal was being struck. *She had the chance of a good marriage if she stayed silent.* But there was more to it than that. The rejection of her father was not so cavalier – Emma wanted to escape because she hated the jeweller's shop. Hated the dark bitterness of David Hawksworth. Hated being under his control, seeing her life ordered and her youth slipping away. For months she hadn't laughed. For months she had met up with Bessie and not relaxed. She *couldn't* relax, because day by day she was haunted by Ricky's death, swamping her in the crushing atmosphere of the jeweller's shop. Piece by piece her cheerfulness was dying, bit by bit her feistiness was corroding. As she walked into the shop in the morning she heard the clocks ticking, and every one of them seemed to grin at her and tell her that she was stuck, stuck, stuck. That she would never get away. That it was doubtful that anyone would want the daughter of Frederick Coles, and that before long, if she didn't escape, she would turn into a spinster, shuffling around the forbidding jeweller's shop like a dry ghost.

Of course there was another way, Emma told herself. She could risk it. Could risk telling Leonard

Hemmings about her father. She paused, remembering what Frederick had written the previous month.

Thank you for confiding in me, my dear, about Leonard Hemmings. He seems a good man, a very good man. But now you have to stand back from me and go to him. I know you will always love me in your heart, but to the world it must seem that I am out of your life. Leonard would not accept the situation, Emma, why expect him to? Few men would. So don't risk it. Don't risk your happiness for me. What good would such a grand gesture do? It would spoil your life and make mine even more unbearable.

She had written back to him, almost angry.

I would never desert you! You're my father and I could never be ashamed of you. Besides, you did nothing wrong, and one day I'll prove that.

Back came the reply, tender and determined.

You could never desert me in your heart. But the world is not kind, and you need some kindness, Emma. Be brave, by all means, but be brave with someone, not alone. Take your chance. Don't let my experience destroy your life. Stay quiet. Stay safe.

Emma hung her head, pressing her forehead hard against the door. Dear God, she hated this shop, hated her uncle – but was that enough of a reason to lie about her father? If Leonard Hemmings married her, she would escape. She would have freedom. She would have a home of her own, and be able to help her father more. Or was she lying to herself? *Would* she help her father more? How could she, if her husband knew nothing about him? But if she risked it and told Leonard the truth, and lost her chance . . . Emma swallowed, her throat dry. If she went along with the deception, she would be lying and rejecting her own father. But if she spoke up – what then? Distressed, she took in another deep breath. She had been lying to Leonard's mother when she said her son had already proposed, but she knew he was about to ask her. And she knew she would accept.

At that moment – with the clocks ticking around her, and her uncle clearing his throat – freedom was worth any price.

When Leonard left the jeweller's shop, I ran after him. I ran after him and called his name, and he turned and grinned at me, with such happiness it made me ache. He put out his arms and hugged me, and I let him. In the street, in full sight of anyone who wanted to look.

And as he held me, he whispered, 'Emma, I love you. Will you marry me?'

In the next street the church bell started to ring, chimed over the town and echoed in Holland Street. It echoed over our heads, Leonard's head resting against mine, my eyes closed against the Burnley surroundings.

I nodded, trying to find my voice, then whispered back to him, 'Yes, yes, I'll marry you.'

And in speaking the words, I felt something I couldn't understand, something between relief and shame. I felt my father's image fade like a shadow in the noonday sun, whilst Ricky's face shimmered in front of me for one lingering instant, then disappeared. Opening my eyes, I looked for both of the *men I had loved, but there was only Leonard there, and I knew I had made my choice.*

And must live by it.

FOURTEEN

Unusually agitated, Leonard Hemmings paced the drawing room floor, staring out of the window towards the front path. He was sure he had arranged for Emma to arrive at two thirty, and now it was three o'clock. Of course, normally he would have collected her in the car, but she had been adamant that she wanted to come under her own steam. Glancing at the clock again, Leonard kept pacing, wondering if she had changed her mind and decided not to accept his proposal, even though she had seemed delighted by the prospect. She might have had second thoughts and couldn't face telling him. In fact, she might now be in the jeweller's shop, avoiding him, whilst he was strung tight as piano wire.

It was the kiss, Leonard realised suddenly. He had been too amorous. But she had responded. Not passionately, but tenderly. Perhaps he had frightened her. He had been mad for her, he thought longingly, desperate to hold on to her and make love to her. But he had drawn back; he was a gentleman, and would wait until they married. Only now he was wondering if they *would* marry, or if he had scuppered his chances.

The door opened behind him, Leonard spinning round. 'Emma!'

'No, dear, your mother,' Elizabeth replied, smiling wanly. 'Do stop pacing, you'll ruin the carpet.'

'She's late.'

'Why didn't you pick her up?'

'She wanted to come on her own,' Leonard explained, turning back to the window and staring out.

Dear God, Elizabeth thought, I do hope he'll settle down after they marry. She had come round to accepting Emma slowly, but seeing how determined her son was, and Grant's enthusiasm, had made it difficult to object. Her husband saw Emma as a charming, intelligent addition to the household, and had no obvious misgivings. But Elizabeth wasn't convinced. She wasn't convinced at all. In fact, there was a certain feistiness about Emma she didn't like. And her age was against her. When Elizabeth had mentioned grandchildren to her son, Leonard had laughed and said there was plenty of time for that.

The thought made Elizabeth uneasy. Her intuition nudged her, and the idea of another woman sharing the house was not ideal. Not that they would be living on top of each other. Elizabeth and Grant would have the first and second floors, whilst the newly-weds would have the ground floor. It was, after all, the perfect solution until the couple decided exactly where they wanted to live . . . Staring at the back of her son's head, Elizabeth wondered for the hundredth time what all the rush was about. If she was honest, she had had some anxiety that there might be a baby on the way. But after meeting Emma, all doubts were laid to rest on that score. The young woman was too respectable to trap Leonard that way. Too respectable and too composed.

Not that Leonard was composed. Her son was, in fact, smouldering. Sighing, Elizabeth walked up behind him and stared over his shoulder at the pathway.

'She'll come.'

'What if she's had an accident?'

'Oh, Leonard, how you do go on.'

'But she's half an hour late.'

'Time will come when half an hour without the presence of your wife might seem like a blessing,' Elizabeth teased him. 'You're sure that Emma is the right young woman for you?'

'I've waited for years to find the right young woman,' he replied evenly. 'I don't think I'd make a mistake now.'

Famous last words, his mother thought, walking around the room and rearranging the cushions.

'You've talked to her about the living arrangements?'

'Yes, that we'll live here until we decide where we want to buy a house.'

'But she didn't express a preference as to where you might like to live?'

'I thought we could settle somewhere between here

163

and Burnley, you know, so Emma wouldn't be too far away from her home town. But when I suggested that, she said she wanted to live near here.'

Good for seeing any grandchildren, Elizabeth thought with relief.

'Live in Yorkshire?' his mother went on lightly. 'Unusual for a Lancastrian.'

'All that stopped with the War of the Roses, Mother.'

'If you say so, my dear.'

Irritated, Leonard kept staring out of the window, willing his mother to leave the room. He didn't want to talk – even about Emma and their future life together. He wanted to just wait until he caught that first sight of her, that moment when she walked up to the door and into his life for ever.

Sitting on a stone wall, Emma folded her hands on her lap and stared at her shoes. After she married Leonard, she would have better footwear, shoes that hadn't been soled and heeled repeatedly. Shoes that would be in fashion. Maybe even light-coloured shoes, the kind no one in Burnley wore because it was a mill town and not a place for any show of flashiness. And some Red Seal silk hose . . . Pausing, Emma shook her head. Why was she thinking about shoes? Something so stupid, so idiotic? But she knew why. Thinking about something that mattered – like her father, or Ricky – would be too upsetting. Might even make her change her mind.

It had taken her a long time to get to the Hemmings'

house outside Leeds. She had wanted to make the last journey on her own, because she knew that after this day, she would be different. Betrothed, spoken for, a young woman with a fiancé and a married life to come. She thought then of their last kiss. Leonard had kissed her before, naturally, but this kiss had been different. There had been an urgency about it. A longing, which had not coincided with her own feelings. Of course she knew that in marrying him she would have to make love with him, but she had mentally skirted around that issue. She could imagine cuddling him, lying next to him, and she loved the feel of his hand in hers, but that was affection. Not sex. Sex was something else . . . Sighing, Emma thought of the conversation she had had with Bessie a month earlier.

'Oh, and when Doug kisses me, it makes me all warm in my bits.'

Emma laughed. 'In your bits?'

'Down there,' Bessie had replied, pointing between her legs. 'Aw, you know, that tingling feeling.'

Well, Emma hadn't had that tingling feeling with Leonard. With Ricky, yes . . . Her eyes closed, suppressing the memory. She wouldn't think about him, she had to forget him. Think about her fiancé, her soon-to-be husband. A husband she would have to have sex with. Only that year there had been a divorce case in which – for the first time – women jurors had been chosen. But the male judge had decreed that some of the letters and photographs had been too abominable and beastly for the women to see. Emma tried to imagine what on earth could be so abominable and beastly. She knew it was about sex, but *what* about sex? She had no one to ask. Bessie had filled her in on some points, but Bessie wasn't sexually active and her knowledge was limited. In fact, so worried had Emma become that she had gone to the local library and tried to find a book to help, then lost her courage when she saw the male librarian looking her way.

But it wasn't just the sex that was worrying her. The reason she was sitting on the stone wall and not hurrying up the pathway to the Hemmings' house was something altogether different. Her father. For all Frederick's enthusing – or perhaps *because* of that unselfish enthusiasm – she felt her betrayal deeply. To turn her back on him, to chose a comfortable life over him seemed selfish and unkind. Not like Emma. Not like her at all. In his letters, Frederick had supported her, and that morning an extra – unexpected – letter had come to the jeweller's shop. A letter urging her on, encouraging her to marry Leonard.

So why was she still sitting on the stone wall? Emma asked herself. Her father was happy for her. Bessie was encouraging her. And certainly there was nothing in Burnley or in Holland Street to keep her. Her thoughts turned back to that morning. In the narrow kitchen, she had made a simple breakfast – toast and jam – for herself and her uncle. In silence they had eaten it. And in silence David Hawksworth had then left the room and opened the jewellery shop.

His tall, slightly stooped figure had ducked under the door frame and disappeared into the ticking womb beyond.

Emma had washed the dirty plates and put them away. As she did so, she told herself that there weren't too many silent breakfasts left to endure. Then, after she had finished the cleaning, she had put on her outdoor clothes and walked to the doorway that marked the divide between the shop and the living quarters.

'I have to go out, Uncle.'

He had tensed, but did not turn or look at her. 'Very well.'

'I won't be back until late tonight. The chores are all done and I've made you something for your dinner. It's in the meat safe.'

She hadn't been able to tell, from looking at his back, if he was annoyed or relieved. And when he didn't answer her, she had walked out.

In the street, she had waved to Jack Rimmer and walked on, catching a tram out of town. And yet to her surprise, she had felt no sense of relief. Only a terrible emptiness. Which she was still feeling now. *Get up*, she told herself, *come on, Leonard's waiting. He's a good man, he'll look after you* . . . But she didn't move, just kept looking round at the well-to-do houses. Not overly rich men's houses, just plush, with a healthy injection of money. Houses that told society you had done well, but houses that weren't ostentatious enough to provoke envy. Nothing too grand, for a girl who had come from very little.

Nothing she couldn't adjust to. And besides, before long, Leonard said they would buy their own home.

So why was she feeling nothing?

'Are you all right?'

Surprised, Emma looked up to see a man watching her. He was poorly dressed, with a rattling bike. A knife-grinder, going from house to house, sharpening blades. He was obviously barely making a living, probably one of the soldiers home from the war, finding it hard to get a job. A million unemployed and rising, the paper had said that morning.

'I'm fine,' Emma replied, getting to her feet.

'You don't look fine. You look like someone with all the worries of the world on her shoulders.'

She thought the same about him.

'No, not me,' she said, taking in the man's poverty, at odds with his well-modulated voice. Pity rose up inside her, and, moved, she pointed to the basket attached to his handlebars. 'Are those for sale?'

'The knives? Yes,' he replied, taking them out and holding them up for her to see. He was obviously desperate to make a sale. Emma had only sixpence in her pocket. But she had security in front of her, and a husband. This man had damn near nothing.

In that moment, she made the decision to make the best out of marrying Leonard Hemmings.

Smiling, she looked at the knife-grinder.

'I want that one, the fruit knife, please.'

'It's sixpence,' he said happily, taking the offered coin and handing the dainty little knife over to Emma. 'Thank you.'

'Oh, I needed it.'

'I don't think you did. So thank you, thank you very much,' the man replied gently, then got on his bike and rode off.

A couple of minutes later, Emma was walking up the pathway to greet Leonard Hemmings. Her husband-to-be. In her pocket was her talisman, the little fruit knife. Which she knew she would keep as a memento. A trinket for her new life.

FIFTEEN

September 1921
'Come in, come in. Bring your shoes, your boots.
Come in!'

His eyesight deteriorating rapidly, Mr Letski was standing at the door of the cobbler's, calling out his mission statement to all and sundry. His simian features were intensifying with age, as his back curved over and his winter waistcoat – of mouldering brownish pony skin – gave off an odour of musk and shoe polish. Behind the counter, Bessie watched the old man, smiling affectionately. He had promised to sign over the cobbler's to her. Lock, stock and barrel. Her ambition was close to becoming reality.

'Come in, come in. Bring your shoes, your boots.
Come in!'

'Mr Letski,' Bessie called out, wiping her hands on her brown overall. Not the most flattering or feminine of garments, she had to admit, but survivable. 'Mr Letski!'

He turned, staring intently at her as she came into focus. 'What?'

'I've someone for you to meet,' Bessie went on,

pinching Doug Renshaw's arm and forcing him out of his seat. 'Mr Letski, this is Doug, Douglas Renshaw.'

'Renshaw! Ah, Renshaw.' He nodded. 'Bring me your shoes, your boots—'

'No, he's not a customer, he's a friend of mine,' Bessie cut in. 'You were saying that we needed some help in the back. You know, with the outer room and all that junk.'

'Junk?'

'You said it was junk, Mr Letski,' Bessie went on. 'And Doug could clear it out for you.' She jabbed the young man playfully in the ribs with her elbow.

'Aw, yeah.'

'And then he could clear out that gutter round the back, where it leaks into the kitchen. And the outside lav. It needs looking at, Mr Letski.'

The Russian moved over to Doug, staring at him very closely to bring the stranger's face into focus. The bright blue eyes, weak smiling mouth and baby curls made Letski pause.

'You're a boy. I need muscle—'

'He's very muscular,' Bessie interrupted, grinning impishly. 'Aren't you, Doug? He looks right soft, but he can shift himself when he needs to.'

'How much?'

'His rates are very competitive.'

The Russian made a rumbling sound in the back of his throat, Doug's eyes opening wide. 'Such a boy, to do a man's work.'

'My mother used him for the attic, and she said he

171

did a right good job,' Bessie went on, even though her boyfriend had damn near put his foot through the bedroom ceiling. But then again, Doug was a cracker in other ways. He always made her laugh, and he made her tingle. And that was more than enough for her. After all, she had brains for both of them; all she needed was a way to make sure that Doug was in her life. The shop was the best way forward. But as well as her career needs, Bessie had bodily needs. And although Doug Renshaw was limited in brains, he had brawn in all the right places. Get him working with her in the shop, and their future would be set.

'He looks puny,' Letski said, jabbing Doug in the shoulder.

'He's not puny!' Bessie replied, on the defensive. 'He played football for the school. Didn't you, Doug?'

'Yeah, right,' he agreed, staring at the weird little satyr in front of him. Not that he was put off. Doug found thinking for himself exhausting, especially as Bessie was more than willing to take the stress off him. He had been working on the markets, then at the sewage works, but Bessie hadn't liked that. Said that she couldn't go for a man smelling like a slop pot. And Doug hadn't liked that, because although there were better-looking girls in Burnley, Bessie Holmes was red hot. Saucy as you liked. Not that she'd let him go all the way; she wanted a ring on her finger before that happened. And although the thought of marriage had been enough to dry his mouth up eighteen months earlier, Doug was coming round to the idea.

If he married Bessie, he would never have to worry again. His life would be easy, like a child's. She would make all the decisions and run everything, and he would enjoy his time in bed with her. Seemed ideal, really.

'He's a likely lad,' Bessie told the Russian. 'Try him out. See how well he works. You need someone to do the heavy work around here, Mr Letski. And I could learn how to do some more cobbling.'

'Let me hear you.'

Doug frowned. 'Eh?'

'Let me hear you,' Letski repeated, pulling him over to the door and opening it. With a delicate push, he nudged him into the street, whispering, '*Come in, come in. Bring your shoes, your boots. Come in.*'

'I don't have any—'

'Just say it, Doug!' Bessie said encouragingly. 'Call it out, in the street.'

'People will think I'm daft.'

'Why?' she teased him. 'Did you want to keep it a secret?'

Jabbing Doug in the small of the back, the Russian repeated the mantra, watching as the newcomer took a breath.

'Come in, come in! Bring your shoes, your boots. Come in!' Doug shouted, startling a woman and child who were passing.

But Letski was entranced. 'Ah, he'll do,' he said, patting Doug's chest admiringly. 'You have big lungs, no?'

'Yeah, big lungs.'

'A man with big lungs,' Letski said happily, peering at Bessie. 'We take him on, I think. Yah, we take him on.'

Waking slowly, Emma lay thinking and enjoying the memory of her wedding day. The marriage had been a very quiet affair, Leonard and she opting for a registry office service. The reason behind their choice was simple: Emma had few friends and family, and Leonard didn't want to remind her of that fact, so he was more than willing to have a simple wedding. His mother didn't like the idea one bit, but then Elizabeth was keeping quiet, unwilling to cause any ructions. Because all her hopes lay in the grandchildren to come, the family Leonard had hinted at wanting. It wasn't the time for Elizabeth to show any further doubts about her daughter-in-law. Instead, she and Grant attended the registry office in their best outfits. Emma wore a pale silk dress and Leonard a grey suit. Only Emma's bouquet was elaborate, a heady concoction of summer roses, baby's breath and lilies, tied with white ribbon, a garland of the same flowers in her hair. Sighing, Emma rolled on to her back and remembered how she had taken off the headdress and saved it, wrapping it in tissue paper and putting it in a sealed box.

As the wedding day had come closer, she had become more nervous, but Leonard had been so understanding. Never mentioning Ricky, never talking about anything in Emma's past that might upset her. And gradually Emma had found herself relaxing with him, a real affection taking the place of gratitude. Not the love she had felt for Ricky, but a deep bond she believed she could build on. She would, as she had promised, make Leonard Hemmings a good wife.

He was obviously determined to be a good husband, and had been a gentle and considerate lover. Not exciting, but giving Emma a security and affection that was obviously genuine. Far away, Emma could hear a church clock chiming, but as it was Saturday, she didn't rush to get up, knowing they could have a lie-in. Leonard was due to wake at any moment, but she didn't want to stir him yet. She just wanted to look at him, at the man she had had so many second thoughts about. The kind man who had proved to be exactly as he had seemed. No shape-shifter, with no clutter of emotions, no mood changes. Smiling, she laid her head on his chest. She hadn't fallen in love with her husband, but she had grown to love him with a fondness that was real, if not passionate. And if their sex life meant little to her, Leonard would never know it. To Emma, the lack of physical satisfaction seemed a small price to pay for contentment.

Slowly, she had been incorporated into the Hemmings house and family. Leonard's parents shared their home and goodwill generously, but as time had gone on, Emma realised that her husband spoke less and less about *their* new home. Instead, there had been significant decorations to their rooms, Emma able to choose the wallpaper and – with the help of her mother-in-law – some pieces of suitable furniture. She had to be careful. After all, the new furniture was taking the place of her mother-in-law's precious items, and tact had to be employed in order to make the rooms more modern whilst not offending Mrs Holmes. Which would not be necessary if the newly-weds had their own home.

But references to house-hunting had all but stopped, and when Emma brought the subject up, Leonard had asked why she would want to move on.

'Aren't you happy, sweetie?'

'How could I not be?' she had answered him only the previous night. 'But we did talk about having our own place.'

'Think of the money.'

'Think of the privacy,' Emma had countered, Leonard pulling her on to his knee. 'We *will* move on one day, won't we?'

'Soon, soon.' He kissed her gently. 'Living here, we can save money for somewhere nice.'

'But we could find somewhere *now* that was not so nice.'

'Only the best for my wife,' he had said, smiling. 'We can be happy here for a while longer, surely?'

All of which made perfect sense, except for the fact that Emma once again had found herself living in someone else's home. It was a far cry from the desolate jeweller's, and far enough away from Burnley to feel safe, but it was still someone else's house. And home. If she was honest, Emma didn't care about Leonard's residential ambitions; she was only interested in getting a place she could feel was hers, a place that had no imprint of another person. Why, she thought, staring at her husband's sleeping face, did it matter so much about the money? They could be just as happy in a small flat. They didn't need a big house.

Sensing her watching him, Leonard opened one eye. 'What are you thinking?'

'About us having our own home.'

'I thought we agreed to put that to one side for the time being.'

'No, you agreed to that,' she said, teasing him to keep the subject light-hearted. 'I never agreed to it.'

He reached out and touched her cheek, moved by the youth and prettiness of her. 'Aren't you happy?'

'Of course.'

'But not happy enough?'

A sudden shaming made Emma pause. How could she push her luck? Only weeks earlier she had been locked into the claustrophobic atmosphere of the jeweller's shop, her uncle hovering around her all the time, the clocks ticking at the hours and days like crows pecking at a corpse. She had been so afraid that she would never escape. And yet now here she was, with a man who loved her, and she was *still* asking for more.

'Forget I said anything.'

He rolled on to his side, looking at her. 'Does it matter a lot?'

'No, not really,' she replied. 'I'm being a demanding, horrible wife.'

'Are you homesick?'

She blinked, wrong-footed. '*Homesick?*'

'Well, you're living in Yorkshire now, Emma, it's a long way away from Burnley. Perhaps you miss your uncle?'

She wanted to laugh, but shook her head instead. 'No, my uncle was very good to me, but I'm much happier with you. And I like it here, I don't miss my home town.'

To her surprise, Leonard seemed unconvinced. 'I want to make you happy, you know that.'

'You do.'

'But you seem . . . sometimes you seem so distant. Like you're thinking of the past.' He had always presumed that Emma was thinking of Ricky, and his reluctance to think about his rival – albeit a dead rival – had prevented him from pressing her. 'I know you've lost people . . . Was it very hard for you?'

Turning away, Emma lay back against the pillows. 'I don't think about the past.'

'You can tell me anything,' Leonard said, his voice soft with kindness. 'There's nothing you have to hide from me, darling. You should know that nothing would affect the way I feel about you. I want you to trust me,' he added tenderly, staring into her face. 'I'm your husband, I want to know all about you. Everything about you. After all, you know everything about me.'

The conversation was catching Emma off guard, and silently she cursed herself for bringing up the subject of their move. God, she had so much to be grateful for. A home. A husband. An escape, But she had to keep her side of the bargain, and she had to stay silent. As ever, the thought skittled in her brain, bringing with it the familiar ache of guilt. She had, if she was honest, used Leonard, used his love to get her out of Burnley, and she wasn't even being honest with him. Surely he deserved that? Slowly she traced his cheek with her forefinger. She knew he loved her desperately, so could she trust him? Could she confide about her father? Or would Leonard be shocked – not so much by the facts, but by her duplicity? Not for the first time, Emma found herself torn between her natural honesty and her own survival.

'Leonard,' she said, her voice very low. 'Would you love me whatever?'

'Whatever,' he replied, frowning. 'What is it? I know there's something you're hiding from me.'

'It's . . .' Emma paused, searching for the words that would minimise the shock, then glanced back into her husband's face. In that moment, she knew that she couldn't tell him. That by unburdening herself, she would burden him. That in her relief, she would shake his equilibrium. If he knew about her father, and knew that she had lied, how would he manage the knowledge? After all, the chances were that it wouldn't be just between them. Something they could talk about in private. Leonard would have to hide the facts from his parents – or tell them. Which would be difficult, and would lead to even more suspicion on Elizabeth's part. Leonard might be able to assimilate her secret, but Elizabeth and Grant would not find it so easy. They weren't in love with her. They loved their son – and would see Emma's actions as deceitful.

Not for the first time, Emma could imagine the exchanged looks over the dinner table, the slight alteration in their voices. All the petty hints that the trust had gone, that nothing would ever be as it was. Then she remembered her uncle's tone of voice when he spoke to her – with the underlying but everlasting inflection of judgement. And when she remembered David Hawksworth's attitude, she knew she could never confide.

'There's nothing, Leonard.'

'But . . .'

'I was unhappy at the jeweller's shop,' she said finally. 'I hated the place, and I didn't like my uncle. I suppose I feel guilty.'

'Oh, is that all!' he replied, laughing and kissing her. 'My God, Emma, what a little sin. When you get older, you'll have much worse things to confide.'

'And you'll forgive me, of course.'

'Everything,' he said, his mouth moving over hers. 'I would forgive you everything.'

SIXTEEN

November 1921

Coughing, Frederick stood up, then gripped the side of his bunk, struggling to breathe. The autumn had begun mild, but was now savage, the prison chilled, the tiled walls holding no warmth. Even though Frederick had grown used to the cold, he found it harder to cope with the damp, and a recent leak in the cell next to his had made matters worse. Reg Spencer, who had become reasonably friendly with him, explained how the plumbing system was breaking down, and commiserated, but it still took a week to get the pipes fixed. No doubt the damp would have dried up in the summer months, but weeks of rain had perpetuated the problem, and after a while the base of Frederick's cell walls was mottled with mould.

Asking for a transfer, he was told that there was no other cell available, except on the North Wing. And no one chose to go there. But as Frederick had never been any trouble, the guards took pity on him, Reg intervening with the Governor. The result was a promise that the problem would be fixed. Trouble was, he didn't say when . . . Coughing again, Frederick sat down and stared at his hands. He would think about something else, he decided, something that pleased him. Like Emma . . . Her letters had kept him sane since his imprisonment, just as her insistence on his innocence had kept him focused. At times, though, it was difficult. Frederick was, against the odds, becoming used to his incarceration. As the first two years passed, and he entered the third year of his sentence, he realised that he was in danger of becoming institutionalised. He was liked by the other prisoners, and treated well by the guards – all but Stan Thorpe, who could never resist a chance to provoke him – and as the months passed, his life on the outside seemed to become remote, unreal to him. His daughter was married and settled. She had – to his intense satisfaction – listened to him and kept her father's secret.

Emma had always been Frederick's main concern. How to watch over her as she grew from a child into a girl. How to keep her in school. How to keep her safe and happy. How to make a home for her. Indeed, the one real pride of his life was how he had succeeded as a father. He had no doubts about that. As a father, he had been exemplary. In fact, the only reason why he could bear the injustice of his imprisonment was because Emma believed he was innocent. Told him that, over and over again. Never doubted it. She would write about how she was going to find a new solicitor and see if he would take over Frederick's case – when she had saved a little money.

And he had written back and said that his present solicitor was fine, and that no one could do anything until there was fresh evidence.

Coughing again, Frederick slumped back on his bunk, staring at the grey prison trousers he was wearing. So unlike his usual dapper wear, the suits he had been so proud of. Which had made him look elegant. Perhaps a little too showy for an accounts clerk . . . An old memory made Frederick wince. The memory of Gregory Walmsley at Oldfield Mill, standing in his office and pointing at the desk. His face had been stony, his voice ragged.

'Frederick, not you, I don't believe it . . . not you.'

No, not me. Not bloody me! Frederick thought, turning over and facing the cell wall. Idly he started to count the tiles, but found that this time he couldn't push the memory away. He didn't do it. He didn't steal the money. He hadn't stolen anything in his life. But Gregory Walmsley – who had become a friend – thought he could. Bloody hell, Frederick mused, his eyes focused on the tiles. How *could* he believe it. *How?* Didn't he know him? Slowly he began to count the tiles again, but the memory of his trial stomped back into his head.

Of course he should have pleaded guilty and avoided the trial and all the disgrace that followed. But how could he, when he *wasn't* guilty?

'So who took the money?' his solicitor had asked him, over and over again. 'If you want people to believe you're innocent, you have to tell them who's guilty.'

'I can't.'

'Frederick,' the man had gone on impatiently, 'you have no defence unless you protect yourself! Are you saying that someone else took the money but you don't know who?'

'I *do* know who it was.'

The solicitor had stared at him incredulously. 'You know who it was? Then let's get him arrested and tried.'

'I can't tell you who it was.'

'Are you mad!'

'No,' Frederick had replied emphatically. 'If I could, I would. But I can't name him.'

'All right,' the solicitor had countered, his voice impatient. 'Stay silent. But if you do, you'll not get off. You know that, don't you? Just saying it wasn't you, that it was someone else, isn't going to be enough. Name the man and save yourself.'

'I can't,' he had replied stubbornly.

'Why stay silent?'

'I have to.'

'Why? Just explain to me why.'

'I can't explain, but I have no choice.'

'The jury has a choice.'

Frederick had winced, but had stuck to his guns. 'I didn't do it. And I trust the legal system. I'll take my chances.'

I'll take my chances . . . Jesus, he thought, he certainly had done that. And lost. But he hadn't been lying to his solicitor; he *had* had no choice. Coughing again, Frederick thought of the name of the guilty man. He spoke it inside his head. Over and over, the syllables well worn and ugly. The name was so familiar to him. So well known . . . How many times had he dreamed that he was back in the courtroom, turning to the jury and saying:

'It was him. It was . . .'

But he always woke up before the name left his lips. Even in sleep, he couldn't utter it. And he never would. Just as he would never confide the truth to anyone. Not his solicitor, not Emma. He had chosen his route. Gambled, and lost. And besides, his punishment was deserved, Frederick thought. Too harsh, too severe for his own fall from grace, but deserved none the less. Which was something he could never let his daughter know. Eleven years of imprisonment and the loss of his good name was a small price to pay for her faith in him.

Stop thinking, Frederick told himself, stop thinking. Perhaps becoming institutionalised wasn't so bad after all. The Moors Prison was his home now, the guards and inmates his familiars. When he had moved beyond the panicky loss of freedom, he had found, if he forced himself, that he could make a reasonable life inside. His daughter didn't need him any more, thank God. And by the time the remaining eight years of his sentence had been served, she would had grown away from him, into her new life. As she should. By then she would have children, a home of her own. Frederick knew that Emma would never break contact with him, and so he decided that he would live vicariously through her, in a way that would make his incarceration bearable. His life inside would be quiet and uneventful, but through Emma he would live on the outside.

There was nothing to stop Frederick Coles from walking with his daughter in his mind. Nothing to stop him reading her letters and imagining her home, her neighbours and her new husband. When she wrote about Leonard making her laugh, Frederick was there. When she described having her hair cut short, in the fashion, he could imagine it as though she was standing in front of him. With every letter that came, he would mark out another week of his sentence. In the prison, he would be a calm and peaceful inmate; but in his mind, Frederick Coles would break down the walls, step over the mould, put on his best suit and whistle as he walked through Towneley Park.

SEVENTEEN

Rigid in the narrow doorway of the shop, Adam Hawksworth looked older, a little less sure of himself, but he still had an expression of smug superiority. Having returned from New Zealand, he was about to ask his father for money. Indeed, he had been watching a number of customers coming and going, and was brooding about being poor when his bloody father was obviously doing all right. For a long time he had wanted to get in touch, but something always stopped him. He couldn't stand his father, for a start, couldn't stand David's cold ways, his insistence that Adam should get a proper job and settle down.

If only his mother was still alive, Adam thought. She would have supported him; she had always been behind him. Looking round, his gaze fell on the jewellery cases and the glisten of gold under the glass. Curious, he moved forward and looked down. His father had never found out about his petty thieving, because Jenny had always covered up for her son. She didn't approve of his stealing, no, not that. Had been angry with Adam for once, until he had promised never to take anything again. Promised over and over, as Jenny hugged and soothed him. Swore he would never steal again from the jewellery shop.

'But in a way, it's mine.'

She had looked at him, bemused. '*What?*'

'Well, the shop belongs to Father, and I'm his son; why shouldn't I help myself now and again?'

'Because it's not right!' his mother had said firmly. 'You have to earn your money.'

A sudden noise made Adam turn. His father was standing on the step that led into the shop. Motionless, David studied his son, the last person he had expected to see that morning. The last person he had expected to see *any* morning. His first instinct was to take Adam in his arms, hold him as he had done when the boy was born, before he became the sulky bone of contention between his parents.

But David couldn't make the move; he was too rigid, too locked into the past.

'What are you doing here?'

'Hello, Father,' Adam said, in a tone just the right side of polite. 'How are you?'

'Well. And you?'

'Fine. I was in New Zealand.'

'I know,' David said, his legs feeling weak, without substance. This was his son, the child he had once loved so much, and he was desperate not to drive him away again. 'Are you staying in Burnley?'

'No, I'm just passing through,' Adam replied, frowning. 'I've got a new idea, a new job.'

'A job?'

'Well, not some regular day job,' he said huffily.

'Something more creative. But I need money to get me started.'

Inside, David could feel his guts churn. Money. Always money. If he was penniless, he knew he would never see his son again. It was just the money that kept Adam coming back.

'I can't give you any.'

'Why not?'

'I need to know more about this job.'

'You want to interrogate me more like!' Adam retorted. 'Christ, you hate me, don't you?'

'I never hated you!'

'You always hated me!' Adam threw back. 'My mother loved me, but you never did.'

Shaken, David stared at the man who was his son. The man he didn't know or understand. A long time ago, Jenny had given birth to him, and David had felt such pride then, walking out with his wife and child. No one would ever know how much it meant to him to have fathered a child. A son. No one would ever realise that he had been terrified of being childless, his sexual inadequacy denying him a family. But now that child, that son, that longed-for offspring, was standing in front of him, hating him.

'Adam . . .'

'Just some money! That's all I need. You've got money, don't deny it. I'm your son, why can't you help me out?'

'I want to know more—'

'Oh, go to hell!' Adam snapped, rounding on his father. His temper was up, his good-looking face flushed as he raised his hand, David ducking. Stunned, the older man straightened up, his face ashen.

'Get out!'

Adam's hand dropped to his side, his expression suddenly sly. 'Dad, I didn't mean—'

'Get out!' David repeated. 'I don't know you any more. And until you're my son, and act like my son, I don't *want* to know you.'

'I'm pregnant.'

'Oh, bloody hell!' Bessie replied, putting down the shoe she was holding and staring at Emma. 'That was quick!'

'*Come in, come in. Bring your shoes, your boots . . .*'

'We're closed now!' Bessie said, turning to Mr Letski, who was standing, confused, in the doorway of the back room. 'Shop's closed for the day.'

He frowned. 'No shoes?'

'Nah.'

'No boots?'

'Not until tomorrow,' Bessie said kindly, leading the old man into the back of the shop and calling for Doug. A moment later, Emma could see the three of them standing in the kitchen, Doug settling the old Russian in his chair and putting the kettle on to boil.

Closing the door behind her as she walked back into the shop, Bessie blew out her cheeks.

'He's almost blind now and getting deaf. I mean Mr Letski, not Doug.'

Smiling, Emma sat down on one of the high-backed stools. 'Can you believe it? I'm going to have a baby.'

'Well, it happens,' Bessie replied, grinning. 'When you get all tingly down there.'

Both of them laughed, Bessie looking hard into Emma's face. She had known from the start that her friend had made a bargain, but she had certainly made the best of it. And her happiness was deserved. Taking her hand, Bessie listened to all the news, thinking that now, finally, Emma might have a real family. A husband, a child, a place where she was loved and needed.

'Leonard's thrilled, as cheerful as any man in Yorkshire,' Emma went on. 'Although that's not saying much.'

Watching her, Bessie noticed that all her friend's spirit had come back. Her feistiness, her sense of fun. Then Emma laughed again, talking about her husband with real fondness. It might not have been a love match for Emma at first, but she was obviously content. The promise she had made – to make Leonard Hemmings a good wife – she had kept.

'Blimey,' Bessie said, teasing her. 'A baby is a hell of a Christmas present. I'm giving Doug a pair of socks. Are you happy?'

'Yes, of course I am,' Emma replied, 'I was a bit taken aback at first, but Leonard's over the moon. And his parents.'

'You'll stay living with them when the baby's born?'

Pausing, Emma chose her words carefully. 'They want us to be one big happy family.'

'How lovely.'

'It's not that bad!' Emma mocked her. 'We all get on well, and they've really made me feel at home. And since my mother-in-law heard about the baby, I can do no wrong. I'm perfect now; any doubts she had about me before have gone.'

'What d'you want, a boy or a girl?'

'Leonard wants a boy.'

'Doug wants five children.'

'But you're not even married!'

'No, and I won't be having five children either!' Bessie replied wryly, dropping her voice. 'He asks me to marry him all the time, but I want to get the business sorted first.'

'But if you got married, you could still sort out the business.'

'Maybe,' Bessie agreed. 'But I like to take it one thing at a time.'

A moment passed between them, Emma choosing her next words with care.

'How's my uncle?'

'Same as ever,' Bessie replied. 'You going to see him?'

'No . . . I write to him, though.'

'Does he reply?'

'No.'

'Old bugger,' Bessie said thoughtfully. 'You know that his son came back?'

'You're joking! Adam?'

'Yeah, fetched up a couple of weeks ago, to touch his father for money. There was a real showdown and your uncle threw him out.'

'Good God. It's a different life here,' Emma said thoughtfully. 'Not much happens in the suburbs. Not like living in Burnley.'

'Maybe not, but you wouldn't want to bring a baby up round here, would you?'

Shaking her head, Emma glanced out towards Market Street, watching the passers-by hurrying under an unexpected downfall. Despite her own exciting news, the Burnley streets still seemed depressing to her, and although she was delighted to see Bessie again, she was looking forward to Leonard collecting her later. In fact, she realised that she had cut all the old ties and had moved on from her past completely. A past that was now unfamiliar, almost hostile to her. Having spent her childhood in the town, Emma had expected to feel some kind of nostalgia, but her new life was safer and she had no hankering to return.

It was pleasurable being able to buy herself clothes and furniture for their home. It was unusual and exciting for her to have the freedom to be in charge of her own life. She was in control, as a wife and mother-to-be. She was grown up, steady, secure. The friends of Leonard's parents all welcomed her, her husband's close friends accepting her into their life readily, although Leonard did seem to want to keep her to himself. But then, that was what you expected when you were first married, wasn't it? Still gazing out on to the cobbles, Emma noticed the hoarding advertising Pears Soap. In the past she had never been able to afford it, but now she had the finest soap and soft towels, and hot water on tap. Her food was different, too; no parched meals with her uncle, but vegetables with butter and meat. Lots of meat now that she was pregnant. Emma smiled to herself. Oh, her life had certainly changed. And if, sometimes, she felt that it might be a little *too* safe, she shrugged the thought off. How could she be too safe? Too secure?

'When's the baby due?'

'June next year. I have to get through the winter first.'

'Summer baby. Nice,' Bessie replied. 'What are you going to call it?'

'Sarah if it's a girl, and Grant if it's a boy. After Leonard's father.'

'Yeah, well it wouldn't be after his mother, would it?'

Smiling, Emma reached out for her friend's hand and squeezed it tightly.

'I don't know if I ever did say thank you for being such a good friend. You stuck by me when Dad went to prison; no one else round here did.'

'My mother would have gone mad if she'd known, God rest her soul,' Bessie replied, thinking of Mrs Holmes, who had recently passed away. 'Ricky's death was the end of her. I should thank you for helping me when she died. It hit me hard, after Ricky.'

'You know we'll always help each other, we always

have and always will,' Emma said sincerely. 'I'm so glad you've got Doug.'

'Oh, he's no bloody good for anything,' Bessie replied, winking, 'but a cracker in bed.' She paused, looking at Emma with affection. 'I don't suppose I'll be seeing much of you from now on, what with the baby coming.'

'Don't be daft! I'll visit as usual.'

'I like it here in this crummy old town,' Bessie went on, looking out of the window. 'But it's not for you. You got out, Emma, and you have to stay out. Enjoy your new life and family. Life was hard for you here; don't come back.'

Anxious, Emma stared at her old friend. 'God, Bessie, don't talk like that. You sound like you're saying goodbye.'

'It's *you* that should be saying goodbye, Emma. To this town. To the old memories. We'll be friends, no matter what. But this place was no friend to you.'

'No,' Emma agreed. 'But you were. If I hadn't been able to confide in you, at times my life would have been unbearable. You know how heart-breaking it was when Ricky died, and then having to hide so much from Leonard . . .'

'You had no choice.'

'No, but being able to talk about it helped,' Emma replied, her tone serious. 'We'll always talk to each other, won't we? We'll never have secrets. Promise me, Bessie, we won't have secrets, will we?'

A little while later Emma was sitting in the car, Leonard driving them home. Moving out of Burnley, they headed away from Lancashire, towards Yorkshire, the boundary of the counties marking Emma's transition. At one point she was tempted to look over the countryside towards the Moors, and the prison where her father was incarcerated, but she kept her head averted. And then, at the last minute, she turned and stared out of the back window, longing for just a glimpse of the prison that had been so much a part of her life.

'Wow, sit down, darling!' Leonard admonished her, surprised, 'Haven't you seen a prison before?'

She slumped back in her seat, silent.

'Grim place, that. Not the kind of place any man would want to end up. Mind you, I suppose it depends on the crime . . .'

Emma could hardly speak. Just stared into the side-view mirror of the Austin, straining to get a glimpse of the jail.

But it was too far away, and as the car moved further and further on, Emma panicked inside. She was leaving Burnley, Lancashire, for the suburbs of Yorkshire. Only this time she was leaving for good. She was carrying Leonard Hemmings's child. She was a respectable wife, with no ties to Holland Street or the vast edifice glowering on the Moors. But instead of comforting her, the thought frightened her. By moving on, into her new role, she was taking herself further and further away from her past. And her father. Suddenly the thought tore at her. How could she be happy when he was still suffering? How could she leave her father behind when she knew he was innocent? How could she become a parent when the parent who had done so much for her was being abandoned?

'I have to go back!' she said suddenly.

Leonard stopped the car and pulled over to the side of the road. 'Are you all right? Did you leave something at Bessie's?'

Yes! she wanted to scream. I left my childhood, my memories, and my father. I left him because I wasn't brave enough to face you. To tell you the truth. I sacrificed my father for a comfortable life. And before, it bothered me, she wanted to say. But now – now that I'm carrying my own child – I can't bear to think about what I've done.

'Are you all right, Emma?'

Her head bowed, she placed her hands over her stomach. Nausea filled her mouth and throat, coupled with panic.

'I just felt homesick,' she lied. 'It's being pregnant. Your mother said it makes women emotional, and she was right.'

Emma could feel Leonard's hand against her cheek, stroking her face, comforting her.

'It's fine, darling. Everything's all right. I won't let anything happen to you, my love,' he said, his voice muted. 'Don't be afraid of the future. I'm with you. It's our future and no one can take it from us.'

'It's our future and no one can take it from us' . . . How those words soothed me at the time, dampened down the panic and made me believe that everything would be well. It took me a long while to really understand the full reason for my fear. At the time I thought it was being pregnant for the first time, deserting the familiar and leaving my father behind. But I had already left him and made my choice, so why it affected me so much that day, in that old Austin car, I didn't understand.

Perhaps it was a premonition of sorts. Perhaps it was just a childish wish to see the jail and know it was still standing, still holding my father. Perhaps it was the farewell – not just to my past, but to my own childhood – because from then onwards I would be carrying the next generation and have responsibility for a new life. I was growing up, no longer my father's beloved child, the centre of Frederick Coles's universe. I was the centre of Leonard's universe, and I knew that when the child was born, it would usurp me.

But that wasn't what frightened me. What

unnerved me that day was something I only came to understand many years later. You see, we can run away, put a thousand miles between our past and our future, but until we can come to terms with our past, it follows us like a ghoul. I was changing so rapidly. A wife, a mother-to-be, but in my heart I was still the lonely girl who had taken the long journey in secret over the Moors. I might be better dressed, and more secure, but that other me was still walking around the jeweller's shop, listening to the clocks ticking away the hours. In reality I had no reason to panic, but panic I did, because Emma Coles was still as real as Emma Hemmings.

And I missed my old self. She had been brave, willing to fight and loyal to a fault. By contrast, the pregnant woman in the Austin car was someone who had compromised with life. Who had manipulated her past to secure her future. Nothing too bad, nothing too heinous – but it wasn't my judgement that made me pause. It wasn't even Leonard's, or the world's.

It was the person who had not yet been born. One day in the future, my child would judge me – and I knew then, with a horrible certainty, that I would be found wanting.

EIGHTEEN

Knowing that Leonard was at work at the brewery, Emma turned to her mother-in-law. Elizabeth was frowning, trying to tie up a Christmas wreath, a short snort of impatience coming from between clenched teeth.

'Here,' Emma said, 'let me help.'

'I hate ivy,' Elizabeth replied, stepping back and watching Emma hang the wreath on the door. She had grown fond of her pregnant daughter-in-law, and was pleased to see that she was making her son an attentive wife. But there was still something nagging at the back of Elizabeth's mind, and although Grant tried repeatedly to reassure her, the feeling remained. A suspicion that would never go away. 'I can't see why anyone puts it in a wreath.'

'It's pretty,' Emma replied, standing back and arching her aching back. 'There, that's the finishing touch. The house looks marvellous with all your decorations.'

'Next year there will be even more decorations,' Elizabeth replied, 'what with a new baby around. I remember when Leonard was little. We made such a fuss that first Christmas, and of course he was too small to remember a thing.' She looked Emma up and down, noticing the slightly swollen stomach and the flush of her cheeks. 'How are you feeling today?'

'Not sick any more, thank God. I feel a lot better, thanks.'

'Being pregnant is hard work.'

'You can say that again,' Emma replied, smiling. 'My ankles have started swelling and Leonard was laughing at me when I told him. Mind you, he did rub them last night.'

'Men have no concept of how women suffer,' Elizabeth retorted. 'If they had to have children, the species would die out. But you have to take things easy, Emma, don't take any risks. You've got a way to go yet.'

Smiling, Elizabeth turned away – then noticed that Emma's coat was on the hall table. 'Are you going out, dear?'

The lie was difficult, but necessary. 'I have to see my uncle. I missed him when I last went to Burnley and I should see him at Christmas.'

'But Leonard's at work, he can't drive you.'

Emma smiled easily. 'I can get there under my own steam, you know.'

'But it will take the best part of a day to get there, see your uncle and come back. And it's dark at four.'

'Elizabeth,' Emma said kindly, 'stop worrying. It's only nine o'clock in the morning and I feel fit. And I feel like getting some exercise. I'll be back before it's late, I promise.' Walking to the door, she turned.

'Don't tell Leonard, he worries so much. And anyway, I'll be home before he is.'

Hurrying down the road, she made for the bus stop to catch the bus that would take her not to Burnley, but over to the Moors. When she got closer, she would have to change buses – she had worked that out – and with luck she should arrive at the prison around twelve. Which would give her plenty of time to see her father and return home. Reaching into her pocket, she stared at the letter she had received via Bessie. They had made a pact that any correspondence from the prison should be sent to Bessie and then forwarded to Emma in Yorkshire. Which was exactly what had happened. Pleased to see Bessie's handwriting, Emma had picked up the letter and taken it upstairs, waiting for Leonard to leave for work before she opened it.

> *Hello there,*
> *Letter from the prison for you. Hope all's well.*
> *Love, Bessie*

And with her letter, another. A note from Reg Spencer, a man she knew as one of her father's guards.

> *Dear Mrs Hemmings,*
> *Forgive me getting in touch like this, but I'm one of the guards at the Moors Prison and I think you should know that your father's ill. He*

didn't want me to bother you, but being Christmas and all, I reckon a visit from you would cheer him up no end. He's not been himself for a while. Nothing serious, but you'll see what I mean.

Like I said, I hope you'll forgive me writing to you, but I remember how you used to visit and I know how much you care for your dad.

Best wishes,
Reg Spencer

The message had come at the right time. All the previous week Emma had been struggling with her conscience, and now fate had intervened, giving her the perfect reason to follow her instinct. Now she *had* to see her father, and he was ill . . . Pushing the letter deep into her pocket, she stared down the road, willing the bus to come. She hadn't liked to lie to Elizabeth, but her father came first, and when the bus pulled up at the stop, she climbed on hurriedly. Frederick had been ill, Reg's note said. Nothing serious, but he wasn't himself . . . What did that mean? Emma wondered, knowing that her father would never have sent for her himself. Especially not now that she was pregnant. In his letters he had said nothing about being ill, but when she sent him a photograph of herself and Leonard, he had replied with sadness in his words. Nothing anyone else would have noticed, but obvious to her.

The bus moved easily along, and by the time half an hour had passed, Emma was disembarking and going for the tram, which was due on the hour. Glancing up at a church clock, she heard it strike, and fifteen minutes later was relieved to see the tram arrive, on time. She knew that everything depended on her timing. In order to get to the jail and home again – and in that way invite no questions – she would have to make sure she stuck to her route. Leonard might think it strange of her to rush off to see her uncle, but he would understand. After all, even people who didn't get on that well made an effort at Christmas. Trundling along, Emma saw the first flakes of snow begin to fall and frowned. She had hoped it would keep away until the following day; snow on the Moors could be difficult and hold up transport. But, she consoled herself, it had been an unusually mild winter; how could one day's snowfall cause a problem?

It was nearly eleven fifty when Emma finally arrived outside the prison gates, knowing that at twelve, visiting time would begin. An extra visiting hour, because of Christmas. Around her grew the queue of people she remembered from the past. Grim-looking men, hard-faced women, older couples, and one woman with a child under her coat. All of them waiting, in silence, outside the iron gates. Looking up, Emma could see the glass and barbed wire on top of the walls, and felt her heart lurch. The place was more terrible than she remembered, and she realised, with guilt, that her absence had been a relief. Shamefaced, she stood in the snow, feeling the light flakes land on her hair and face as she stamped her boots to keep her feet warm. She knew from past experience that on the stroke of noon the gates would open and the visitors would begin their long, silent procession into the entrance yard. From there they would be hustled into the visitors' room. Above her the clock struck suddenly, making her jump, as the jail doors opened and two guards stood on either side of the queue, watching them pass.

The smell, the size, the colour, the depression of the jail crushed into Emma, the echoing sounds and barked orders taking her back to the first days of her father's incarceration. Jesus, she thought helplessly, this is a desperate place. Then her gaze moved across the yard and she saw – segregated and double-wire-fenced – the dead bulk of the North Wing. The place where Ricky had been killed . . . Closing her eyes for an instant, she turned, then moved on into the visitors' room, taking her seat on the low bench, the empty prisoners' bench opposite her.

In silence they all waited for the inmates to be shown in. After another minute, Emma heard the sounds of feet and orders, all mingling, echoing in the cavernous belly of the jail. Finally, the door of the visitors' room opened and the first men came in. Craning her neck to see, Emma looked for her father's dark head of hair. A little taller than most of the inmates, Frederick was usually easy to spot, but this time Emma was surprised not to see him and jumped when a man sat down opposite her.

For a moment she wanted to tell him to move, that her father was coming – but then she realised that it *was* her father. Reg Spencer had not been exaggerating, Frederick was ill, and not himself. Not himself at all. Not charming, not glamorous, not dapper. Aged, and with the beginnings of a stoop, his face colourless, his thick hair spattered with grey. Shocked, but determined not to show it, Emma reached for her father's hand.

'No contact!'

Jumping, she withdrew it and smiled at Frederick. He had obviously been looking forward to seeing her and had made an effort. His uniform was pressed and neat, but his weight loss had made his collar loose, and his hands shook slightly. In a little more than two years, Frederick had aged a decade.

'Dad . . .' Emma said, her eyes filling. 'I had to come and see you and say happy Christmas.'

'You shouldn't have come, love. You know I asked you not to,' he said, his voice as well spoken as ever, but muted. 'But I'm glad you have. I don't want you worrying about me.'

'You've lost weight.'

'I had a chest infection.'

'I brought some food,' Emma said helplessly. 'I want you to eat it all, Dad, all of it . . . Oh God, are you all right?'

'I'm fine. Like I said, I've been ill, but now I'm fine,' he said, trying to sound light-hearted. 'I got your letter, love. I was so glad about the baby. How are you feeling?'

'I'm fine, Dad,' she said, choked. 'But I'm worried about you.'

How could she ever have rejected him? How could she have lived her life outside and not come to see him?

'I don't want you getting upset, Emma. You don't know how pleased I am to hear about your new life and now this baby. It's all wonderful for you. And it's what you deserve.'

'What about you, Dad?' she countered, looking round. 'What about what you deserve? Not this. Not being here.' She paused, lowering her voice as one of the guards glanced over to her. 'You should never have stopped me visiting you.'

'It was for the best.'

'I miss you.'

'I miss you too,' he said honestly, 'but this way is best, Emma. When I come out, we can meet up again. But not in here.'

'Why not?' she said, leaning towards him. 'I can come over, like I used to. No one needs to know.'

'You would have to lie to your husband and his parents. And that's not right. It's too much for you.'

'*What about you?* You need me, Dad, you know you do,' Emma responded. 'You're not well, I can see that, and I can't just walk away and leave you again.'

'Yes you can, and yes you will,' Frederick replied, his voice harsh. 'How dare you make this any more difficult for me? Don't you realise that your life is what keeps me going? Knowing you're all right, happy; that's what keeps me alive. Don't you jeopardise that for me, Emma. It wouldn't be a kindness.' He paused, smiling. 'There now, we've quarrelled and we never do that.'

Fighting tears, Emma was staring down at the table between them. 'Are you all right? I mean, are you really better, or is there something else?'

'No,' Frederick said firmly, 'I'm not dying, love. I was just ill, and this place doesn't do a lot for any man. It ages you; I suppose you can see that better than I can . . .' He stopped, thinking of her last letters. 'I liked the photographs. That husband of yours looks a good fellow.'

'He is,' Emma said, glancing back to her father. 'He's very kind.'

'You need that,' her father replied, changing the subject. 'I'm so glad to see you, Emma. I wouldn't have asked, but I wanted to see you. It's Christmas, after all. And this time next year, you'll be a mother.'

'Yes . . .'

'You'll enjoy that. I remember how happy we were when you were born. Children are a blessing.'

She nodded, but she was studying her father's face with distress. Frederick's illness might not have been serious outside, but in the damp conditions of the old jail, he was struggling. Was it really serious? she wondered. After all, Reg Spencer had written to her, so he must be worried. Emma thought about the note from the guard: *He's not been himself for a while. Nothing serious, but you'll see what I mean . . .*

And she did see. She saw a man who was aged and changed, and, more frighteningly, someone whose inner light had been extinguished. Her father, the dapper Frederick Coles, was a shell of his old self. A

208

carapace, a walking, talking automaton. All the fire had been extinguished. He was, Emma thought with queasy unease, a damp squib of a man. And why had it happened? Because he had been jailed – for something he hadn't done. Oh, and how that innocence, the irony, would stifle him. To be guilty of something and be punished was harsh. To be innocent and have your life scraped away, cell by cell, was hell.

'I'm going to see your solicitor, see if there's any news.'

'Nothing, love. I would have told you.'

'Nothing at all?' Emma countered. If her father stayed in the jail for the next nine years of his sentence, she knew she wouldn't be taking him out alive. 'Dad, we have to do something to prove you're innocent.'

'There's nothing we *can* do.'

'Maybe there is,' she persisted. 'I'm going to talk to—'

'Let it be!' Frederick snapped, surprising her.

'Why?'

'I don't want you getting involved in this any more. It was a mistake to see you, Emma. I knew I shouldn't have allowed it. But I wanted to see you again, to tell you how happy I am about your news.' He held her gaze desperately. 'Keep writing to me, love. Please, keep writing.'

Mute, Emma stared at her father, her mind swimming. He was losing his will to live, she could see that. Her marriage, and now the coming baby, had not helped him, whatever he might say. On the contrary, Emma's escape had allowed him to relax. Knowing she was safe, that he had no responsibility for her, had snuffed out the fire that had kept Frederick going. He might pretend that he was living through her, but the lack of hope and the long years that stretched ahead of him were going to kill him. He might not know it, but Emma did.

'Dad, I want you to take better care of yourself,' she said firmly. 'We *will* find some new evidence and clear you. You're innocent, and one day everyone will know it.'

He nodded, as though he didn't believe it. Or even care.

'Just keep writing,' he said, then turned as the bell sounded. 'Visit over.'

'I've only just got here!' Emma said desperately. 'Just a little longer.'

'Rules, my love,' Frederick replied, getting to his feet and falling into line with the other inmates. 'Take care of yourself.'

'I love you,' Emma called after him, watching as the row of men moved into the corridor, taking her father with them.

Urgently she searched the tops of their heads, but Frederick was no longer the tallest, and as she sank back down on the bench, she felt her heart shatter like ice.

NINETEEN

Restless, Leonard walked back to the car, climbed inside and slammed the door closed. In silence, he stared ahead into Holland Street. David Hawksworth had been emphatic – his niece had not visited him. Not that day, or any day for a long time. She wrote letters, he had said simply, but didn't call. *Sorry*, he had said, watching Leonard pause, obviously shaken, *she's not here* . . . So why hadn't she told him where she was really going? Leonard wondered. Surely she would realise that he would call for her at her uncle's and find out that she hadn't visited?

'But it's past four,' Leonard had insisted, staring at the old grandfather clock on the wall. 'And if she's not here, where is she? God, she might be hurt.' He had turned, catching the look on David's face. A look that alerted him. 'Do you know where she is?'

'No. Why should I know where your wife is?'

'You just looked . . . Are you *sure* you haven't seen Emma?'

'I haven't seen her since she left here and married you,' David had replied, turning away. 'She's your responsibility now.'

211

Back in the car, Leonard let his anger subside. What a bastard David Hawksworth was, and how right Emma had been about him. Looking round, Leonard expected at any moment for Emma to appear. To wave at him and run over, jumping into the car, happy that he had made the trip to collect her. But long as he stared, his wife did not come down Holland Street. Surely she would know that he would follow her to the jeweller's shop? If she had been hiding something, she would have been more careful . . . Slowly, Leonard relaxed. Emma was up to something, something for Christmas, some kind of secret she would tell him about later. That was all; she had gone shopping! That was why she had said she was going to be away for the day – she had needed time on her own, without being rushed.

Starting up the car, Leonard smiled with relief. He had been letting his imagination run away with him. Thinking that his wife had had an accident, or been lying to him to cover up some assignation. For a stupid instant, he had even suspected that she might be seeing someone else. The thought made Leonard wince. Emma, of all people. She was happy, carrying their child. She wasn't the type to cheat on him. All she had done was to tell a white lie, to get some time alone. Not that he wouldn't have words with her when she did come home. Scaring him like that.

By the time he returned home, Leonard was buoyed up, and was surprised to find his parents waiting at the door, looking anxiously at the passenger seat.

'Where's Emma?'

Leonard stopped in his tracks, the snow falling on his hair. 'She isn't home?'

'No. No, she isn't,' his mother replied, Grant moving towards his son and pulling Leonard indoors.

'No one's seen her since this morning.'

Inside, Leonard turned to his mother. 'What did she say this morning? What did she say? Where did she say she was going?'

'I told you,' Elizabeth replied, trying to keep her voice calm. 'She said she was visiting her uncle.'

'She never got there.'

'*What!*'

'Her uncle hadn't seen her. In fact, she's never visited him.' Leonard stopped short, noticing the look of suspicion on his mother's face and blundering on. 'She must have gone shopping to surprise us. That's typic- ally Emma; she wanted some time to buy presents . . .' He trailed off, suddenly lost. 'Where is she?'

'I'll take the car out,' Grant said shortly, looking over to his son. 'You come with me.'

Stunned, Elizabeth stared at her husband. 'Where are you going?'

'We have to follow the route Emma said she was taking,' Grant replied, his tone solemn. 'There might have been an accident. Or she might have got held up coming back over the high ground.'

'I'll drive,' Leonard said, taking the car keys from his father's hand and turning to his mother. 'It's seven o'clock. We'll bring her back, I promise. We'll bring Emma home.'

213

Stuck out on the moor, Emma was staring at the passengers around her and cursing her bad luck. She had made good time and caught every connection she had planned, but the last bus had engine trouble and stalled on a steep incline. At first she had expected the trouble to be fixed – after all, northern winters were always cold and the weather was frequently inhospitable – but this particular driver was inexperienced, and instead of getting the engine running again, he had flooded it. Now, as the snow continued to fall relentlessly, Emma sat with the other passengers and waited for help. But help didn't come, and as three thirty turned into six, she knew that she was going to be found out.

What was she going to say? That she had seen her uncle and that the bus had broken down? Why not? It was partially the truth, and although she hadn't see David Hawksworth, who would know? God, Emma thought to herself, worried about her father and her husband, why did this have to happen now? If only things had gone her way, she could have made the prison visit and been home before Leonard.

Banging her fists on her lap, she stared out of the bus window. She was suddenly tired of the lying. Tired of covering up. It was true that she was worried about her father – but surely she had a *right* to that concern? Surely it was natural for a woman to want to see her own flesh and blood? Wasn't that normal? But the situation *wasn't* normal, and she knew that. Miserably, Emma thought back to the prison. Her father's deterioration had thrown her, unnerved her – and made her feel guilty. By not visiting, she had managed to put the reality of Frederick's situation to the back of her mind, but now she had seen it again, in all its squalor and hopelessness – so how could she go back to pretending her father didn't exist? Huddling into her coat and biting her bottom lip, Emma reproached herself. Didn't Leonard deserve better? Didn't she owe him the truth, after he had done so much for her? Couldn't she trust him, after they had grown so close?

Suddenly the bus engine spluttered into life, the vehicle humming under her feet. But the relief was short-lived. Emma knew that by the time she returned home it would be late and everyone would be waiting for her. Waiting for her explanation. And despite what she had seen and felt that day, despite her father's decline and her own guilt, she would have to lie again. And again, and again . . .

Finally, just after eight, an exhausted Emma walked up the pathway to her home. But before she could turn the key in the lock, the door was opened, Leonard grabbing hold of her.

'Oh, thank God, thank God you're all right!' he said, burying his face in the nape of her neck and holding her tightly. 'You're so cold, Emma. Come in, darling, and sit down.'

Without speaking, she followed him, expecting to see her in-laws, but there was only Leonard, pouring her a brandy and sitting her in front of the fire. Taking off her coat, he wrapped a rug around her, looking into her face desperately. *Lie to me,* his expression said, *lie to me* . . . And Emma knew then that he suspected something. That she was seeing someone else. That his young wife was seeing another man . . . The ridiculous thought almost made her smile, her teeth chattering against the glass as she sipped her brandy. What did he know? She braced herself. *What did Leonard actually know?*

'Where were you?'

She kept sipping the brandy.

'You told my mother you were going to see your uncle in Burnley. Why were you so long?'

She was dazed, upset, and couldn't think clearly. In fact, all she wanted to do was to lie down and sleep. Tomorrow she would explain, tomorrow she would think up some lie that would put Leonard's mind at rest. But not now. Now she was too tired to think clearly. Tired and sick of lying. And sorry, so sorry that she had scared her husband so much.

'Emma, *did* you see your uncle?'

He was getting angry, she could hear it in his voice.

'Well, did you? Answer me!'

There was a moment's pause, and then she nodded. And as she did so, she realised that Leonard – kindly, caring Leonard – knew she was lying.

Her hand shaking, she put down her glass and looked at her husband.

'I'm sorry if I worried you.' She paused, staring into his face, which had paled. 'What's the matter?'

'I went to your uncle's, Emma,' he said, for once cold with her. 'I went to surprise you and pick you up. He said you hadn't been there today. *That you'd never visited him . . .*' Breathing heavily, Emma leaned back in the seat, Leonard continuing. 'I told myself that you'd wanted a day on your own. To do some Christmas shopping.' He glanced around her feet. 'But you've no bags, Emma. You've no bags, no presents.'

Her head was swimming. She could hear Leonard talking, but it was mingling with the sound of the prison gates creaking open and the bus engine coughing hoarsely as the snow fell.

'I was . . . I was . . . I'm sorry,' she said stupidly, blindly.

'*Emma, look at me!*' he said, his tone sharp. 'Please tell me the truth.'

'Leonard . . .' She trailed off, unable to tell another lie.

'Tell me the truth, Emma. Are you seeing someone else?' Troubled, he caught hold of her wrist, surprising her.

'No! No! I would never do that to you.'

'But what *have* you been doing to me?' he retorted. 'I love you, Emma, but I have to know what you've been doing. You *have* to tell me where you've been.'

'Nowhere.'

'*I don't believe you!*' he snapped, letting go of her wrist and turning away. She could hear him breathe in, trying to control himself. But when he turned back to her, his face was blank with confusion. 'You are my wife . . .'

'Of course I am!' she said, her tone pleading. 'And

217

I've never done anything you would be ashamed of. I would never cheat on you.'

'So where were you?'

'Leonard, stop shouting at me, please! I'm so sorry I worried you, I won't ever do it again, but please, please trust me.'

Shaking, he bent towards her. His eyes stared into hers, then suddenly he changed, almost pleading with her.

'If you're in love with someone else, whisper it.'

'No!'

'Whisper it,' he commanded her. 'No one will overhear, my parents need never know. If you've fallen in love, Emma, tell me, we can sort this out.'

'I haven't fallen in love with anyone!'

'Just tell me, don't lie!' he snapped. 'Just tell me!'

'I'm not seeing anyone else,' Emma said, tears rolling down her cheeks.

'So where were you?'

'I was just . . . I was just . . . thinking.'

'I know there's something you're hiding, Emma. I've always known, since I met you. There's a secret you've never confided in me. But you can,' he urged her. 'You can tell me. Are you unhappy, is that it? Do you want to go back home?'

'No, no!' She looked at him, her expression bewildered. 'I don't want to leave you.'

'I know you want a home of your own,' he hurried on. 'I should have listened before now. We'll move, find somewhere before the baby's born. Then you can have your own house, and run it your own way. I should have known how important that was to you, I should have—'

'You've done more than enough,' Emma said desperately. 'There's nothing more you could do for me, Leonard. You've been the kindest of men, the best of husbands, the most loving person I could have hoped to marry. It's not anything to do with you.'

'I've lost you.'

'No! No!' she reassured him, watching as he slumped into a chair opposite her. She realised then how much he meant to her; and she also realised how much he loved her. Desperately, blindly. His face was losing colour as she leaned towards him, her voice pleading with him. 'Leonard, you're the best husband any woman could have. Look at me, darling, please look at me.'

But he wasn't listening. All he could think of was that his wife was unhappy – and the reason for that unhappiness he put down to his own stubbornness. They should have their own house, they should have their own space. Emma was unhappy sharing with his parents, and now that the baby was coming, she was getting more and more upset. *That* was what had caused her to go out, to get some air. Some space. It wasn't anything dreadful. She wasn't in love with anyone else, she wasn't going to leave him. She just wanted her own home.

'We'll move next week. Tomorrow.'

'It's not that,' Emma said hurriedly. 'I'm not unhappy here, Leonard. Please, calm down, you're getting all worked up.'

But he wasn't taking any notice.

'Emma, I understand now. I've talked to people, and having a baby is difficult for a woman. You need to feel safe in your own home, making a nest.'

'Leonard, it's not your fault—'

But he persisted. 'It will all be all right, Emma. I promise you. I'll sort this out. Very soon everything will be perfect again.'

'Leonard, please stop, darling, please calm down.' She reached for his hand, and he grabbed at it.

'I can make your life perfect, Emma. I can make you safe and happy. You don't have to be afraid of anything.' His voice was speeding up with panic. 'I've got it all worked out. I know you had to spend some time on your own, to think. I understand. But there's nothing to be worried about, my love.'

And then Emma started shaking violently. She was exhausted, cold and desperate. Hysteria was close, panic and confusion making her giddy. All she wanted was some quiet, a moment to think, but Leonard had pushed her too far and she felt cornered.

'*There's nothing to be worried about?*' she repeated. 'You want to know where I've been, Leonard? Are you *sure* you want to know, are you really sure?'

He nodded.

'I've been visiting my father. In the Moors Prison. He was jailed for theft over two years ago.'

'But your father's dead,' Leonard said dumbly, his face losing colour.

'I was afraid to tell you the truth.' She paused,

watching Leonard's face. He was confused, she could tell that, but he also looked badly shaken, and his hands were trembling as he clenched his fists.

'Your father's not dead . . . ?'

'Let me explain—'

'He's alive. *He is in jail?*'

'I would have told you. In time,' she stammered. 'I would have told you—'

She stopped talking suddenly, frowning as she noticed Leonard slump further into his seat, his eyes blazing.

'When?'

'I *would* have told you—'

'When would you have told me?' he roared. 'When, Emma? This week, next week? When our child was born? Or in ten years' time?'

'Leonard, listen to me.'

'I *have* listened to you! And you've told me that you've lied from the day I met you. That you've *kept* lying, and if I hadn't found you out today, you would never have stopped lying!'

Panicked, Emma moved over to her husband, terrified of his anger, the injury she had caused him. 'Leonard, calm down, darling. I didn't dare tell you—'

'But it wouldn't have mattered!' he shouted, suddenly distraught and pushing her away. 'I love you, why would that have mattered to me? Didn't you know me? Didn't you trust me, Emma? Jesus, did you have to lie to me, every day?'

'Leonard,' she said hurriedly, 'don't upset yourself

so much, my love. We can sort this out, you know we can. We're a team, you and me, we can sort anything out.' Moving back to his side, she touched her husband's forehead and felt the sheen of sweat, loosening his collar and feeling for his pulse, which was unnaturally quick. 'Leonard, breathe deeply, darling. Breathe deeply.'

His eyes were fixed on hers, but suddenly his look was no longer angry; rather bewildered. And Emma knew in that moment that he *would* have understood. That if she had been brave enough to tell him, Leonard Hemmings would have been able to accept the truth. Would have married her despite her past. Desperately he reached out and caught hold of her wrist, pulling her towards him, his expression changing from pain to fear. He was trying to talk, Emma realised, just as she was trying to break free and summon help. His mouth was working, trying to form words, his right hand clutching his left arm, his eyes still fixed on hers as – within a second – the life went out of him.

In an instant, Leonard Hemmings had gone from husband to corpse.

TWENTY

In the days that followed, the family doctor told Emma that Leonard had died from a heart attack. It was, he said, something that could not have been predicted or avoided. He had had a weakness in his heart. Alone in her room, Emma heard the noises from below, the doors opening and closing as her parents-in-law moved about. The house was very quiet, the double bed very empty, her hand straying often to the pillow where her husband had laid his head. Deeply in shock, Emma trembled at every sound, only one thought remaining a constant in her mind. *I have to keep the baby. I have to keep the baby.*

Shattered by the death of their son, Elizabeth and Grant Hemmings kept their distance. They had overheard the argument and knew the reason for their son's demise: *Emma*. Emma and her lies. Emma, their daughter-in-law. All Elizabeth's suspicions had been proved right. Emma was not to be trusted. It was Grant – deep in grief for the loss of his son – who tried to remonstrate with his wife. How could Emma have told Leonard about her father? The girl had been in an impossible situation. But the only reason Elizabeth could tolerate Emma's presence in the house was the baby she was carrying. She could only make some bitter sense out of her son's death with the birth of her grandchild. It was the only bond that held the three disparate people together.

Emma clung to the baby in her womb. She breathed evenly, fighting panic, when she cried for Leonard. She looked to the window seat and imagined him sitting there, turning and smiling at her. She regretted her stupidity, her lack of courage. *And she hated herself.* For injuring a good man who had loved her so much. For using Leonard Hemmings – and then repaying his kindness so cruelly. The only way she believed she could be forgiven was by bearing Leonard's child. By devoting her life to her baby. To his offspring. She would tell the child all about its father. What Leonard had been like, what he had said, done. She would raise the infant well, and in time – if it was a boy – he might take over the family business. And – Emma swore it to herself – she would let the child bond with Elizabeth. Let her mother-in-law close, let her spoil, take care of, even monopolise the child. *Anything*, Emma begged silently. *Just let the baby live.*

She held tight to the baby for another week, even bearing up under the strain of Leonard's funeral. She forced herself to eat, to take exercise. She looked at Elizabeth and said nothing, just touched her stomach in silent complicity. Another week passed. The baby held on. Ashamed and heartbroken, Emma walked around the Hemmings house, out of place, avoiding eye contact with anyone. More alone than she had ever been in her life. Her rock had gone. Her protection, her husband, was dead. And she was alone again. But not completely, because she had his child inside her.

Then one morning, Emma woke to find herself lying in wetness. Throwing back the bedcovers, she saw the blood over the sheets and felt the cramps deep in her stomach. Shaking, she grasped her night-gown. But the loss of blood had made her dizzy, and she fell, heavily, the sound reverberating around the quiet house.

She had lost her child. Her child, and Leonard's. The baby had lost its grip on life and on its mother. For two days Emma lay in the matrimonial bed, alone. No husband by her side, no child in her belly. Staring up at the ceiling, she thought she heard her father's voice, then realised she had been dream-ing. She wanted to die. To close down. To give up. Because there was nothing left to fight for. Her marriage, her dream of family, was over. What was the point in going on?

Those were the days that changed the course of Emma's life. If she had wanted, she could have given in, let herself stay with the Hemmingses as the young widow who had now lost her child. But she wasn't going to do that . . . Struggling to her feet, she looked around the comfortable bedroom. If she was honest, she had been fond of Leonard, but she had not loved him. She could hardly spend her life grieving. It would be hypocrisy. And she had had enough of lying. It would not be fair to Leonard's memory. So what was there to live for? she asked herself. What? She thought of Ricky, remembered falling in love with him, and despite her pain, she didn't rage against the gods for taking him from her. Didn't curse her luck. Didn't count up all her losses and let them crush her. Instead, she remembered. And she knew in that moment that she would – one day – find love again. Not a compromise love. Not a hidden half-love. She would love fully again, and a man would love her in return . . . She sighed and leaned against the wall, again thinking of Ricky. She had nothing left except hope. And that drove her on.

In silence, Emma packed her cases, taking nothing from the rooms where she had spent her married life. Finally, when she had finished, she left the little fruit knife on the table beside her bed. It had proved to be an unlucky talisman. A blade that had cut her deeply. Slowly, she walked towards the door. Her in-laws were nowhere in sight, and so she left them a long letter she had written, thanking them and asking their forgiveness. For Leonard's death, for her lies and for the loss of their grandchild.

It was Christmas Eve.

PART THREE

I regret the sweet breath of your friendship
And the spite of your loss.

Anon.

I went back to Burnley a widow. There was nowhere else to go. I had no money set aside, and none was offered, even for me to make a fresh start. To the Hemmingses, I was over. In the past tense. Finished with. They would make an idol out of their son, keep his clothes and photographs, but I would be expunged from his life. I had been an appendix, something easily erased. Because the baby was dead. The last link to their son was gone.

I cried more then than I thought I could ever cry and keep sane. But I took nothing with me when I left, laying my wedding ring beside the bed. How could I keep it? I hardly needed it to remind me I had been a wife. And I left behind the first toys we had bought for the baby, along with the cot. All I *did take was Leonard's hairbrush and a small brown donkey I had bought for the baby. I would cry with it in my hands, clutching it, sometimes even holding it against my stomach. But the grief of losing my child drove me back into the world again. Away from the safety of Leonard and the promise of family life.*

Of course I knew I had destroyed him. Cheated

him from the start and lied until the end. But I hadn't wanted to hurt him. That had never been my plan. I should have known that intentions rarely coincide with events.

When I reached Holland Street that Christmas Eve, the jeweller's shop was in darkness. There was a light on in the tobacconist's and in Jack Rimmer's hardware store, but I didn't enter either. Instead I stood in the porch of the jeweller's shop and stared at the sign, which said CLOSED. We Will Reopen on Boxing Day. Gradually my gaze moved past the sign, into the shop beyond. I could make out the old grandfather clock and hear the ticking, even from where I stood. My dread of that place was not lessened by my absence, but intensified. All my dreams of breaking away had been an illusion. My escape had been perfunctory, and now here I was again, back in Burnley, back at my uncle's shop.

Shivering in the cold, I stood in that doorway and wanted to walk away again. But where could I go? There was nowhere for me. No home, other than this. No husband, no safe house. This was all there was. And I realised something about myself then, something vital. I was a survivor. I had lost everything, but I still wanted to live. To go on, however hard. However tough. I owed it to my husband and my dead baby. And most of all, I owed it to myself.

Then suddenly a lamp went on in the back room, my uncle's tall, angular form momentarily silhouetted against the light. Without any apparent surprise, he *unlocked the door and stood back for me to enter, the clocks chiming the hours behind him, the stuffy interior unchanged and sucking me in.*

TWENTY-ONE

Burnley, Spring 1922

Like many a northern town that winter, Burnley had plenty of flu deaths. People who had struggled through the harshness of the war years had found the peace difficult to adjust to. There was still work for the returning soldiers, even though the mills were beginning to be threatened by cheaper foreign imports. The larger mills, like Lowerhouse Mill, with its impressive five storeys, employed many Burnley workers, making cotton cloth and weaving calico. Besides the mills, there were the timber yards and the sewage works. Or if a man fancied something less physical, there were many pubs in Burnley needing landlords to slake the workers' thirst.

As for entertainment, there was always the theatre, and new cinemas were being opened regularly, the Charlie Chaplin talkies coming over from the USA, along with stories of the movie stars' lives in Hollywood, and jazz. With the film stars came the glamour and the fashion. Hampered by their elaborate clothes in wartime, women taking over men's work had found it a necessity to simplify their own attire. And once they had rid themselves of the long skirts, corsets and intricate hairstyles, they had no desire to return to them. Newly freed from their restrictive clothes, women adopted more casual drop-waisted dresses, and softer, seamless underwear.

'My God, that's a sight for sore eyes,' Doug said, eyeing his new wife up and down in her flesh-coloured bra and pants. 'You look a treat, Bessie.'

Making a sultry face, she sat down on the bed next to him, taking off her glasses and rubbing her eyes.

'You know something, Doug? I could get used to this marriage lark,' she said simply, wincing as she heard the footsteps overhead.

Mr Letski had managed to lose much of his eyesight and most of his hearing, but otherwise he was in excellent health, although his mind wandered and he sometimes held long conversations with Bessie in Russian. Providing she nodded occasionally and make a few insignificant noises, he was happy to continue, but if she was busy in the shop, he would buttonhole Doug, who just stood looking at the Russian with a blank expression on his face.

'Humour him,' Bessie would say kindly, because she was very fond of the old cobbler. 'He's let us move in and live here; the least you can do is listen to his bloody stories. Anyway, they're interesting.'

'They're in Russian! I don't talk Russian.'

'Really?' she would reply, her tone sarcastic. 'Well, pretend.'

Because of her fondness for Mr Letski, Bessie was determined that no one in Burnley should think that she and Doug were taking advantage of him. So she spoke to a solicitor and then put a notice in the paper asking for any of the old man's surviving relatives to come forward. No one did. And after another couple of months had passed, Mr Letski – with a happy flourish – signed over the cobbler's to Bessie.

'I can't believe it, it's all legal now,' she said, Doug kissing her neck and making her laugh. 'Get off! I want to talk about the business. I'm glad it's sorted. I didn't want anyone thinking that we're taking advantage of Mr Letski.'

'I'd like to take advantage of you,' Doug said, pulling a face as Bessie jabbed him in the ribs. 'Oi, that hurt!'

'You big kid,' she teased him, rolling on to her stomach and staring at her new husband. Not much to look at, and a bit dopey, but she loved him. And he was terrific in bed. Hurriedly Bessie put her thoughts to other matters. 'I saw Emma yesterday. Went over to the jeweller's shop.'

She paused, thinking of her friend. Emma had been crossing Holland Street, carrying a basket, and had stopped dead, pausing at the corner. Although Bessie had known what had happened to Leonard and that her friend had lost the baby, it was still a shock to see Emma standing there, unnervingly calm. Hurriedly she had run over to her and hugged her, Emma fighting tears as she held on to her old friend. Upset, Bessie had told her how sorry she was, Emma nodding, unable to trust her voice.

'It was as though time had stopped,' Bessie told

Doug. 'As though Emma being married and living in Yorkshire had never happened. I heard that bloody old woman Mrs Carter talking about her the other day. Saying how Emma had got above herself and it was no surprise she was back in Burnley. *That's what comes of people who think they're above the rest. And her with that father of hers.* Christ,' Bessie went on violently, 'I thought people would be sympathetic. I mean, Emma's not had much luck, has she?'

'They think she messed up.'

'What!'

Doug shrugged. 'I reckon people think Emma had it made and that she dropped the ball. Wrecked her chances.' Dumbstruck, Bessie stared at her husband. She told Doug most things, but not everything, as beer had a way of making him jabber. So she hadn't even told him the *real* reason for Leonard Hemmings's untimely death – and yet here he was, like everyone else, thinking Emma had failed. 'She's unlucky.'

'*Is she buggery!*' Bessie snapped back. 'She lost her baby, and she wanted that child so much. Even more after Leonard died. I remember getting a letter from her when she said she was going to live for the child . . .' She stopped, moved. 'But she will come through, she always does. You'll see, one day Emma will show everyone. I know her, she'll survive.'

'She showed everyone when she married well and left Burnley. Now she's back, she's not impressing anyone.'

Much as Bessie hated to admit it, it was the truth.

To see her friend relegated from wife and expectant mother to David Hawksworth's drudge was almost unbearable. And if it was bad for her, what was it like for Emma? How did she feel, having seen her life smashed to pieces, her security destroyed? To be dependent on her uncle again, knowing how he felt about her and her father? Bessie didn't know, but even the thought of it shook her. The jeweller's shop had not changed, had stayed like an insect fixed in amber, unmoving, unfashionable, the world going past its fly-blown windows.

And going past Emma inside.

Carefully David Hawksworth wound up the clock he had spent a week repairing. Then he listened, satisfied by the steady, resonant ticking sound. He would be paid well for the repair, and that pleased him, because money had been tight. Now that he had Emma to support, he would need more income. He had expected to resent her as bitterly as he had done previously, but a sea change was slowly coming over David Hawksworth. Emma had lost everything. Respect, status and hope. She had been secure, and life had cheated her, and David felt bitterly sorry for her.

For the first time David saw some similarities between them. He had been held back by his family, and now Emma had been robbed of her good fortune. He was unaware of the part his half-brother had played in Emma's downfall; he only saw a young woman whom life had injured. He had been half expecting her return when he heard about Leonard's death, and when he had seen her on his doorstep, David had felt an unexpected sense of justice and relief. It was *right* that she should come back. She needed him. After all, no one else did.

Suddenly reminded of his son, David hung the clock on the wall and started to put away his tools. He had been surprised to see Adam when he visited, looking strong and relatively prosperous. But instead of welcoming his son and listening to his stories of his travels, David had immediately begun to interrogate him. And when Adam had asked for money to start up a business, his father had reacted violently. The argument that had followed had been vicious . . . Gripping the tools in his hand, David stared at the scuffed top of the work table. Had he been *so* wrong to hope that his son would want to come into the business? Wasn't that what most men would like? To pass on their profession to their offspring? But he knew he shouldn't have been so hard on Adam, making an enemy out of his own child until there was nothing but hostility between them. He would, David thought desperately, have done anything to turn back time. How easy it was to move the hands of a clock, to make it read any hour, to reverse them, turn them forwards or stop them. If only life was like that, he thought longingly. If only you could arrest time, hold it, or change it. Give yourself enough time to wipe away your regrets.

Unusually emotional, David clenched his jaw and fought an unwelcome desire to lose his temper. To bang on the table, to scream at the top of his lungs, to rage against the gods. To say that life was a cheat, that it went too quickly, that before you knew it you had made all the wrong moves and played the wrong suit. With the wrong partner. Or lost every hand and never got back into the game. His fists clenched, he forced himself to take in some deep breaths. He could see what he had to do now. He would make amends, he told himself. He would change. He had been a happy man once; surely there was some warmth in him still? He had loved once; surely there must still be some love in him.

Distracted, David thought of his niece. Emma's return had showed him a way to correct his past. He would take care of her and make a proper home for her. As he should have done for his wife and his son. As he should have done before, for Adam, for his own child . . .

'Uncle?'

He turned at the sound of Emma's voice. 'Yes, what is it?'

'I've made you something to eat,' she said quietly.

Surprised, David studied her. Why didn't I see it before? he wondered. Why didn't I realise how much you hurt? How much all the gossip – about your father and about your marriage – must rip at your heart? I should have known. I should have known.

'Uncle?' Emma asked timidly. 'Would you like me to bring your food up on a tray? You could have it here as usual.'

Turning, he shook his head, his voice seeming to

come from a long way off. 'No, Emma, I'll eat with you . . . if you want me to.'

Taken aback, she smiled faintly and walked downstairs, laying two places at the table. She watched her uncle come down the narrow back stairs into the kitchen, taking a seat next to hers. His long legs knocked against the table support, but he pretended not to notice, Emma serving him and then herself. The long memory of their argument sat like an unwelcome guest between them, David breaking his bread and then passing Emma the butter. Surprised to find that her hand was shaking, she took it, keeping her face averted. She had been back at the jeweller's shop for three months, and in all that time she had not eaten with her uncle. He had been as he always was, remote and cool. In silence, Emma had kept house and tidied up the shop after they closed. In silence, she had starched her uncle's shirts and pressed his suits, although his underwear was sent, as usual, to the Chinese laundry off St James's Street. Unwilling to provoke any outburst or find herself thrown out again, she had been subdued. Besides, she had plenty to think about.

Many times she had hoped that her uncle would speak to her. Not about Leonard, or even the lost baby – that would have been too personal – but about *anything*. The shop, the news, the Palmers next door. But he was not forthcoming, and she didn't press him. She didn't mention her father either, reverting back to her old secrecy. Of course Frederick knew what had happened to his daughter, and a flurry of letters between them had given her some comfort. But her father wasn't there, wasn't able to put his arms around her and let her grieve. His sympathy was immense and heartfelt, but remote. And she longed for closeness. Longed for *someone* to hold her.

Emma knew she could have visited Bessie as often as she liked. Knew that there was always a welcome waiting. But Bessie was married now, and Emma was still too raw to spend too much time there. She knew it was wrong of her, but she couldn't bear to watch the newly married couple being happy, when she had so recently lost her own chance of love.

'You're very quiet.'

She looked up, surprised from her day-dreaming and equally surprised to find herself in the jeweller's shop. 'I was thinking.'

'About what?'

'Things . . .'

His immediate reaction was to back off, but this time he persisted, pushing himself on.

'I can't imagine how difficult everything is for you, Emma. I lost my own wife, as you know.' He paused, wondering why he was confiding now. But it seemed that he couldn't stop, that some instinct propelled him on. 'She died after we'd been married for a while. But I did love her. She was very dear to me.'

Surprised by the confession from such an unexpected source, Emma stole a wary glance at her uncle.

'She died of influenza, as you know. And by that

time we weren't so close. But I never stopped loving her, never stopped wondering *why* I lost her. Why it had to happen.' He clenched his fists tightly. 'It made me a bitter man. Cold and remote, but I wasn't always like that. Truly I wasn't. I knew how to laugh, to be happy; it's just that I let myself change. And I forgot how to love properly.' He cleared his throat. 'I'm only telling you this because I want you to know that I understand something of what you're feeling. You think . . .' His voice faltered, caught out in mid-sentence. 'You think your life is ruined.'

'Maybe it is.'

'No,' he contradicted her, his fists still tightly clenched, his back hunched as he stared at the tabletop. 'That's what *I* thought, what I believed. That's what made me what I was, bitter, angry with everyone . . . But I was wrong, Emma. And I want you to know that. Don't be like me. You see, I know now that if I had *really* loved Jenny, I would have been grateful for loving her, not embittered for losing her.'

Touched, Emma took a moment to reply. 'I know you're trying to help . . .'

'But why should you listen to me?' he said. 'Why me? I'm hardly the man to give you advice.'

'I did care about my husband,' Emma said, her voice low. 'I loved him, perhaps not enough, but I did love him. I grew to love him. *I did.*' She paused, close to tears. 'I should clear away the dishes . . .'

'No, wait,' David said, clearing his throat again, determined that he would break through his niece's reserve. He had failed with his son; he would not fail with Emma. 'Listen to me, please.'

Nodding, she sat down again.

'I've been cruel.'

Bending her head, Emma traced a line across her plate with her fork. *Don't cry*, she told herself, *don't cry. This is not Bessie, or your father. Don't cry.*

'And I'm sorry for anything I might have said to upset you. Now, or in the past,' David went on, staring at the mute young woman in front of him. His usual reticence made him want to leave the table, run away, but this time he couldn't. This time he had to make amends. 'I should have understood more. Should have realised how difficult it was for you, living here. How attractive I made it for you to leave and get married.'

'It was my choice.'

'But if I had made your life easier, would you have made that choice?' David asked, facing her. 'You can't reply, can you? Because we both know the answer.'

She was moved by his honesty, by the unexpected understanding.

'Emma,' he went on, 'if there's *anything* I can do to make things better for you . . .'

Her voice was barely audible. 'There's nothing.'

'I want to help you.'

And she knew in that moment that he was genuine, that the argument, the bitterness between them had eaten into him. He was sorry, she was sorry, for everything that had happened. For all she had had, and lost. For all he had had, and lost. They were both bitterly upset and regretful, and suddenly any old injury was not worth hanging on to. She had to live here, with her uncle, make a life again. What that life would turn out to be was down to her. But David Hawksworth was trying to make amends. It might be late and more than overdue, but he was trying.

Slowly Emma looked at him, her eyes filled with tears.

'I miss him. I miss Leonard . . . and . . .'

She stopped, but David knew what she had been about to say: *my father*. In fact, he had been thinking about Frederick for some time, and had guessed that Emma had been visiting the prison the terrible day that Leonard had come looking for her. And he had come to realise that in all honesty he could hardly have expected her to turn her back on her own father. She was a grown woman; of course she could make up her own mind and do what she thought was right. Just as he had done for so long.

'I don't know what to say,' he stammered. He was mellowing, and could see the damage his bigotry had done. He felt a tightness in his throat, a sympathy that threatened to overwhelm him. 'You'll feel better, Emma. One day. You'll be happy again . . .' He blundered on, not knowing what to say, or how to say it. Just knowing he had to try. 'Please forgive me . . . forgive me. I'd do anything to make things better for you. I *will* do anything to make things better.'

And then Emma began to cry, loudly, inconsolably.

For a moment David Hawksworth stared at her, and then he moved, unlocking his arms and his reserve, and taking hold of her. He was sure she would push him away, but she didn't. Instead she clung to him as though her heart would break.

TWENTY-TWO

'Well,' said Florence, leaning against the doorway of Jack Rimmer's shop. 'From what I've been seeing, Emma and her uncle seem to be getting on better. Not before time, either.'

Clattering two pails together, Jack hung them from string on the awning outside.

'They're too low, you'll do some passer-by's head in.'

'Only if he's seven foot tall,' Jack replied shortly. 'How's Harold?'

'I don't know. What don't you ask him yourself?'

'By God, he's not in the doghouse again, is he?' Jack asked, feeling more than a little pity for Harold Palmer. But then again, it boded well for Jack. When Harold was being ignored he had a drinking partner, and he was feeling like a pint. 'You two not talking?'

'I don't see what business that is of yours!' Florence snapped, then immediately went on, 'I'm his wife, and I think I'm entitled to a little holiday. Just mentioned it, I did, and he went mad.'

'Doesn't sound like Harold.'

'You have no idea what that man is like indoors,' Florence said, making herself out to be the victim when everyone in the neighbourhood knew that she ruled her husband with a rod of iron. 'He can be very . . . hurtful.'

Smiling to himself, Jack hung up another pail, Florence watching him.

'Do they sell?'

'Nah, I just put them up for decoration. Of course they sell!'

'I would have thought a woman only needed one good bucket to last her. I mean, I've had mine for years.'

And if I had too many customers like you, Jack thought, I'd have been out of business long ago.

'Anyway,' Florence went on, tapping the underside of one of the pails and hearing a satisfying clunk, 'I heard that Adam was back again.'

'Nah.'

'Sure, a friend of mine – well, not a friend, sort of an acquaintance; she used to buy papers from us, and her husband's tobacco, until he ran off with that tart from the Red Fox pub. You know the one – blond hair and a squint . . . Anyway, this acquaintance of mine—'

'I thought that barmaid died.'

'She did!' Florence said impatiently. 'What's that got to do with anything?'

'You brought it up,' Jack replied, turning away from her and pouring a bag of nails into one of the numerous drawers behind the counter.

'Well, she said that Adam Hawksworth was back and he'd been seen in Bury. Then in Manchester.'

'So?'

'I thought you'd be interested,' Florence replied, somewhat miffed. Dear God, what was the point of talking to a man? They were never interested in the important things in life. 'I mean, after that argument Adam had with his father, I thought he'd go back to New Zealand. Maybe he's thinking of a reconciliation. I mean, I don't care for the man, as you know, but David Hawksworth seemed very cut up after that last run-in with his son.' She paused, pursing her lips with pleasure as an idea came to her. 'Of course if Adam wanted to come back into the jewellery trade and Emma was there, with her feet tucked nicely under the table, it wouldn't go down well with the son, to see his cousin getting what was rightfully his.'

Folding his scrawny arms, Jack stared at his neighbour. 'I thought you liked Emma?'

'I do! I'm just thinking aloud.'

'Well I'd keep your thinking to yourself,' Jack warned her. 'Emma needs a home now more than ever. If she's getting on with her uncle, good for her. And if he wants to teach her the trade and bring her into the business, he wouldn't go far wrong.'

Flushing, his neighbour retorted sharply, 'What's the matter with you, you old fool! Did you hear me criticising Emma?'

'You were damn near criticising her,' Jack replied, 'and as for being an old fool, you're only a few years younger than me, Florence Palmer.'

Taking in a deep breath, Florence stormed off, entering the tobacconist's and standing in front of her husband with her hands on her hips. Then she remembered that she wasn't talking to him . . . For one ghastly moment she hovered between wanting to confide and wanting to keep punishing him.

Infuriated, she finally pointed to the counter, one long bony finger jabbing the air. 'And another thing – I don't want liquorice next to the bloody sherbet.'

Pushing her hair away from her face, Emma turned her attention back to the book on her lap. Her uncle had given her several to read, all about jewellery and repairs, and although she had found them difficult, she had been eager to learn. The reason was twofold – she would please her uncle, who was trying so hard to make up for their previous ill feeling, and she would keep herself busy. Her mind, in particular. She didn't object to keeping house, tidying the shop, or studying – in fact she welcomed it. In return, David Hawksworth was treated to something he'd never thought he would experience again – the beginnings of a real emotional bond with someone. As he talked to Emma, he found himself enthusing again, and slowly the jewellery business – which before had always come second to his thwarted teaching ambitions – now seemed a skill. Something worthwhile, which required no little intelligence. He also discovered, by teaching Emma, how much he knew. And as the days passed, spring into summer, he found a pride in his work.

'I was thinking,' he said, looking round at the interior of the shop, stuffy in the summer heat. 'Perhaps we should decorate?'

Smiling, Emma looked up from the book she was reading. 'I like that idea, Uncle.'

'The shop is a little . . . old-fashioned,' he went on, looking around and seeing it for what it was – a glowering, mean-spirited place. 'Perhaps a coat of paint and a change to the window . . .'

Jumping to her feet, Emma joined in. 'We could change the layout of the window,' she began, feeling her way and not wanting to appear to be criticising. 'I was looking in a magazine – one of Bessie's – and it had some lovely ideas. From London.'

Slowly, David turned, pleased to see some animation in his niece's face. He wouldn't tell her, but she could have done anything with the shop and he would have agreed to it.

'Ideas from London . . .'

'Well, we wouldn't have to go that far.'

'Perhaps a new window would bring in some more custom.'

'It's summer, and people walk about the town when the weather's good,' Emma went on. 'They look in the windows. That's why Jack Rimmer's always busy – he always has lots going on. We couldn't do that, of course, but we could make a little display.'

'Like what?'

'Maybe put something in the middle of the window,' Emma continued, thinking aloud. 'Make it a feature. Like engagement rings. Lots of people get engaged in the summer. I heard that more people get engaged in the warm months than at any other time of year.'

Impressed, David looked at his niece. 'You know the strangest things, Emma. All right, you do your display. We'll see how it goes, shall we?'

'I can do the window?' she asked, incredulous. The window that was off bounds to everyone except her uncle. The window that had been an outward show of his character. Gloomy, without colour. But not for much longer. 'Are you sure?'

'Yes, I'm sure.'

'It'll be the best window in Burnley,' Emma said, rolling up her sleeves, her voice more animated than it had been for a long time. 'No one will ever walk past this shop again without stopping.'

She worked for the rest of the day, hanging a temporary card on the door – DECORATION BEING UNDERTAKEN. WE WILL REOPEN TOMORROW. Then she carefully took everything out from the window and cleaned the glass thoroughly. When the space was cleared, she was surprised to find it much bigger than she thought, and for a moment she stood in the window looking around her.

'How much?' a lad called out from the street, teasing her, Emma smiling and jumping down into the shop beyond.

As David worked in the room under the eaves, Emma laboured in the shop. She had a clear image in her head and was determined to make it work. A while later, David came down from the workshop and stood watching his niece, the window cleaned out but still empty. Hesitant, he approached her. In his left hand were the keys to the shop – and the safe.

'You'll need these,' he said simply.

A cleaning rag in one hand, Emma paused, staring at the ring of keys. She knew instinctively that the gesture meant a great deal. Not only was her uncle trusting her, he was pushing aside her past. Letting go of the shadow of Frederick and Ernie Coles. His stepfather was a villain, and his half-brother was a proven thief, but David Hawksworth had meant it when he said he wanted to change. And he was prepared to prove it.

'Go on,' he urged Emma, 'take them. When you've finished with them, give them back to me.'

Her palm sticky, she took the keys, feeling the cold weight of steel. She wanted to talk about her father then. Wanted to open up the last forbidden communication with her uncle. But she resisted the temptation. It would be too much, too soon. And besides, she didn't want to alienate him now.

'I'll take good care of them,' she said.

'The combination of the safe is 14-6-18-94.'

Emma repeated the numbers, touched by the trust he had put in her.

'It's my son's birthday,' David went on, his tone tight. 'I wanted the safe combination to be simple, so he could always remember it. You see, I wanted Adam to work in the business with me.'

Emma nodded, unsure of what to say.

'I wanted to keep the shop in the family. Pass it down to my son . . . But even though he didn't want it, it *is* going to stay in the family, isn't it?' David said quietly. 'You're family.'

The afternoon slid into evening, the summer light fading around nine, David coming down from the eaves workroom and watching his niece. But Emma was too busy to stop. Pink-faced with exertion and summer heat, she moved from the safe to the shop, then climbed into the window to work on her display. Numerous times she arranged the old velvet display boards, wiping them over with a damp cloth so that the velvet fluffed back to life. Innumerable times she polished the stones in the rings, making an interlocking heart shape with them. Finally, satisfied, she wiped her hands and walked out on to the street. The tobacconist's and the hardware store had closed, but the jeweller's shop hummed with light. Stunned, her gaze travelled over the interlocking pattern of rings, diamonds and gold reflecting back the evening light, the design fascinating and compelling. The rings were not of particular value; there wasn't the market for anything too expensive; but the display made the jewellery glimmer. It made the rings fit for Bond Street. Made the plain gold bands seem cultured and classic. With the dark background and the heavy cloth, the jeweller's window shimmered magically in the summer night.

'Good God,' David said as he walked out and looked at the window. He had lived in this shop much of his life, resented it, run it because he had to, but run it without love. And it had been obvious to everyone. A miserable place, it had served as somewhere people went when they had to, not from choice. David Hawksworth's own bitterness had made the shop sour. But love had brought the window back to the living world. Love had opened its brilliant eye and made it wink at life again. And Emma had done it.

'It's marvellous,' he said at last.

She nodded, accepting the compliment. 'We'll make a fortune.'

'Yes,' David agreed, his tone awestruck. 'I think we might.'

TWENTY-THREE

Smiling, Frederick looked at the local newspaper photograph Emma had included in her letter. It was of David Hawksworth and his shop, the heading over the picture reading: JEWELLER'S SHOP REFURB-ISHMENT. And underneath there was a short article.

> *The well-known Hawksworth jeweller's, Holland Street, has been run by Mr David Hawksworth for over twenty-five years.*
> *Now Mr Hawksworth has updated his stock and made an inviting window display, featuring his new jewellery. When asked about his modernised window, Mr Hawksworth said that his niece, Miss Emma Coles, had helped him. 'Without Emma, I would never have known what to do,' he admitted, and confided that he was training her in the jewellery business.*

Well I'll be damned, Frederick said to himself, looking at the photograph again. Who could guess how life would work out? he thought. He had been terrified for his daughter after Leonard died. Her letters had been so odd then, so strained, Emma trying to explain what had happened and at the same time trying not to worry her father, whilst Frederick could feel the heartbreak in every word. He was with her every step of the way, but not being able to comfort her was intolerable. Who was holding his child? Who was letting her cry? Who was there for her? Only his half-brother, and that thought had chilled him.

But in Emma's recent letters she had told him that David had changed and was trying to make up for their previous difficult relationship. Frederick hadn't believed it. Yet here was the proof, he thought, looking back to the newspaper article and the photograph of his half-brother. David had done the right thing by his niece, he had come up trumps . . . Curious, Frederick peered at the grainy image. David looked older, though that was to be expected, but the hard lines around his mouth had softened and he was smiling. Well, not exactly smiling, but he seemed content.

For a moment Frederick felt something close to jealousy, but he curtailed it. Emma had had a rough time and she needed her uncle – just as Frederick needed to know that his daughter was safe. It was an unexpected bonus that they were getting on, but nothing to worry him. Unless he let it. Emma loved her father, Frederick knew that only too well, and no one would supplant him. His half-brother was looking after his daughter in his absence, David wasn't trying to usurp him. Or was he?

Annoyed with himself, Frederick put the cutting to one side. He had no right to be anything other than grateful to David Hawksworth. His half-brother could have turned his back on Emma, as so many had done. But he had taken her in. Not once, but twice. He had been there for her at a time when Emma had been grieving. He had even changed, tried to make her pain less. Surely that deserved some thanks? Surely it was only fitting that Frederick should feel relief? Gratitude that his half-brother had stood by his child?

But it should have been me, Frederick thought, unaccountably distressed. *It should have been me.*

In Manchester, Adam Hawksworth was walking down Deansgate, cutting up towards St Peter's Square, the Burnley newspaper in his hand. Furious, he read the article again, then screwed it up. His father was bragging in the news! His damned father, pleased as punch with his shop – *which his niece had helped him with*. The same niece who was being trained up in the business. Whoever heard of a woman jeweller? Adam thought, enraged. It was *his* legacy, not Emma Coles's.

To be honest, he hadn't wanted to work in the business. But when the New Zealand farming enterprise hadn't been successful, he had come back to the north of England. After all, he knew he could always return home. Until his position had been taken over by his cousin, the jeweller's door being slammed in his face once and for all. By his flaming *cousin*, daughter of Frederick Coles... Adam stopped walking suddenly, checking his reflection in a nearby window. He was handsome enough, with his thick black hair. Good teeth were something of a novelty in poorer towns, but Adam's teeth were strong and unusually white, making a gentleman out of him and giving him a blistering smile. He was charming too – but he was at a loss now.

His easy early life, adored by his mother and without any structure, had not prepared him for hard work. Of course, his father would never know that his mother had given him money, enough to set up a business in New Zealand. She had wanted him to get away, and when his father had finally thrown him out, she had seen that as an advantage. Urged on by her, Adam had gone to find his fortune, coming home very occasionally to visit her, or writing asking her to send more cash. On a couple of occasions he had come back to the north of England and met up with her, but never his father. For a while, Adam *did* find his fortune in property – and then lost it again. At the same time, he broke up with a woman he loved. Trouble was, by that time his mother had passed on and there were no more handouts coming Adam's way.

There was no one praising him either. No one making excuses for him, as his mother had always done. Women were attracted to him, but when they got to know him, they found him difficult, sulky, demanding. And sly, at times almost feral. His mother had thought the world of him, but he was glad that Jenny had never found out that he could be a mendacious, venal type if crossed. Well, who wasn't sometimes? It was life, he told himself, and he had got along in whatever way he could. Sometimes he had made the wrong choices, fallen in with the wrong people, but that happened to a lot of people. Didn't it? He had been in a few fights too, but he wasn't going to be walked over. A man had to stand his ground. Still smarting, Adam thought of the newspaper article again, burning with the injustice. He might not have wanted the business, but it was one thing to be able to turn it down, quite another to have it taken away from him.

Disconsolate, he sat down on a bench in St Peter's Square, staring morosely at the pigeons. He had seen an advertisement for a room to let and wondered how he would pay for it. Digging into his pocket, he found enough money for two nights, no more. Looking around him, Adam realised then that he would have to find some money. That he would have to find work too, whatever kind of work. The thought was not an appealing one. He didn't like the mundane dreariness of a job. The nine-to-five routine bored him; his lack of application had been the reason for his failure in New Zealand. Not that Adam saw it that way. He was talented, he told himself, he was special. Not the kind of man who could do just any type of work. Not physical, demeaning work, but creative work. Didn't anyone understand that? No, no one. Except his mother, Adam thought, and now she was dead. She had been the only one who had seen his promise, always known he was unique. Yet despite all her encouragement, his paintings hadn't sold, and although he had written a couple of good songs, he hadn't got any money for them either. Not in England or in New Zealand. And when he bought a sheep farm, he had tired of that within weeks, selling it on as quickly as he could, and only finding out afterwards that he had been cheated and given half its worth. Because Adam Hawksworth was no businessman.

And so, adrift, he had come home. But there was nothing for him here either. Silently he shuffled the coins in his hands, as an idea came to him. He had some friends. Old friends, a few likely lads who would find him something to do. Perhaps not too respectable, but not too bad. Nothing like Ernie Coles. Now there was a *real* villain . . . Adam kept jingling the coins. He would go back to the Acorn pub in Mumps, Oldham; there were always a few chancers in there. Someone would have a job for him. As a lookout, or a driver. Adam could drive; he had learned in New Zealand. He sighed, pleased with himself. That was the solution, he thought, he would just do something on the sidelines. Not directly criminal, just something to put money back in his pocket. It wouldn't be for long. And it wasn't like being a real villain – it was just a way of tiding him over.

When he was straight again, he would find something worthy of his talents. But until then, he would do what he could.

Drawn by the window display, Mrs Irene Knight stopped outside Hawksworth's jeweller's and studied the display trays. Her hat was arranged at a slight angle, flattering her angular but attractive face. Even past fifty-five, and widowed for the last four years, Irene had never neglected her appearance. It was fine for married women to let themselves go, but she wasn't prepared to grow old, or plain. And if she didn't have a husband to admire her, she would do the job herself. It wasn't simple vanity on Irene's part; it was a way of keeping herself in the world. She had seen too many widows to envy their usual route to invisibility. Her husband's death had come as a shock, especially as she had no children to console her, but Irene had a backbone of iron. Under the slender, well-veneered exterior of a respectable, well-to-do woman, she was solid working class. Her father had been a miner in Doncaster, her mother a seamstress. When a chance had come for Irene to go down south and work as a maid for a wealthy family, her parents had urged her to go. At first she had been reluctant and homesick, but six months after she left Doncaster for Somerset, she had softened in appearance and manner.

The country suited her, and when her mistress died and left her some money, she had been canny enough to open a small tea shop by the seaside. Drawing on her northern grit and working twenty hours a day, she made herself a good little business. People came to her tea shop. Regulars, and locals, and tourists.

And then, one summer, Raymond Knight walked in for a cup of tea . . . They were married within four months; Raymond, a veterinary surgeon, working long hours, Irene selling on the tea shop and becoming a full-time vet's wife. It was, she knew almost immediately, the best decision of her life. But the magic didn't last, and many people didn't even get a little of it, as she knew only too well. So when Raymond died during the war, Irene chose to be grateful for what she had had, not bitter for what she had lost.

Peering further into the jeweller's window, Irene was startled to find a young woman looking back at her from inside. A pretty young woman who smiled, inviting her in.

'Was there something I could show you?' Emma asked the stranger.

'There's a little opal ring, on the right-hand side of the central display,' Irene replied. 'I'd like to see it, please.'

Getting the ring out of the window, Emma placed it on a velvet cloth, the stranger picking it up and staring at it. Then, to Emma's astonishment, Irene took out an eyeglass and stared at the opal from every angle.

'Good . . . good,' she said at last, putting it on the third finger of her right hand.

Amused, Emma watched the woman, judging her to be middle-aged and comfortable. A visitor from out of town, probably, certainly not with a northern accent.

'Is it for a relative?'

'No, I was thinking of it for myself,' Irene replied, smiling, her dimples appearing suddenly and giving her a mischievous look. 'As a widow, I can afford to indulge my fancies from time to time. No husband to nag me.'

Immediately taking to her, Emma pulled another couple of opal rings from out of the window and offered them up.

'These might interest you.'

Irene looked at both of them carefully through the eye glass. Emma was curious.

'Are you in the business?'

Irene smiled. 'I've been in many businesses, my dear. Been a servant, a shop owner, a vet's wife, and learned how to handle a nice little legacy. Dealing in jewellery,' she winked, making Emma smile again, 'women can be very resourceful.'

'I believe that.'

Holding up the magnifying glass again, Irene looked back to the rings, too engrossed to notice the tall, middle-aged man who had walked in from the back room. Watching her uncle's face, Emma was amused to see his expression as he noticed his customer. There was – yes, it was there – a flicker of interest.

As though she had just heard his footsteps, Irene looked up, her right eye massive behind the magnifying glass.

'Oh, hello,' she said cheerfully, David putting out his hand to shake hers. 'I was looking at your rings. Very nice, very nice too.'

'Has my niece been helpful?'

'She's a lovely girl, lovely,' Irene went on, putting down the magnifying glass and turning her cool blue eyes on David. 'You have some quality in this shop. And not just in your staff.'

The compliment found its mark, Emma noticing with surprise that her uncle was flushing around his neck. David Hawksworth, she thought excitedly, was embarrassed. And she had never seen him embarrassed before, not by any remark – even one from a delightful, attractive widow.

'I like the opal,' Irene said firmly, turning back to David. 'I dare say you and I can agree a good price.'

He shifted from one foot to the other, tongue-tied, Emma intervening to rescue him.

'Mrs . . .'

'Mrs Irene Knight,' she said, making a little mock bow. 'Widow, lately moved from Somerset to Burnley. How do you do?'

'I do well,' Emma replied cheerfully. 'And this is my uncle, Mr David Hawksworth. A widower, who has owned this jeweller's shop for the last twenty-five years. Haven't you, Uncle?' she prompted him, David nodding mutely. Gamely, Emma continued. 'I've had an idea. Why don't you take Mrs Knight into the back parlour and have a discussion about the pricing in private?'

Dimpling up, Irene smiled at David, who had suddenly and mercifully recovered his powers of speech.

'Good idea, Emma,' he said, guiding Irene into the back room. 'Good idea . . .'

Watching them, Emma smiled inwardly. The David Hawksworth of old had been too closed down, too bitter to be reached. But this new, improved version was certainly interested in Mrs Knight. Craning her neck, she could just make out their silhouettes in the parlour, and hear the sound of Irene's full-throated laugh, followed by her uncle's guffaw. For a moment she didn't realise what it was. She had never heard her uncle laugh before, and found herself laughing too. Shaking her head, she began to tidy away the display trays, thinking of Irene and wondering how she could arrange for this delightful newcomer to become an even more delightful regular. They might make a good pair, she thought, around the same age, with the same interests, and Irene seemed like a woman who was strong enough to know her own mind.

And then suddenly Emma paused, putting down the display tray and thinking of Leonard. How life played tricks, she thought. Here she was, only in her early twenties, back in Burnley, wanting to play matchmaker for her uncle. Wanting to make *him* happy, with a partner and a love in his life. As for herself . . . Emma shrugged, jerking away the memory of Ricky, then of Leonard. Of the men in her life. The men who had come and gone. She had had her chance of happiness and had lost it. But oddly enough, she didn't feel envious as she had done with Bessie and Doug Renshaw. She felt excitement for her uncle. A genuine hope that she could make something special happen for him. That she – who had bungled love – could hopefully secure it in David Hawksworth's life.

For Emma, it was far better to be an outsider, making the magic happen, than to be an insider, seeing it fade.

TWENTY-FOUR

Summer was holding her own, even on the Moors. As swallows circled overhead and grasshoppers chirruped in the long grass, the bus meandered up the dusty road towards the Moors Prison. Impressive in his new prison uniform, Jim Caird traced his finger down the bus window, his thoughts settled. His family came from Burnley, his father working in the mill, his mother staying at home to look after a bunch of kids. Never particularly academic, Jim had been expected to leave school and follow his father into the mill, but he had had other ideas. He was fond of his family, but wanted to have a part of his life away from them. Didn't crave the huddle of Cairds that would populate the mills and come home together. There was nothing wrong with his gaggle of brothers, but Jim was more of a loner. Not unsociable, but needing time to think. And the rest of the Cairds didn't spend much time thinking. They played football, drank beer and went to watch Burnley Football Club playing, the group of them a ready-made circle of friends. But as the oldest, Jim was almost remote, more responsible, not needing his brothers to make him feel safe in the world. Or rather he was the oldest *now*, after his elder brother had been killed in the war. That death had changed Jim irrevocably. His closest ally and confidant had been unexpectedly and terribly taken away from him, and from that day he realised that life could play hideous tricks on anyone.

Soon after the death of his brother, Jim went to the mill and worked alongside his father, going to night school to get the qualifications he needed to enter the prison service. In living memory, none of the Caird tribe had ever gone for further education, but Jim wasn't going to be teased out of it, whatever his siblings said. Instead, he hauled up his basic education by a couple of years and finally obtained the qualifications he needed. It had been tough, but Jim was like that – determined when he set his mind to anything.

Impressed, his parents had bragged about their eldest son all over Burnley. Our Jim, they said proudly, had qualifications. He was going into the prison service. Not the mill, not the sewage works or the timber yard; he was going over to Strangeways in Manchester to work his way up from trainee guard. And so he did, although it took him several years to make the transition from trainee to prison guard. On the way he made a few friends and fewer enemies, keeping his usual reserve up, like a boxer keeps up his guard. He met and went out with a couple of girls in Manchester, and then moved back to Burnley, finally obtaining a post at the Moors Prison. Working there would mean a lot of commuting, but Jim wasn't worried about that. He would work in shifts, four or five days on, then a day and a half off. Time to think, and he liked time to think. As for the journey to and from work, that didn't faze him either. He finally had a job he wanted, and he was going to make the best of it.

Yet the reputation of the Moors Prison was not welcoming; Jim knew about the old jail, and how renovations were intermittent and patchy. He had heard about the plumbing, the overcrowding – and about the notorious North Wing. After some careful questioning, he had also heard about the terrible death of Richard Holmes. But that was down to a shortage in staff, he was reassured at his interview; the wing was secure now. Neither the Governor nor the interview board mentioned that the prison had the highest number of murderers and rapists in the north-west. They didn't mention the solitary confinement for paedophiles, or the growing number of mentally ill who had been incarcerated in the Moors Prison when there was nowhere else for them to go.

But Jim had done his research well, and through a friend had made the acquaintance of Reg Spencer. It was Reg who told him about the reality of the jail, describing the conditions without pulling any punches. After all, he was one of the longest-serving members of staff. By the end of their conversation – during which time Jim had bought Reg and himself a few pints of beer – Jim was convinced that he wanted the job. Despite the drawbacks – or maybe because of them – he wanted to work at the Moors Prison.

So, at the age of twenty-six, Jim Caird was setting out on his first day at work. His parents had been delighted, crowing to everyone that their son was going up in the world. Smiling to himself, Jim decided that it was a small world if being a prison guard was a major achievement. Turning back to the bus window, he looked out, his reflection looking back at him in the weak morning sun. His hair was very short, dark blond, his eyes deep set, his cheekbones high. At first sight he gave the impression of a man who was strong, his physique backing up his facial appearance. He didn't have the bulk of Reg Spencer, but years of swimming at the Burnley Baths, playing football with his brothers and amateur boxing had made him muscular and quickened his reactions. Besides, he was a man who was always aware of his surroundings, and alert to a fault.

The bus picked up speed as it moved downhill, and Jim stared as the prison came into view. He wasn't afraid of the edifice, but he could imagine how terrible it would seem to a man who had a long sentence to serve. Or to the relatives of inmates; the prison glowering, dark against the skyline, the sound of the hooter echoing across the bleak landscape. Glancing upwards, he noted the usual barbed wire and broken glass at the top of the wall, and as the bus shuddered to a halt outside the side gates, he heard the sound of the iron doors being opened.

'First shift leaving,' a voice called out, as the

guards from the previous shift filed out. 'Second shift on board. Move yourselves, lads, we haven't got all day.'

Following three other men, Jim moved into the side entrance of the prison, the doors slamming closed behind him, the guard on duty looking him up and down.

'We have a virgin amongst us, gentlemen,' he said slyly. 'Be gentle with him.'

There was no malice in the teasing, the man slapping Jim on the shoulder as he showed him into the second entrance to the prison. Locking those doors behind the four men, the guard on duty turned to Jim.

'Right, you're with Reg Spencer,' he said, pointing Jim towards the doors on the left. 'As for you three, look on the rota.'

When the other men had dispersed into the guards' room, the officer in charge turned back to Jim. 'You know Reg, don't you?'

'Yeah.'

'He's a steady pair of hands. And he spoke well of you. In this place you listen to the other guards and take advice, hear me? They know what they're talking about, they're not just pissing in the wind. You'll start with Reg for the next few months, then we'll see how you get on.'

Jim nodded. 'I told the board I wouldn't object to working on the North Wing.'

The guard on duty pulled a face. 'Not many volunteers to work there. Why?'

'Probably because not many others want it,' Jim replied, smiling faintly.

'Well, be that as it may, you'll have to prove yourself here first. You were at Strangeways, weren't you?'

'For three years.'

'Hard prison, but it's different here,' the guard went on, putting a key in the door and turning it, letting Jim pass through. As he closed the barred gate, he said: 'You can make a good life here, if you fit in, and I think you will. A word to the wise – don't get close to the prisoners, and watch out for Stan Thorpe. He's one of the guards, been here for years, and he's a bigger bastard than most of the inmates.'

'Thanks,' Jim said simply, turning as he heard footsteps behind him.

Dressed in a pressed uniform and sporting his impressive moustache, Reg Spencer walked over to the newcomer. 'OK, lad, this is the beginning of your life at the Moors Prison. Good luck, you might need it.'

Emma had to admit to herself that over the past two months Irene had made life at the jeweller's shop even easier. Now that the attractive widow was visiting more often, it had been simple for Emma to suggest that she might like to help out in the shop – a suggestion that had been welcomed by her uncle. In fact, to Emma's amusement, she was finding it almost effortless to manoeuvre herself out of the jeweller's shop in order to allow her uncle and Irene time to themselves. Having talked to Irene at length, Emma had discovered that she had wanted to return to the north for a change of scene. But she had found not working dull, and was soon bored. And more than delighted to help out at the jeweller's.

Finding some of her afternoons free, Emma had taken advantage of the situation and visited her father. David was too preoccupied with Irene to ask questions, and it allowed Emma to relax, without having the constant worry of getting back to the shop quickly. It had occurred to her to confess about her visits to her father, but she had decided against it. Her uncle was beginning to relax and enjoy his time with Irene; he was even smiling occasionally. Why did he need to know about Frederick? Why cast a shade over his newly discovered happiness? Besides, it was a matter of real pleasure to Emma that she had been so successful as a matchmaker. At first she had wondered if her uncle would draw back and find excuses to remain aloof. But David Hawksworth had not been lying – he wanted to change. And if life (and his niece) had done him the kindness of offering him a second chance of happiness, he would take it.

As for Irene, she was clever. But then Emma had known that from the start. Having taken rooms on the outskirts of town, Irene had been wondering if she would stay in the north-west. Whether she even liked it, after the mellowness of Somerset. It was true that her family had originally come from Doncaster, but in reality, what had that to do with her? Her life had been spent elsewhere, and if it hadn't been for her lucky visit to Hawksworth's jeweller's, she would have moved on. But fate had intervened and she had met David Hawksworth. All this she had confided to Emma, both of them making an unspoken pact to bring the new romance to a glorious conclusion. David needed a wife, and Irene needed a husband. And besides, it would be good for business.

And good for me, Emma thought, walking along Deansgate and revelling in her day off. She hadn't been to Manchester for a while. The last time had been when she had gone with Bessie and Doug to see the new Chaplin film, *The Kid*, all three of them laughing and mimicking Chaplin's gait as they walked back across Deansgate towards the tram station. But today she was alone, and feeling more peaceful than she had done for a while.

Florence Palmer might try and scare her with horror stories about how Irene would move in and edge her out. And then where would she be? But Emma wasn't worried. In fact, she wasn't thinking ahead any more, trying to second-guess the future. Her life had been so unpredictable, so traumatic, that she didn't want to know what was coming next. Better to live day by day than tempt fate. Or hope too much. Or plan. Or even dream . . . Her own desire for emotional happiness Emma had put on hold. Her grief for her losses did not allow her to expect much personal joy, and she was content knowing what she was doing for her uncle. Let him be happy, Emma thought, it's a good way to say thank you.

But Bessie wasn't about to let the matter drop, and had challenged Emma the previous night.

'You'll find someone else one day.'

'I'm not interested,' Emma had replied genuinely.

'You're too young to give up.'

'I didn't say I was giving up, Bessie. I just said I wasn't interested in love at the moment.'

'Bloody hell! You sound like an old woman!' Bessie had remonstrated, blowing out her cheeks. 'You're good-looking. You could come out with us. Doug knows plenty of young men.'

'It's too soon,' Emma had said, her tone edgy. 'It's far too soon, Bessie. It will be too soon for a long time.'

'Yeah, well don't leave it too long, or you might wake up one morning and see that your choices have dried up. It happens faster than you think, Emma, and your experiences – bad as they were – can't wreck your life for ever. You have to move on.'

Which was true, and Emma knew it. But she wasn't moving on anywhere for a while. The shock of Leonard's death, and the loss of their baby, had changed her. It hadn't hardened her, but her mind had put the grief to one side. She did cry for her lost family, often, but alone, or in the dark. In the daylight, she functioned without thinking of them. They were her companions only when life was asleep. When she wasn't working, or learning about the business. Their ghosts came out to visit when the shop closed, the lights were turned off and the street was silent outside her window. Hardly knowing if she was awake or dreaming, she would see Leonard again, and remember the cot they had bought for the baby. She would think of her husband's kindness and then remember how his life had slipped out of her hands. How she had seen the moment when he had swung between living and dying. The moment of loss, when he had gone from her. Moved on, out of her sight, out of her reach. And all that was left was his body. Which wasn't Leonard at all . . . As to the loss of the baby, that had become befuddled in Emma's mind. The terrible days after her husband's death had blurred until the memory was as spotted as a fly-blown mirror.

So how could she – so raw, so guilty – think of loving anyone again? How could she deserve happiness? Surprised that she had walked so far without realising, Emma stopped outside a shop window and looked in. The memories slid back, the sunny day warming her as she stared at a pair of new gloves. They would be expensive, she thought, but pretty. Very pretty . . . Slowly, she walked on, enjoying the sunshine as the clouds shunted over the rooftops and the gold lettering glittered on the pub sign overhead. She was enjoying the weather so much that she didn't notice the man approach her, and jumped when he said her name.

'Miss Coles?'

Turning, Emma smiled as she saw her father's solicitor, Cedric Overton.

'I thought it was you. How are you, my dear?'

'Very well,' Emma replied. 'And you?'

'Good. Busy, but that's nothing unusual,' he went on, a briefcase under his arm and his hat in his left hand.

'Is there anything new about my father's case?'

He gave her a sympathetic look. 'Nothing, I'm afraid.'

And then Emma did something she didn't fully understand. Following some uncertain hunch, she asked: 'I've been talking to my father a lot recently. I'm visiting him again, as you know, and he's opened up about his case.' She paused, wondering why she was saying these things. 'In fact, he's told me a good deal more than I could have guessed.'

'Really?'

'Oh yes,' Emma went on. 'He's told me things I never knew before.'

'Indeed?'

'He should have told me sooner. But still, I know now.'

Naturally, Mr Overton took this to mean that Frederick had confided in his daughter. And because of that, he confided in her too.

'Personally, I could never understand why he wouldn't name the person.'

Stunned, Emma stared at the solicitor, aware that she had inadvertently uncovered something of tremendous importance. She chose her next words carefully.

'The person who was really guilty?'

Overton nodded, changing his briefcase from under one arm to the other. 'He said he could never

276

give me the name. But then you know all this?'

'Yes, yes,' Emma went on hurriedly, 'but I wanted to talk to you about it. I wanted to know what you thought.'

'I think now what I've always thought, my dear. Unless your father names the person who was responsible for the theft, he will remain in jail. His defence – that it was someone else, but without giving a name – was too flimsy. I told him that at the time. I've told him over and over again since. But he won't give the person up.'

Emma was finding it hard to swallow, the saliva drying in her mouth. Keep calm, she told herself, act normally.

'But he's serving a prison sentence for something he didn't do. Why would he endure that for someone else?'

Overton looked into her face and shrugged.

'I don't know . . . I must admit, I did wonder if he'd told you the name of the guilty man.'

'No!' she said hurriedly. 'I'd have been in touch with you right away. Why would I let him rot in jail if I knew the person who was really responsible?' She paused, trying to control her emotions, Overton suddenly looking at her with a suspicious expression.

'Oh my God. You didn't know about any of this, did you?'

Shaking her head, she looked down. 'No, not until you just told me.'

'Damn!'

'No, don't blame yourself, I'm glad I know,' Emma

said, reassuring him. 'I'm going to see my father at the end of the week. And I'm going to ask him outright to name the guilty man.'

'Why would he tell you if he wouldn't tell me? Why would he tell you now, after being in jail for three years?' Overton said, his tone flat. 'I think your father intends to serve his sentence without ever disclosing the truth. He must have a very good reason to keep quiet.'

Emma's temper flared suddenly.

'Have you seen my father lately, Mr Overton? He's had a bad winter and a poor spring. He's got a lung infection . . .'

'I know.'

'. . . and a cough he can't shake off. He's getting older and looks ill. He's also getting used to the idea that he's in jail, and he's changing. In fact,' she said brokenly, 'he's giving up. And now you tell me that he knows the real thief and won't expose him? That Frederick Coles would rather rot in jail than speak out?' She turned away, staring into the distance.

Around them, shoppers passed by, joking and laughing in the October sunlight. Back in Burnley, her uncle would be talking to Irene, flirting, maybe even starting to speak of a future. But in the Moors Prison, Frederick Coles was serving another's man sentence – and she didn't know why.

'*Why* would he do it?' she asked, her tone incredulous. 'Why would he do such a stupid thing! He's giving his life away.'

'He must have a good reason.'

'What reason?' she hurled back. 'Mr Overton, look me in the face and tell me. Make me understand – what reason on God's earth would make a man give up his good name and his freedom to shield another?'

'I don't know,' Overton said simply, sighing and shaking his head. 'But until someone can answer that, your father will stay in jail.'

Emma's voice was barely a whisper. 'You know he could die there? My father could sacrifice his life for someone else.'

'He must have his reasons,' the solicitor repeated.

'And I want to know what they are. I want him to tell me why any sacrifice should be that great.'

TWENTY-FIVE

Having been working as a guard at the Moors Prison for three months, Jim was slowly growing to know the inmates he was responsible for. He knew which to avoid, and which to mistrust, and he knew which were the harmless ones. Like Frederick Coles. Jailed for theft and given eleven years. The sentence had been long, Reg told him, because Frederick hadn't pleaded guilty and the money had never been recovered. His legal team had told him that it would go better for him if he pleaded guilty and gave up the money – which had been considerable, as it had consisted of the week's takings and the workers' wages. But he denied having the money and doing the robbery. Said it was someone else.

Going by pure gut instinct, Jim believed him. And so did Reg, who, after watching Frederick for several years, had to admit he thought the sentence was wrong. In fact, most of the guards believed Frederick Coles was innocent and treated him differently to the other inmates. Not in an obvious way, but with a little more respect. All apart from Stan Thorpe, who had taken a dislike to Frederick, thinking that he believed he was better than the usual type of thief. There was another reason, too. Thorpe's fascination with Frederick's daughter had intensified over the years. Emma had changed, grown up, since she had visited her father when he was first jailed. Life had ironed out her naïvety and she was more composed. And with her composure had come a different look about her face. A stillness that was compelling, hiding as it did a feisty nature underneath. In fact – although he would never admit it – Thorpe was smitten by Emma, even changing his rota to coincide with visitors' day. He would let the visitors in and then stand back, watching Emma as she entered, and again as she talked to her father. Her good looks and respectability stood out against the coarseness of many of the visitors, and he found himself staring at her.

Reg had noticed and told Jim Caird, both of them keeping tabs on the repellent Thorpe.

'What yer fucking staring at!' Thorpe barked, suddenly realising he was being watched. His bad temper and bad breath had not lessened with time, and although he could have already retired, he was holding on grimly to his peck of power.

'Calm down, Stan,' Reg said, Jim watching the altercation between the older guards. 'No one's staring at you. You're not exactly a vision of loveliness. And you're even more bad-tempered than usual. What's the matter with you?'

'It's usually my bloody stomach, but now my bleeding teeth are playing me up,' Thorpe admitted, waggling one of his canines and grinning unpleasantly at Jim. 'I suppose yer'd like to knock it out fer me?'

'Not really.'

'*Not really*,' Thorpe parroted back, moving closer to Jim and marking him out as his next victim. Meanly he studied Jim's strong face, the high cheekbones and even jaw line. Tough he looked and tough he was. But Thorpe wasn't going to let him intimidate him. Others might steer clear of Jim Caird, but Thorpe wasn't backing down. 'Yer a bit thick, aren't yer? Hey, aren't yer?'

'You're right, Mr Thorpe,' Jim said coolly, 'but thick enough to break your arm.'

Blinking, Thorpe stepped back, Reg smiling as they watched him walk off.

'Lesson one, you put that bugger in his place. You should have no trouble with him now, Jim. A bully never picks on anyone who can hold their own.' He sighed. 'He'll be off down to the visitors' room now, hanging about waiting for Emma Coles to come and see her father.'

'I saw her the other day,' Jim said. 'Striking young woman.'

'That she is,' Reg agreed. 'And that filthy old bastard Thorpe's fallen for her.' He winked at Jim. 'You reckon she'll be interested?'

Jim didn't think so, but his curiosity was great enough for him to go down to the visitors' room himself and watch Emma's arrival. For once, she was late, Frederick already waiting at the table for her as she walked in. There was another difference, Jim noticed: she seemed ill at ease, unable to meet her father's gaze. Standing by the wall, Jim found himself trying to eavesdrop and then walked a little way off, ashamed of himself.

Then, spotting Thorpe, he moved over to the older man.

'I can manage here on my own.'

'Fuck off,' Thorpe said belligerently, playing with his loose tooth, his eyes fixed on Emma.

'You could call in at the sanatorium. The doctor's there, he could pull that tooth for you.'

'A doctor ain't a dentist!' Thorpe replied ungratefully, his breath foul as he breathed through his mouth. 'Fucking killing me, this tooth.' His bad-tempered gaze slid from Emma to her father. 'Look at that sod, thinks he's too good for this place. Thief, that's what he is, only people don't think so, because he was so flaming dapper. Not so dapper now, hey? No one stays dapper in this place.'

Irritated, Jim kept his tone even. 'Look, why don't you get that tooth out? You'll feel much better, and it'll only take a second.'

Against his better judgement, Thorpe considered the suggestion. He could just run over and get the bloody thing pulled, then come back and still see something of the Coles girl.

'Yeah, all right,' he agreed, walking off and leaving Jim alone.

With Reg Spencer on the other side of the visitors' room, Jim knew they had plenty of cover. Not that

that was what he had been worried about. He had simply wanted Thorpe out of the way so he could look at Emma Coles. And as he looked at Emma, he found himself remembering everything he had been told by the other guards. About the scandal, and how Emma had had the nerve to visit her father, alone, when she had been only fifteen. Jim also remembered the rest of her history. The death of Ricky Holmes, and then her husband, leaving her a very young widow. A widow who had had to return to her uncle's shop in Burnley . . .

Pacing the visitors' room, Jim glanced over to Emma a few times, but not often enough to invite comment. Because of his tough looks, he was popular with girls, and his reputation as an ex amateur boxer gave him a masculine allure. The fact that he was in very good physical shape didn't hurt either. He ran several miles a week, in all weathers. Down the town streets he would pound, timing himself with a stopwatch, then making a jump at the low wall by the Methodist church. If he was fast, he would be delighted and whoop with pleasure. If he was slow, he would come out the next day and push himself even harder.

Jim had run past Hawksworth's jeweller's a few times and he knew the shop; in fact he'd already known something of Emma's story, as his mother had related it to him after she found out he was guarding Frederick Coles.

'Oooh,' she had said, her fleshy face turned to Jim. Years of childbearing had not aged her, and although the weight had piled on, it had given her a cherubic look. 'It were a right do, that were. Frederick Coles a thief. They never found the money, and his daughter . . . everyone was talking about it, poor kid. Had to go to her uncle's.' She had paused, putting her head on one side. 'Visiting her dad, is she?'

'Yeah, comes every week.'

'That's nice,' Mrs Caird had gone on. 'Pretty, is she?'

'Yeah,' Jim had said reflectively. 'Must be hard to see your father in jail.'

'Oh yes,' Mrs Caird had replied. 'Thing was, no one would have been surprised if it had been Frederick's father. Ernie Coles was born for jail.' She had patted the back of her son's hand, leaving a smear of flour on it. 'Funny, isn't it, how life turns out?'

Now, despite himself, Jim tried to listen in on the conversation, moving a little closer as he passed by the wall. Emma was wearing a fitted blue coat, her hair cut short as was the fashion, her expression cautious as she studied her father. Having only ever seen affection from her before, Jim was curious at this turn of events, Emma's voice raised a little higher than usual.

'So, who was it?'

'Ssh!' her father said suddenly. Again, Jim thought, this was unusual. Normally there was never any harshness between father and daughter. 'I have my reasons . . .'

Reaching the end of the room, Jim turned,

infuriated that he would miss out on some of the conversation as he retraced his steps.

'You don't understand,' Frederick was saying as Jim walked past again. 'You have . . . it's trust.'

'But I don't understand – who is he?'

As though suddenly aware that they might be overheard, Emma glanced up and caught Jim's gaze. But instead of appearing uneasy, he looked back at her levelly. His expression was calm and thoughtful, his bearing erect. And although she had seen him several times before, Emma was suddenly struck by him and found herself flushing, glancing away in confusion.

Relieved, Frederick took the diversion as a means of defusing their argument. 'Emma, this is one of our new guards, Jim Caird.'

Jim put out his hand, Emma taking it and feeling an immediate physical attraction. Something she had not felt for a long time.

'I've heard all about you,' she said, trying to sound calm. 'My father speaks highly of you. Says you've got the makings of a governor.'

Smiling, Jim nodded. He was obviously sure of himself at his work, but there was a certain lack of confidence in himself as a person that she found endearing.

'I'm sorry if I embarrassed you,' she said sincerely. 'My father has a way with words.'

'No offence taken,' Jim replied, then, after smiling again, he walked off.

Outwardly he seemed unperturbed, but inside Jim

Caird was cursing himself. Why had he not thought up some witty remark to amuse Emma Coles? She had been welcoming, flattering him, but he had just stood there like a tailor's dummy, with all the eloquence of a brick wall. He could easily understand how Stan Thorpe could fall for her; she was good-looking and something special. But *he* had missed his chance. At the moment he could have made an impression, he had floundered . . . Walking slowly up and down the room, Jim studied the prisoners and their visitors, finally plucking up enough courage to glance back to Emma and her father. But they were deep in conversation and didn't even look up.

But unless he was mistaken, she *had* noticed him. There had been a connection between them. Emma might be preoccupied with her father now, but in time he would make her notice him again. After all, he would be able to see her many times when she visited. He would take it slowly, get to know her father better – and then her. Perhaps have a chat when she came to the prison. Bump into her by accident, strike up a conversation . . . Jim walked the length of the room and then turned, walking back again and passing the Coleses. Yes, he would take it carefully. He liked this girl, liked what he heard of her – and besides, he was fascinated.

Jim Caird was a man who knew what he wanted. And he wanted to get to know Emma Coles. There had been a frisson of electricity between them; he was man enough to notice it, and he knew she had. Who cared about her past? About her father's crime or her grandfather's notoriety? He didn't. Other people might hold it against her, but who was he to judge? The Cairds were poor stock themselves, most of them hardly educated, a gaggle of relatives running amok in Burnley. Never in trouble with the law, but never amounting to anything much either.

Jim knew all about stigmas; he worked with people most would steer clear of. Worked where others dumped their criminals and forgot them. But not Jim. He didn't like many of the inmates, and he had known some hard cases in Strangeways. He didn't pretend to understand why a man killed, and he didn't want to make excuses for him either. Jim Caird's greatest gift was not compassion – it was acceptance. All his life he had been able to accept situations and actions others found reprehensible. He could talk to killers and divorce their actions from his own moral code. They were – in his eyes – responsible for themselves and what they had done. He was not judging them, or absolving them. He just accepted them.

And so, following his own view of the world, he found himself keen to pursue his interest in Emma Coles. Who she was, who her relatives were and what they had done was nothing to him. He had more sense than to believe in his own virtue. God knows, bad luck could have landed *him* in trouble easily enough. He had been a bit of a rough lad himself at one time. Just teetering on the edge of violence. He hadn't been good, but he had been lucky. Perhaps at another time *he* would have been the one in jail.

For an ordinary man, Jim Caird was pretty extraordinary.

TWENTY-SIX

October 1922

Staring through her magnifying glass, Irene peered at the ring and then clicked her tongue.

'What is it?' David asked, bending down towards her.

'Pinchbeck.'

'*Pinchbeck?*' he repeated, taking the glass from her and staring at the piece. 'You're right. Hardly worth more than a couple of bob.'

Smiling, he straightened up and stared at Irene. If he had had any idea that the romance had been organised, the thought wouldn't have worried him. He would have been grateful, if anything. What he did know was that he had a new love in his life. Something he would never have believed possible only a year previously. In fact, over the last few months the thought had made him a little giddy, and once or twice he had actually laughed out loud, stifling the sound before anyone overheard him and thought he had lost his mind.

Irene Knight. Irene Knight . . . He repeated the name over in his mind as he turned away from her

and opened the safe. Irene Knight. *Irene Hawksworth*
. . . He paused, taking in a breath. How far had he
come? How far in a few months? Did he really just
think of Irene like that? Did he really just give her his
name? Was that what he wanted? Leaning into the
safe to keep his face averted, David considered the
possibility. If he did marry Irene, what would it
mean? She was interested in the shop, knew about
jewellery and would be the perfect help. But what
about Emma? David frowned, suddenly remembering
his niece. He could hardly usurp Emma for his new
love. Not after all she had suffered; it would be
brutal. Besides, he had made a promise to take care
of her, and he would keep his oath. Anyway, he had
grown very fond of his niece. She might be
Frederick's daughter, but David now thought of her
as his child.

And not simply as a replacement for Adam. Even
though he had had a letter from his son, a garbled
note about how he was a bad father and how Adam
was going to make a fortune in London, there had
been no further communication. No forwarding
address had been given and no follow-up visit made.
Adam was out of reach again, off limits. For a
moment, David wondered why he was *still* trying to
please his son. But the answer was obvious. Adam
might well be vicious and greedy – but who had made
him that way? Would a better father have made him
a better son?

If Adam could see him now, David thought, he
would see that his father could be loving, kind even.

Emma would tell him that, and Irene. In fact, if Adam came home they could all live together, be a family again. Surprised by his own sentimentality, David began to wind the clocks, Irene watching him in silence. What was he thinking? David asked himself. Adam would never come home. But Emma *was* home, was part of his family. And he wanted her to stay with him. His surrogate daughter . . . Slowly David kept winding the clocks, checking the time on each of them. If he *did* marry Irene, there would be no reason for Emma to leave. She would still have her own room, and work in the shop. Of course, Irene would want to run the home in her own way – wives were like that – but he couldn't see any real problem occurring, as the two women got on.

'What is it?' Irene asked suddenly, walking over to David and touching his arm.

He looked down at her, at the angular face with its intelligent eyes, and wondered how he could even hesitate. He had to grab his chance, otherwise she might walk out of his shop. Right into some other man's shop and some other man's life.

'Irene,' he said, clearing his throat as he always did when he was nervous. 'I've been thinking. I know this might come as a surprise . . .'

She doubted it.

'. . . but over the past months I've become very fond of you.'

I care for you too.

'I know it hasn't been very long . . .'

Long enough.

'. . . but I hope you might feel something for me.'

Go on, Irene willed him silently. *Go on, say it.*

'I was wondering if we might think about—'

'Puddings!'

Stunned, David and Irene turned to see Florence Palmer standing in the doorway of the shop with a bag in her hand.

'Well?' she demanded. 'Are these yours?'

'What?' David said dimly.

'These puddings,' she repeated, slamming them down on the counter. 'They were delivered to me, but I didn't order them.'

Softly, Irene began to laugh, David glancing over to her, his expression baffled.

'What on earth . . .'

'I'm talking about pudding!' Florence went on, glancing from one to the other and wondering why they had both started laughing. 'What the hell's so funny?'

'Nothing,' David stammered. 'No, they're not our puddings.'

'You sure?'

Helpless with laughter, Irene leaned against the counter.

'I'm sure,' David replied, Florence staring at him with ill-disguised annoyance.

'You're off your head, David Hawksworth! I always said you'd go that way one day. It were a perfectly simple question, nothing funny. All I asked was – are these puddings yours?'

Ignoring her completely, David turned to Irene, his expression tender. 'Will you marry me?'

And Florence Palmer fainted.

'Come in, come in. Bring your shoes, your boots . . .'

'Your turn,' Bessie said, nudging her husband awake, Doug pulling on his trousers and stumbling downstairs. In the dark shop, Mr Letski was standing at the door, calling out his sales pitch to the empty night. The old Russian was virtually blind, and had become senile. In the daytime, he was childlike and easy to deal with, but at night he came to life, going back to his glory days.

Gently taking the old man's arm, Doug closed the door. 'No sales today, Mr Letski,' he said patiently. 'You have to go back to bed.'

'There are spies,' the Russian whispered, his accent even more pronounced with age. 'There are spies under my bed.'

'Nah, not any more,' Doug replied, yawning. 'I checked earlier and threw them out.'

'How many were there?'

'Six,' Doug said, plucking the figure out of thin air. 'I beat them all up.'

'Good,' Letski said, pinching Doug's forearm. 'You look like a chicken, but you're not so puny, hey?'

'Not for a chicken,' Bessie said, walking downstairs and putting the kettle on to boil.

It struck her as strange that she had not yet got pregnant. But as she said to Emma, she had a ready-made child in the old cobbler. Patient to a fault, she had taken over the care of the Russian, Doug helping her out, both of them running the shop together. Time had turned the tables on Bessie's critics, and now everyone was pleased to see that she was taking responsibility for an aged foreign man, with no family of his own. Inheriting the cobbler's shop was only what she deserved.

But although he could be demanding, Bessie had grown used to caring for Mr Letski, and had even adjusted to his nocturnal jaunts, although his new habit of unlocking the shop door had worried her and she had pressed Doug to add a new bolt.

Making tea for the three of them, Bessie sat down at the kitchen table.

'He beat up all six spies,' Letski said admiringly, pointing to Doug. 'Six spies.'

'They certainly seem to be going up in numbers,' she replied. 'I'd have thought by now that we'd have got rid of all of them.'

'They train plenty, plenty spies,' Letski went on, tapping his nose with his forefinger. 'Communists.'

'What's a Communist?' Doug asked, Bessie rolling her eyes.

'A Communist is a person who hides under beds at night.'

'What for?'

'To steal the chamber pots,' she replied, her tone exasperated as she dropped her voice. 'Don't talk about Communists, Doug! You know how it gets him going.'

But Mr Letski's attention had already wandered.

Sipping his tea, he looked round at the kitchen and then banged down his tin mug.

'We have a sale!'

'Yes, right . . .'

'Nah,' he said firmly, 'we have a sale. Put shoes in window.'

'We *mend* shoes, Mr Letski,' Bessie said patiently, 'we don't *sell* them.'

'Why not?'

Bessie paused, thinking. 'Yeah, why not?' she asked, turning to Doug. 'Business has been slow, we *could* start selling shoes. I was in St James's Street the other day and there was a sale on, and there was a queue of women. We could do it, Doug. We could.'

Getting to her feet, Bessie hurried into the shop beyond and turned on the light, glancing round. The place had hardly changed since she had first come to work there. The same lathe, the same lasts for the shoes, the same rows of rubber soles and boxes of steel heel tips. And, of course, the metal tips for the clogs. Breathing out, she walked around, Mr Letski watching her from the doorway.

'We need a new sign too, something more modern,' Bessie went on, picking up the poster on the counter and staring at it. The woman depicted was wearing her hair up, in the old style, her dress long, her shoes button-up boots. 'God, this went out before the war! No one wears stuff like this any more – except the old folk.'

'Who are customers,' Doug said timidly.

'Yeah, I agree. But we could have them *and* new

customers too. And Mr Letski's right, we should sell shoes. Over there,' Bessie said, waving one hand across the shop. 'We could put up shelves and put out all the new styles, display them like in the shops on Market Street.'

'How are we going to pay for it?'

'You have to speculate to accumulate, Doug,' Bessie told him, knowing he wouldn't understand a word she was saying, but carrying on anyway. 'And handbags. Just a few to begin with. Women like handbags and we could buy them to match the shoes.'

'Oh, I don't know . . .'

'You're no businessman,' she reproved her husband. 'I can see the sign now. We'll have it in big red letters – SALE.'

Doug looked at his wife. 'But we can't have a sale before we get some shoes in the shop.'

She sighed expansively. 'Yeah, I know that. But when we get the shoes in, we could have a sale right away. You know, get people's interest and give them a bargain at the same time.' She turned suddenly, kissing the old cobbler loudly on the top of his head. 'Good idea, Mr Letski! You're a marvel, you are, a right marvel.'

When Emma returned to the jeweller's shop later that day, Irene was waiting for her. With her glasses in her hand and an alert expression on her attractive face, she ushered Emma into the back room and closed the door. Surprised, Emma watched her make them both a cup of tea, Irene finally taking a seat next to her. 'I want to make one thing clear, and very clear,' Irene began. 'I am not going to be one of those awful women who try to take over.'

'Really?' Emma replied, bemused. 'Where's my uncle?'

'Gone out,' Irene told her, moving her chair closer to Emma and dropping her voice. 'What would you say to us getting married?'

'You and me?' Emma teased, Irene laughing.

'No, silly! Your uncle and me.'

'I would say that it was the best piece of news I'd had for months!' Emma replied, giving Irene a quick kiss on the cheek. 'He proposed! I'm so glad – although I have to say, I thought it would take longer. My uncle's not exactly a hasty kind of man.'

'You gave us plenty of room,' Irene said, nudging her. 'Every time I came to visit, you went out. Many women wouldn't have been so obliging. Especially as they might resent another woman coming on to their patch.'

Emma shook her head.

'This isn't my patch, Irene. My uncle needed to meet someone and be happy. I'm only glad I could help – and particularly glad it was you that walked into the shop that day. You made it easy for me to welcome you,' she said, taking the older woman's hand and squeezing it tightly for a moment. 'I like you.'

'Oh, and I like you, my dear. And I know your uncle thinks the world of you. But . . .'

'Yes?'

'Well, you might say that this is none of my business, but I'll be joining the family soon and perhaps there are some things I should know. Not to interfere, but to understand. I don't want to step on David's feelings without knowing it.' She looked into Emma's face. 'I asked him about you and how you came to live with him.'

Alerted, Emma was suddenly on edge. 'What did he say?'

'That you had no one and needed a home,' Irene answered. 'But then the other day, that Mrs Palmer next door – who has a grudge against David for some reason or other – she let slip something about your *grandfather*.'

'What did she let slip?'

'That he was a rogue.'

'He is,' Emma replied honestly. 'But I don't see him. In fact, I've never seen him in my life. My father kept me well away.'

Irene nodded, her usual confidence faltering. 'But then Mrs Palmer said something about your father . . .'

Emma stiffened.

'. . . and when I mentioned it to David, he ignored me as though he hadn't even heard what I said.' Irene paused. 'I'm really not trying to interfere, and nothing would make me change my mind about marrying your uncle. He's a fine man, under that dour exterior, and I reckon we'll make a good match. But I'm not one for secrets, Emma, never was. I like to know the facts – however bad or difficult – just so I know where I stand.'

'Why didn't you ask Mrs Palmer what she was talking about?'

'I wanted *you* to tell me,' she replied, 'not some gossip with bad hair.'

Smiling distantly, Emma looked down at the table. She had liked Irene from the start, but had grown unused to sharing confidences. For years she had kept her secrets and they had cost her dear, her father never knowing that he had inadvertently been the cause of her husband's death. Her uncle didn't know about her prison visits, not in the past, or now. If she confided in Irene, would the knowledge be safe? Or would she feel an obligation to tell David?

'You can trust me, Emma.'

'I . .'

'You can trust me.'

Emma nodded.

'Tell me about your father.'

The temptation was enormous. To be able to talk about her beloved father, to be able to discuss her worries about him. To have someone she could tell when she went on her visits, someone who would cover for her, make excuses, be on her side. But was it too much to ask for Irene to keep her secret? Wasn't confiding putting a wedge between the couple? A wedge that might cause problems later?

'There's nothing to tell,' she said finally.

Irene sighed, folding her hands on her lap. 'I suppose I would have said that too, if I was in your position. But you see, I think I know a little more than you imagine, Emma. Florence Palmer has a big mouth when she's had a drink, and I have big ears sometimes – when I think I should hear something. And I've heard a couple of things over the last weeks.'

'Like what?'

'Like your father still being alive,' Irene said, bringing Frederick Coles into the jeweller's shop for the first time in many years. Bringing him eerily back to life.

Slowly, Emma nodded. 'Yes, he's still alive.'

'And in prison?'

'He didn't do it!' Emma said vehemently. 'Whatever that busybody Florence Palmer said, or anyone else for that matter – my father's innocent.'

'And you love him very much,' Irene replied, her voice understanding. 'I can't imagine how difficult it must have been for you to come and live here with your uncle, not being allowed to even talk about your father or what he'd done. You *couldn't* talk about it, could you? I mean, that much was obvious when David ignored my question. And besides, I've never heard any reference to your father in all the time I've been coming here. What was he supposed to have done?'

'Stolen a lot of money from Oldfield Mill.' Emma paused, taking in another breath. 'My father told everyone he hadn't taken the money. That someone else had – only he wouldn't say who it was. So no one believed him. Not the police or the jury. They

301

thought he was lying and that he had hidden the money for when he got out of prison. His solicitor, Mr Overton, advised him to tell them where the money was, so they could recover it. He said that the sentence would be lighter if he did ... but my father didn't know where the money was. *Because he didn't take it.*'

She stopped talking, surprised at the outpouring and relieved at the same time. She hadn't known how much she had needed to confide in someone. Infrequent talks with Mr Overton, or the guards at the prison, were limited, and she knew that she must have exhausted Bessie's patience long ago. Not that her friend ever said so, but there were only so many times the story could be repeated.

'How long is your father's sentence?' Irene asked carefully.

'He got eleven years and he still has eight to serve,' Emma told her. 'There was another thing that counted against him at the trial – *his* father, Ernie Coles.' She raised her eyebrows. 'Well, you've already heard about him from Florence Palmer.' Emma looked at the woman next to her. 'I'm afraid I'm not from good stock, but you can't hold it against my uncle. Ernie Coles was just his stepfather and he got away from him as soon as he could. David Hawksworth is many things – some of them I don't fully understand – but he's respectable, I know that for a fact. An honourable man.'

'You can say that when he denied the existence of your father?' Irene asked, impressed by Emma's divided loyalties.

'My uncle has his faults, but he's changed so much, I can't hold what he was against him now.'

'I see,' Irene replied thoughtfully. 'I did hear that you used to visit your father in jail . . .'

Emma said nothing, just stared at the tabletop.

'That must have been hard. You were only fifteen when he was first incarcerated. Of course, it would be a little easier now, but still not a pleasant duty.'

'It isn't a duty,' Emma said, looking at the woman next to her and knowing that Irene had already guessed. 'I visit my father because I want to. Because he needs me to. Because he has no one else.'

'And because you worry about him?'

'Yes, yes, I do,' Emma confessed, her voice low. 'I don't think he's going to be able to serve out his sentence. I can see he's getting weak, and he's changing. I don't think he has the same fight in him. Maybe at first he believed that some new evidence would come out and exonerate him, but not now; now he looks like he's resigned.'

'But if he knows who the real thief is . . .'

'Oh, I know what you're going to say!' Emma replied heatedly, getting to her feet. 'I've asked him over and over again to give me the name, but he won't. He says he can't. I don't know why. I don't know why anyone would give away eleven years of their life for something they didn't do.'

'They wouldn't – unless they had a damn good reason.'

Emma turned back to Irene. 'What reason? No one can explain what reason would be good enough. Not his solicitor, not me – and God knows I've thought about it.'

Calmly Irene filled up the tea cups, gesturing for Emma to sit down again. Thoughtfully, she then sipped her tea, taking a few minutes without speaking. A couple of times she seemed about to say something, then stopped herself, having another drink of tea as though she wasn't quite sure of what she wanted to say. Then, finally, she drained her cup and leaned back in her chair.

'Well, it's a difficult one,' she said simply, Emma frowning.

'You're not worried, are you? I mean, none of what I said is going to make a difference to you and my uncle, is it?'

Tapping the back of Emma's hand, Irene gave her a patient look. 'Good God, my dear, you don't get to my age without having some experience of life, and you don't survive at all unless you can adapt. I was just thinking about your father, and you. How hard it must be.'

'But you can't tell my uncle.'

'Of course not! Unless he's already guessed.'

'Has he said something?'

'Not a word,' Irene replied. 'As far as I know, David is unaware of your visits. But I think I can help you.'

'How?'

'Well, you helped me get to know your uncle. Without your matchmaking, I dare say I wouldn't be marrying again. So I reckon I owe you something,

Emma. I can't help you directly with your father's case, but I can make sure you visit as much as you like – with your uncle being none the wiser.' She winked at Emma, smiling wickedly. 'When I was little, my parents took me to the circus. Well, I don't remember much about it, apart from one performer who could juggle all these plates at once. I thought it was impressive, and the image stayed with me. It's not unlike life, in a way.'

'In what way?'

'We're women, my dear, and women have to be a little sly sometimes,' Irene said, her eyes bright. 'Not for badness, but to keep all the plates spinning at the same time, without dropping any.'

TWENTY-SEVEN

Vicious-tempered with toothache, Stan Thorpe walked the upper gangway of the South Wing. Holding his cheek, he looked over the mezzanine, through the suspended netting, down to the lower floor. As he did so, he saw Frederick Coles walk past and felt a peevish jolt go through him. Only the previous week Thorpe had tried to start a conversation with Frederick, but he had ignored him. Well, maybe not ignored him, but carried on talking to Jim Caird instead. Which had made Thorpe feel like a bloody fool. After all, he was one of the most senior guards in the prison, and Caird was one of the newer men.

Pushing his tongue against his swollen upper gum, Thorpe cursed under his breath, his mouth sour. He would go back to the doctor in the sanatorium, even though he was a bastard and had told Thorpe he needed all his teeth out. Get some dentures, he'd said. Yeah, right, Thorpe had glowered, false teeth like an old man? Brooding, he stared down into the floor below, watching Frederick. It was visiting day tomorrow, Thorpe thought; Emma would be coming to see her father. And he, Stan Thorpe, would talk to her. Yes, this time he would talk to her. Have a little chat. If he could just take something for the fucking toothache, which was driving him out of his wits.

'What are you looking at?' a voice asked.

'Mount Everest,' Stan replied bitterly, turning to Reg. 'Why hasn't Coles gone out for his exercise?'

'Not feeling too good.'

'Soft sod.'

Reg sighed. 'He's losing weight.'

'Not as dapper as he once was, and that's a fact,' Thorpe replied, jabbing his tongue against his gum and wincing. 'I can remember when Frederick Coles was a good-looking bloke.'

Sensing the delight in Thorpe's voice, Reg said, 'I hear you've changed your shift tomorrow?'

'Yeah, so?'

'You've been on every visiting day for the last two months.'

'Yeah, so?'

'Why?'

Slowly Thorpe turned. He couldn't bully Reg Spencer, but he wasn't about to be pleasant.

'What's it to you?'

'Just making conversation.'

'*Just making conversation*,' Thorpe mimicked. 'What are you, some kind of social secretary?'

'I just wondered why you wanted to work the visitors' shifts. Wondered if it had anything to do with Emma Coles,' Reg continued. In fact, he had been talking to a worried Frederick about Thorpe's growing obsession with Emma, and had promised to try and help. 'The visiting day shift is an easy one. You should let the other guards have their turn.'

'I've been at this fucking prison longer than anyone! I've a right to cut myself a bit of slack.'

'We used to take the visiting days in turns,' Reg went on. 'You know that.'

'You want to do something about it?' Thorpe challenged him. 'Go and have it out with the Governor, then. Go and report your colleague to the top brass, see how popular that makes you.'

Unmoved, Reg studied the other man, then walked off, his hands behind his back.

Even more enraged by Reg's interference, Thorpe walked down the iron steps to the lower floor. He didn't know, but he suspected that Frederick Coles had complained about him. Obviously Coles had noticed his interest in his bloody daughter, and asked for him to be moved. Fucking Coles, Thorpe thought, enraged. Just because he was popular with the guards and one of Reg Spencer's favourites, what right did he have to run the prison? Stamping down the iron steps, Thorpe's toothache made him even meaner than usual. He had noticed that Emma looked uneasy when she caught him staring at her, but he didn't expect her to go crying to her father. And now this . . . As he moved down the polished corridor between the cells, the inmates stopped or stepped back. Thorpe's temper was legendary and no one wanted to be his next whipping boy. But they needn't have worried. Thorpe had spotted his next target and was headed straight for him.

'*Coles!*'

Frederick turned at the sound of his name. 'Yes?'

'Your visiting privileges have been cancelled for tomorrow,' Thorpe said flatly. 'I found a knife in your cell.'

'You can't have!' Frederick replied. He had never been in trouble and had been a quiet prisoner, never the type to invite attention. He knew that Thorpe was lying; what he didn't know was why. 'You can't just stop my visiting rights.'

'It's in the prison regulations,' Thorpe continued, his tone sly. 'You can take it up with the Governor, but then he would have to know that I'd found a knife in your cell – and that would go on your record. You don't want it to go on your record, do you? Not blotting that clean file of yours.'

'*I didn't have a knife in my cell,*' Frederick said emphatically, standing up to the guard, the other inmates watching him. 'And I want my visiting rights.'

'*You want your rights!*' Thorpe parroted. 'Well, talk to the Governor about it.'

'*You* put that knife in my cell,' Frederick said, his tone deadly. 'Why?'

'I don't know what you're talking about. And you better watch your mouth, making accusations like that. I'm a prison officer, you should respect me.'

'You're not going to make trouble for me.'

'Coles, you've made it for yourself,' Thorpe replied, his tone dismissive.

'You put the knife in my cell deliberately – so you could drop my visiting privileges. I know you, Mr Thorpe, you're a bully.' Frederick could see the man take in a breath, but went on. 'I want my visiting rights back! I want to see my daughter.'

And then he realised what the episode was about, as he saw Thorpe's eyes flicker. Emma had always known that the guard watched her, and had ignored it, but the previous week she had been irritated and complained to Frederick. Obviously Thorpe had overheard, and been humiliated, because it was common knowledge that he was besotted with Emma.

'You can't do this, and you know it,' Frederick said, dropping his voice. 'You know I didn't have a knife in my cell. *You put it there.* Now if you just walk away, I won't say a word about this to anyone.'

'*You* won't say a fucking word!' Thorpe hissed. 'That's bloody good of you. I find a weapon in your cell and *you* won't say a word about my disciplining you.' He moved closer to Frederick, his breath foul. 'You want to mind your step with me, Coles. I could see to it that you didn't see your daughter tomorrow, or for a quite a while.'

Beside himself, Frederick raised his voice. 'I *am* seeing my daughter tomorrow.'

'You want a bet?'

'You can't stop her coming,' Frederick went on, his temper suddenly escalating. 'Where's this knife

310

anyway? This one you've supposed to have found in my room?'

There was a flicker of surprise in Thorpe's eyes, and a momentary hesitation. 'That doesn't concern you.'

'I would say it does.'

'Well I wouldn't,' Thorpe continued, aware that he was losing ground in front of the other inmates and keen to put Frederick in his place. 'Get back in your cell.'

'Why don't you make me?'

His toothache raging, and feeling unexpectedly threatened, Thorpe pushed Frederick towards his cell, his voice unpleasant.

'I'll personally explain the situation to your daughter tomorrow. Have a little chat with her.'

Without thinking, Frederick pulled back his fist and was about to take a swing at Thorpe. But luckily, before he could strike, his arm was caught in a tight grip, and he spun round to see Jim Caird.

'What's all this?' Jim asked, his voice composed.

'You see that!' Thorpe hollered. 'That fucking bastard was going to hit me.'

'I didn't see anything,' Jim replied, nudging Frederick out of the way.

'He was about to hit me!'

'No he wasn't,' Jim contradicted him, Frederick moving to the doorway of his cell and watching the clash between the two guards.

Frederick's temper had cooled, and he realised then that if he had struck Stan Thorpe, he would really have been in trouble. Any attack on a guard was viewed seriously by the prison authorities. It could mean a curtailing of privileges and, in serious cases, even put a question mark over the inmate's parole.

Breathing heavily, Frederick watched the younger man square up to Thorpe.

'I think there was a misunderstanding . . .'

'Look, Caird, you little shit!' Thorpe snapped. 'You're in no position to tell me what to do. I've been here longer than anyone. I know this prison inside out, and how it runs. You're still wet behind the ears.'

As ever, Jim wasn't about to back down.

'I know you can't take away a man's visiting rights. Not without seeing the Governor about it first.'

'You know the rule book now, do you?' Thorpe countered, knowing that the younger man was right and blustering in front of the watching inmates. He had run the wing for many years with a mixture of bullying and victimisation, and he didn't like being confronted. 'Coles had a knife in his cell!'

'He's not the type,' Jim replied. 'He hasn't ever been in trouble and he's never been violent. You're just picking him out to bully. I wouldn't put it past you to have planted that knife yourself.'

Thorpe's eyes were bulging. '*You what!* So you're a friend of fucking Mr Coles, are you? Or maybe a friend of his daughter? I've seen you watching her, looking at her—'

'Mr Thorpe . . .'

'*Mr Thorpe*,' he mimicked, his jealousy obvious to everyone. 'I suppose you think you have a chance there? Hey? Fine, good-looking young man like you? Well, I suppose you might have. I mean, no decent man would want the offspring of prison rabble.'

It was too much for Frederick. Lunging for Thorpe, he struck out at the guard, hitting him on the upper lip before Jim could stop him. Reeling back, Thorpe stared at Frederick. A moment passed whilst everyone held their breath, Thorpe's mouth filling with blood. Working with his tongue, he felt around his mouth and then spat out a tooth into his hand.

Enraged, he stared at Frederick, his eyes hostile, dangerous.

'You've had it, Coles. Oh, you've really had it now. You'll be lucky if you ever see your pretty daughter again.'

TWENTY-EIGHT

Standing on the pavement facing Hawksworth's jeweller's, Adam stared at the window, trying to work up enough courage to enter. His foray in London had not been a success, and he was down on his luck and in need of funds. Even prepared to beg his father for help. Why not, when the old man owed him. Adam paused, swallowing and trying to draw up his nerve. He was just going to go in and talk to his father. And if his cousin was there, so what? She could hear what he had to say. She wasn't anyone to worry about. Not with her background. Who was she to judge him? Yet still Adam couldn't move.

Instead he waited, surprised to see a middle-aged woman come out of the jeweller's, arm in arm with his father. Incredulous, Adam stared at the unlikely couple, watching them as they walked down Holland Street and disappeared around the corner. *His father was seeing someone!* It was inconceivable. How could he be walking out with a woman? Galvanised, Adam crossed the room and walked into the jeweller's, a pretty brunette coming out of the back to greet him.

'Good morning,' Emma said, smiling. 'Can I help you?'

So *this* was his cousin grown up, was it? The woman who had been so helpful to his father and usurped his inheritance? This was her.

Curtly, Adam jabbed his finger at one of the clocks.

'You mend clocks?'

She noticed the tone and cooled her own. 'My uncle, Mr Hawksworth, does, yes.'

'Been at it long, has he?'

Curious, Emma studied the thick dark hair and the perfect teeth, a dim memory stirring. She felt she knew the man, but wasn't sure. He seemed to remind her of someone in her childhood, but not someone she could place.

'Mr Hawksworth has run the jeweller's for over twenty-five years.'

'Your uncle, you say?'

'Yes, my uncle,' Emma repeated. 'Is there anything you would like to look at in particular?'

'I remember,' Adam said suddenly, smiling his blistering smile and catching Emma off guard. 'There was a piece about him in the local paper a while back. And it mentioned you – how you were learning the business.'

Cautious, Emma wondered who would remember such a trivial matter in such detail – unless it was somehow important to them personally. Cagey, she returned the smile, her voice even.

'I'm learning, rather slowly, though.'

'Well, it's a man's job, isn't it?' Adam replied. 'It's a shame your uncle doesn't have a son to train up. That's the way of things usually, isn't it? A family business passes from father to son.'

And then Emma remembered the old photograph of the boy. Much younger than this man, but with the same thick hair and spectacular teeth. And the cynical halo. The boy she had seen once, long ago, when she and her father had visited the jeweller's shop.

'You're Adam, aren't you?'

He bowed mockingly. 'I certainly am. And you must be my cousin, Emma.'

'Yes,' she replied, her tone wary. 'I thought you were abroad.'

'I was. Then I was in London.' He was puffing himself up, unable to resist the temptation to brag. 'But I thought I'd come back up north, you know, have a look at where I came from. I saw my father just now. He was with a woman.'

Emma nodded, careful with her words. 'Yes, he was.'

'Who is she?'

'Why don't you ask him?'

'I'm asking you,' Adam replied, somewhat taken aback by Emma's increasing hostility. Bloody hell, he thought, what a cheek. Her father was in prison, and her grandfather a bleeding thug; who was she to put on airs? 'I was just asking a question.'

'But it's my uncle's business.'

'He's my father.'

'So why don't you stay and talk to him when he gets back?' Emma replied, feeling uncomfortable and watching as Adam walked around the shop.

'It looks better, I'll give you that. A lot more modern. I never thought the old man would change the place.' He turned, his tone lighter, attractive. 'That was down to you, though, wasn't it?'

'I helped.'

'I suppose you've got my old room too?' he asked, suddenly moving to the back staircase and running upwards.

Unable to leave the shop, Emma watched him, then realised she couldn't object anyway. It had been his old home; he had every right to look around.

Knowing how much he had discomforted her, Adam moved around upstairs, walking to his old room and pushing open the door. On the walls were his familiar posters, his football boots still hanging from the back of the door. Time shuffled back, took him to the days when he was a boy, his mother walking into the room and putting her arms around him.

You're special, Adam, she had said. *Special. And one day everyone will know how special you are. Listen to me – you have to believe in yourself and get on in life. I'll help you all I can, you know that, but you mustn't let anyone or anything stop you.* He could almost feel her lips against his hair again, her voice low. *My life has been spoiled, because I let your father ruin it. I was so different once, so different . . . I don't want you to change. I don't want that for you.*

Never listen to anyone, never let anyone ruin your dreams. She had been urgent, insistent, her own frustration passed on to her son as a white heat. *You have to live for me, Adam. You have to live for both of us.*

He missed her more than he could bear; could almost feel her in the room with him, her presence next to him. His life had been so certain when his mother had been alive. She'd supported him. Whatever he did, she was behind him. It was all excusable. And he had meant it when he said he would send for her. He would have done, when he was settled. Only he never got settled, and never had enough money . . . He flopped down on the bed, miserable to the point of distraction. This was *his* room. *He* should be here, and his mother should be with him. If she had lived, he would have been a success. His mind wandered, running over her words. She had drummed ambition into him, flattered his meagre talents into genius, telling him that the means justified the ends. That conscience was for other people.

There are people who don't achieve, people who're scared. You have to go out and grab your life, she told him. *Grab it and let nothing stop you.*

Trouble was that even with all her pushing and his lack of scruples, Adam didn't have the abilities to make his name. And that had been the hardest thing to accept. That he was – for all his mother's effusive praise – a nonentity. A man without prospects, who had bummed his way around a good part of the world and was now back where he started. With nothing to show for it. A driver for petty criminals, that was all. Just a bloody driver . . . Angrily Adam got to his feet and stared out of the window. He would get money from his father; he would beg, plead, do anything. And however reluctant he might be, his father would pay up, because he wouldn't want his son around. They had never got on. Besides, he had his little apprentice – and some new woman in his life.

Adam seethed, staring down into the Burnley street. *What if his father was going to get married again?* The thought hadn't occurred to him until that moment and left him limp as a glove. If he did marry again, it would push Adam even further away from the family and the shop. He might not want the shabby jeweller's, but he wanted to know that – if all else failed – he had something to fall back on. *But what if he didn't?* Adam thought desperately. His cousin was downstairs now, well and truly accepted into the business. And there might well be a new wife in the wings. His temper spluttered. How could his father even think of marrying again, when he had ruined his mother's life? How could the bastard dare to be happy? Adam scratched his nails down the window glass. It couldn't happen, he thought. His poor mother had been so unhappy, what right had the old man to try for peace of mind? What peace of mind had he even given her?

For another half an hour Adam stared out of the window. He thought about going downstairs, but decided that he had nothing to say to his cousin, and she would hardly follow him upstairs. Not when she had the shop to look after. In fact, for a while Adam felt himself go back in time, and he became a boy again, in his old room, looking at his football boots and waiting for the bell to tinkle over the door to announce a customer's arrival.

Finally, the bell *did* sound, only it wasn't a customer . . . Jolted back into the present, Adam walked to the top of the narrow stairs to eavesdrop.

'Your son's upstairs,' Emma said quietly.

'Adam!'

'Yes, Uncle, he's been here for a while.'

Adam could hear his father's familiar footfall and tensed. But David didn't ascend the stairs, just stayed below, talking to Emma.

'What does he want?'

'I should go,' Irene said, her tone hurried. 'You have enough to worry about.'

'Stay here,' David replied firmly. 'You've no reason to rush off. Adam didn't say he was coming, so he'll have to take us as he finds us. Frankly, I'm surprised he did come back, after the argument we had last time.'

'He's in his room.'

'It's *your* room,' David corrected his niece. 'I'll go and talk to him.'

A few moments later, Adam watched as his father stood in the doorway of the bedroom. He had to admit that David looked better than he had the last time they met. He had put on a little weight and seemed more relaxed. Unaccountably annoyed by his father's show of health, Adam folded his arms and leaned back against the window ledge.

'London didn't work out,' he said simply, shrugging. 'I need some money, Father.'

'And I'm supposed to give it to you, just like that?'

'You look like you're doing all right. And you look well, Father. Have you got something to tell me?'

'Like what?'

'I saw you,' Adam went on, his tone less certain in the face of David Hawksworth's formidable presence. 'With some woman.'

'My fiancée.'

'Fiancée,' Adam scoffed. 'Aren't you a little old for that?'

'What d'you want?' David replied, aware that Emma and Irene could probably hear much of the conversation.

'I've told you, money. I've no cash, so I can't get out of your hair.'

There was a momentary pause before David answered. 'You don't have to go, Adam. You could stay here, work here, if you wanted.'

Surprised, Adam took in a breath. This was the last thing he had expected – the extended olive branch. So the old man *had* changed, he thought, sensing vulnerability. A weakness he could exploit.

'You want me to stay? As what?'

'My son, what else?'

'But you've got an heir,' Adam said, his tone sly. 'My cousin, she's training in the business.'

'That wouldn't mean that you couldn't,' David hurried on. 'It's a family business. You could have trained here long ago; I wanted you to.'

'You never did!'

'Oh, I did,' David replied wearily. 'It's just that your mother filled your head with such wild ambitions.'

'She wanted the best for me!' Adam hollered back, ever protective. 'She knew I had talent.'

'She spoiled you. She did what she thought was right, but her advice didn't help you in the long run.'

Sneering, Adam faced up to his father. 'My poor mother, how easy it is for you to blacken her name now she's dead. You can say anything about her now, can't you? Now she can't defend herself.' He moved towards his father, his voice rising. 'Have you told your fiancée about my mother? What a bad influence she was on me? Of course, I suppose your new wife will be a perfect match. Everything my mother wasn't.'

'Adam, why do we have to fight every time we see each other?'

'You make us fight!' he hurled back. 'You're talking about my mother like she's to blame for my life. I'm just struggling at the moment, that's all. I have some irons in the fire and soon I'll be back on top. You can tell your fiancée that. Your son is no down-and-out, oh no. Adam Hawksworth is going to prove himself.'

Wearily, David sighed. 'Why all the bluster? Why can't we just sit down and talk? Work something out?

I don't care if you're a success or struggling, Adam, you're family. And perhaps it would be best for you to come home for a while.'

'So you can keep your eye on me?' he countered. 'Or so you can wear me down, like you did my mother?'

'What I did—'

'Was wrong!' Adam snapped. 'My mother was full of life and you bled it out of her. And now you look at me and want me to settle down. Why don't I just cut my wrists, Father? That would really slow me down.'

'Stop getting so overexcited,' David warned him. 'I can never talk sensibly to you.'

'That's the point, you never talked anything *but* sensibly to me. My life here was sensible, you made my mother so sensible she died of being sensible. You crushed all the life out of her.' He stopped, suddenly remembering why he had come. Jesus, he had to keep himself focused. But somehow, seeing his father so happy with his fiancée and his little shopkeeper niece was too much. *He* wasn't happy, Adam thought self-pityingly, he wasn't happy at all. 'I need some money, Father. Just a loan.'

'I don't have much—'

'You have plenty!' Adam retorted. 'You must have, to do this place up and get married again. That costs money.'

'Your cousin only gets a small wage, and Mrs Knight will be living here as my wife, not earning a salary,' David explained calmly. 'We don't make much money, but I can give you something to tide you over. What are you going to do? Where are you going?'

'Like I say, I have options,' Adam replied truculently.

'Why not stay here, just for a while?'

'I don't want to stay here, in this bloody town! What is there here for me!' Adam snapped, his grand illusions getting in the way of his limited common sense. 'I'm going to make it big. You'll see, my name will be known, you mark my words. I have talent, and talent isn't always recognised at first.' He paused, flustered. 'What's it to you, anyway? Since when did you care? You were quick enough to throw me out before.'

'You chose to go!'

'You threw me out!' Adam snapped, flopping down on the bed, his expression sullen. 'I need somewhere to sleep for tonight.'

'You can sleep in the parlour, on the sofa.'

'Not in my old room?'

'No, Adam, not in here. But if you want to come home, we could make other arrangements.'

'You never give up, do you?' Adam countered, looking at his father slyly. 'Got a guilty conscience, Dad? Want to make everything all right, have us all as one big family? No chance, I'm not staying here. No one with a grain of sense would stay here. Look at the place! It's a dump. You might have done it up a bit, but it's a crummy shop in a crummy northern town, with nothing doing. And you're a crummy northern man, with no ambitions left. That's why you want me home,' he said cruelly. 'So I can be a loser like you. So you can look at me and see yourself and not want to scream. Because you're going nowhere, are you? You're always going to be stuck here, with your creepy shop and all the things you want to hide, pretend never happened. Like your revolting stepfather. Oh, and your half-brother – how *is* Frederick, by the way?'

Stepping forwards, David was about to strike out, but stopped himself. Instead he walked to the door, then paused.

'I'll put some money in an envelope for you, Adam, and leave it on the counter in the shop. Take it and go. I don't want you in this house a moment longer than you have to be.'

'No worry,' Adam called after his father. 'I wouldn't stay here if you begged me.'

Sitting down on the bed, Adam breathed in to steady himself. It was always the same – an argument. Only this time he had gone too far and he knew it. He shouldn't have brought up his father's past. What was the point? But somehow David Hawksworth inflamed him to such a point that he always said terrible things. Perhaps secretly he wanted him to strike out, or explain the past. But his father would never do that . . . Slowly Adam got to his feet and walked downstairs. Pausing at the bottom of the steps to compose himself, he took in a breath. Much as he loathed the shop, it was his home, and somehow – even with all its depressing memories – he was reluctant to leave. The place had never meant happiness to him, only security.

The one thing Adam Hawksworth had never experienced in the outside world.

'Is this the envelope from Father?' he asked Emma, picking it up and weighing it in his hand. 'Feels pretty heavy . . .'

Without replying, Emma stared at him. Irene had left with David, trying to console him as they hurried down Holland Street.

'Are you happy here?'

Emma ignored the question. 'Why did you have to say all those things?'

'They were true.'

'So what? It didn't make them any less cruel.'

'Oh,' he said, feigning terror. 'Don't be cross with me! I couldn't bear it!'

'And why did you have to mention my father?'

'Why not? He *is* your father, after all,' Adam replied, changing the subject quickly. 'How much is in the envelope?'

'More than I'd have given you.'

'How much would you have given me?'

'Nothing.'

Adam raised his eyebrows. 'I can see that you've got a lot of your grandfather in you. Same kind of temper.'

'I don't know why you're such a snob,' Emma replied, her tone freezing.

'You don't have to be a snob to want to steer clear of Ernie Coles.'

Slowly, Emma looked her cousin up and down. 'You're hardly a prince yourself.'

'But I'm not related to Ernie Coles. I don't have that to live down to.'

'You don't need it, you're repellent enough.'

Flinching, Adam pushed the envelope into his pocket.

'You've got a nasty mouth on you, Emma. A very nasty mouth. You should be careful that it doesn't get you into trouble.'

Walking to the door, Emma opened it and stood back to let her cousin pass. Hesitating for an instant, Adam paused on the doorstep.

'You can have the shop, with my blessing. You can rot here, because that's what happens in this place, people wither away.' He looked around, shivering. 'You won't see me again.'

'Oh, you'll be back,' Emma said dismissively. 'You're not man enough to survive on your own.'

TWENTY-NINE

Reg Spencer was confused. He decided that he might have to intervene with the Governor after all – although a part of him resented having to take a stand. He had loathed Stan Thorpe for years and known him to be a bully, but he hated being put in a situation where he had to give evidence against one of his own. There was an unspoken creed amongst the guards that they always backed each other up. It was a way of sending a message to any troublesome inmates – or any that might be thinking of becoming troublesome – that they would be outnumbered, or at least outsmarted. But this was different.

Reg knew that Frederick Coles would never have had a knife in his cell. He wasn't the type, and was too keen to keep his nose clean to risk some show of bravado. Besides, he wasn't violent and never had been. He hadn't made friends with any of the other inmates either, had just kept himself to himself. Always polite, but reserved. He was, as most of the guards knew, a very unlikely kind of prisoner. At first they had expected him to change and show his true colours, but as time went on it became more and more obvious that Frederick Coles *was* the placid, good-mannered man he appeared, and always had been. He was courteous, gentlemanly, and the person least likely to cause trouble. A peacemaker, at times. But one who knew his limitations. Frederick Coles had learned that in order to survive prison you kept to your own type, or you kept to yourself.

That he would have a knife in his cell was ridiculous, Reg decided. Why would he risk being found with one when it meant automatic loss of visiting rights? Which was the one thing Frederick Coles would *never* want to lose – after all, it was his daughter who had kept him going. From the first he had lived for her visits, and then, courageously, he had banned her completely from visiting him when she married.

Reg knew only too well what that had cost Frederick Coles. The slowing-down of his optimism, his hopes for freedom. He even suspected that, dreadful as his son-in-law's death had been, some part of Frederick welcomed the return of his daughter. But the lifting of his spirits had not lasted long, and Reg could see in Frederick what he had seen many times before in other inmates – a hopeless acceptance. His illness hadn't helped either. Frederick wasn't a weakling, but the jail conditions had aged him and he had even confessed to Reg that the idea of the years stretching ahead of him was wearing on his nerves. Nothing more – Frederick wasn't the kind of man to moan – but it was enough to tip Reg off. And make him watch Frederick Coles just that little bit more.

So why would a man who was subdued and accepting of his fate suddenly have a knife in his cell? It didn't ring true. What *did* ring true was Stan Thorpe's spite. He had been looking for another victim to bully for a while, and his fascination with Emma Coles had unfortunately focused his attention on her father. But there was more to it – the smitten Thorpe had noticed Jim Caird's recent interest . . . Breathing out, Reg stared down the corridor, still thinking. Naturally a young woman like Emma Coles could never be interested in a pig like Thorpe, but he was blind to the fact. Actually fancied his chances for a while – until he had noticed Jim Caird exchanging a smile with Emma Coles. Then a few words, here and there . . . And soon a festering bitterness – as painful and abscessed as his teeth – had grown inside Stan Thorpe. And had culminated with him planting a knife in Frederick's cell.

It was typical of Thorpe, Reg mused, his way of punishing the man. And a way of driving a wedge between him and his daughter. Because, by Christ, if Thorpe wasn't going to have a chance with Emma, no one would. And she would be punished for her lack of interest too, being cut off from her father. But Thorpe had underestimated Frederick, and picked the wrong man to victimise. Unfortunately Frederick's attack – deserved as it was – would only serve to heighten Thorpe's hatred of him. And of Jim Caird. The young interloper, the quiet strong man who was everything Stan Thorpe could never be.

Christ, Reg thought irritably, what a bloody mess.

The atmosphere on the wing was full of static, and Thorpe had lost two teeth, Frederick keeping to his cell. In fact it was the perfect simmering mood to invite trouble. A hothouse cauldron in which every word or movement could be misinterpreted. Reg knew the atmosphere only too well, and knew what it could lead to. He thought suddenly of Ricky Holmes and that terrible Sunday . . . Which was why he knew he should go and see the Governor. To explain what had happened and stop Thorpe. He knew the whole matter would go on Thorpe's record and count against him, but if Reg left it, circumstances would accelerate. Thorpe was vicious and had to be stopped. The only trouble was that it would mean Reg Spencer coming down on the side of a prisoner, not a guard. It would mean that he would cross a line no one chose to cross. Ally himself to an inmate, rather than a colleague.

And, Reg asked himself, was Frederick Coles worth it?

Hands behind his back, he walked on. Perhaps he should sleep on it, see if everything settled down of its own accord. After all, he was due for his retirement soon; it would be a sad day if he left with a shadow hanging over him. He had made a lot of friends at the prison, men he liked. And they liked him – but if he went to the Governor and took an inmate's side, would they still like him? Was it worth losing comrades for? Was it worth losing your good name? Stan Thorpe was a bastard, that was true, but what would it mean to Reg if he exposed him? Frederick

Coles had got by pretty well so far, and Jim Caird had his eye on the situation. That much was certain. Was it worth Reg Spencer nailing his colours to the mast now?

Well, *was it*?

Smiling, Emma thought about Jim Caird – and about what Frederick had written. He had teased her and mentioned that Jim asked about her. *He's smitten, I think, and you could do a lot worse. Jim Caird is a very steady, honest and tough young man. Nothing showy about him, but a real strength there. A tough man . . .* Then he had gone on to ask for her to forgive his matchmaking. But Emma hadn't minded. In fact the idea of Jim Caird was actually making real inroads into her psyche. She wasn't interested in him as a boyfriend; still too raw from Leonard's death and the loss of their baby – not that anyone knew about that, apart from the Hemmingses and Bessie. There were some things too deep to share, Emma had decided, and losing her baby was still unbearable. But she *did* long for male company, her uncle being caught up with Irene, making plans for their wedding. She was delighted to see him so happy, but missed the closeness they had developed and knew that when Irene came to live at the shop, she would have the monopoly of David's affection.

Which was just as it should be . . . Deep in thought, Emma walked out of the jeweller's and straight into one of Jack Rimmer's buckets. With a resounding clanking noise she stepped back, Florence coming out of the tobacconist's and rounding on Jack.

'I told you! I said one day you'd knock someone out!'

'I'm not knocked out,' Emma said, rubbing her forehead, Jack bobbing up and down in front of her.

'Are yer all right? Are yer? Are yer?'

'I'm fine.'

'She's stunned!' Florence went on, determined to make a drama out of it. 'You can see it in the girl's eyes, she's stunned.'

'I'm not stunned . . .'

'And with her being a bridesmaid soon.'

Mystified, Emma turned to her neighbour. 'Who's going to be a bridesmaid?'

'You are,' Florence replied, 'what with your uncle getting married. He'll need a bridesmaid.'

'It's not going to be a big do,' Emma explained, taking the damp cloth offered by Jack and putting it on her forehead. 'Just family.'

'Speaking of which, I saw Adam the other day. Proper put out he looked, as well he might be,' Florence went on, hoping that Emma would fill her in. When she didn't, Florence continued. 'I bet it didn't go down well about his having a new stepmother . . .'

'Does it hurt?' Jack asked Emma urgently. 'Well, does it?'

'No, it's nothing.'

'. . . I mean, Mrs Knight hooking your uncle,' Florence carried on, staring, fascinated, at the bruise beginning to form on Emma's forehead. 'That were quite a lucky chance, her being a widow and your uncle being a widower. And them getting together. I mean, as you know, Emma, your uncle and I don't see eye to eye sometimes, but I wish him well.' She paused, before adding, 'At his time of life a person deserves some luck. I just hope Mrs Knight knows what she's letting herself in for.'

'A good marriage,' Emma said succinctly, thanking Jack and walking off, Florence running after her.

'Of course, you must feel a little put out, love. Who wouldn't? You having been the lady of the house, so to speak, for so long. And now another woman coming in and taking over.' She paused for effect. 'Anyone can see that Mrs Knight – well, soon it will be Mrs Hawksworth, won't it? – that she's a nice person. But people change, when they get their feet under the table. A guest isn't a wife, is she?'

'No, Florence, a guest is not a wife,' Emma agreed.

'You're always welcome over at our place, love. You know that, always have been. And if things get difficult – not saying that they will, but they do say it's always trouble when there are two women in a house. Anyway, you're always welcome to come and have a little moan. Get things off your chest, if you like. I'm a good listener, always have been. Just ask Harold. You ask my Harold and he'll tell you what a good listener I am.'

Amused, Emma paused at the corner of Holland Street. 'Thanks for that, Florence,' she said pleasantly. 'I'll bear it in mind.'

'You do, you do, love,' she replied, 'and don't worry, things will work out fine. You don't want to listen to other people, going on and putting thoughts in your head. You'll be fine.'

Laughing inwardly, Emma walked on towards the tram stop. She was still smiling as she nodded to a couple she knew and then caught her reflection in the window of a shop on the other side of the road. For quite a while Emma hadn't been interested in how she looked. She had taken care of herself automatically, had her hair trimmed in the fashionable style, and wore modern clothes. Clothes not dissimilar to the ones she had bought when she was married to Leonard, although cheaper, coming from the market or the shops off St James's Street. But she wasn't really interested in how attractive she appeared, and hadn't been since the death of Leonard.

So it was with some surprise that she found herself studying her reflection and looking herself up and down critically. What was she thinking? she wondered suddenly, turning away from her reflection, embarrassed. No one was looking. Why should they? She was a widow, no catch for anyone. No catch at all. Better to put those thoughts out of her mind once and for all, she told herself firmly. She had had a chance at happiness and been hurt. And hurt someone she cared for. What right had she to expect another chance? And besides, who would be interested?

Oh, but there *was* someone interested, Emma

remembered – Jim Caird. And she must be interested in him, otherwise why would she be looking at her reflection in shop windows? Flushing, she turned away. She was being stupid, she told herself briskly, getting on the tram and paying her fare. That was what it was, stupid. Her father was just teasing her, playing a game, talking about Jim Caird like that. She would have to tell him off, she decided, tell her father to stop being mischievous. In fact, that would be the first thing she would tell him when she arrived at the prison. But she still thought about the dark grey of Jim Caird's eyes and the way he had smiled at her. And the way her stomach had fluttered . . .

Looking out of the window, Emma watched the Burnley streets, seeing the headline: TREASURE OF DEAD KING FOUND IN EGYPT. Jim had been telling her about that only the other day, when he had bumped into her on the way out. He had told her about how Howard Carter and the Earl of Carnarvon had found this burial place, filled with gold artefacts and a gilded coffin . . . Still thinking of Tutankhamun, Emma watched as the tram skirted Towneley Park and headed out of town. Jim's voice had been deep as he told her about the tomb, deep and even. The kind of voice a woman believed in, the kind that sucked her in. Before long Emma hadn't been sure what he was talking about, only that she didn't want him to stop.

Oh God, she thought, flushing again and then turning her mind to other matters. She was relieved beyond measure that Irene knew about her prison visits. To have someone to confide in, to trust, was priceless. To know that any delays in her journeys would be covered, accounted for by Irene, made the trips less tortuous, the stress lessened. Perhaps in time she might even be able to tell her uncle about them. But then again, would it drive a wedge between them? Dismissing the thought, Emma got off the tram and took the bus out towards the Moors Prison. She was setting off in daylight, but soon the November night would draw in, and she dreaded that. Hated the winter darkness as the old buses wound their way towards the grim jail. Just as she hated waiting for the bus to return to collect the prison visitors. But it was worth it, she reassured herself, worth it just to see her father.

Finally reaching her destination, Emma got off the bus and glanced round. It was a perfect day, skylarks coming over from the Moors, late butterflies making darts into a picture-book sky. Even the sun was still warm, with that last poignant stab at late autumn before the chill came in hard.

Entering the anteroom off the visitors' room, Emma paused, then smiled shyly as she saw Jim Caird walking over to her.

'Hello,' he said, his delight in seeing her obvious. 'How are you today?'

She nodded. 'Fine, thank you.'

But before he showed her into the next room, Jim hesitated, uneasy. 'I've got some bad news for you.'

'Not my father! Is he all right?'

'He's fine, honestly,' Jim replied, hurrying to

reassure her. 'It's just that the visit has been cancelled.'

Stunned, Emma stared at him. '*Cancelled!*'

'We couldn't contact you in time to stop you coming over. We did send a postcard, but I don't suppose you got it.'

'No,' Emma said sadly, 'I didn't. Why's the visit cancelled?'

'There was an incident.'

'What kind of incident?' Emma said, her senses alerted. 'What happened?'

'I can't discuss it.'

'I think you can,' Emma replied heatedly, then lowered her tone. 'I've not come all this way to see my father just to be turned away at the door. I should know *why* I can't visit him. Is he ill?'

Hesitating, Jim looked round, then ushered Emma towards a passageway off the anteroom. As he closed the doors after him, he said, 'Don't tell anyone I've talked to you about this, all right?'

'I promise, I won't tell anyone.'

'A weapon was found in your father's cell.'

'No, that can't be right,' Emma replied, her tone assured. 'Not my father. He's never violent, why would he have a weapon? What kind of weapon?'

'A knife.'

'I don't believe it,' Emma said firmly. 'My father hated knives. When I was a child, he used to shout at me if I even touched them in the kitchen. He would never have a knife.' She shook her head impatiently. 'Oh, come on, Jim, you haven't known my father for long, but you must realise how stupid this is!'

He did realise and nodded. 'I don't believe it either.'

'After all, why would he *need* a knife?'

'Some inmates use them for protection.'

'Are you saying that my father needs protection?'

'No, that's the point, your father gets on very well here. He keeps himself to himself and he hasn't made enemies,' Jim went on. 'I don't believe for one moment that he would risk having a weapon, knowing that if it was found, his visiting rights would be stopped.'

'Never,' Emma said, her face pale. 'Someone must have put that knife in his cell.'

'I agree,' Jim said, after a moment's pause.

'So why can't I see my father?'

'The authorities *think* a knife was found in his cell. We might not believe it, but they do, and they have to stick to the rules,' Jim explained, his tone apologetic. 'I'm really sorry you had to come all this way just to hear this.'

She shrugged hopelessly. 'What can I do about it?'

'Nothing.'

'*Nothing?*'

'No, your father's visiting rights have been stopped for a month.'

'God . . .'

'It's better that he doesn't contest the decision, not without having evidence that someone planted the knife. Otherwise the punishment could be extended.'

'*For something he didn't do?*' Emma replied, folding her arms as she leaned against the wall. 'My

339

father's innocent. Of this, and of the theft at Oldfield Mill. I mean, I know every prisoner says that, but he really *is* innocent. And now this – something else he didn't do. I wonder he doesn't lose his mind in here.' Her tone was bitter, unlike her. 'And he's not like he was. You didn't know him when he first came here. He was very smart, very dashing, not what you'd expect. Not like he is now.'

'I know it upsets him sometimes when he sees other prisoners leave, finish their sentences.'

Her heart shifted. 'Does he talk to you about it?'

'A little,' Jim admitted. 'Sometimes it gets to him, the years he still has to serve. They seem to get longer, not shorter. I believe he misses one inmate quite a lot. They weren't close, but they used to play cards sometimes.'

'And he's gone?'

'Apparently he was released a while ago,' Jim told her. 'But don't worry too much, I keep an eye on your father. I won't let him get too low.'

Grateful, she held his gaze, liking him more as every minute passed. 'Thanks for that – and for telling me what went on. I know you're not supposed to.'

'I'm just sorry you had to come all this way. I like your father.'

'He likes you too. He wrote and told me all about you,' she said, smiling as she remembered Frederick's teasing in his letters. 'Will you tell him that I came? Tell him I'll write to him and come as soon as I can. Will you tell him that?'

Jim nodded. 'Course I will.'

'Will you keep talking to him?'

'Yeah, of course. Some of the inmates you can't relate to, but your father's different. He's told me all about you.'

She grimaced, but felt excited that they had been talking about her. And that Jim Caird had obviously taken an interest.

'God, I hope he hasn't told you everything.'

'No, not everything. But he did tell me about your husband's death. I'm so sorry, that must have been terrible for you.'

Caught off guard by the unexpected show of sympathy, Emma nodded. She had struggled to come to terms with Leonard's death, but she was still haunted by the argument and by her actions. And many times she woke, startled, thinking she was losing her baby again.

'I lost my elder brother in the war,' Jim continued. 'I know it's not the same, but it still hurts. I'm close to another brother, Tommy, really close.' He paused. 'But I still miss the one that died.'

For a moment Emma wanted to confide. But she daren't. Couldn't lie and say, *I miss the husband I loved so much.* Because she *hadn't* loved Leonard, and the fact tormented her. She missed his kindness, the security he had given her. The brief, sweet time she had had with him. They had been good friends, laughing, happy with each other, content. But she had not been in love. She had felt guilt for his passing, and a massive regret for having lied to him and inadvertently caused his death. But she didn't miss him as a wife should miss her husband. As she should mourn for a lover. No, she missed him and grieved for him as a beloved friend. And in that moment, Emma realised something she had not known before, *that she would never have grown to love Leonard Hemmings*. She would have grown old without longing for him. Without feeling incomplete apart. Without an all-consuming hunger for him.

And somehow, knowing that made his loss even worse.

'Perhaps, some time, you might like to talk about it,' Jim said, breaking into the silence.

'You run out of words, don't you?'

'I know,' he agreed. 'I felt that about my brother. I kept thinking about all the things I should have said to him. Things he should have known. But if I had said them, would they have come out right? Sometimes, when you most want to, you can't find the words. Or they sound strained.'

'Yes,' she agreed, surprised by his sensitivity. 'Or insincere.'

'But I found that it helped me to talk about my brother.'

Slowly she raised her head, her eyes meeting his. 'I can't talk about him. I can't talk about my husband.'

'I'm sorry, I didn't mean to upset you.'

'You didn't,' she said hurriedly. 'I can't talk about Leonard, but I *want* to talk. I'd like to talk to you. About my father, anything . . .' She paused, feeling foolish because she had opened up so quickly and, in doing so, shown her obvious liking for this man. For a woman who had been guarded for so long, Emma was shaken by her openness. 'Sorry, I'm not making sense.'

'You're upset,' Jim replied, walking her to the exit. 'Go home and get some rest.' He paused, looking at her, feeling a real pull towards her. 'Will you be all right?'

'Fine.'

'Could I call and see you on Saturday afternoon?' he said suddenly, taking his chance. He could see Emma flush, but she didn't reject him. 'We could go for a walk, something like that?'

'Yes, I'd like that,' she agreed, her voice soft. 'Tell my father I came to see him, will you? Tell him I love him.'

'I'll tell him,' Jim replied, closing the door and locking it after her. And then pausing, his heart beating very quickly, his whole being concentrated on the Saturday to come.

THIRTY

Almost as though it was something they had been doing for years, Jim took Emma's hand. She felt a jolt of affection for him, stealing a glance at him as they walked along. They were comfortable together, but there was something more. An attraction that was unnerving. Jim had felt it from the first, and touching Emma – even holding her hand – had intensified his desire for her. As for Emma, she was suddenly struggling with an emotion so intense it was threatening to overwhelm her. It was similar to what she had felt for Ricky. But much deeper, down to her gut. The feeling made her mouth dry, her heart speed up; it made her chatter, unlike herself.

'I was thinking,' Jim said, sliding his hand into the crook of her arm, drawing Emma closer to him. But the movement was so natural, she hadn't noticed it until she realised she could feel his warmth. 'Why don't we go for a day out? I could take you to the seaside?'

'Yes, I'd like that,' she replied. 'I've not been to the seaside for a long time. Well, since I was a child. Dad took me, after my mother died. He bought me a kite, so we could fly it on the beach. Only there was no wind and it didn't take off right . . .' She paused, grabbed at a breath, hardly recognising herself. 'I mean, we wouldn't have to get a kite. I don't really like kites.'

She stopped, mortified, Jim looking at her with a smile on his face.

'Are you nervous?'

'Yes.'

'Me too,' he said, smiling more broadly. 'I've been looking forward to taking you out for so long, Emma. Thinking about it over and over again, and wondering if you'd accept. Then wondering where to take you. Then wondering if you'd like me.'

'I *do* like you,' she said, flushing.

'Well, I like you a lot,' he admitted, shaking his head and speaking from the heart. 'I mean, frankly I feel a bit light-headed.'

'Me too,' she said, awestruck.

'Dry mouth?'

She nodded. 'Yes.'

'How's your stomach?'

'Churning.'

'Mine too,' he said, then laughed. 'We're either very ill, or falling for each other.'

'Could that happen so quick?' Emma asked, her voice hardly more than a whisper, she was so excited.

'It can happen in a minute. One of my brothers fell in love like that.' He clicked his fingers, then, without thinking, he kissed her.

Taken aback, Emma froze, then felt a warmth

from her head to her feet, a deep longing that fired up inside her. As Jim's arms tightened around her, she clung to him, his lips finally moving to her ear and whispering, 'He was right.'

'Who was?'

'My brother.' He kissed her gently again. 'It's happened to me – I'm in love. How about you?'

'Oh, yes,' she said eagerly. 'Oh, yes!'

In the months that followed, Jim Caird visited Emma many times. He told her how Frederick was doing, and passed on letters and snippets of gossip. But he never mentioned anything about Stan Thorpe. Instead he talked about his own family, and his multitude of brothers, about his parents and how he had been brought up. And he kissed her. He kissed her a lot. Then he made jokes about being under educated and needing night school, and Emma relaxed with him and finally told him about her past. About the time after her father was jailed. After another few dates, she told him about Ernie Coles – although Jim already knew about her grandfather. In fact, he knew more about him than she did.

'Ernie Coles,' he said, smiling as he threw some bread into the park lake, the ducks swarming to catch it. 'My God, my father knows him.'

'He knows him?'

'Yeah, Tommy does too. He's the brother I'm closest to.' He raised his eyebrows. 'My parents weren't too pleased about it, I can tell you. Warned Tom off good and proper.'

'Did my grandfather want your brother to do something?' Emma asked uneasily.

'Run a couple of errands for him. Pass on some messages.' Jim lit a cigarette and stared ahead, taking Emma's hand. 'But that's the way it always starts – with something simple. Then once you're hooked, it gets easier and easier to do more and more. We come from a rough neighbourhood, Emma; I was brought up seeing how easy it was for lads to slip into thieving.' There was a long, uncomfortable pause before Jim spoke again. 'You know that I believe your father's innocent?'

'I know.'

He nodded. 'He's not the type to steal.'

Emma thought for a long moment before speaking again. 'He knows who the real thief is.'

'*He does?*' Jim asked, turning to her. 'Who?'

'He won't tell me. I tricked his solicitor into confiding in me.'

'But why wouldn't your father expose the person?'

'I don't know. I really don't know.'

Sighing, she changed the subject. It wasn't fair for her to go on about her father all the time, which she did with Jim because he was such a willing listener. Besides, she knew that Jim wasn't supposed to be discussing her father's case. It wasn't illegal, just something prison staff and visitors avoided, to circumvent any divided loyalties. But then again, Emma thought with pleasure, Jim was becoming much more than a prison guard . . . If she could have stepped out of herself, she would have been amazed at the change in her. Love had transformed a pretty girl into a beauty. Emma glowed, and because she loved Jim as much as he loved her, she felt a different kind of security.

Smitten, Jim was proud of his girlfriend, and if he wasn't with Emma, he was talking about her. In fact, after he had been introduced to Bessie, the three of them had been spotted in town, the rumour mill grinding into action. Not wanting to risk bringing Jim to the jeweller's shop – which would open up questions about how she had met him – Emma kept him away from Holland Street. But it was no good; the news was out. Much as Emma tried to shrug off Florence Palmer's teasing about her having a new man in her life, she hated the idea that it was public knowledge – feeling that it was somehow disrespectful to Leonard. Surely she should grieve for him longer?

But Emma knew that the crying she had done for his loss and the loss of the baby had been so intense she would never forget either of them. She would think of them both for the rest of her life, but she couldn't survive without love. Couldn't function as a person without affection. And slowly she began to realise that it wouldn't lessen her grief for the ones she had lost if she allowed herself to love again. After all, wasn't that the very thought that had kept her alive? The will to survive, to be loved again?

'You're miles away,' Jim said suddenly.

Jumping, Emma thought back to what he had been

saying earlier about her grandfather, and turned the conversation back to Ernie Coles.

'What does he look like?'

'Who?' Jim asked, inhaling on his cigarette.

'My grandfather.'

'You've never seen him?'

'No,' she admitted, 'never.'

'He's about six foot three, bullet head, very big build, short hair, almost bristly, grey now. He has an aura about him, someone you wouldn't push around. And it's not just his size, either, it's the look in his eyes. Something makes you back off – makes *everyone* back off.'

'He sounds frightening.'

'He is,' Jim replied, grinding out the stub of his cigarette with the heel of his boot. 'That's why Ernie Coles is called on to stop trouble, or sort people out.'

'But he must be getting on now. He must be more than sixty.'

'Doesn't look it, because he's kept himself fit. He works out at the gym over the Black Knight pub in Hanky Park, with the boxers. That's where he learned the tricks of the trade, how not to get hurt and how to knock a man out with a punch.'

Despite herself, Emma was fascinated. 'But surely he can't still fight?'

'He could, if he needed to. But Ernie Coles doesn't need to fight much – his reputation does all the fighting for him. And no one's had the nerve to challenge him, either. None of that older man being usurped by someone younger. No one's taken on Ernie Coles and won.'

'People talk about him.' Emma grimaced. 'He's famous round here.'

'That's his power; he has the charm of violence.'

'*The charm of violence*,' Emma repeated. 'My father has the charm of a good man . . .'

'And your grandfather has the charm of a villain,' Jim finished for her. 'I don't blame your father for not wanting to have anything to do with Ernie Coles, and I admire him for keeping you away. But Ernie is still your grandfather, and you did ask me about him.'

'I did, yes,' Emma agreed, changing the subject. 'My uncle and Irene are getting married next week. The upstairs of the shop is an unbelievable mess. Boxes everywhere, clothes. And Irene can't work out what to wear, and who to invite. Honestly, it's a madhouse at the moment.' Emma paused, trying to sound casual. 'I wondered . . . Oh, it's nothing.'

Jim glanced over to her enquiringly. 'Now that's not like you. You always speak out. What about the wedding?'

'Well, it's going to be a very small affair, hardly anyone there actually, just them, a few friends and me . . . and I thought I might feel a bit lonely on my own.'

'And me being your boyfriend . . .'

'You are, aren't you?' Emma said happily, laying her head on his shoulder. 'Will you come to the wedding?'

'Of course I'll come.'

'There's one problem, though,' Emma went on. 'My uncle doesn't know I visit the prison, so I can't introduce you as a prison guard or he would wonder how I knew you. But I want you to be there.'

'It's not a problem,' Jim said simply. 'I can say that I work at the prison, but that I was introduced to you through Ricky Holmes. I know Bessie now; it would work.'

Relieved, Emma smiled. 'That's perfect!' She looked at him, relieved. 'You always sort things out, don't you?'

'I have that kind of boring mind.'

'You're not boring, Jim.'

His heart quickened. 'Knowing you isn't exactly boring either,' he replied, kissing her hurriedly and then taking her hand. Together they stared out on to the park lake.

'I wish I didn't have to ask you to lie,' Emma said suddenly.

'It's a very small lie. Hardly a lie at all.'

'There are no harmless lies. There are no small lies either,' Emma said, her voice hardly audible. 'One day I want to live without lying about anything. Live openly, everyone knowing who I am, where I live, what I do. I want to be able to tell the world: *This is me, all of me. Take me or leave me, but this is my life and my history.*'

Touched, Jim stared at her.

'Rough times in the past, hey? Want to tell me about them? We all have them, but they're always harder when you can't share them,' he prompted her carefully. 'What happened?'

'I lied to my husband,' Emma confessed, the words out of her mouth before she had time to check them. But she had to say them; this time she had to be open. If she and Jim were going to have a future, he had to know everything about her. 'I let him – and his family – believe that both my parents were dead because I knew they wouldn't want me if they knew about my situation. So I disowned my father,' she said, her voice cracking. 'My father wanted me to, he urged me to. Told me to take the opportunity for a good life. He said that we could write to each other and that it would help him if he knew I was happy. But you know something?' Emma asked, her tone bitter. 'I wasn't happy. I didn't love Leonard Hemmings. In fact, God forgive me, I used him to get away from my uncle. I used him to escape. I lied to everyone, including myself. I did try to be a good wife; Leonard never knew I wasn't in love with him, but that didn't matter. *I knew.* And then . . .' Her voice plunged. 'I was pregnant and he found out about my father. That he was still alive and in jail. That I was visiting my so-called dead father behind his back. Leonard had a heart attack. The shock killed him, and his parents overheard the argument. Then I lost the baby.'

Jim's grip tightened on her hand.

'I wanted that baby so much. You'll never know how much. But I couldn't hold on to it. I lost the baby, I couldn't keep it alive. I wasn't good enough, or didn't try hard enough. Maybe it was my

352

punishment . . .' She was crying silently, Jim's throat tightening with pity. 'I came back to Burnley, to my uncle's shop. I ended up exactly where I started.'

'No,' he said gently, 'not where you started, sweetheart. Because you survived.' He slid his arm around her and pulled her to him, kissing the top of her head.

'Only Leonard's parents and Bessie know about the baby. And you now.'

Emma sighed raggedly, amazed that she had confided in him, and suddenly aware that from that moment he would see her differently. He might now dislike her and step back. Fall out of love with her. Leave her. Her heartbeat slowed, and she was unable to speak another word. She had laid out the bald facts of her life, put them down on the table for him to read like a newspaper. Whatever Jim chose to do from that moment on would mean that she still had him – or that she was alone again.

'Sorry, I shouldn't have told you all that.'

Jim didn't reply; he was just staring ahead.

'I'm not a very nice person, you see. I'm not very brave, or very honest.'

'You didn't love him?'

'What?'

Jim looked intently into her face. 'You said that you didn't love your husband?'

'No, I cared for Leonard, but I wasn't in love with him. Why? Does that matter?'

'It matters to me,' he said evenly. 'You see, since I've known you, I thought I was up against the ghost of your dead husband. I thought that you had loved him and lost him, and believed that you would never love anyone like you loved him. I thought he would always be in your heart, that there would never be room for someone else. *For me . . .*' He paused, pulling her to him tightly. 'You lied because you had to, Emma. You took a chance and it backfired on you. Your husband died because he had a weak heart; you didn't kill him.'

'It *feels* like I killed him. I see his face, the moment he died, and it feels as though I murdered him.'

'No, he died because he had a heart condition,' Jim replied firmly. 'He could have died playing football, or running for a bus. He could have died a year earlier, or a year later. But he didn't die because of you, Emma.'

'The shock . . .'

He shrugged. 'Life is full of shocks. What about your shock when your husband died? What about the shock of losing your baby? What about having to come back home and face everyone? What about the shock of your father's imprisonment? God, Emma, your life has been filled with shocks; isn't it time you forgave yourself for wanting to be happy?'

She considered his words, her voice small. 'But I don't deserve to be happy.'

'One day I'll remind you of that. One day I'll quote those words back to you and you won't believe you ever said them.' He squeezed her hand, looking into her face intently. 'I think you're the most remarkable woman I've ever met. I want you to be in my life, for the rest of my life,' he said, putting his hand over her mouth to stop her talking as he hurried on. 'I'll be here for you today and every tomorrow of your life. Just love me.'

'I *do* love you!' she said eagerly.

'For ever and always?'

Nodding, she touched his face. 'For life, Jim. For the rest of our lives.'

On a chill January morning, Mr David Hawksworth married Mrs Irene Knight at the registry office in Burnley. The bride wore a pale cream suit and a cloche hat, the bridegroom stern but happy, a carnation the size of a tea cup in his button hole. Afterwards, a few friends enjoyed a wedding breakfast with them, Emma relieved that Jim had come with her, although she was surprised to feel Irene tugging her arm soon after the meal began.

'Come over here,' she said, urging Emma towards the hallway.

'It's your wedding breakfast,' Emma replied. 'Don't you think your new husband might miss you?'

'This won't take a minute. I want to say something important to you, Emma, and now seems like the right time,' Irene said, her hand gripping Emma's tightly. 'I've been watching Jim Caird for a while now, seen him with you and chatted to him. He's a very solid chap, very strong. I like him. And he loves you.'

Emma flushed, Irene rushing on before she had time to speak.

'I've never asked you about your marriage, my dear, it wasn't my business, but reading between the lines, I'd say that it wasn't a love match.' Emma glanced down, surprised, as Irene carried on. 'I think you made the best of a good friendship with a good man – which is why I want to tell you to grab Jim Caird and love him for all he's worth.'

'But—'

'Jim Caird is a quiet man, but there's a lot of fire in him. And I think you know it. You want a *man*, a man in bed next to you. A man you can trust and call your own. A man who makes your heart shift.' She pointed to the next room, where they could hear chatter and laughter coming from the wedding breakfast. 'Your uncle isn't handsome, but I'm in love with him, and I want that for you, my dear. That's all I wanted to say. Don't let the past – or any guilt you might feel – ruin your future.'

THIRTY-ONE

Feeling around the back of his gum with his tongue, Stan Thorpe leaned on the railing and looked down into the corridor below. He had waited for his opportunity for a while, but for some reason, every time he was on duty, Frederick Coles was working in the kitchen, or was in his cell. And besides, Thorpe had been posted with Reg Spencer – and he knew only too well that Spencer was on to him. So he waited, knowing that one day Frederick Coles would be vulnerable. From his perch, he could watch the inmates, and he stared at one of the men who had just been jailed, a whip-thin young man, with sparse dry hair and puffy eyes, the look of slum breeding stamped on every one of his features. At any other time, Thorpe would have singled him out instantly as his new whipping boy, but his attention was fixed on Frederick Coles.

That he had had the nerve to hit him! And worse, that Jim Caird had sided with the bloody inmate, not his colleague. Reg Spencer had also made it clear that he would never support Thorpe's version of the story. Of course he had overreacted, Thorpe knew that, but he'd been so put out that it had seemed a good idea to plant a knife in Coles's cell – knowing it would stop his visiting rights. Weeks of trying to get his fucking daughter's attention only to be ignored for *Jim Caird* had inflamed Thorpe, and as he sucked on the hole where one of his teeth had been, he seethed inwardly. Of course, Coles, being the bleeding gentleman everyone took him for, had decided not to bear a grudge. Thorpe smiled grimly; *he* might not bear a grudge, but by Christ, Thorpe was bearing a grudge big enough for both of them. One which had increased as time had passed.

Aware that he was being observed by Reg across the landing, Thorpe nodded curtly, watching the other man retrace his steps. Above him the clock said 6.15; Reg's shift finished at 6.30 – not long to wait until Thorpe would have Coles to himself. Because what Reg didn't know was that the guard who was due to relieve him was going to be delayed by an hour. His wife had had a fall and he was going to be coming in late – so the message went. Thorpe knew all about it, but he had made sure Reg Spencer didn't. And whilst Thorpe waited for his chance, he thought about how he could make Frederick Coles's life more difficult. He knew that having visitors banned for a month would hurt, but that wasn't enough. Thorpe had wanted the pleasure of telling Emma that she couldn't see her father; he had wanted to see the look on her face, her punishment for ignoring him, and at the same time he had wanted to see her. But even that pleasure had been denied him by Jim Caird, who had intervened and greeted Emma Coles himself.

Which had done nothing for Stan Thorpe's temper. And so he had plotted, and bent his mind on a way of making Frederick Coles's imprisonment harder. Verbal abuse was too obvious, and could be overheard by the other guards, most of whom seemed likely to take Coles's side, so it had to be something more inventive, and ultimately more damaging ... Thorpe's masterstroke had come when the authorities finally sent someone in to treat the damp in several of the cells. The prison doctor had examined Frederick and decided that his cough was due to poor conditions that had taken their toll on his health. And so his cell had been one of those marked out for repair. It had taken five months for the workmen to finally arrive at the prison, and when they did, Thorpe was on duty. It was Thorpe who told them that they could miss cell number 78, as it had already been seen to ... The thought made him smile triumphantly. It was January already; by the time the bitter northern winter had chilled down the tiled walls, Frederick Coles would be coughing up blood. And no one would be any the wiser, no one would be able to point the finger at Thorpe. The list had gone missing; there was no evidence to say *which* cells had been listed for repair, and it was easy enough for Thorpe – if questioned – to say that the workmen had got it wrong.

All he had to do was wait, Thorpe thought to himself, his tongue working around his raw gums. As the weather hardened, the damp would start coming in, chilling Frederick Coles's cell and making a sick man out of him. Thorpe knew Coles's type. Already struggling after three winters, he would never get through another with his weak chest. And besides, he was changing, that was obvious; he was getting institutionalised – which was always the first sign that an inmate was losing hope. Naturally his illness, or even his demise, would be no one's fault. Just one of those things, nothing to say that Stan Thorpe had had a hand in it. It was just Mother Nature being a bitch. Just down to an old building that had seen better days.

Thorpe stared down into the corridor below. Frederick Coles's door was closed. He would be reading inside, Thorpe mused. Reading another of his fucking books, like he was some kind of intellectual. Yeah, he thought, well you keep reading, Coles, stay in your cell and breathe in all that damp air. That's all you have to do, just keep breathing.

And then Thorpe had another idea – one that would hurry his victim's decline along even faster. He would make sure that no extra food or treats from his daughter reached Frederick Coles. If he made sure he was on duty on visiting day, he could confiscate anything before anyone was the wiser. Tell the girl that he was going to pass it on. So what if she asked her father about it? Frederick Coles would know who had taken it, but he'd stay quiet. After all, what could he do about it? He had attacked a guard, that was a good enough reason for any man to bear a grudge. Oh yes, Thorpe mused, all the fruit Emma Coles brought in, along with the pastries and the chocolate, none of it would ever reach her father's cell. Deprived of the additional nutrients, Coles would falter more quickly . . .

'Stan?'

He jumped at his name, turning to see Reg standing there, looking at his watch. 'I should be off now.'

'Fine, see you.'

'No,' Reg said, frowning, 'I'm not going until I'm relieved. I'll wait for the next guard to come on shift.'

Piqued, Thorpe exhaled sharply. 'I can manage on my own. Caird's on the next landing.'

'Nah, I'll wait until I'm relieved,' Reg repeated, leaning on the iron banister next to Thorpe. 'How are your teeth?'

'Fucking great, how are yours?'

Reg sighed, looking down into the corridor below, his gaze travelling to the door of cell number 78.

'I can manage on my own,' Thorpe said. 'I'm the most experienced guard in this place.'

'I'm in no rush to get off,' Reg replied, his tone steady. 'I've got all the time in the world.'

Without Reg Spencer having to say another word, Thorpe realised that he was suspicious. He had known and worked with Reg for many years and could judge him to a nicety. Reg was – without using words – giving Thorpe the gypsy's warning. Even by simply looking at the door of number 78, he was pointing out that he knew what was going on. Of course, Thorpe realised, Reg didn't know *what* he was planning, or what he had already set into motion; he was just feeling his way. Picking up on his instinct. Which was how many of the guards worked in the prison environment.

Irritated, and yet even more determined, Thorpe sucked on one of his back teeth.

'What d'you think about Caird?'

'Good guard,' Reg replied. 'But you don't like him, do you?'

'I don't like anyone.'

'Well, at least you're constant,' Reg said, folding his arms. 'All died down, has it?'

'Has *what* all died down?'

'That misunderstanding between you and Coles?'

'Misunderstanding?' Thorpe repeated, his expression feral. 'He bleeding hit me.'

'You asked for it. Talking about his daughter that way. I thought you liked her.'

Biting his tongue, Thorpe refused to rise to the bait. 'She's nothing special.'

'Jim Caird wouldn't agree with you.'

'Well, I remember when Ricky Holmes was interested in her too,' Thorpe said spitefully. 'Didn't get him far, did it?'

Taking in a breath, Reg kept his voice steady. 'It's a good landing this. We should keep it that way, Stan. Keep it nice and quiet. We don't need any trouble here. No grudges.'

'Who's got a grudge?' Thorpe countered, all innocence.

'You know what I mean,' Reg replied, glancing at

his watch again. 'You didn't hear anything about my relief being held up, did you, Stan?'

Stan's expression was guileless. 'Nah, not a word. Not a word.'

Shaken, Bessie leaned against the outside prison wall and lit a cigarette, blowing the smoke out into the winter air. She had been to visit Frederick on a whim, the cobbler's being temporarily closed because of a burst pipe. It wasn't the first time she had been to the Moors Prison – she had visited Frederick a couple of times a year since he had been incarcerated – but this time she had seen a real difference in him . . . Inhaling, she waited for the bus that would collect her and the other visitors. Cold, she stamped her booted feet on the snowy ground and remembered the night she had come with her mother and stood outside, waiting for news. That terrible night when Ricky had gone into the North Wing . . .

Shivering, Bessie inhaled again to steady her nerves, thinking of Mr Letski and how they had to lock all the doors at night because he was wandering again. The neighbours had told her that he had been found down at the sewage works, roaming about in his nightshirt, and since then the doors had been locked and barred. Sometimes, in the early hours, they would hear him rattling the locks, then the shuffle of feet as he returned to bed.

At other times they would wake to the old sales pitch: *'Come in, come in. Bring your shoes, your boots. Come in!'* rendered in a very loud, heavily accented voice.

Laughing, Bessie would nudge Doug and he would go and quieten the old man. If it was her turn, Bessie would go downstairs and play cards with him. His favourite was poker, a game he remembered from the old days, and one that he excelled in. Even senile, Mr Letski could be counted on for two things – remembering every card played, and never taking off his moleskin waistcoat. Bessie had tried numerous times to get it away from him, but even when he was asleep, the old man had a primitive bond with the article and would waken instantly if Bessie even touched it. Life, Bessie realised, had turned out pretty bloody good for her. She loved Doug, found the old Russian amusing, and she owned the cobbler's – her ambition fulfilled. The only shadow that hung resolutely over her life was the loss of her brother Ricky. And visiting the Moors Prison had brought his death back to her.

Sighing, Bessie watched the smoke curl from her cigarette, and pulled her knitted cloche hat down over her cold ears. She had been unpleasantly surprised by Frederick Coles's condition. Perhaps Emma didn't see the same deterioration, as she visited so often, but to Bessie it was shattering. Frederick was as courteous and amusing as ever, smiling when he saw her. But his skin was thin, the veins showing underneath at the temples, and his hair lacked lustre and colour, mostly grey now. But more shattering was his hacking cough, Frederick bending over double a couple of times, then brushing it off as though it was nothing, when anyone with half a brain could see that it was serious.

The cold of the prison wouldn't be helping, Bessie thought, seeing the bus approach and stamping out her cigarette. And everyone was saying it was a bitter winter. Climbing on board, she took a seat and watched as the bus pulled away, the prison slowly disappearing over the horizon. Bessie didn't want to lose anyone else she cared about to that chilling place, didn't want to see Emma lose her father after losing so many other things. Frederick might pretend that everything was all right, but he was lying. He had the look of an inmate who had grown accustomed to being imprisoned. It was a look without hope, even without energy. Bessie thought back to what she knew and wondered, as had Emma, why Frederick wouldn't expose the real thief. He had kept his secret for so long, she thought, probably expecting it to come out without any intervention of his. But it *hadn't* come out, and judging from the look of Frederick Coles that day, he might end up taking it to his grave.

It was past seven when Bessie arrived back in Burnley, walking up Market Street and jumping when someone touched her shoulder. Turning, she smiled when she saw Emma, but not before her friend had noticed something in her eyes.

'What is it?'

Bessie pulled a face. 'You just scared me to bloody death and you ask what it is?' Hurriedly she tried to change the subject. 'So, how's your fiancé? More in love with you now than he was yesterday? Honestly, you two are a couple of real lovebirds—'

Emma cut her off.

'Don't change the subject. I know something's worrying you.'

'Mr Letski—'

'It's not about him. You've just been to see my father.'

Bessie paused, the snow beginning to settle on both of them as they stood under the gaslight. 'He's not well, is he?'

'I know,' Emma replied, her tone adrift. 'I spoke to one of the guards, and he said they were keeping an eye on him. And Jim said that he had seen the prison doctor yesterday.'

'He's got a terrible cough,' Bessie went on tentatively, feeling her way. 'He's aged a lot. I don't want to worry you, but I saw your father a few months ago and he was a different man.'

Pulling a scarf over her hair, Emma stood silent, listening. Her expression betrayed nothing, her eyes fixed on Bessie.

'He's slipping away, isn't he?'

'He's ill,' Bessie agreed. 'And he's . . .'

'Giving up,' Emma finished for her, nodding. 'I know. I've seen this coming on for a while, but lately he's gone downhill. He doesn't complain, and I take in food and all kinds of treats, but nothing's doing any good. It looks as though he isn't even eating them. When I asked him about it, he just looked blank. Jim wouldn't tell me anything, until we had an argument and he said that Dad's cell was bitterly cold and damp. I wrote to the Governor, but he didn't write back . . .' She paused, the snow mottling her red scarf. 'I have to get him out of there. I have to get him home, or he'll die.'

Bessie didn't doubt it, but pretended otherwise. 'Oh, come on, your father's tough, he'll get by. He's done more than three years of his sentence already.'

'With seven years to go,' Emma replied. 'You know he won't make it. *I* know, Bessie, that's why I wanted you to see him, to see what you thought. Whether I was imagining it or not.'

'You're not imagining it.'

'So I have to get him out!' Emma snapped back, turning under the snowfall. 'My father *has* to tell me who the guilty man is. Then we can get the sentence overturned and bring Dad home.'

'But if he hasn't told you so far . . .'

'He has to tell me now!' Emma replied emphatically. 'When I see him next week, I'm going to insist that he tells me. I want whoever did that robbery to decay slowly in jail. To fall apart, just like my father has. I want the guilty man to hear the sound of the doors slamming closed and see the hours and years creep past. I want him – because he's the one who deserves it – to rot. I want his body to grow old and die there. Because he's letting that happen to my father.'

'Please, love, listen to me,' Bessie said, clasping her friend's hands.

But Emma snatched them away, her face flushed with anger and anxiety. 'No! I don't want to listen to anyone any more. I know what I have to do – I have to get my father out of that prison as soon as I can. Or, God knows, he'll come out as a corpse.'

THIRTY-TWO

February came in sullen, the weather bleak, the days short and savage with cold. In Burnley, Mr Letski broke out of the back window of the shop and walked – barefoot – almost a mile before Bessie caught up with him. At the tobacconist's, Florence was ill with influenza. So ill that she didn't colour her hair for weeks and the grey regrowth finally gave away her age. Next to the jeweller's, on the other side, Jack Rimmer had a sale and cut everything to half price, a couple of local lads putting frogs in his buckets to scare him when he lifted them down. In Hawksworth's jeweller's, David spent the quiet winter afternoons in the workroom up in the eaves, whilst Irene and Emma ran the shop together. And in the Moors Prison, Jim Caird was wondering how he was going to break the bad news to Emma.

Her father had been taken into the prison infirmary that morning, coughing up blood, his temperature dangerously high. As he watched Frederick being carried out on a stretcher, Jim wondered about the rate of his decline, and what had prompted it. Everyone knew that Frederick had a weak chest, and the weather had been bitter, but the speed of his deterioration had been shocking. Thoughtful, Jim walked into Frederick's cell, shivering at the cold, and touching the tiled walls. Damp, they ran with water, the sheet on Frederick's bed chilled. *God*, Jim thought, staring at the bed. *Where are the blankets?* All the inmates had blankets, extra in the winter. Alerted, he looked at the shelf opposite Frederick's bunk, two photographs of Emma resting on it, and a cake tin. Picking the tin up, Jim shook it, then opened it, surprised to find it empty, with no evidence of having held anything for a while. And yet he knew that Emma brought in food for her father; she cooked for him, made cakes and pastries . . .

Uneasy, Jim looked back to the bed. How could anyone sleep with so little to cover them, and in such damp? Turning over the pillow, Jim's gaze fell on a pile of letters, the handwriting Emma's. Putting them in his pocket, he walked to the door just in time to see Stan Thorpe's approach.

The older man looked anxious, hurried.

'I heard Coles got taken to the infirmary,' he said, trying to pass Jim and get into the cell. 'I should check his things.'

'I've already done that,' Jim replied, his eyes hard.

'He had some . . . some laundry due to come back. Blankets and stuff.'

'Is that why he didn't have them on his bed?'

Thorpe shrugged. 'You know Coles, keeps himself to himself. You would think this bleeding cell was off bounds the way he goes on. Must have something to hide.'

'It doesn't look like he had *anything* to hide.'

'What's that supposed to fucking mean!'

'I think you know,' Jim replied, his anger rising as he pushed the man aside and strode up the iron stairs, Thorpe following.

'What's Coles been saying, hey? Whatever that bastard said, it's not true. You want to remember – he hit me. He's got a grudge against me, has Coles.' Thorpe watched as Jim turned at the top of the stairs and moved towards Reg Spencer on the mezzanine. 'I warned him! I told him to keep himself warm, with that cold. I said, you have to look after yourself in here . . .'

He was still talking when Jim reached Reg, the older man alerted by the intense look on Jim's face.

'Can we open Thorpe's locker?'

Surprised, Reg nodded. 'You'd have to have a good reason.'

'I think I've got one,' Jim replied, signalling to one of the other guards and getting the man to waylay Thorpe, as he and Reg headed for the guards' locker room.

Once inside, Reg stared at the younger man. 'Whatever you think, you'd better be right. Breaking into another man's locker is serious.'

'This *is* serious,' Jim agreed, watching as Reg reached for a spanner and broke the lock on the third attempt.

Hurriedly, Jim pulled back the door.

'Jesus . . .' he said simply, Reg looking over his shoulder. 'Look at all this. That bastard Thorpe's been confiscating Frederick's bedding, and the food Emma brought in for him.' He pulled out a pile of stale cakes and biscuits, throwing them down on the floor as his temper broke. '*I'll kill the bastard.*'

'No you won't,' Reg warned him. 'You've got a career here, lad, no point ruining that. Don't risk spoiling your record by fighting that shit. Believe me, Thorpe's going to be thrown out for this.'

'He's damn near killed Frederick Coles!' Jim said angrily. 'Why didn't Coles say anything?'

'You know what he's like, never wants to cause trouble. He never let anyone in the cell unless he could help it.'

Jim's expression was dangerous. 'Christ knows how long this has been going on for. Why wouldn't he report Thorpe?'

'He didn't want any more trouble,' Reg repeated, resigned. 'He knew what Thorpe was like. How he bullied people. I bet he was afraid that Thorpe would stop his visiting rights again.'

'He wouldn't have had any for much longer. He wouldn't have been alive for anyone to visit!' Jim snapped, his vehemence shaking Reg. 'This must have been going on for weeks. We should have known. I should have said something after that fight they had. I should have realised that Thorpe would have to get his own back.'

Guilty, Reg kept his face averted. He knew that he should have gone to the Governor a long time ago.

God knows, he had wanted to. But he hadn't wanted a mark on his record, hadn't wanted to get a name for splitting on one of his colleagues. Instead he had left well alone, letting a man suffer for the sake of a bloody report . . . Ashamed, Reg picked up the confiscated blankets and some of the food, walking to the door. If he had spoken up sooner, Frederick Coles wouldn't be in hospital, coughing up blood.

'I'm going to see the Governor,' he said grimly. 'You better let Frederick's daughter know that her father's in hospital. They've had a phone put in at the Gordon Arms. You can call there and ask the landlord to pass Emma a message.'

'How bad is he?'

Reg paused before replying. 'He might rally, or he might not. Either way, Jim, get his daughter here. And you stay on; she'll need you.'

THIRTY-THREE

'Dad?' Emma whispered, sitting down beside the iron hospital bed. 'Dad?'

Frederick didn't reply; he had fallen asleep again. Sighing, Emma leaned back in her chair. Her father had been so pleased to see her, even joking that it was worth faking an illness just to get a hospital visit. But he hadn't been faking; one look at his face had told her that.

Watching him sleep, Emma sat holding her father's hand, Jim waiting beside her. Outside the barred windows, the snow banked up against the panes, the daylight fading, the soft lamp beside the bed throwing the far side of her father's face into shadow. Silently, Emma studied the well-known features, noted how the skin was tight over the cheekbones, the cleft in her father's chin dark as an ink mark. Lying against the white sheet, his left hand still bore his old wedding ring, although it had become loose, his knuckles enlarged as the flesh had diminished.

'Dad?' Emma said, thinking he had woken, then leaning back as she realised he was still deeply asleep.

Turning to Jim, she held his look. The previous

day, he had proposed to her in a curious manner, by leaving a note in her handbag that she had found when she was alone. Giddy with happiness, she had written under his question, *WILL YOU MARRY ME?* simply: *WHEN?*

That night Jim had waylaid her in Holland Street and she had waved the note in front of his face, making him read it.

'You ass!' she had teased him. 'Why didn't you ask me in person?'

'Because I couldn't have borne you saying no,' he had replied, showing a rare flash of vulnerability. 'But you said yes!' he shouted, picking her up and swinging her around, not caring who saw them. 'You said yes!'

Yet before they had had a chance to celebrate their news, Emma had been summoned to the jail. And suddenly all her attention was focused back on her father.

'How bad is he?'

'He's better,' Jim told her. 'So the doctor said.'

'Honestly?'

'Yeah, honestly,' he replied. 'He'll be all right, love, he will.'

'No he won't,' she contradicted him. 'Not unless I get him out of here.'

'Emma . . .'

'I *won't* let him stay,' she replied, her tone emphatic. 'Somehow I'm going to find out who really broke into Oldfield Mill – and then they'll have to let my father come home.'

'He won't tell you.'

'Then I'll find out another way.'

'Like how?'

'I don't know,' Emma said, her tone fierce. 'But I will. Or he'll die here. He's giving up, doesn't talk about finding new evidence any more. Just accepts his sentence as though there's nothing anyone can do about it. That's why he's so ill: he doesn't believe he's got a chance. Just thinks his life is this place . . .' She glanced away, feeling Jim's hand on her shoulder. 'No one can live without hope. If I could just give him that, something to hold on to, something to make him believe he can get out. That one day everyone will know the truth, and his name will be cleared. I want to see my father walking in Towneley Park again, with his head up, not sick and forgotten in this place.'

Moved, Jim kept his voice steady. 'You don't think that he was just—'

'Telling me a story, to make me feel better?' Emma said, finishing his question. 'No, Jim, I don't. I *did* wonder about that, once. But I remembered that it wasn't my father who told me about the other man – it was Mr Overton. If Dad had just wanted to make me feel better, he would have told me himself, wouldn't he?'

'Yes, he would,' Jim agreed. 'What about the solicitor?'

'He doesn't know anything. He was as frustrated about it as I was,' Emma replied, staring at Frederick's sleeping face. 'I asked my father to name the man again. Today, when I first saw him. But he ignored the question, pretended he hadn't heard. In the past, I've written to him asking the same, but he would never tell me. I don't suppose he ever intends to.'

'Then I don't see how we can find out who the real thief is.'

'I never said "we"; I said *I* would find out,' Emma said, her tone quiet but firm.

'I know you didn't say "we". But I did,' Jim replied, standing up to her. 'You can't do this on your own. From now on, everything you do will be with me. You're not alone any more, Emma.'

'But you can't get involved . . .'

'I *am* involved.'

'I don't want to ruin your career.'

Impatiently, he sighed. 'God, Emma, don't be so stupid! I *am* involved, I want to be involved. What kind of a man would I be if I *wasn't* involved?'

'Oh Jim, I know you mean well,' she said gently. 'But how *can* you help me?'

'I'll do my best.'

'You always do that,' she said, smiling and placing her hand over his. 'I'm going to talk to Mr Overton again. Just to see if there was anything we overlooked.'

'I could come with you.'

'You're not supposed to get involved with individual cases. You know what the authorities would say if they found out you were helping me. They might even take you off my father's wing, and that would be a real blow. He needs you; *I* need you to look out for him.'

'You keep telling me what I'm not supposed to do, or what I can't do. Well, I'm going to do what I think is right,' Jim said, his tone direct. 'You talk to Mr Overton, and then we'll go through your father's case step by step together. We'll look at the evidence as though we were the jury. With an open mind, without being prejudiced about what's already known.'

She raised her eyebrows doubtfully. 'How can we do that?'

'By stepping back,' Jim replied. '*You* can't – so that's where I come in. I can judge the situation without so much emotional involvement. I can look at the evidence anew because, in all honesty, I haven't seen it before. I've heard about the case, spoken to you and your father about it, but I haven't looked at the bald facts. We don't talk about the inmates' crimes, so I don't really know that much at all.' He paused, staring at her. 'Can you show me the newspaper reports of the case?'

She nodded.

'You kept them?'

'Every one.'

'Good. And give me anything else written at the time.'

Again Emma nodded. 'There was a lot of gossip too. People talked about my father's past, and of course about Ernie Coles.'

'Is there anyone you can talk to about that?'

'Jack Rimmer, the old hardware shop owner,'

Emma admitted after a moment's thought. 'He knows all about what was going on around that time. He would know all the gossip too. He's reliable, and fond of my father. About the only person in Burnley who is.'

'I can ask around about Ernie Coles and his colleagues.'

'Why?' Emma asked, surprised. 'My grandfather wasn't involved in the theft at Oldfield Mill.'

'I know that. But he and his crowd were known villains at the time of the crime. They might know something. Whether they'd *tell* us is another matter.'

Emma shrugged. 'I suppose I could ask them . . .'

'*Are you bloody mad!*' Jim snapped. 'You stay away from anyone like that, d'you hear me? They wouldn't let some woman just walk in and poke around. People don't care that you're trying to help your father; they'll only worry that you're asking questions that might damage them. It's a closed world, with no room for amateurs, especially a woman. You can't take them on; you wouldn't know where to start. And you *wouldn't* be helping your father. Be sensible. He needs you, so don't endanger yourself. Stay away from people like that.'

'So who *is* going to talk to them?'

'I will.'

Her expression baffled, Emma stared at him. '*You?* You're a prison guard. Why would they talk to you?'

'Remember I told you my family had had some dealings with Ernie Coles? Well, it goes a bit deeper than that,' Jim admitted. 'I wasn't involved directly, but let's say that if I had to – *if I had to* – I could reach him.'

Surprised, but not willing to push him for further information, Emma nodded. 'What can I do?'

'Like you said, talk to your father's solicitor – and research the case. We'll study it together and see if anything got overlooked.'

He paused, looking back to the sleeping man. Frederick was breathing irregularly, his lungs straining. Watching him, Jim thought of the confiscated goods in Thorpe's locker, and of the fight the two men had had previously, which had led to Thorpe's ill treatment. The injustice almost choked him, but there was one question he had to ask. He didn't want to ask it, but he had to know, once and for all.

'Are you sure?'

Flinching, Emma turned to him. 'About my father being innocent? Do you really have to ask that?'

'Yes, I do,' Jim replied. 'He's not my father, and it's not my cause. So I have to know, before I take an important step that might cost me dear. *Is there really another man? Is there a guilty man out there, waiting to be discovered? Is your father innocent?*'

Her expression calm, Emma faced him. 'I don't think my father is innocent, I *know* he is. In fact, I would stake my life on it.'

PART FOUR

Darkness reigns at the foot of the lighthouse.

Japanese proverb

I had not expected to find – or deserve – a man like Jim Caird. But from the moment I had confided everything to him, and made a clean breast of it, I had no doubt he was committed to me. From the moment he took my side, I was no longer alone in the world. There was someone with me, someone I could talk to and trust. I didn't have to pretend or lie to Jim. He knew me, all my faults and weaknesses, and he accepted them. Knowing he was in my life made me even stronger.

But I doubted that even Jim knew how determined I was to get my father out of jail. Seeing his decline forced me to act. I would dream of the faceless, nameless man, confront him, and try to grab hold of him. But when I awoke, there was nothing there. Instead I would look at the time and wait until morning, until I heard the sounds of Irene going downstairs and my uncle beginning to wind the clocks.

Suddenly – from being so alone – I had allies. I had always had a friend in Bessie, but the presence of Irene at home radically changed the atmosphere in the jeweller's shop. Due to her it became a place of sanctuary, rather than a depressing prison. She was quick-witted and clever, never once making me feel my place and delighted that I was engaged to Jim, whilst still covering for me on my prison visits to my father. As for my uncle, he was a changed man; not demonstrative, but he had lost his melancholia and welcomed his new existence. And so my life altered and became more smooth, exciting. I was loved and I loved in return, and my future looked hopeful again.

But then came the news that my father was dying. And I wasn't going to let him die. Not in the Moors Prison, not out on that chill landscape, not away from his home and the streets he had once loved. When I dreamed of the faceless man, sometimes he disappeared, to be replaced by my father. And when I dreamed of him, he was always younger and full of vigour, tipping his hat to Ricky Holmes and swaggering in his smart clothes. I dreamed that he had floated out of the prison, up into the clouds, and then down into the streets again. A free man, a man with his name restored. A man I was proud to call my father.

When I woke, I knew he was in the Moors Prison. And I knew that – many times – Jim was there, keeping an eye on him as he worked his shift. Standing watch for me. We both cared for my father, but I think only I realised that time was getting very short. Hope does not last indefinitely. There is an old Arab proverb – 'A man who has health has hope.

And a man who has hope has everything.' Well, my father was running out of health and out of hope.

And so I determined that I was going to find that faceless man and put a name to him.

I didn't know then how much that discovery would cost us all.

THIRTY-FOUR

'Well, I ask you!' Florence said, jabbing her husband with her elbow. 'Emma's walking out with that Jim Caird. And I heard – and I reckon it's true – that they're engaged. And only just over a year since her husband died. It's a scandal, that's what it is.'

Harold sighed, trying to read his paper. 'Oh, let the girl alone. She deserves some happiness.'

'She's a widow. What would you say if I was larking around after you were dead? Going with every Tom, Dick and Harry.'

'It's one man,' Harold remonstrated, 'and she needs a friend.'

'*Friend!*' Florence said, craning her neck around the door to watch the couple pass. 'You must be blind. Mind you, I suppose David Hawksworth will be glad to get his niece off his hands again. Him being married now.' She took in a breath, secretly relishing Emma's romance. 'If you ask me, that family marries too much. Far too much, too much for anyone.'

Harold was thinking that one marriage was more than enough for him. If he had wanted to have his ear bent further, he would have told his wife about the latest gossip in Burnley – the rumour going around that Frederick Coles was dying in prison. Which would account for why Emma was looking so worried lately, he thought, peering over the top of the paper stack he was getting ready for the evening delivery. Imagine having your father in jail, and worse, *dying* in jail. With all the gossip that would follow . . . Harold could imagine it only too well. How people who had so conveniently forgotten Frederick Coles for years would be talking about his death. And bringing up the whole sordid case again. The theft at Oldfield Mill . . .

Wincing, Harold thought of David Hawksworth and wondered how Frederick's half-brother would take the news. Or whether, as before, he would ignore what was going on. But if you could ignore a scandal, you could hardly ignore the death of a relative. Even one who had been boarded up at the Moors Prison for years. Still thinking, Harold put down the papers and began to count the boxes of matches, making a note of the number in his pocket book. His life – and his wife – might not be the most exciting in the world, but at that moment he wouldn't have traded places with anyone in the Coles family. Not in the past, or in the days to come.

'What can you remember, Jack?' Emma asked, sitting in the back of the hardware shop as Jack Rimmer perched on a high stool. His expression was strained, as though the effort of thinking back was actually painful to him.

'There were some talk about your father being framed . . .'

'By who?'

'God, luv, if I knew that, I would have shouted it from the rooftops.' He paused. 'How *is* your father?'

'Very sick.'

Jack nodded, thinking. 'There were some tough lads in Hanky Park, and – oh, that's a thought.'

'What?'

'That pub – what's it called? Yes, the Black Knight, in Hanky Park. Salford. That's a real hang-out for anyone criminal, or in mind to become criminal. And for the rough types . . .'

'Like my grandfather?'

Startled, Jack blew out his cheeks. 'Why the interest in your grandfather?'

'He knows people.'

'Yeah, the kind of people you won't want to know. Listen to me, Emma, if your father thought you were even asking after Ernie Coles, he'd go mad. Ernie and Frederick weren't close, to put it mildly, but if your grandfather had known anything, d'you think he'd have let his son go to prison for something he didn't do?'

Emma shrugged. 'Like you say, they weren't close.'

'No, but they're flesh and blood. Even if they live different lives, Ernie wouldn't have let his son go to prison for nothing.'

'Unless he bore my father a grudge for rejecting him?'

'Nah,' Jack said firmly. 'Ernie Coles is too big a man for a grudge. Blood's blood – if he could have helped your father, he would have done.'

Emma was unconvinced. 'But he's never visited him in jail. Not once, in over three years.'

Jack whistled softly. 'Being Ernie Coles's son didn't help your father at the trial; what d'you think it would do for him inside, if Ernie came visiting? Every hard man in the prison would want to prove something, would want to take on Frederick to settle a grudge with his father. Or to prove a point. Nah, Ernie stayed away because he knew it would be safer for your father.'

'So why didn't he write?'

'You don't know anything at all about your grandfather, do you?' Jack asked, shaking his head. 'Ernie Coles *can't* read or write. He's barely educated. It doesn't matter in his world, though. No one needs to be a scholar.'

Thoughtful, Emma mused aloud. 'But my father loves books; he educated himself. Passed that accountant's exam, worked hard for his qualifications. I don't suppose my grandfather encouraged him much.' She glanced over to Jack. 'They couldn't be less alike, could they?'

'No, not really.'

'Must have been hard for my father, growing up with Ernie Coles. No wonder he wanted to put so much distance between them as soon as he could get away from home.' She flushed. 'All the more reason why he would *never* have turned out to be a thief.'

'Muck sticks, luv; people judged him by his father's standards.'

'But my grandfather's never even been arrested, let alone spent time in jail!' she said hotly. 'And he's done enough to serve time. It should be him in there, not my father.'

'Yeah, well you're not the first one that's said that,' Jack replied, getting to his feet and shouting at a group of local boys who were clattering the tin buckets outside.

Following him, Emma leaned against the counter. 'But if Ernie Coles knows everything that's going on, and everything that went on in the past, he might know something that would help his son without even realising it.'

Jack laughed hoarsely.

'Well, that would make your grandfather a fool, and one thing he isn't is a fool.' Annoyed, he rapped on the window, shaking his fist at the boys as they scattered. 'Now, you see that? If Ernie Coles had been in here, those lads wouldn't have dared to try it on. He wouldn't have had to say anything, he would just have needed to be here.'

Folding her arms, Emma kept talking.

'I've never heard of my grandfather coming back to Burnley. He must live somewhere. Doesn't he have a home?'

'The Acorn in Oldham, luv,' Jack told her. 'It's a rough pub, that, full of all sorts, but you could say that Ernie Coles lives there. He has an understanding with the landlord – and a woman nearby.'

'The Acorn,' Emma repeated thoughtfully.

She would pass on the information to Jim, and let him follow it up. Her grandfather might be a hard man, but Emma knew that Jim could handle himself, and besides, the Caird family had old history with Ernie Coles. And yet could she *really* ask Jim to get involved? She knew he wanted to help, was more than eager, but Emma was reluctant to endanger his career or his reputation. The memory of Leonard flooded her brain momentarily, reminded her of what her history had cost another man, and made her pause.

Walking to the door of the hardware store, Emma smiled at Jack Rimmer. 'Thanks.'

'Any time, luv. I like to talk about villains – just as long as I don't have to mix with them,' he replied, pulling a face and then staring hard at her. 'You don't get involved, luv, you hear me? Your young man can ask around for you, but you stay away.'

'I was just—'

'I know you, and how much your father means to you. But you're a woman in a man's world in places like Hanky Park and the Oldham back streets. And you're not tough enough for it. You're strong, Emma, but you're not slum rabble.'

'I'm Ernie Coles's granddaughter.'

He laughed without humour. 'That's no protection! If you got to him, you might have a chance, but there's plenty of people who would welcome an opportunity to hurt you before you got that close.'

Unnerved, Emma paled. 'Well, perhaps you're

right . . . I'll tell Jim what you told me and let him deal with it.'

'Best thing, luv,' Jack said, relieved, watching her as she left the shop.

Outside, on Holland Street, Emma thought about what Jack had said, and decided that her grandfather's reputation was far-fetched. Ernie Coles had become one of the north-west's bogeymen, a legend to titillate respectable citizens. It was true that he was a hard man, but he was no murderer. A thug, but not that dangerous, surely? Still thinking, she walked towards the jeweller's shop. She would tell Jim about the Acorn – but only after she had gone there herself.

After all, Ernie Coles was her grandfather. And, like Jack had said, blood was blood.

THIRTY-FIVE

March bit down cold, the weather sinking its teeth into the north-west, news coming from the prison – via Jim – that Frederick had been moved into another cell. He was out of the infirmary, not well, but partially recovered, although the prison doctor told Emma he was worried about the prolonged cold spell. All the blankets Stan Thorpe had confiscated had been returned, along with others, and every week his daughter brought food to supplement her father's prison diet. But the guards could see the deterioration continuing. Too much cold and the damp conditions had weakened Frederick Coles, and although no one was prepared to predict disaster, both Jim and Reg Spencer kept a weather eye on their charge.

'I heard that Stan Thorpe was fired,' Jim said with some pleasure, 'without his pension.'

Reg nodded. 'Serve the bastard right. But you watch him, he'll not be able to stay away. This place was his life.'

'The authorities will never have him back, will they?'

'No chance,' Reg said coldly. 'It was his own fault;

he had been asking for it for years.' He turned to Jim. 'Does Emma know what he did to her father?'

'No,' Jim replied urgently. 'What good would it have done to tell her? Thorpe was thrown out, Frederick was given another cell . . .'

'But the damage was done.'

'Some,' Jim agreed, 'but he could recover.'

'Not here he won't,' Reg replied, moving away and beginning his head count of the inmates.

Jim knew he was right about that, but would never have told Emma what the common consensus was in the prison. Instead he was waiting for her to contact him so they could go over all the old reports of her father's trial. Musing, Jim walked along the mezzanine gangway, the noises of the men's voices below echoing in the vaulted ceiling above his head. They had been lucky on the wing: hardly any fights had broken out for a while, and nothing serious. Jim was pleased about that, because although he wasn't afraid of violence, he didn't invite it. Having grown up in a rough area, he had seen too often what drink and fights could do. In fact, at one time he had been the junior boxing champion for the Burnley Council School, training twice a week at the Black Knight in Hanky Park.

It had been a fairly long way to cycle, but the best place in the area to train. They had had a gym over the pub, Jim remembered, sawdust on the floor, and a square ring raised up about two feet, with worn wooden steps at the corners. On the walls the landlord had hung mementos of his own glorious past, as well as a couple of posters of the present-day boxing champions, and one of Johnny Weissmuller. He wasn't a boxer, the landlord had explained, but he'd swum one hundred metres in less than a minute. *And if that doesn't make a man a bleeding hero, I don't know what does.*

The regulars had all teased Jim when he first came to the Black Knight, mocking his muscles and sparring with him. One old hand even knocked him out cold. Jim grimaced at the memory, then remembered something else. How one day he had been hitting a punchbag, and a burly man had come over, putting out one huge hand and stopping the bag swinging. He had had a venal look, his eyebrows heavy, the eyes deep set, the gaze unwavering. Intimidating.

''Lo there,' he had said.

Jim had looked at Ernie Coles and remembered what his father had told him. Immediately he had been on his guard. 'Hello.'

'You're Frank Caird's boy,' Ernie had gone on, his voice a deep bass, his speech slow, which had made every word more pronounced and more threatening.

'Yeah, that's right.'

'I know your brother, Tom.'

Swallowing with difficulty, Jim had held the big man's gaze. He hadn't needed to ask who he was; everyone knew Ernie Coles, and Jim had realised that he was bound to bump into him at the gym, where he worked out. Slowly he had watched as Coles had turned away and taken off his jacket. His bulk had been impressive, his arms and neck well muscled, with no excess weight around his middle. Taking in a breath, Ernie Coles had then picked up some weights and begun to do bicep presses.

'Yeah, I know Tom . . .'

Uncertain of what he should do, Jim hadn't moved, just remembered the state his brother had come home in only a few days earlier.

'You want to be a professional boxer, Jimmy Caird?'

'Yeah, I'd like to be. But it costs money,' Jim had said diffidently. 'My family don't have the cash, so I'll be getting a job. A regular wage.'

'Shame to waste talent,' Ernie Coles had gone on, changing hands with the weights. 'A young man with talent should be encouraged. And money shouldn't come into it. Not enough to stop you doing what you want.'

'I dunno,' Jim had replied awkwardly.

'I do,' Ernie had answered. 'What if I spoke to your parents and got them the money to have you trained up? It would be an investment; you could pay me back when you started fighting. It's a good game, good money.'

The only thing Jim had known at that moment was that Ernie Coles didn't do people favours. And he had been smart enough to remember his father's warning and put two and two together. If they borrowed money from Coles, they would be in his debt. He would own Jim and his career. And if it paid off, he would organise the fights and the deals, taking a big percentage for himself. Which was what a manager did, Jim had thought, watching Ernie Coles as he began to pound the punchbag. But this would be no ordinary manager, Jim had realised; what else would he be asked to do apart from the fights? What other jobs would he be pressed into? Illegal jobs, putting pressure on people outside a boxing ring?

Wondering how he could refuse without offending Ernie Coles and making a dangerous enemy, Jim had realised that he had to make a choice. He could go for the fight game, with Ernie Coles, or study for a respectable job. And learning how to box might turn out to be an advantage either way.

'My parents don't borrow money from anyone, Mr Coles,' he had said finally, his voice steady. 'Thanks for the offer, but I can't take it.'

Ernie Coles had stopped lifting the weights, his pale, watery blue eyes intense. 'You might regret that. Don't make a decision now, think it over.'

But Jim hadn't wanted to think it over. He had wanted to settle the matter there and then.

'I never really thought I had a future in boxing. I'm going into the prison service.'

Mirthlessly, Coles had laughed. 'That's going to be your regular wage?'

'Yeah.'

'Not much money in it.'

'No,' Jim had replied carefully, adding the afterthought, 'But you get a pension.'

That time Coles had laughed with real humour. '*A fucking pension!* Well, there you go, lad, if it's a life with a pension you want, then you'd not work well with me.' He had put out one huge hand, shaking Jim's hard. 'I'll tell you what, though. One day we'll talk again – and then you can tell me if you made the right choice. There's pensions and pensions, Jimmy Caird, remember that.'

But the years had passed and Jim hadn't bumped into Ernie Coles again, not to talk to, at least. He had seen him a few times at the Black Knight, but soon afterwards Jim had moved on and started his studies. And now here he was, engaged to Ernie Coles's granddaughter . . . Breathing out, Jim glanced at his watch, waiting for the end of his shift. He would have to work another shift in the morning, but after that he had a day off. On the way home he would call for Emma and see how much information on her father's case she had managed to get together. He wouldn't tell her what he was going to do next, or anything about his experience with Ernie Coles.

He wanted to keep Emma away from the man who had once offered him a job. The same man who had broken his brother's nose.

Walking out on to the street, Irene looked down the road and frowned. Emma hadn't said anything about visiting her father, and yet it was past six and she hadn't come home. Of course she had no intention of giving Emma away, but she was feeling a little guilty about having to lie to her new husband.

Walking back into the jeweller's, she smiled at David and dropped into one of her cover stories.

'Of course, I forgot, Emma's visiting Bessie tonight,' she said uneasily. 'We'll have our food now.'

'Emma's been over to Bessie's a lot recently. Talking about her new life, I suppose. Emma, engaged to be married.' David sighed. 'She hasn't said anything about *when* they want to marry, has she?'

'No, dear, she hasn't.'

'I hope it's a long engagement,' David replied, sitting down at the kitchen table. 'To be honest, Irene, I don't want her to leave. Me and Emma, we had some bad times, but we've got over that. I like having her here.'

'So do I, love,' Irene replied honestly. 'But it's right that she'll have her own home and family. It's the way of life. She must feel a little bit crowded in here, what with me moving in. It's only natural for her to want to have her own space and home to decorate and make her own. And Jim's, of course.'

'Do you like him?'

Surprised, she nodded. 'Oh, yes, I've told you that before. I like Jim Caird a lot.'

'He seems a good man.' David glanced at his wife, suddenly anxious. 'I worry about the shop. About the future. I mean, I know you and I could run it for years, but I want it to go on after me. It's not much of a place, I know . . .'

Irene hushed him. 'It's a grand place, and all the better for having you in it.'

Moved, he looked into her face. 'I got so lucky with you. I didn't really deserve you, I've not been a good man, not really. Oh, I did what was morally right. Did what my conscience dictated, but I didn't feel for people, not really. Not until I met you – you taught me how to care.'

'I think you're too harsh on yourself,' Irene replied, winking at him cheekily. 'I knew you were a good man from the moment I saw you.'

'Good, maybe. Good in that I was an upright citizen, and law-abiding. But not good like other people are good.'

'I don't understand, my dear.'

He felt around for the right words.

'You and Emma, you both care about other people because it comes naturally to you. But I did what was *expected* of me, not what I felt compelled to do out of love.' He felt suddenly foolish and stared down at the table, clearing his throat. Patiently, Irene waited for him to continue, knowing how hard it was for him to express his emotions. Finally, David continued. 'I've been thinking a lot lately, about the past, and how I've acted. When Adam came back that last time, I should have tried to mend some bridges, tried to keep him here and be a proper father to him.' Exasperated, his voice became curt. 'Oh, what am I talking about? My son's no good. He'll never come back here. He didn't want the shop when he was a boy, and he's not going to change his mind now.'

Gently, Irene patted her husband's hand, her intelligent face questioning. 'Perhaps you should ask yourself the most important question – would he be the right person to run the shop?'

'He's my son!'

'I know that, my dear, but Adam's not like you. He's not reliable. Could he make the best of the opportunity?'

Putting down his knife and fork, David glanced at his wife. 'That's what I'm talking about, Irene. I wanted my son back, because I wanted to make things right between us – not because it's right that he should be here.' He cleared his throat again, nervous. 'But it wouldn't work out, I know that now. I'm never going to be close to my son. But . . .'

'Yes?'

'I was hoping Emma might want to take over one day.'

'The jeweller's niece taking over the jeweller's shop?' Irene said, smiling. 'Why not?'

'We could retire in a few years, wouldn't have to work all our lives. Not like Mr Letski, going crazy in the cobbler's.'

Irene laughed. 'I don't want to go crazy – even in a cobbler's.'

'So you wouldn't mind if I left the shop to Emma?'

'Why would I mind! It isn't my shop.'

'You're my wife, the shop is half yours.'

'David, my love,' she said simply, gesturing for him to continue eating. 'Whatever you do is all right with me. I'm just happy to be with you, that's all that matters.'

He paused, staring at his plate.

'But before I mention anything to Emma, I thought I should try one last time. Maybe write a letter to Adam, say what I feel, apologise.' He paused, shrugging. 'But we don't have an address, do we?'

'No, love.'

'Well, when he comes back, we'll get an address,' David said, picking up his knife and fork again. 'I'll try to talk to him, but we always argue. If I get an address, I can write to him . . . People respond to letters, don't they? They read them over and over again, think about them. Perhaps I should have written to him a lot sooner.'

'You did your best.'

'No,' David said ruefully, 'I didn't do my best.'

'You tried.'

'I wasn't a good father to him. We were too dissimilar, and he was so close to his mother. Jenny was always telling him how wonderful he was, how he could do anything, how he was always right, how he was special. But life doesn't like special people. Especially when they've nothing to be special about. I know why she spoiled him now – to make up for my treatment – but it ruined him.'

Anxious, Irene hurried to console her husband. 'You just tried to make him see life how it is.'

'But was that kind?' he asked, turning to her, his voice anguished. 'Reality is too hard for some people. I should have known he was weak. I should have known that the truth was too much for my son.'

THIRTY-SIX

'It's a matter of some concern,' the Governor of the Moors Prison said briskly, staring at the young guard in front of him. He had heard good things about James Caird, but lately he had begun to hear other things – not so good. Like Caird becoming too involved with Frederick Coles. Well, thought the Governor, it happened. The fact that Jim Caird was going out with Emma Coles also came under the heading of 'things that happened', but the latest information to reach him had caused real concern. Apparently Jim Caird had been out and about asking for information about Frederick Coles and the robbery at Oldfield Mill.

Irritated, the Governor looked at Jim, at the pressed uniform and the even, calm expression. One of the guards who had been picked out for success, but not the way he was going now.

'You like your job, don't you?'

'Yes, sir,' Jim replied.

'You would like a career in the prison service? I mean, a life-long career.'

'Yes, sir. I worked hard to get my examinations to

enter the service. And it's been everything I hoped for.' Jim paused, suddenly feeling under threat. 'It's my life.'

'And you want to keep your job?'

'Yes, sir,' he repeated, trying to keep the unease out of his voice. 'Have I done something wrong, sir?'

'I think you know.'

'No, sir.'

'Are you going to deny that you have been showing an interest in the case of Frederick Coles?'

Jim hesitated before answering. 'No, sir, I'm not going to deny it.'

'So you *have* been asking questions, in all kinds of places? Talking to criminals and generally trying to dig up everything about the Coles case?'

Surprised that the Governor could have found out, Jim held the man's gaze.

'May I ask who told you, sir?'

'No, you may not.'

'But what I do on my own time, sir, is surely my own business.'

The Governor sighed, his suit too big because he had lost weight from a bout of food poisoning, his glasses smeared with fingerprints from putting them on and taking them off continuously.

'Who told me is not important. You know the unwritten law in the prison: guards don't get too involved with the prisoners.' He paused, sitting down, but keeping Jim standing to attention in front of his desk. 'It looks bad to have an officer trailing over an old case. Looks like he might not agree with it – and people might presume that the prison authorities took the same view.'

'I did what I did on my own time.'

'No matter, I heard about it. And so will other people,' the Governor replied. 'We have to have people working here who believe in the system one hundred per cent.'

'I do, sir.'

'I don't think so,' the Governor countered. 'I understand that you're going out with Frederick Coles's daughter, Emma?'

'We're engaged, sir.'

'Ah,' he said simply, taken aback. 'That *would* put you in a difficult position. But you have to choose which horse to ride – because you only have one arse. You can go sniffing about trying to undermine the case – which, I might add, was tried by a British jury, who found Frederick Coles guilty of theft – or you can do your job here and stop trying to be a bloody hero.'

Flinching, Jim kept his voice expressionless.

'I'm not trying to be a hero.'

'So what *are* you trying to do, Caird? Make me and the prison service look like idiots?'

'That was not my intention.'

'Well, maybe it wasn't, but you're on a slippery slope here, and I suggest that you think about your next move very carefully,' the Governor went on, staring at Jim's file on top of his desk. 'I've been reading your record; it looks impressive. You seem like the kind of man we want here. A man who could progress up the ranks. You chose your career very well, and a promotion wouldn't be out of the question next year.'

Jim didn't say a word.

'I'm not suggesting that you give up your fiancée, Caird, I'm just saying that you should stop trying to impress her by playing amateur detective.' He paused for a long moment. 'I want to make myself perfectly clear – you could flourish in your career at this prison, even end up as chief warden. But not if you carry on with this absurd charade. The man is guilty. He was found guilty and sentenced. His daughter may not be able to accept it, but you have to.'

Taking in a deep breath, Jim took a moment to answer.

'I still say that what I do on my own time is my own concern.'

'*Then you're a bloody idiot!*' the Governor replied. 'You can't hunt with the hounds and run with the foxes. It's called divided loyalties. I think you have to decide what you want most – Emma Coles's good opinion or your career.'

'But what if it wasn't just *her* opinion, sir? What if it was proved to be mine?'

The Governor gave him a hard look, his irritation obvious. Of course, if Caird had been an ambitious man, he would never have become engaged to an inmate's daughter. Not that Emma Coles was the usual rabble offspring. But a more political man might perhaps have chosen a less contentious bride

. . . He looked Jim up and down. Divided loyalties always led to complications – unless he could nip any further rebellion in the bud.

'Are you saying that you think Frederick Coles is innocent?'

'He might be.'

'Jesus, Caird, I didn't take you for a fool!'

Unnerved, Jim stared at the Governor. He *couldn't* lose his job, he thought. He couldn't – he had studied and worked for it for years. Gone to special classes to educate himself enough to secure a position in the prison service. It had been his ambition, one he had fulfilled, and one he had enjoyed. He liked the work and he liked being good at it, knowing that he had managed – despite drawbacks – to achieve something in life. It was true that he loved Emma. True that he was seriously considering Frederick's innocence – but did another man's good name matter more than his own security? Breathing in deeply, Jim considered his options. If he lost his job, how could he support a wife? He would have a black mark on his record and he knew only too well that no other prison would hire him with a question mark hanging over his head. But then again, could he let Emma down? Could he renege on a promise to her? Smash her hopes, lose her good opinion, her love?

'Who told you what I was doing, sir?'

'Caird, that's not for you to know.'

'It must have been someone who knows me, and has a grudge against me.'

'Or a loyal employee.' At that moment, Jim knew

exactly who had reported him to the Governor. A man who hoped to get his job back at the prison by betraying another man.

'It was Stan Thorpe, wasn't it?'

An instant's hesitation confirmed it, the Governor brushing aside the question as he hurried on. 'Well, I've said what I meant to say, Caird. I leave the rest to you. Either you decide to act like a proper member of the prison service, or you'll have to look for another job.'

Dressed sombrely in a dark winter coat and hat, Emma got off the bus in Oldham and looked about her. She wasn't familiar with the town, having only visited a few times before, but it looked unwelcoming, chilled with the winter night. Down Moss Row, the lights of the pub threw sullen reflections on the wet surface of the cobbles, the banks of terraces that surrounded the Acorn uniform and grim. Many had windows boarded up, others were serving as cheap shops, a few flophouses hanging torn sheets at the windows, one with a man sitting silently on the steps outside. He was smoking a squib of baccy, the pungent smell reaching Emma as she paused at the entrance of Moss Row.

Her courage failed her in that instant. Suddenly, faced with the sleazy, eerie atmosphere, she found herself remembering what Jack had told her when she'd reminded him she was Ernie Coles's granddaughter: *That's no protection! If you got to him, you might have a chance, but there's plenty of people who would welcome an opportunity to hurt you before you got that close.*

And now Emma could believe it. Holland Street was poor, but nothing like this. This place was more like the Moors Prison, with the same oppressive aura. Hesitating, Emma thought about leaving, but she had come so far and she wasn't going to back down now. Slowly she moved into Moss Row, past the silent man, who didn't even glance up, her steps echoing in the narrow passageway. Instinctively she looked around for another exit, but there was only one way in, and one way out. And that was behind her.

Taking her time, Emma drew closer to the Acorn, the sounds of voices coming muted into the freezing air. Exhaling, she could see her breath on the indigo night, the overhead lamp making it into a mustard halo for an instant before she walked on. Then, just as she reached the double doors of the pub, she saw two men come out. One in workman's overalls, the other thin, coughing up a gob of spittle into the gutter. When they saw her, the thin man put his head on one side.

'Want a drink, luv?'

She shook her head.

'Yer a long way from home, aren't yer?' he went on, looking her up and down. 'Lost?'

'No,' Emma said, her voice falling quiet, showing her nerves.

'So why are yer 'ere?' the man went on, his companion moving a little way away and relieving himself against the wall. 'Can I 'elp yer?'

'I came to visit the Acorn.'

Interested, the man leaned towards her. 'Now why would yer want to go in there?' he said, Emma smelling the cheap beer on his breath and trying not to step back. 'I could take yer somewhere. Somewhere nice, quiet.'

'No, no thank you,' Emma began, sensing trouble and trying to turn.

But he caught hold of her hand and clung on to her. 'Nah, there's no point taking that tone, I were just being pleasant.'

'Aw, come in and fucking leave her alone!' his companion called out, his voice reverberating around the narrow passageway, his impatience obvious. 'I wanna 'nother drink.'

Shrugging, the thin man let go of Emma's arm. 'Yer not my type anyway, luv,' he said, touching her cheek briefly. 'Mind yer, if yer want to make a living round 'ere, I'd get a little more friendly. Know what I mean?'

Watching him walk off with the other man, Emma took in a breath and then moved into a deserted doorway to control herself. Her legs were shaking, her heart thumping unpleasantly fast, her mouth dry. Jesus, what was she doing coming here? Jim had been right to warn her off. And she should have listened to Jack Rimmer as well. They had known what they were talking about. This was no place for a woman on her own. And at night . . . Fighting panic, Emma was about to leave when there was further movement from the pub. Ducking back into the shadow of the doorway, she watched a prostitute come out with her client, followed soon after by a man throwing a pail of water into the gutter.

Curious, Emma studied the man. Wasn't her grandfather supposed to have an understanding with the landlord? And this was evidently the owner of the Acorn. But he was obviously not a man to approach, Emma thought, taking in the bald head and the leather apron around his thick waist. His boots, metal-tipped and studded, clacked against the uneven cobbles as he glanced around him. Still hiding, Emma watched him and wondered about the woman Ernie Coles was involved with. Was she on the game? Was she like the woman who had just walked past with her client? Emma wasn't an innocent; she had seen many women like that visiting the prison, but not in everyday life. And then she realised how pathetic she would seem to them. How out of place, how naïve, how stupid, thinking she could just walk in and ask questions.

Uneasy, Emma realised she was out of her depth, and understood why her father had protected her from Ernie Coles and the life he led. Then, hearing a noise, she jumped back into the shadows, watching the silent man get up from the steps where he had been sitting, and walk down the passageway. He was middle-aged, limping badly, his clothes stinking as he came towards her, his tongue flicking over his lips.

'Hey!'

She said nothing, just shrank further back into the dark doorway.

'Hey, I can see yer!' He looked round, then put his finger to his lips and grinned, most of his teeth missing. 'Sssh, I get it! Yer don't want anyone to know yer there.'

Still Emma said nothing.

'Hey!' the man said more loudly, weaving towards her, Emma putting up her hands to silence him.

'Be quiet!'

The man stopped, stared at her, his eyes rheumy, unfocused. 'I can see yer.'

'Go away.'

He wasn't about to move, just kept staring into the darkened doorway. 'I thought yer came past me, and yer did. What are yer doing? Hiding?'

She nodded, keeping to the shadows. 'Yes, I'm hiding.'

'Right,' he said, drunkenly tapping the side of his nose with a filthy forefinger.

'Just go away, please.'

'I can't do that,' the man replied, his voice quieter.

'Why not?'

'Well, I could . . . but yer'd have to give me some money.'

'What!'

'Yer want to hide, yer have to pay me.'

'I—'

'Pay me, or I'll tell on yer.'

Sighing, Emma felt in her pocket and handed the man a shilling. 'Now get away.'

He took the shilling, stared at it, then ambled off, weaving his way towards the doors of the Acorn.

Taking in a slow breath, Emma prepared herself. She had come too far to turn back now. But just as she was about to step under the lamplight, there was a hurried clatter of movement and shouting. Bursting through the pub doors, two men fell into the alleyway, yelling at each other and fighting. Both men were obviously drunk, both missing punches as their arms flailed around, but they hit each other enough for one to have his nose broken, the other man spitting out a clot of blood.

Realising that she had to get out of Moss Row as soon as possible, Emma was about to leave the shelter of the doorway when a heavy footfall sounded on the cobbles close by. Holding her breath, she stepped back into the darkness, but from where she stood, she could see the figure of a man under the lamplight. He had paused and was lighting a cigarette: his bullet head, with its cropped hair, tipped downwards towards the match. She could see the flame light up the pale, dead eyes momentarily, then watched as he inhaled. His bulk threw a huge shadow on to the cobbles of Moss Row, his shoulders massive under the cheap coat. And she knew – without being told, and without knowing *how* she knew – that this was her grandfather. The man she had come to see. The man she had believed would help her.

Fascinated, she studied him, watched as he moved towards the two fighting men. His shadow fell across them, then, without any apparent effort, he hauled one man off the other and flung him against the wall.

'What the fuck—' The man stopped, seeing Ernie

Coles, his tone shifting to a wheedling pitch. 'I were . . . We were . . . It were nothing.'

Emma's grandfather watched as the other man scrambled to his feet and ran out of Moss Row. But the first drunk was too slow and Ernie grabbed him again. Even without him saying a word, Emma could see the power her grandfather wielded and she stayed hidden, kept in the shadows, out of sight, because she was suddenly terribly afraid. Then she watched as Ernie Coles, showing no emotion, dragged the drunk upright and punched him in the gut. The man vomited, bending over and gasping for air – and in that moment, Emma ran.

Without looking back, she ran away from the passage, away from the threat of the pub and its customers. She ran until she was breathless, away from the narrow dark terraces, until the streets became busy with lights and people and she was back in the centre of the town. Still shaking, she climbed on to the first tram home. Silent, she sat in her seat, trying to calm herself. But all she could see was the big man with the pale eyes. The man her father had expunged from their lives. The man who was every bit as intimidating as his reputation. Every bit as chilling. Every bit as dangerous.

She *was* Ernie Coles's granddaughter – but the thought was no comfort at all.

'What the hell were you thinking of!' Jim snapped, taking Emma by the shoulders and shaking her. 'What were you doing? Have you any idea what could have happened to you?'

Overwhelmed, she tried to push him away, but Jim held on to her.

'You could have been hurt!'

'I wasn't!' she retorted. 'Nothing happened!'

Jim could hardly believe what Emma had just told him, or rather, what he had managed to prise out of her. That she had been to the Acorn on her own, to find her grandfather . . . Exhausted from having just come off his late shift and from his run-in with the Governor, he had arrived at the jeweller's shop, knowing that David and Irene were out for the night and thinking that it was the perfect opportunity for Emma and him to go over the case notes.

But instead he had discovered what she had really been up to.

'You're a stupid woman!' he said, shaking her again. 'A stupid bloody woman!' Struggling, she tried to push him off, but he was incensed and not about to relax his grip. 'I said *I* would look into it.'

'He's not your father, he's mine!' Emma retorted.

'We agreed—'

'*I* didn't agree,' Emma replied, her face flushed. 'I didn't want to get you involved. And I thought I could do it on my own.'

'So now you don't trust me!'

'Oh, let me go!' she snapped, frustrated. 'You don't own me! I can do what I like.'

'And get yourself killed, you bloody moron,' he said, looking into her face and suddenly kissing her. He kissed her mouth, her cheeks and then drew back, staring into her eyes. 'God, Emma, what if something had happened to you?'

But she didn't answer, her arms going around his neck instead, her lips against his. For several minutes they kissed, until Emma finally drew back.

'I was so scared.'

'Serves you right,' he teased her. 'Never do anything like that again.'

'My grandfather was so frightening. So sinister.'

'I've been thinking' Jim said suddenly. 'We should set a date for our marriage.'

She looked at him, incredulous.

'Not now! Not with all this worry about my father.' Then she paused, suddenly apologetic. 'It's always about him, isn't it? I'm sorry, Jim, but it matters to me so much.'

'I know that. I understand,' he replied, thinking of what the Governor had said to him earlier. 'But we have a life too.'

'And I *want* that life. With you,' she said, her expression loving. 'But I have to clear my father's name first. You understand, don't you?'

Reluctantly, Jim nodded. 'But we might not succeed, we might not find out anything to help him.'

He stopped short, seeing the expression on Emma's face. A look of disappointment that tore into him. And he knew then that if it came down to choosing between his career and his love, he would always choose Emma. The loss of his career would be devastating – but the loss of her would ruin his life.

'What d'you mean?' she asked uneasily. 'Why

would you say that? Do you think it's useless?'

'No,' he said, his voice gaining confidence. He wasn't going to lose Emma – and if he was careful, he wasn't going to lose his job either. He would just have to be clever and keep his movements secret. And hope – and pray – he wasn't found out. 'We just have to get on with it. Get moving, straight away . . .'

Jim didn't know what was going to happen, but he knew that Frederick Coles didn't have another winter in him, not served at the Moors Prison. If they were going to get him out, they had to do it soon – or it would be too late.

'And afterwards, Emma, you'll marry me then?' he asked. 'Whatever happens, you'll marry me?'

'What could happen to stop me?' she said, kissing him gently. 'I swear it on my life.'

'Promise me too that you'll never go back to that pub?'

'Never,' Emma said, shaken as she thought back. 'I saw my grandfather for what he really was. You know, I was going to talk to him,' she said, blushing as she glanced away and sat down. 'I was going to be a heroine and find out something that would save the day . . . I can't believe he's my grandfather, that we share the same blood.'

'Now you see why your father kept you away from him?' Jim replied. 'And why I tried to warn you off? I told you about my brother. Well, when Tommy told Ernie Coles he wasn't going to work for him any longer, Coles hit him with a tyre iron and smashed his nose.'

'God,' Emma said, shaken. 'You never told me that.'

'Why would I? You didn't need to know. But now you understand why I know all about your grandfather? In his book, my brother had let him down. Cried off a job at the last minute – and no one lets Ernie Coles down. So he punished him. Rough justice, but if you run with those types, it's what you get. Tommy was seventeen at the time, but it taught him a lesson he never forgot. Kept him straight. Did him a good turn, in fact.' Stroking Emma's arm, Jim smiled at her. 'So, did you get the information together?'

'All the newspapers and notes,' she said, pointing to a stack of papers on the sofa. 'And I spoke to Jack Rimmer. He told me about the Acorn and a place called the Black Knight.'

Jim nodded. 'I know them both.'

'You know *all* these places? How?'

'I used to go there, when I was young. Before I made my choice.'

Confused, Emma looked at him intently. 'What choice?'

'I had every chance of being a deadbeat. I had little education. A good family, but not an ambitious one. We were straight, but no one round our way would have been surprised if we'd gone bad. Ernie Coles and Foster Gunnell – another hard case – picked their boys from our street, and others like it. They talked about good times to draw us in. Not difficult, if you've never had money or anything much to call your own. Gunnell always promised – and still does – the high life and women. He made a fortune from property and shops, mostly through overcharging on the rents, and lived big. But your grandfather didn't offer glamour. He promised power, fear and money. He could get respect from anyone. Ernie Coles would have crushed a man like Stan Thorpe without breaking into a sweat. So imagine how tempting it was for us. We could flog ourselves for life at the sewage works or the mills, for a small wage and no respect. Or we could cross the line. Work for the other side. Get what we wanted, however we could. It's a miracle that out of all my family, not one of my brothers has become a criminal. Tommy came closest, but my father put an end to that.'

'And you were never tempted?'

'Of course I was,' Jim admitted openly. 'I was going to be a boxer once. A real fighter, get into the money and the fame. Your grandfather offered me the money to make it happen. And that was the choice I had to make. The moment I decided that I wanted to feel clean in myself. Wanted to like myself, look myself in the eye.' He paused, shaking his head. 'I'll never have money, Emma, or be able to afford a big house, but I can offer you security. The knowledge that I won't cheat in any way, or change how I feel about you.'

Moved, she touched his forehead, running her finger between his brows. 'Will you always love me?'

'Always.'

'How d'you know?' she asked, suddenly remembering her past. 'People change, life changes them, things happen.'

'Yes, they do,' he agreed. 'Marriages break down and people give up when they don't feel safe. When the bond isn't there – that connection that nothing on earth or in heaven can break.'

'We have that, don't we?'

'Oh yes,' Jim said emphatically. 'We have it now, and it can only grow. If you love someone, *really* love them, you know them, accept them, make allowances for all the petty, stupid things they do. Because you do them too. If you love someone like that, you'll always win out. If you've got someone with you, beside you every inch of the way, you could go to hell and back and never be afraid.'

Touched, Emma laid her head on his shoulder. She could feel the strength of his body under the prison uniform and knew that he meant what he said. This was a man a woman could trust; someone who would never back down, or buckle. He was quiet, because he had no need to shout. He was reserved, because he had no need to court attention. He was his own man, and he was now hers . . . Touching the back of Jim's hand, she traced the pattern of his fingers and then laced them tightly with her own.

THIRTY-SEVEN

Flapping, Sheila Caird laid out another cake on the table in the front room, giving three of her sons a mildly warning look not to touch. The chocolate cake – the result of a gruelling morning's baking – was for their special visitor, Jim's girl, Emma Coles. Having already met Emma a couple of times, Sheila liked the young woman, but she was always nervous around her. It wasn't anything Emma had said or done; Sheila was nervous around anyone new. The house was too poor, too cramped, too shabby. She was too stupid, too anxious. In her own small world, running her terraced house and her family, Sheila was confident. But anything, or anyone, who came into the sphere rocked her axis.

Her husband, Frank, was the opposite. Where Sheila hung back, Frank was outspoken, lighting innumerable cigarettes with his nicotined fingers, a fug hanging over the table where they were sitting, Emma having been invited over for tea. The Cairds had long ago ceased to notice the smoggy overhang, or the fact that their father had kippered his offspring, Frank lighting up another cigarette as he leaned towards Emma.

'Good to have yer here,' he said sincerely.

His wiry frame belied his strength, which had been honed by decades working in the Burnley mills. Frank Caird might only weigh nine and a half stone, but he could lift double his body weight and had very clear ideas about his family. Like keeping them all in line. His sons might be bigger and taller than their father, but Frank could control them by force of will.

'So,' he went on, his accent broadly Lancastrian, 'I hear that our Jim's taking a look at yer father's case for yer. I hope the authorities don't hear about it; it wouldn't do him any good. But hey, our Jim knows what he's doing, always has done.'

Emma was surprised that Frank knew about Jim's involvement, and worried that it might lead to some bad feeling with the Cairds. She was also feeling nervous about being here on her own, but Jim had sent a message to say that he had been held up at the prison and would be along later. Smiling uneasily, Emma considered Frank's remark about the authorities. The thought unsettled her.

'Well . . . he volunteered to help,' she said apologetically. 'I don't want him to think he has to.'

'He's fallen for yer,' Frank replied, Sheila embarrassed and interrupting him.

'Some cake, luv?'

'Fallen for yer good and strong,' Frank went on, ignoring his wife, although he put out his plate for a

422

slice. 'And I'm right glad, because he needs a good woman.'

'Another slice for you, luv?' Sheila asked Emma, trying to stem her husband's flow.

'That would be lovely.'

'A better lad would be hard to find. Even with yer trouble,' Frank went on, blithely unaware how tactless he was being. 'And I bear yer no grudges, Emma. Not even if yer grandfather *is* Ernie Coles.'

Dropping the cake she was holding, Sheila shot her visitor an appealing look.

'Pay no mind to him, luv,' she said, her voice timid. 'My Frank's got a big mouth, but he means no harm.'

'Her grandfather *is* Ernie Coles,' Frank persisted, baffled. 'I'm only talking the truth.'

'But yer making her feel right awkward,' Sheila said shyly, looking down at the floor and the ruined chocolate cake. Sighing, she called for the family dog and watched as he ate it. Of course, if they hadn't had a visitor, she would have cut off the bit of cake that had hit the floor and put the rest back on the table.

Still staring woefully at the dog, Sheila turned to Emma. 'What Frank means is that we're pleased to . . . know yer.'

'Pleased to know yer! To know yer? She's Jim's fiancée!' Frank replied impatiently. 'Not someone from the Jehovah's Witnesses.' Coughing shortly, he flicked some ash into the grate, then leaned back in his seat. The house was uncomfortable, with little furniture, but he ruled it like an emperor. If Sheila could see the worn curtains and the waxed tablecloth and cringe, her husband thought that Emma Coles was lucky to be courting their eldest son. 'I've worked hard all my life, brought up five sons, with the help of our Sheila, and no man could have had a better wife . . .'

Warmly, Emma smiled at the timid woman standing over them with yet another cake.

'We don't stand on ceremony here. We've not got money fer that, or inclination. But we're honest people.'

Flushing, Emma misread what he was saying and leapt to her family's defence.

'My father's innocent.'

'Cake?' Sheila said, to no one in particular, Frank leaning towards Emma and smiling broadly.

'No, don't yer go taking offence. If yer say yer father's innocent and our Jim says the same, then that's good enough fer me,' he replied, sucking on his cigarette, a flurry of smoke momentarily clouding his face. 'So, yer going to get married, hey?'

Emma took in a breath. 'Well . . .'

'Good idea,' Frank went on, taking her strangled reply as a yes. 'We could have a big wedding, hey, our Sheila? All the lads could muck in and we could take over the Co-op dance hall. Cost a bit, but that's what money's fer, family occasions.'

'Mr Caird—'

'It's Frank, luv,' he said, nodding. 'Now yer going to be part of the family.'

The arrival of Jim stopped the verbal assault, Emma looking at him with relief as he came into the kitchen. Drenched from a downpour, he took off his coat and put it on the rack to dry, smiling at his mother and taking some cake.

'Sorry I was late,' he said to everyone. 'Did you have a good chat?'

'We were talking about yer wedding,' Frank said, nodding as though he approved and the event could go ahead.

Amused, Jim winked at Emma. 'It's not for a while, Dad.'

'No point hanging about.'

'No point rushing,' Jim said firmly, turning as he heard the front door open.

Hoping that Jim was going to walk her home, Emma was momentarily surprised when he asked one of his brothers to see her back to Holland Street. Then, before she could say anything else, Jim turned to another brother who had walked in, falling into a deep and muted conversation with him.

'Those two – Jim and Tommy,' Frank said, glancing over to Emma and offering up an explanation. 'Thick as thieves they are, and lately they've been chatting like a couple of washerwomen over at the public laundry.'

Donald, Jim's other brother, helped Emma on with her coat, and they walked to the door together.

Spotting them, Jim hurried over and kissed Emma on the cheek.

'I need to stay, talk to Tommy. Donald will see you home,' he told her. 'I'll come over to the shop tomorrow, all right?'

She smiled in agreement, then, after saying goodbye to Jim's parents, left with Donald Caird.

As soon as they had gone, Jim pulled Tommy into the kitchen and sat down, his brother taking the seat opposite, his hair still wet from the rain. Jim shivered momentarily, Tommy walking over to the fire and kicking it back into life with the toe of his boot. After a couple of moments, the flames caught, a sick red glow mottling the walls, Frank calling out from the front room:

'Have yer made a bloody fire in there? We're not made of money.'

Smiling, the brothers ignored him, Jim holding his chilled hands out to the warmth. Watching him, Tommy studied the firm features, like his own, but stronger. He admired his elder brother, wanted to be like him, had even considered becoming a prison guard, until he realised he would have to study for it. And studying had never been his strong point. He was better in the mill, with his father and brothers, having a pint after work, and playing snooker in the pool hall off St James's Street. No point trying to better himself, Tommy thought, when he had no reason to. No governor to draw a promotion from, or pretty woman to impress. Tommy's girls – like all the other Caird brothers' women – were mill girls, or factory workers. Appealing because they were young, but none of them lit up with ambition. Which was fine by Tommy; he wasn't a man who looked for – or needed – a strong-minded woman. Which was more than he could say for Jim.

'So, what did you find out?'

Tommy picked up the poker and riddled the coals, making a few flames dart uncertainly up the chimney.

'There were some rumours going around about the Coles case,' he began. 'Some people – most, actually – thought Frederick was innocent, but when he didn't name anyone else, they shrugged it off. Even though they still talked about it.'

'You said there were rumours?' Jim prompted him. 'What kind?'

'About Foster Gunnell and his lot. They'd been working around that area, doing some jobs, a few breaks-ins, and a robbery at the post office.' He dropped his voice, making sure that their parents wouldn't overhear. 'Someone said there was a Frenchwoman involved.'

'*A woman?*'

Tommy nodded. 'I had to go careful, asking questions. You know how it is, you don't want to look obvious.'

'I'm grateful.'

'No trouble,' Tommy replied, secretly pleased that he was impressing his idol. 'It's just that if Dad gets wind of me talking to some of these types . . . You know what he was like about Ernie Coles.'

'I remember only too well,' Jim said wryly. 'What about this woman? Was she working for Gunnell?'

'And Ernie Coles.'

The name nudged them apart, moved between them like a combine harvester slashing its way through corn.

'Ernie Coles,' Jim repeated slowly. 'What was the woman's name?'

'I dunno. And no one knew, or would tell me.' Tommy took in a breath, looking into the fire. 'I can't push it too much, or people clam up. It's taken me days to get this much information. And quite a bit of money.'

'You know I'll give you any money you need,' Jim reassured him. 'I had to spend enough to get something out of Gordon Moore.'

Tommy raised his eyebrows. 'Bloody hell, Jim, I wouldn't dare talk to that bugger!'

Hesitating Jim realised that a week earlier *he* would have thought twice about it. But now that the pressure was on, he was moving faster, trying to uncover as much as he could before he was found out again.

'I'm taking over now, Tommy. I'll get the information.'

'As a prison guard?' his brother replied, smiling ruefully. 'Oh yeah, they're going to open their hearts to you, aren't they? The only reason some of them would even give me the time of day was because they remembered my run-in with Coles, and the fact that I'd once worked for the bastard.' He touched his nose, the broken bridge flattened. 'You could say that I'm walking around with my own personal calling card.'

Laughing, Jim slapped his brother on the knee. 'Tell me about this Frenchwoman – she was involved in the jobs?'

'Some said so.'

'Thieving?'

'Yeah. Well, it's not uncommon, Jim, for a woman to steal from shops now. Or the market. Most of the pickpockets are kids or women. Think about that old hag in Salford – Ma Taylor – she fences everything for this area.'

Jim nodded. 'She might be worth talking to.'

'She wouldn't talk to you or to me,' Tommy said, his tone disgusted. 'She's as suspicious as a snake and about as vicious.'

'So who *is* the woman who ran around with Coles and Gunnell? I take your point about shoplifting, but maybe she was more important. If she got involved in the break-ins, it would mean she was trusted, a part of their circle.' Jim paused, remembering something Emma had told him. 'It couldn't be Ernie Coles's woman, could it?'

'I dunno,' Tommy said, baffled. 'I don't know anything. How did you hear about her?'

'From an old friend,' Jim replied. 'He said that Coles had a woman in Moss Row. Seems that she's been part of his life for a while.'

'But if she was his age, she'd be about sixty – how many women do you know who'd be doing burglaries at sixty?'

Thoughtful, Jim stared into the fire.

'I spoke to one of the prison guards, Reg Spencer, asked him what he knew, because the guards hear everything in prison. We're not supposed to talk about individual cases, but he didn't seem to mind.

Told me about Foster Gunnell falling out with Ernie Coles when Gunnell made a move to take over his territory. Apparently Ernie talked him out of it – with his fists. Gunnell's never challenged Coles again, and they agreed to a truce. He also told me about how they divided up their men.'

'Oh yeah,' Tommy said, remembering. 'Gunnell took over a couple of Coles's men, because they couldn't go back to Coles after they'd turned on him and thrown in their lot with Gunnell. One of those men got killed in an accident a year later, didn't he?'

'Drowned,' Jim said, looking at his brother doubtfully. 'In the North End mill stream, got caught under the wheel. I bet that wasn't a bloody accident.'

Falling silent, Tommy stared ahead, thinking about the way Ernie Coles had picked up the tyre iron and smashed it across his nose. He could remember the sound of the metal hitting the bone, the crushing, soft collapse, and then the pain and the taste of blood. Tommy hadn't had anything to do with Coles since that night, but he had kept bearing a grudge and was more than willing to help his brother find out anything that would damage the man who had attacked him.

'The other man that used to work for Coles?' Tommy said enquiringly. 'Anyone got a name?'

'No,' Jim replied. 'No one's mentioned a thing. What about you?'

'He was young, that's all I know.'

'From around here?'

Tommy shrugged. 'Who knows? I could ask.'

'No, don't,' Jim said firmly. 'You've done enough; I don't want you asking around any more. If Coles got to hear about it he wouldn't like it. I'll find out about the other man, and the woman.'

Laughing mockingly, Tommy stared at his elder brother. 'They won't talk to you! You're on the wrong side.'

'But they won't know that,' Jim replied evenly. 'I wasn't always a prison guard, and I don't have to advertise the fact now. Besides, who knows me in Oldham or Hanky Park?'

'Why there?'

'Because the Acorn is Ernie Coles's watering hole and the Black Knight in Hanky Park is where he and Gunnell do business.'

'You can't just walk in there and start sniffing around. I'd leave it alone,' Tommy said, anxious. 'Honestly, Jim, there must be another way.'

Sure, Tommy had asked around himself, but nothing serious. He hadn't approached anyone dangerous. But his brother was now talking about going to notoriously rough pubs, where the worst types hung out. And suddenly Tommy Caird didn't think it was a lark any more. Didn't want to settle his own personal grudge with Ernie Coles. Getting the information was costing money, money they couldn't afford to give away, and it might cost a lot more. Suddenly there was a very real chance that his admired brother might get in over his head.

'You've done enough, Jim.'

Surprised by the remark, Jim glanced at his brother. 'What d'you mean?'

'All this, it's asking for trouble if you push much more,' Tommy went on, hating himself for sounding like a coward and yet aware that Jim could soon be walking into something from which he might not be able to escape.

The memory of the man drowned in the North End mill stream came back eerily. He had become entangled in the slats of the mill wheel, the papers said, but Tommy – and everyone else – knew he hadn't. Knew without being told that he had been tied to that wheel, and drowned as it turned, filling his nose and mouth with water, pushing the air out of his lungs.

And he didn't want it to happen to his brother.

'You've done enough.'

'This is for Emma.'

'So let her do it.'

His voice warning, Jim looked his brother up and down.

'Let her do it?'

'Look, she's bound to think that her father's innocent,' Tommy hurried on. 'We'd think the same about Dad. But honestly, how likely is it? If Frederick Coles *did* know the man who was guilty, why didn't he tell someone?' He gripped Jim's arm as his brother attempted to stand up. 'Don't get angry with me! I'm just saying what everyone else would think if they knew what you were doing. Emma has to believe her father – you don't.'

'Jesus!' Jim said, brushing off his brother's grip. 'You think she's lying!'

'No. But her father might be,' Tommy replied, standing up and facing his brother, his voice tight. 'You've got a good job at the prison, you've done well in life . . .'

'Be very careful what you say next,' Jim warned him.

But Tommy persisted.

'You're in love with Emma, fine, I get it. But you don't have to risk yourself for her father. It's not about her – it's about him.'

'You don't understand, do you? Frederick Coles's story *is* about Emma. It's what she believes, what she held on to when her life fell apart; it's what makes his imprisonment bearable. Proving her father is innocent is her reason for living.'

'What about you?' Tommy said bluntly. 'Aren't you that?'

'What the hell!'

'Because if you aren't her reason for living, you *should* be.'

Ducking as Jim threw an unexpected punch, Tommy lost his balance and fell to the floor. Surprised, he scrambled to his feet and lurched towards his brother, catching Jim under the chin and splitting his bottom lip. With fury, Jim then grabbed Tommy, spun him around, and caught his neck in a head lock, talking directly into his ear.

'How dare you speak to me like that! *You* want to back off, fine. But don't try to make out that you're

433

doing it for my bloody benefit,' he hissed, finally letting go and watching as Tommy slumped into the nearest chair.

Rubbing his neck, Tommy glowered at his brother, his throat burning, but before he could say another word, Jim had walked out. Tommy could hear him saying something to their parents and then heard the slam of the front door as he left, but he didn't move. Cursing himself, he knew what a mistake he had made. Not just by questioning Emma and her father, but by trying to convince his brother to back off. Jim Caird had never backed off from anything.

And this was to be no exception.

THIRTY-EIGHT

In his cell, Frederick was writing Emma a letter. He had told her about the new guard, who had replaced Stan Thorpe, and also about the work that had been finally done on the damp course. He was, he wrote, feeling better. And besides, spring would be here before long . . . He had known from the start that there would never be an appeal, or any new evidence. There couldn't be, because he was the only person who knew the guilty man, and if *he* didn't give up the name, there was no other way it would be disclosed. The secret was his – and Frederick knew he would never pass it on. At first, his course of action had been endurable. But as the years passed, his sacrifice had not lessened, but intensified.

He told himself repeatedly that his sentence would end, that he would get out, albeit a lot later than he should have done. But instead of the memories fading, they increased. Frederick dreamed repeatedly of the grim day he was arrested, of his parting from his daughter, and of the way people in Burnley had judged him. And worse, the way his friend Gregory Walmsley had accepted his guilt so readily and sent him spinning downwards from respectable accounts clerk to thief. Throwing him out of society's reach, into that hinterland of mistrust and criminality. And the Moors Prison, which had become his home for eleven years.

Of which he hadn't even served half . . . Frederick leaned back on his bunk and stared up at the green-painted ceiling. He could recall how content he had been working at Oldfield Mill and coming home to pick up his daughter from school. Even after his wife died, and there had been only the two of them, life had been happy. But the world didn't want to know him any more, and even when he got out – *if* he got out – the world would still turn its back. He might dream of a warm sun, and a walk with his daughter, but there would always be people to remind him of what he was.

And all because he had stayed silent. Kept the name a secret. Protected the real thief. For his action, Frederick had been barred from living, exiled from commonplace life. From catching a bus, buying a pint of beer, choosing summer fruit from a barrow on the market. Nothing enormous, or even important to most people – but important to him. To be a respectable man again, to have his good name returned . . . Frederick realised that he was clenching his fists and relaxed, counting the wall tiles. He could do it, he told himself, he could serve the sentence and keep the secret. He could hold that name to himself without ever uttering one syllable. And when he got out, he would move away from Burnley, with Emma.

But she would be married by then . . . His thoughts scattered. And then what would there be for him? A lonely life, bumming in some unqualified job – because who would hire an accounts clerk who had been jailed for theft? Yet if he opened his mouth, if he told his solicitor the name, he would be freed. Overton would inform the police and they would arrest the guilty man, and Frederick would walk out of the Moors Prison. He might even get an apology, people flocking around him in Burnley, saying that they never believed he had been guilty. It would be so simple. If he uttered the name, it would all be over.

The temptation was so intense that Frederick almost called out for a guard, but the moment passed, and instead he looked back to the tiled walls and continued to count. Determined, steady, soothing himself until the frustration passed. For reasons that mattered to him more than his freedom, Frederick Coles was going to serve another man's time. He could stop it – but he knew he never would.

Come in, come in. Bring your shoes, your boots! Come in, come in!' Mr Letski cried, his accent pronounced, his eyes bright with pleasure as he stood by the front door of the cobbler's and called out his refrain. The fact that it was Sunday and there were few people about meant that Bessie allowed him his moment of glory. If anyone did pass, they merely smiled at the old Russian, or nodded, humouring him.

'I don't see how you're going to manage,' Doug said, staring at Bessie with admiration. 'Having a baby, and having to cope with Mr Letski.'

'I've been having this baby for months – why the sudden interest?' she teased him. 'Anyway, where are you going?'

'Nowhere! But it's you that's having the baby.'

'And you that made it happen. So you can adjust yourself to the idea of helping out,' she replied, glancing over to Mr Letski in the doorway. 'I've got used to getting up in the night anyway – what with seeing to him, a baby might not be that much more trouble.'

'My mother said—'

'*Your mother!* Hah!' Bessie replied, dismissing Mrs Renshaw with one deadly phrase. 'You know what your mother said to me the other day? That she wanted to die when she had you, the pain was so bad. I said that I wanted to die when I *married* you.'

'You never!'

'It was a joke,' Bessie replied, moving past her husband and staring at the shelves, then reorganising the new delivery of footwear.

Sales had been quite brisk in the last few months, and Bessie's line in handbags hadn't failed either. In fact, she thought to herself, she might open a dress shop one day. Even work her way towards St James's Street. Now that would be something, and if the baby was a girl, she could see a brilliant career for the future Miss Renshaw. A profession, a shop of her own. Maybe *two* shops in time. She might even end up in Manchester, somewhere like Kendal Milne. Or even Southport . . .

'You'll have to give up work, of course.'

Slowly Bessie turned to her husband, her smile rigid. 'Oh aye?'

'Well, being pregnant, you'll have to give up working in the shop. You're going to be a full-time mother when the baby comes,' Doug said, looking round. 'I can take over.'

'And I could shoot myself in the eye, but neither is likely. No one's running this shop but me – and you better get used to the idea.' She winced, touching her stomach. She had had indigestion all morning and it was getting worse. 'Give up work, as if! This place is a little gold mine.'

'But what about the baby?'

'There are things called prams, Doug, and cots. You put babies into them, so you can get on with your work,' Bessie said, spelling out the obvious. 'My grandmother took my mother to the mill in a basket. She used to work the last spot on the row, so she could have a bit more room. Many women did that in those days. They had to; no one was around to look after the baby, and they had to work.'

'My mother could help out.'

Stunned, Bessie stared at her husband. 'Your mother brought you up – I would have thought that was reason enough for not wanting her too near our child.'

'Hey!' he said, looking affronted. 'My mother did the best she could.'

'That's what I mean,' Bessie replied, walking to the door and standing next to Mr Letski. She nodded to a passing customer, wincing again with stomach ache, but covering it well.

''Lo there, Mrs Thomas.'

'Come in, come in. Bring your shoes . . .'

'Hello there, Mrs Renshaw.'

'. . . your boots . . .'

'Looks like it's going to be cold again.'

'. . . Come in. Come in!'

'And how's Mr Letski?' the woman asked, Bessie grabbing the Russian by the arm as he made a sudden movement into the street. 'I heard about his getting worse; you must be feeling sad about that.'

'Well, he's not likely to get better, is he?'

'We were saying on the market yesterday that you had your work cut out, looking after him. Shame he's no family, no one to take him off your hands.'

'He's not a bloody dog!' Bessie replied, miffed.

'I know that . . . I was just thinking, him not having relatives, he might be a burden. Mrs Little was saying – she's a widow, you know – that she could take him on. For a little cost, of course.'

Bessie was glassy-eyed. Mrs Little was a harpy, with an eye for making money. She wouldn't look after poor old Letski, she would fleece him.

'We look after him.'

'But you're having a baby.'

'Which won't render me incapable. In fact, I heard that women have children every day and can still talk and cut up their own food.'

Mrs Thomas looked put out. 'I was just thinking of doing you a good turn.'

'Me? Or Mrs bloody Little?'

'Well, really!' the woman snapped, hurrying off.

Hauling the Russian indoors, Bessie turned to the old man. 'You've got an admirer, you have. AN ADMIRER . . .' she repeated, more loudly.

He blinked.

'Mrs Little, she wants to take care of you. And your money,' Bessie finished off, just as Doug walked in.

'What about Mrs Little? What are you talking about?'

'She's got her eye on the old man. But I put a stop to that, once and for all,' Bessie said, her voice faltering momentarily as she touched her stomach again. 'I mean, I'm fond of Mr Letski, and she wouldn't treat him right. Mean bitch, I saw her buying offcuts at the market. And how would he cope, being fed offcuts?' She touched his head fondly. 'Mr Letski has decent food.'

'Look after me.'

'No, she wouldn't!' Bessie said, bending down to the old man. 'SHE WOULDN'T TREAT YOU RIGHT, WOULD SHE?'

Blinking again, the old Russian looked into Bessie's face, and then, as though he hadn't see her for a long time, welcomed her like an old friend.

Bessie, my dear!

'I'VE JUST SAVED YOU FROM MRS LITTLE!' Bessie repeated, shouting to make him hear.

'Yes, lovely shop, lovely shop, well done, my dear, well done.'

Smiling, Bessie looked around. She had built up the business over the years – as if she would let Mrs Little come and take him over! As if . . .

'Pretty lady, Mrs Little,' Mr Letski said thoughtfully.

'What! That old bag.'

'She like me?'

'No, she hates you,' Bessie replied. 'She hates you! GOD! OH, BLOODY HELL, BLOODY HELL!'

'He's not that deaf,' Doug said, startled by his wife's outburst.

'It's not him, it's me.'

'What's the matter with you?'

'I'm having a baby, you moron! Call the midwife.'

THIRTY-NINE

From the first, Jim had been emphatic that he was going alone, whatever Emma said. She had seen the Acorn, and had some idea of what it was like, so how could she seriously think of returning there with him? He was jittery, worried about being followed and spied on, knowing that another slip would mean he would lose his job.

'I can't do it with you,' he said, his voice uncharacteristically cold. 'I can't worry about you. Please, Emma, stay home.'

'What's the matter?' she asked, aware that there was a tension between them.

'Nothing.'

'Yes there is. Tell me.'

Putting down his mug of tea, Jim glanced over to her. 'I had a fight with my brother. I don't like bad feeling, not in the family.'

'And I caused it?'

'No,' he lied. 'It wasn't about you.'

'You're a bad liar,' she said, walking over to him and sliding her arms around his waist. Serious, she gazed up into his face. 'I don't want to bring you any

443

trouble. God, Jim, I wouldn't do that to you. It would upset me so much to think I was hurting you in any way.'

'You're not,' he said, shaking his head and holding her to him tightly. 'Tommy was out of line. Just talking rubbish, that was all.'

'But he was helping you.'

'He's done all he can now,' Jim told her. 'I can do the rest. I've got some leads, a couple anyway. Someone was talking about a Frenchwoman who might have been involved.'

'A Frenchwoman?'

'Yes, and there's a man I want to know more about.' Jim paused, kissing the top of her head. 'Don't worry about me, I can handle myself.'

'What if you can't?' she asked, her voice a whisper. 'If anything happened to you, I couldn't live with it. I couldn't stand to have another person suffer because of me.' She touched his bottom lip, where Tommy had split the skin. 'You've already been fighting with your brother. The brother you're so fond of. What next, Jim? Fighting with your parents? Falling out with the rest of your family? And for what – for me? I don't want that to happen. To be honest, I can't let that happen.'

'It was just a fight.'

'And how many more will there be?' she countered. 'Your brother was against what we're doing, wasn't he?'

'Tommy's a kid.'

'He's a grown man! And before long, your parents

will object. Your father said something the other day; he was worried about your job.'

Jim flinched. 'It doesn't matter.'

'It does!' she said, her voice raised anxiously. 'You haven't been in a situation like this before; you have a lot to lose. You have a choice, Jim, I haven't. I don't want you to suffer for me.'

'I'm going out,' he said, his tone emphatic. 'Stop worrying.'

'Let me come with you.'

'No.'

'But if anything happens to you, what then?' she asked. 'I love you so much, Jim, I couldn't live without you.'

He took hold of her hands tightly.

'We agreed on our course of action. I know you're scared, Emma, but don't be. Tommy panics, he's a kid. My father talks rubbish, don't listen. I'm only going to ask some questions, not hold up a bank.' He smiled at her, trying to elicit some response. 'I used to train in the gym over the Black Knight. I'm not a stranger there. I could go back and it wouldn't seem odd to anyone. As for the Acorn, it's a rough pub, but I was brought up around pubs like that.'

'But—'

'Let me handle this, will you? Trust me, Emma, I know what I'm doing. It'll all be worthwhile, you'll see.'

Watching him leave, Emma stood for a while in the doorway of the jeweller's shop. Behind her she heard footsteps, but didn't turn, Irene walking over to her and putting a hand on her shoulder.

'Are you all right?'

'I don't want to lose him.'

'Why would you?'

'Because he's got divided loyalties and I know how much that can tear a person apart.'

'Jim Caird is a very strong man.'

'He'll need to be. He's going to the Acorn pub,' Emma said. She had explained to Irene the previous night what they were doing and sworn her to secrecy. 'It's the pub where Ernie Coles lives – and now Jim is going there, asking for anything that might help my father's case. And I'm letting him. *It's not his battle!*' she said helplessly. 'God, I should never have let him get involved.' She watched the last glimpse of Jim as he turned the corner of Holland Street, her mouth drying as she snatched up her coat. 'I have to go with him!'

'My dear, I don't think that's wise.'

'*I have to go!*' Emma snapped, running to the door and then pausing. 'Not a word to anyone, Irene, you understand? I'll be safe, honestly. I'll be with Jim.'

Running down Holland Street, Emma paused, catching sight of Jim as he waited for the tram to take him over to Oldham. She knew that if he saw her he would send her back, and so she ran to the next stop, making sure that she was out of sight when the tram arrived minutes later. Climbing on board amidst a group of other people, Emma moved upstairs. Knowing that Jim wouldn't see her there, she paid her fare and watched a group of lads smoking in the back seats. After almost an hour, they reached Oldham, Emma waiting until she saw Jim get off the tram before she ran downstairs. Hanging back, she followed him, taking the same route she had taken before. This time it wasn't completely dark, although the night was drawing in and before long Emma knew the lamps would be lit.

Carefully she followed Jim, who never looked round until he approached the alley of Moss Row. Ducking back, she held her breath, then, after a moment, stepped out again, just in time to see Jim walking up to the entrance of the Acorn. He moved with his head high, almost as though he knew the place and was unconcerned, as he pushed open the doors and walked in. Holding her breath, Emma watched. Fifteen minutes passed, the daylight dipping away, the winter night snaking in. Along with it came the cold, the temperature dipping as she sheltered against a sudden fall of rain. Surprised that Jim was still inside the pub, Emma kept watching the doorway, totally unaware that she was also being watched.

By a big, muscular man with pale, cold eyes.

'I want to talk to you, Irene,' David said quietly, as his wife moved from the closed shop into the back parlour. 'I want you to tell me the truth.'

She took in a breath, her face expressive. 'This sounds very serious, my dear.'

'It is,' David replied. 'I was in the back room.

Came home earlier than I thought from the market and I heard you talking to Emma.' He paused, noticing how his wife's face lost colour, her eyes flickering. 'I don't eavesdrop, Irene, it's not my way, but I couldn't help hearing what you two were saying. Emma was talking about some pub, then she mentioned her grandfather – my stepfather – and Frederick.' He said the name as though it made his throat constrict to utter it. 'And from what I heard, it seems that you and my niece have some under-standing, some confidences you share.'

Sighing, Irene sat down in front of the fire, her ankles crossed, her hands on her knee.

'Sit down, David,' she said, smiling dimly. 'Actually I'm glad you overheard the conversation. As Emma said, divided loyalties are very difficult. I didn't want to keep anything from you, my dear, but you would never talk about your half-brother, and Emma needed someone to confide in. She chose me – before she had Jim.'

Shocked by her honesty, David's immediate inclination was to get up and leave the room. The old David Hawksworth would have done; he would have cleared his throat and left, stiff-backed, then gone upstairs and laboured in the workshop under the eaves, brooding, melancholic. For a moment it was all David could do not to fall back into his familiar mode. But he didn't, because he was no longer that man. He had changed over the months. Loved by Irene and by his niece, he had softened and was now prepared to listen. And besides, he had had his suspicions for a while. Had even wanted to ask Emma if she was visiting her father, but had lacked the courage.

'What did Emma tell you when you talked? How cruel I was? How I pretended her father never even existed? That Frederick was dead?'

'No, she never said anything like that. In fact, David, your niece has never said anything bad about you.'

He was humbled by her words and looked away.

'I was ashamed of him. My half-brother was tried and sentenced as a thief. But I see now – I've been thinking about it for a while – that I was unreasonable. Frederick is Emma's father. What right had I to expect her to reject him? Even after what he did.'

'Apparently Frederick has always said he is innocent.'

'He could hardly say anything else, could he?'

'Well, in reality he could,' Irene responded calmly. 'He could have just kept his mouth shut and served his time. Or he could have named the person who did commit the crime.'

'*He* committed the crime; he was tried in a court of law.'

'No, my dear,' Irene said evenly, 'Frederick has told Emma and his solicitor that he's innocent and that he knows who the guilty man is.'

Shocked, David stared at his wife. If Frederick was innocent, his judgement had been grossly unfair. David might love Emma now, but he had treated her coldly when she most needed him. And if Frederick wasn't a thief, he had let his half-brother down badly.

'Who *was* the thief?'

'Frederick won't name him.'

'Why . . .' David stammered, 'why didn't Emma tell me about this?'

'You never asked her,' Irene said, her tone muted. 'How could she talk to you about her father, David? You've never mentioned him to me, and I'm your wife. I wouldn't have known about Frederick unless Emma had told me, or I'd overheard some gossip. In this shop, Frederick Coles doesn't exist and neither does Ernie Coles.' She leaned forward, taking her husband's hand. 'Why are *you* ashamed? You were a boy, Ernie Coles was your stepfather; you didn't choose him, you didn't want him in your life. And you left him behind as soon as you could.'

'You don't know what that man was like,' he said darkly. 'How his image hung over our lives. No one picked on me at school – no one dared. Frederick and me were a thug's kids, Irene, the lowest of the low.'

'But not from *choice*, my dear. It wasn't your choice. It wasn't your fault. And it wasn't Frederick's.'

Overcome, he hung his head.

'When Frederick was arrested, I hated him. My half-brother, my family, *he had let us down*. Just like Ernie Coles had done.' He clung to her hands, desperate to explain. 'So when he was imprisoned, I put him and Ernie Coles out of my mind. If I didn't talk about them, they were dead. They were out of my life, and they became ghosts, nothing else. With

Emma here, I kept up the pretence. I had to, because every time I looked at her, I remembered Frederick. She looks so like him. She *is* so like him.'

'And Emma needs support now – from all of us.'

'But I don't understand what she was saying to you,' David went on. 'What does she think she can do for her father?'

'Save him.'

'I've been so mean-spirited,' David said, his tone disgusted. 'What I must have put her through all these years. I almost forced her into that marriage, you know. I wanted her out of this shop. And I thought it was the right thing for her. A good marriage . . .' He laughed bitterly. 'I told Leonard Hemmings that her father was dead. Emma felt she had no choice but to carry on the lie. So she did – and look what happened. Her husband died, and she came back here.' He bowed his head further, running his hands through his hair. 'What have I done to her? *Jesus, what have I done?*'

'Nothing that can't be undone,' Irene said hurriedly, moved by her husband's distress. 'We can help her now.'

'How?'

'Give her some money.'

Alerted, David looked up. '*Money?* What for?'

'Apparently they're buying information. Paying people for anything they can tell them to help Frederick's case.'

'Buying information . . .' Hurriedly David rose to his feet and went to the safe. Opening it, he rummaged around and then walked back to Irene with a bunch of notes. 'She can have this! All of this! Give it to her, Irene. When she comes home.'

'No, David, *you* give it to her,' Irene said gently. 'You're her uncle, it should come from you.'

He nodded. 'We could raise more money, as much as they need—'

'David,' Irene said, stopping her husband's torrent of words. 'The money is wonderful, my dear, but there's something else that matters even more.'

'What?' he said desperately. 'Tell me, I'll do anything to make this right.'

'Talk to Emma about her father. Listen to her, to what she says about Frederick. Let her bring him into this place, David, bring him to your table, and into your heart. Let your niece return her father to the family and make him real again. Please, sweetheart, let her bring him home.'

Moving without making a sound, surprisingly for such a big man, Ernie Coles walked over the cobbles and then paused behind Emma. She was standing at the corner, only a foot away from the doorway where she had stood the first time she had visited Moss Row. Only that time she had not been seen. This time she was being watched, her stalker only a foot away. Smelling the scent of her warm skin, Ernie Coles stared at the coat Emma was wearing and the thick, wavy hair. She meant nothing to him; he was just curious as to why a young woman who was obviously a stranger would be watching the pub. For a moment he considered walking away, but his curiosity got the better of him, and he moved forward, touching Emma on the shoulder.

Panicked, she spun round, looking up into the cold eyes of Ernie Coles.

'Oh, God . . .'

'Who are yer?'

'I . . . I . . .' she stammered, unable to form a sentence, then she took a breath to continue. 'My name's Emma, Emma Coles. I'm your grand-daughter.'

The news seemed to leave him unmoved. Expression blank, he walked away. But before he had gone many steps, he called over his shoulder, 'Well, come on.'

Warily Emma followed him, the noise of the pub loud to her ears as her grandfather pushed open the doors. Inside, the thick fug of cigarette smoke momentarily blurred the faces of the drinkers, but she could just make out the landlord behind the bar staring as Ernie Coles approached. Leaning across the bar, her grandfather said something inaudible, then the landlord beckoned for him to come through into the back room. Signalling to Emma, Ernie Coles waited for her to enter, then closed the door. Nervously she looked round, at the varnished walls, yellowed with decades of nicotine, the dusty stack of empty bottles under the window, and the couple of faded deckchairs serving as seats.

Lighting up, her grandfather walked over to the window and sat on the ledge, Emma trying not to stare at him, the noise of the drinkers outside coming intermittently as the doors opened and closed from the bar.

'Who did yer say yer were?'

'Your granddaughter,' Emma replied, taking in the size of Ernie Coles's hands and arms, the skin unwrinkled and icily pale. She remembered then what Jim had told her, that her grandfather still exercised at the gym, keeping himself in shape.

'*My granddaughter*,' he said, his bass voice expressionless. 'Yer good-looking, take after yer father. Does he know yer here?'

'No!' she said, shocked. 'No, my father knows nothing about it.'

'So, why *are* yer here?' he asked, the door opening again as the landlord approached. Passing Ernie some money, he gave Emma a quick look, then moved back into the bar. 'I asked yer – why are yer here?'

'To see you.'

'I don't think that's true,' Ernie Coles replied, putting the money into his trouser pocket and then opening a bottle of beer.

'It's true!'

'Yer father didn't want anything to do with me, and I'm his flesh and blood. And he made certain yer didn't come near me. In fact, I'd go so far as to say that yer didn't even know about me – not if yer father had his way.'

'He . . .' She paused, not knowing what to say and intimidated by the man in front of her. Ernie Coles seemed almost angered to see her. 'I need your help.'

454

'*My help?*' he repeated, amused, although his eyes were dead. 'What fer?'

'My father. Your son.'

'He doesn't want to know me.'

'That may be true.'

'So if he doesn't want to know me . . .'

'I do,' Emma said, her voice faltering. She could see some reaction in her grandfather's eyes, some flicker of interest, and pushed on. 'I need to know you, Mr Coles. I need to know you – and I need your help.'

Taken aback, he looked at the young woman in front of him, and remembered his son. At first he had been doubtful that Emma was his granddaughter, but as soon as he had had time to scrutinise her, he could see that she wasn't lying. There was too much of Frederick in her to be a fake. Same fine good looks, same elegance, no slum breeding showing. It was obvious that Netty's genes had travelled down to his granddaughter, because there was nothing of Ernie Coles in her face or her figure. As for her voice – that was pure Frederick. Well-mannered, smooth, polite. And totally out of place in the Acorn.

And what nerve she had, Ernie Coles thought admiringly. What bloody nerve to fetch up and face him. And even if she hadn't intended to do that, she hadn't backed down when he'd confronted her. Hadn't let him frighten her – which was more than most men managed . . . He kept on smoking, not giving her an answer, whilst Emma stood in the middle of the room, silent.

'Yer father hates me, thinks I'm dirt,' he said at last. 'What d'you make of that?'

'I don't know you.'

He gestured around the rank room. 'Well, what d'yer think, hey? Yer like what yer see? Like where I live?'

'I don't . . . I don't know what you want me to say,' she said, fighting to hold her nerve.

'The truth,' Ernie Coles replied. 'Why don't yer tell me the truth? Yer here, yer want something from me, so I want something back. I want the truth.'

'My father's very ill.'

'What's that to me? He never cared if I were alive or dead.'

'You know he's in jail?'

He nodded. 'I know. Thieving.'

'He didn't do it!' Emma said, her courage building. 'My father's innocent and he knows who the guilty person is.'

A quick rapping on the door made Emma turn, her grandfather watching as a slight woman came in. She was very tall, soberly dressed, her age around sixty.

'This is my . . . This is Marianne,' Ernie Coles said, Emma looking at the woman and realising that there was some bond between her and her grandfather. 'She can't talk. Dumb.'

Slowly the woman passed a note to him and then moved silently out of the room. She left behind an odour of camphor. As Ernie Coles gazed at the note in his hand, Emma wondered what she should say next. And where Jim was. She had seen him go into the pub, but not come out. Unless he had left by another exit . . . More and more she was wondering what the hell she was doing. Her hopes for help were laughable, and she was stuck at the Acorn with nowhere to turn.

'So,' he said finally, 'yer were saying?'

'My father's innocent. He knows who did the job at Oldfield Mill.'

'So why didn't he speak up?'

'I don't know,' Emma said honestly. 'He won't tell me who the person is or why he won't name them.'

'So?'

She was wrong-footed, and blundered on blindly. 'I wondered if . . . if you knew.'

Blinking slowly, Ernie Coles fixed his pale eyes on his granddaughter, his expression unfathomable.

'Why would I know?'

'You're supposed to know everything that goes on.'

For the first time, he laughed. 'Well, yer got that right.'

'So, *do* you know?'

'If I did, why should I tell yer?'

'Because Frederick Coles is your son.'

'That doesn't mean anything to me,' Ernie Coles replied indifferently. 'He didn't want to be my son, so maybe now I don't want to be his father.'

'But—'

'Yer very young and very strong-willed,' he said, 'but I'm not about to fall over just because yer here.

No *I'm yer granddaddy, luv*. That's not my way. I've nothing to give yer, nothing to tell yer.'

'But my father—'

'Has made his choice, like we all do in life.'

'But he's suffering for someone else.'

Getting to his feet, Ernie Coles walked over to Emma and looked down at her. 'And have yer never wondered why?'

'I . . . He must have his reasons.'

'Which he won't tell yer.'

'No.'

'Yer loving father, yer wonderful father, is keeping the truth from yer.' His tone became mocking. 'I mean, I can see how much yer love him. But that's just like our Freddie, always popular, always the good guy . . .'

'You make him sound—'

'How?' her grandfather countered. 'Like a fake? Like he's too good to be true? Maybe I am making him sound like that. Maybe I have a *reason* to talk about him like that.'

Emma held her ground. 'What reason?'

'A good reason,' he said, circling Emma slowly. 'A reason yer father might not want yer to know about. So, Granddaughter, I think yer should leave now. If yer father wants to keep quiet, let him.'

'He never stole that money.'

'Maybe not.'

'He's not done anything wrong!'

'Well, that's another matter. A man might be guilty of many things, apart from thieving.'

'I don't believe you! You're just trying to make him look bad,' she snapped, suddenly defiant. 'My father's an honourable man.'

'And if yer leave now, yer can go away thinking that fer the rest of yer life,' Ernie Coles replied, opening the door and looking at her.

To his surprise, Emma slammed the door shut again. Then, more nervously, she turned back to her grandfather.

'Do you know who the guilty man is? If you do, tell me, please. If I can prove my father's innocent, I can get him out of jail. I can make sure he'll recover. He's lost his good name . . .'

'Yer can live well enough without one.'

'*He* can't,' she replied. 'They branded him a thief, gave him eleven years, and he'll never last that long. He's not you, he's not tough enough. If there's anything – *anything* – that will put me on to the guilty person, please tell me.'

'Yer don't want to know.'

'*I have to know!*' she snapped.

'Not unless yer prepared to see what yer father really is.'

Unnerved, Emma stopped short. From the look in Ernie Coles's eyes, he wasn't bluffing. He knew the truth – and in that moment, Emma realised that the truth might not be what she wanted to hear. She had presumed that when they knew who the guilty man was, her father would be exonerated. But suddenly there was a sweaty, queasy feeling in the room, and she was scared. Scared of the truth. Scared of how it might change the way she felt about her father. Scared of what it might do to her long-held, unshakeable trust.

'What do you know?'

'Yer sure yer want the name of the guilty man?'

'Yes, I'm sure.'

'Because once yer've heard the truth, yer can't unhear it,' he explained, his tone steady. 'Means nothing to me, but it will to yer.'

'Just tell me who it is.'

'Adam Hawksworth.'

She reeled back, as though struck. 'Adam Hawksworth?' she repeated dully. 'My uncle's son?'

'Nah. Yer *father's* son.'

For many years afterwards, Emma would remember the sensation inside her head. A buzzing began, then a dull fizzing sound, the room swirling round like water going down a plughole. Shaking, she reached for one of the deckchairs and sat down, her grandfather offering her a sip of beer.

'No . . .'

'Drink it.'

Slowly she did so, then breathed in deeply, the dizziness finally passing.

'Adam Hawksworth is his son?' she said, confused, frowning as she tried to remember Adam's face.

The young man with the good hair and perfect teeth, the sly son of the jeweller. Only he wasn't the jeweller's son at all. Which meant that her father had had an affair with the late Jenny. Got her pregnant and allowed her to pass off his child as David's son. And for years her uncle had been none the wiser. Jenny had known of course – maybe it was part of the reason she had spoiled Adam so much, still in love with Frederick. Or maybe out of guilt, trying to make allowances for her secret by treating the child as special.

'How d'you know?' Emma asked, her voice edgy.

'Like yer said, I know everything that goes on. And people talk. Jenny told someone just before she died. Shame it weren't her husband.' He paused, taking the bottle out of Emma's hand and having a swig of beer himself. 'Poor old David Hawksworth. He were my stepson, yer know. Pompous little fuck, thought he were better than me. Just like yer father. Only Frederick weren't such a good guy, were he? Nah, he slept with his half-brother's wife and let her have his child and palm him off on poor respectable, po-faced David. They were a couple of right losers, those boys. And they looked down their noses at *me*.'

Shaken, Emma stared at her grandfather with loathing. 'Are you sure about Adam? Are you sure he took the money from Oldfield Mill?'

Breathing out, Ernie Coles shook his head, then drained the remainder of the beer.

'Now listen to me, because I'm going to give yer some good advice. Stay out of it.'

'*Stay out of it!*'

'Yeah, stay out of it.'

'But if Adam is guilty . . .'

'And you go to the police, they'll arrest him.'

461

'And free my father.'

'Which they could have done years ago – if yer father had spoken up and named him. Only he didn't fer a reason – *he didn't want to*. He knew Adam Hawksworth were guilty and he took the rap for him – because he was his *son*. It's justice in a way: Frederick finally took some responsibility for the child he allowed another man to raise.'

'I don't understand . . .' Emma said, trying to think clearly. 'I *have* to name him. Adam did it.'

'Nah, yer father doesn't want that, or he'd have done it already. He's chosen to do the time fer his son.'

'But he *won't* serve his sentence!' Emma said defiantly. 'He's too sick. He'll die in there if he has to do another winter.'

'So yer think that exposing what he did – that he slept with his half-brother's wife—'

'But why would he do that?'

'It were a long time ago. I don't know the full story, but I heard things. Seems David Hawksworth's marriage was rocky and your mother . . . sorry to say it, but your mother was a sick woman . . .'

Emma took in a breath.

'. . . I guess your father needed comfort. You were only a little kid then; perhaps he and Jenny Hawksworth needed each other. Pity is, they had a son, who turned out to be a thief. Now,' he said, sighing. 'Yer think that if that comes out it'll help? Nah, best to keep quiet. Yer father knows what he's doing.'

'He's killing himself.'

'So let him!' Ernie Coles replied. 'There's more than one way to lose yer good name. Think what the gossip would be like if the truth got out. Yer can't blow the whistle on yer father. It's not yer life.'

'Why do you hate him so much?' Emma asked bitterly.

'Mind what yer say.'

'Why should you be the only one to speak up? Why shouldn't I say what I think?' she countered, standing up to him. 'You were no father to him or my uncle.'

'They didn't want to know me!'

'And it's obvious why,' she countered. 'But I don't understand how none of this matters to you. Neither of them are bad men. I don't suppose it ever occurred to you how much guilt my father might be feeling. Maybe he covered for Adam not because he was his own son, but because he wanted to pay back a debt to his brother?'

'Yer think what yer like. Yer want to make them heroes, be my guest.'

'They made mistakes, but they tried to make up for them. Look what your son is doing now – dying in jail for his own child. I don't suppose you would have done that, would you? For all your toughness and your reputation, I can't see you being hard enough for that.'

'Fucking hell,' Ernie Coles said, clapping slowly, his big hands making the sound reverberate around the room. 'Yer a fighter, a tough little bugger, aren't

463

yer? If anyone else had said all that to me I'd have flattened them. Be grateful you're my granddaughter. Now, get out.'

'But—'

'*Get out!*' he snapped, Emma backing to the door and then hurrying out through the pub doors.

Once in Moss Row, she began to run. She never wanted to see the place again, or her grandfather. In fact, she was sorry she had ever spoken to Ernie Coles. Sorry she had asked him for help. Because he hadn't given her any. Instead he had ripped her father's image apart, and shaken her to the core. Her father had slept with his brother's wife. They had had a son, and kept his parentage a secret, deceiving everyone for years . . . Still running, Emma thought of Adam, of the greedy, spoiled young man who had never made anything of his life. The same Adam in whose room she had slept for years. The same Adam who came in and out of her uncle's life, disrupting everyone. *That* Adam. Her half-brother. Finally Emma stopped running, her face set. Anger and disappointment threatened to wind her. Her father was a liar, a cheat – and yet he was trying to make up for what he had done. He was giving eleven years of his life to protect his son. *But to what end?* Emma thought distractedly. If Adam was a thief, why protect him? He would only go on to steal elsewhere. What good was her father's sacrifice if Adam didn't appreciate it, or know the reason for it?

And then she realised that there was only one person who could give her the answer. She would have to visit her father and tell him that she knew the truth. Beg him to expose Adam and save himself.

'Emma!'

Turning, she saw Jim running towards her.

'God,' she said, flinging her arms around his neck. 'I'm so glad to see you!'

He was baffled, his expression confused. 'What are you doing here?'

'I followed you. I waited for you to come out of the Acorn, but I didn't see you leave. I was . . . I was talking to my grandfather.'

He paused, holding her at arm's length. 'Did you find anything out?'

'Yes, everything.'

'The name of the guilty man?'

She nodded. 'And why my father kept quiet.'

A silence fell between them, Emma looking into Jim's face expectantly.

'You know, don't you?'

'Yes,' he admitted finally.

'So why did you come to the Acorn if you already knew?' she asked. 'Why come here to see my grandfather?'

'Because I wanted to ask him something,' Jim replied. 'You see, I didn't want you to find out from someone else, and I was ready to pay Ernie Coles to keep quiet. Only you got to him before I did.'

Moved, Emma took his hand.

'But I *had* to find out, Jim. I had to know why my father's still in that jail.'

'Does it change anything?'

She looked into his eyes and then shook her head.

'I wasn't expecting it, but I can understand how it could have happened. My mother was ill for a long time, not really a wife at all. Jenny's marriage wasn't strong; in a way, it was almost inevitable. Who am I to say that it was wrong for them to try and comfort each other?'

'But now you know who the thief is—'

'I still want to get my father out of jail,' Emma said firmly. 'He's not going to die there.'

That Jim would go to such lengths to protect her moved her beyond words. He had been too late, but that didn't matter. He had stood side by side with her, when no one else would have done. And in the end, desperate to protect her from what he knew would hurt her, he had been ready to face Ernie Coles and buy him off. An act that had taken guts, and had proved – without doubt – the strength of his love for her.

FORTY

Coughing, Frederick stood up and walked to the entrance of the visitors' room. Before entering, he smoothed his hair and straightened his back, holding himself erect as he moved over to the bench and sat down. To his surprise, Emma was already there, her expression welcoming, but somehow changed.

'Hello there, love, how are you?'

'I'm fine, Dad, just fine. How are you?'

He paused. The difference in his daughter was subtle, but obvious to him. 'What's the matter?'

'I want you to tell me something. I know I've asked you this before a few times,' she said evenly, 'but I want to ask you again now, for the last time. And I want you to tell me the truth. Who carried out the robbery at Oldfield Mill?'

He paused, glancing away from her and looking at his hands. A minute passed, then another, Frederick praying that his daughter would speak again, but she didn't. Instead she left him hanging, knowing that he had to answer her. And answer her honestly, because she had asked for the truth. His head bowed, Frederick wondered if she knew already.

467

If she was testing him, or hoping that he would tell her another tale. Something more palatable than reality. But as he wondered about lying, he was suddenly tired of pretending. The winter had done more than undermine his health; it had undermined his courage.

And now the only person who had made that sentence endurable was sitting in front of him, asking for the truth. Suddenly it seemed the least he could give her.

'Adam Hawksworth.'

Emma breathed in the name, taking it on board, relieved beyond measure that her father hadn't lied. 'Why did you take the blame for him?'

'Don't you know?'

'Tell me, Dad.'

'He's my son, Emma. I'm sorry, but he is. Jenny and I had an affair.' He dropped his voice. 'What I tell you now, you must never repeat to a living soul.'

'I promise.'

'My half-brother . . . there were problems in his marriage with Jenny. There was some anxiety that David might never be a father. He was a cold man, and embarrassed by his failings. He loved Jenny, but he shut her out, and your mother was so ill . . . I needed someone. Jenny did too.' He hurried on. 'I'm not trying to excuse what we did. But no one would ever have known, if we hadn't had a child.'

'Are you sure that Adam isn't David's son?'

'One hundred per cent sure,' Frederick replied, his tone firm. 'Jenny took the doctor into her confidence and lied to David about the dates. David didn't realise that Adam was born a month early. He always believed he had fathered the child. Jenny didn't love me and I didn't love her. We just needed each other, and when David believed he was going to be a father, Jenny was hopeful that her marriage would get better. Because she loved him. She said that she didn't want to break up her marriage or mine. That it was a mistake and we should go on as if nothing had happened. So we did. Now and again she would get in touch with me, tell me things by letter. But we never met up alone.' He swallowed before continuing. 'David was so pleased to have a son, and Jenny didn't want to take that away from him. It wasn't only that we were hiding what we'd done – what good would it have been to tell my half-brother the truth?' He paused, shaking his head. 'I have no excuses; there *are* no excuses. But I can't let David know the truth. I can't take his son away from him.'

'But Dad—'

'No,' he said firmly. 'I've done some craven things in my life, Emma, but on this I'm adamant. David Hawksworth must always believe that Adam is his child.'

'But Adam is a thief. He let you go to prison for what he did!'

'I don't care.'

'I do!' Emma retaliated. 'If he stole once, he can steal again. He should be stopped.'

'At what cost?' Frederick asked her, his voice

gathering strength. 'At what cost?'

'What about the cost to *you*, Dad? What about the eleven years you're serving for him?'

'He's my son.'

'*I'm your daughter!*' she snapped back. 'Don't I deserve to have you home? Your name cleared? My name cleared?'

'Emma, don't—'

She cut him off.

'All these years I've believed you when you said you were innocent. And now you can prove it, but you won't. Why would it have to come out about Adam being your son?'

He looked at her with disbelief. 'You found out. Of course it would come out, and then think of the gossip.' He paused, staring hard at her. 'How *did* you find out anyway?'

'You don't need to know that.'

'But I do. Considering this is a time for truth, Emma, I want you to tell me how you found out.'

'Your father told me.'

Stunned, Frederick leaned back on the bench, folding his arms. He was obviously shaken, his face ashen, a vein pulsing at his left temple.

'I see . . . Well, I imagine he enjoyed telling you. Bringing me down a peg or two, putting me on his level.'

'Dad,' Emma said softly, 'forget about Ernie Coles. Let's just think about you. You're not well; we have to get you out of here, and now we have the means to do it. Just give the authorities Adam's name and you'll be freed.'

'He's your half-brother.'

'He means nothing to me,' Emma said firmly. 'How could he, when he let you suffer like this?'

'He doesn't know I'm his father.'

'I don't care about that. He's knows you're innocent!' she retorted. 'He knows another man is doing his time.'

Frederick took in a long breath. 'Let me put it another way. If I give Adam up, how will your uncle feel when the truth comes out? David couldn't live through that; you know it and so do I.'

'*You're* living through it.'

'I can. Because I'm doing something right!' he said, his tone angry. 'Because I'm paying my dues. This is the only way I can repay David – by not taking his son away. By not making him look like a cuckolded husband. By not dragging his name through the mud again.' He raked his fingers through his hair. 'Getting me out of jail by exposing Adam won't help me. It wouldn't help anyone.'

'But Adam's a thief.'

'I know! He was always an opportunist. He'd come back to Burnley after another failure and David sent him to me to see if I could fix him up with a job at the mill. I'd been counting the wages and left them out for him to see. I should have been more careful. Jenny wrote to me about Adam whilst he was growing up. How clever he was, how he was going to do so well. Only once did she write something critical

– when she admitted that he had taken money from her purse.' Frederick paused, frowning. 'But I was so busy at the mill that day.'

'Why was Adam there?'

'David had asked me to see if I could find him a job there. He would never have stuck it, of course, but I promised David I'd take him to see Gregory Walmsley and put in a good word. I did what I promised – only it was the day the wages were counted, and I left Adam in the room on his own. And he took the money. I knew it was him straight away. I knew.'

'And he never returned any of it,' Emma said curtly. 'Something that went against you badly at the trial. Adam must have known you'd been found guilty of the crime.'

'Not at first. Adam left the north again after he took the money. He was always moving from place to place. And he didn't come back, or have any contact with his father, for over a year. When he *did* come back, I don't suppose David told him about my being jailed. And knowing Adam, he wouldn't have asked about it. He would have been too pleased to have got away with it. If he found out later, he'd have been too craven to own up.' Frederick shrugged. 'That's the way his mind works. After something happens, he moves on.'

'Which was more than you did.'

'I understand why you're bitter,' Frederick said, trying to console his daughter. 'I know what all this about Adam being your brother means.'

'No, Dad, you *don't* understand,' she replied. 'It's not that you had an affair, or even that you passed off your child as another man's son. I can understand that, in a way. It's the fact that you're letting your life pass by in this place. It's like you've got the key in your hand, but you won't put it in that lock and turn it. You could be free.'

'I could,' he agreed. 'But the price is too high, Emma. Promise me you'll never expose Adam.'

'Dad—'

'*Promise me!*' Frederick pleaded, his expression desperate. 'This isn't a choice for you or anyone else to make. It's *my* choice. I want to do this because it wipes my conscience clean. It pays off my debt to my brother.'

'And if you died in here, would that be enough for you?' she asked, her tone wavering. 'Well, I love you too much to watch it happen, Dad. I can't come here every week and see you get worse and worse, knowing that Adam Hawksworth is a free man.' She stood up to go. 'I understand why, but I can't condone it. You may be able to stand your punishment, but I can't. I *can't* watch you commit suicide.'

Without another word, Emma pushed back her seat and hurried out, leaving her father staring after her. And behind him, the prison clock ticked the moment away.

FORTY-ONE

Wearily, the Governor beckoned for Jim to enter his office. He did not offer him a seat. Instead he stared at Jim's file, read it again, together with the recently added notes, and sighed expansively. It was an insincere sound, one that was supposed to convey sorrow, but that came over more as exasperation.

'You remember our last conversation?'

Jim nodded, holding his uniform hat in his hand, wondering what was coming next but knowing full well what it was. He had been seen deliberately ignoring the Governor's wishes. God knew who had spied on him this time, Jim thought, and it didn't even matter any more. It could be Stan Thorpe, and if the Governor thought to reinstate that bastard for betraying a colleague, so be it. Maybe he was in the wrong job after all. Despite his external composure, Jim's heart was speeding up and he could feel the pulse in his neck. Get on with it, he willed the Governor, but the man was taking his time.

In fact he took another minute before continuing, during which time Jim stood in the middle of his office with his guard's hat still in his hands.

'So you remember what we spoke about?'

'Yes, sir.'

'And you haven't had a brain injury in the last week?' the Governor said sarcastically. 'Some accident that I don't know about. Some terrible attack that wiped your memory.'

'No, sir.'

'So it's working?'

'Yes, sir,' Jim said, his tone even although he was being baited and the suspense was terrible.

'No excuse, then?' the Governor went on. 'No excuse for you to say that you don't remember or understand.' He stared at Jim's file again. 'I mean, you're an intelligent man. You studied hard to get into the prison service; this was a career you wanted. So why throw it away?'

Jim said nothing, just prayed that he was about to be given another warning. But he knew he wasn't. He knew he had gambled and lost. He had put Emma before his career, and although he had thought the choice had been relatively easy, he was uncertain facing the Governor's stolid anger.

'Have you got nothing to say for yourself? You were seen again, doing exactly what I told you not to. You can't say you weren't warned, Caird. I just want to know why you didn't stop.'

'I couldn't, sir.'

Unmoved, the Governor sat down, staring at him. 'I hope it was worth it.'

Silent, Jim waited for the next words.

'You're fired.'

'Jesus.'

'I warned you. You knew what would happen if you went on with this. I can't have my staff running around making me – and the prison – look bad. You want to be a hero, do it on your own time.'

'But this job is everything to me!'

'Correction, this job *was* everything to you,' the Governor replied coldly. 'Now your loyalties are elsewhere. You're caught up with Frederick Coles and his daughter and some daft scheme to prove he's innocent. Which, believe me, he is not. I thought you were smart enough not to fall for that line, Caird. Every prisoner in this place would have you believe he's innocent. The pity is that you're involved with Coles's daughter, otherwise you might just have dismissed his claims with all the others.'

'Unless they're true.'

Sighing irritably, the Governor closed Jim's file on the desk in front of him. 'Stubborn to a fault. Pity you didn't put all that effort into your job.'

'I did a good job here,' Jim said, his caution leaving him. 'You have no reason to fire me. What I did *was* on my own time, for my own reasons.'

'Which had more to do with the prisoner's daughter than the prisoner's good name.'

Enraged, Jim threw his hat on to the Governor's desk, his expression defiant.

'You're wrong. I would have done the same for any man. After all, that's the point of justice, isn't it? That the guilty are punished, the innocent exonerated? Or at least that's what I thought.' He turned to the door,

476

then turned back. 'You know, I thought this job was everything to me. But now, frankly, you can keep it, *sir*.'

Standing on Holland Street, Tommy Caird watched the door of the jeweller's shop, then the corner, waiting for Jim to come into sight. He knew that his brother was going to meet up with Emma, but he wanted to catch him first. Furiously, Tommy lit up a cigarette and inhaled greedily. His rage was out of bounds, he knew it, but he couldn't stop himself. He had been at work and someone had mentioned a rumour doing the rounds that his brother had been laid off at the prison. One of his work colleagues had an uncle working at the jail, and he had passed on the news.

Never, Tommy had said. *It's his life. He was home last night and didn't say a thing. Laid off? Who lays off guards at the Moors Prison?*

But then he had remembered Jim leaving home that morning, very early, and when he had looked out of the window, his brother hadn't been wearing his uniform. So now he was waiting for Jim, waiting to confront him, angry as hell. Another few minutes passed, then Jim finally appeared round the corner, Tommy catching up with him and grabbing his arm.

'You were fired, weren't you?'

Annoyed, Jim shook him off. They had made up after their previous argument, and he was surprised to see Tommy so angry again.

'What's it got to do with you?'

'*It's your bloody career!* The thing that mattered to you so much. I can remember how you used to swot for those bleeding exams, tell everyone what you were going to do. I was proud of you – we all were. None of us would have worked that hard, or managed to get the qualifications. We used to brag about you, how you'd done so well, and now you've let it all go.'

Infuriated, Jim faced his younger brother. 'This has got nothing to do with you.'

'It has everything to do with me!' Tommy snapped back, a couple of people staring at them as they passed. 'I helped you. I went around trying to find things out – but then you had to take over. And after you'd been warned off at work. You knew it was stupid, but you went on.'

'It was my choice.'

'What bloody choice!' Tommy said, disappointed as he looked at his fallen idol. 'To lose everything for Emma Coles, just to prove her father innocent? I told you to stop. I warned you.'

'Yeah, well, everyone warned me.'

'But you would go on, wouldn't you? And now what? You'll end up like the rest of us, working at the bloody mill or something similar. I admired you,' Tommy said, his tone bitter. 'I looked up to you, wanted to be like you – and now I'm ashamed of you.'

Grabbing his brother's arm, Jim looked into his face, his expression hard.

'You're ashamed of me? You think I did the wrong

thing? Because I stood up for the woman I love, and for what I believe? Because I stood up for an innocent man?'

'You don't know that!'

'I do now!' Jim hurled back.

Stunned, Tommy stopped his tirade, breathing heavily. 'You know who really did the robbery?'

'Yes.'

'So you'll go to the authorities, get Frederick Coles out of jail?'

'No, I can't.'

'You can't? Why not?'

'He doesn't want the person to be named.'

'Oh, that's bloody great!' Tommy replied, incensed. 'So you go to all this trouble and lose your job, but *he* doesn't want to do anything about it. He's going to let you make a sacrifice like that, for nothing?'

'It's not for nothing.'

But Tommy wasn't listening. 'You've ruined your career, your bloody life!'

'I made a choice to honour his decision.'

'And who made that honourable choice for you?' Tommy countered defiantly. 'You're blinded by that woman, besotted by her. You'd do anything for her – but what has she done for you?'

'Loved me!'

Exasperated, Tommy stared hard into his brother's face. 'You bloody idiot! I thought you had more about you.'

'And I thought the same of you,' Jim replied, his

tone warning. 'You judge me and think I've been a fool? Well, *you're* the fool, because you can't see what really matters in life. I did all this for Emma, because I love her, and because loving her is more important than anything – even the job. I got fired because I didn't back down. Because I didn't give in and tell the Governor the truth. I could have,' he said bitterly, 'but I didn't. Because I have to live with what I do, and come to terms with my own conscience. And breaking another man's confidence to keep my job wasn't a good enough reason to lose my own self-respect.' Shaking his head, he looked at Tommy with disbelief. 'Yes, it hurts. I loved that job, and I worked bloody hard for it. I was proud of it, but I let it go – and so should you. You can despise me all you want, go ahead, hate me. I fell off my pedestal; well, that's tough, I'm human. But in the end, whatever you think, I have to live with myself – and what *I* think is more important.'

Resigned, he walked away, entering the jeweller's shop, the door closing softly behind him.

'You lost your job?' Emma asked, legs giving way. Sitting down, she stared at the wooden floor of the jeweller's shop. 'God, I'm so sorry.'

'It's OK,' he said, trying to sound calm. 'It's fine.'

Her sorrow for Jim was intense, her frustration intolerable. In fact, she even wondered *why* she had been so determined to find her father innocent. Looking back, it seemed clear to her that Frederick had made his decision long ago, and would never have changed his mind. But she had persisted, drawing Jim into her vendetta – and now she had ruined his career. *For nothing*. Knowing who the guilty man was had been a pyrrhic victory. Because it would never come out. She had blundered on, terrified that her father would die in jail, but when it came down to it, when she was given the means to get him released, he had blocked it. And Jim had paid the price.

Hopeless, Emma put her head in her hands. It wasn't fair that Jim had been punished, it just wasn't fair. And it was all her fault. He had loved his work, but she had inadvertently taken it away from him. Fired, the damning decision would go on his record, and make sure that no prison would hire him again. In return for everything that Jim Caird had done for her, she had succeeded in hobbling him. By loving her and wanting to help her, he had lost his status, his future. For what? For her. And it wasn't enough. *She* wasn't enough. She hadn't been for Ricky, or Leonard, and she wasn't enough for Jim Caird . . .

Slowly Emma glanced up at him. He smiled, but she didn't react. How long before he hates me? she thought. How long after he's started work in the mill or the factory will he look at me and blame me? How long can he love me when it cost him so much?

'Emma, don't worry.'

'*Don't worry*. How can I not worry? You lost your job because of me.'

'I chose to get involved. You didn't hold a gun to my head.'

'I didn't stop you. And now you've been fired.'

'I can get another job.'

'But not the one you want,' she replied, wrapping her arms around her body as though she was cold to the bone. 'This would have been almost bearable if we'd succeeded. If we could have got my father out. But to be stuck in no-man's-land, knowing what we know and not being able to use it . . . God, Jim, what was the point? I ruined your life for nothing.'

'You didn't ruin it,' he said quietly, putting his arms around her. 'You're not going anywhere, are you?'

She clung to him tightly. 'I'd never leave you. But it's not fair, Jim. It's not fair. It's cost too much and I'm so sorry. I'm so sorry for what I've done to you.'

'Ssh!' he said, soothing her. 'It's all right, I can adjust. It will be fine, honestly, Emma, it will be fine.'

But as he said the words, he knew he was lying. That inside, something had been crushed by his losing his job. His love for Emma had not been shaken, but he felt diminished, and somehow a smaller man.

FORTY-TWO

Unable to sleep, Emma turned over in bed, then opened her eyes. The first thing she saw was the pair of football boots Adam had worn as a boy. The boots she had never taken down from the back of the door, because somehow the room had always belonged to him in part. Even though she had changed the eiderdown and the curtains, the boots had stayed. She stared at them now, thought about her half-brother. She remembered his face and wondered why there was nothing of her father in him, then realised that they were alike in their build, and the shape of their heads. Turning over again, Emma looked around the room she had lived in for so long as the jeweller's niece. When she had been going out with Ricky Holmes; before she married; and when she came back, in those terrible months after the death of Leonard. And she remembered how many times she had imagined her father's release, his triumphant return.

Which would never happen . . . Emma had no anger with regard to his affair with Jenny. The result had been so devastating, she could only too easily imagine how difficult it would have been for both parties. And somehow a passion from so long ago, which had gone so horribly wrong, deserved pity rather than condemnation. She could also understand why her father would not speak. Instead he would tell her to get on with her life; insist that she concentrate on her own existence and be happy with Jim – even though the shock of Jim's dismissal would be another blow to him.

Her stubbornness had ruined so much, for so many people, Emma thought. And yet something inside her *couldn't* let go. Still staring at the walls, she thought back, trying to imagine her father's and her uncle's lives with Ernie Coles. They would have been known everywhere, pointed out, a villain's kids. Because they had both left home as soon as it was possible, it was evident that there had been little love there, and after meeting her grandfather, she could see why. A brutish man, violence in every inch of his body, he would have hung over the family like a threat. Suffocating his sons, he would have held up a mirror to them: *This is me, my life, this is how you get respect. My way.*

But both of them had been better men and got out. They had tried – in their own ways – to make the best of their lives and put their history behind them. They had fought to be respectable, normal, living decent lives. One as an accounts clerk, one as a jeweller. Nothing to make the world spin faster, or the moon turn black. Just simple lives, good lives – which was a miracle, considering where they had come from. No taking the easy route for David or Frederick, no following in Ernie Coles's brutal wake . . . Emma sighed. What if they had had a different father? A man who had encouraged them? David would have become a teacher and flourished, not always fighting with his past, terrified that people would judge him because of where he had come from. And her father, what would he have been? Probably very much as he had turned out. But as a fully qualified accountant, with his own small business. Dapper, elegant and charming, he would have bestrode his world like a paper Colossus, never worrying that his daughter would be tainted by his blood or be hidden from her own grandfather.

Emma knew that Ernie Coles wasn't totally responsible for the way his offspring had turned out. But the fact that he had watched them, known about their lives, monitored their existences from a distance gave her an idea. A glimmer of hope. It was true that he had talked about his son being in jail with all the passion of someone ordering a pint of beer. He had known that Frederick was innocent, but had let it go. Indifferent, cold, hard as bone. *But not completely*. Ernie Coles would never have bothered to follow their lives unless he had had *some* interest.

Getting to her feet, Emma washed and dressed hurriedly, taking care not to wake Irene and David. Then she picked up her bag, and to her surprise, found a note in it. The handwriting was David's.

Dear Emma,

Irene and I have talked and I now under-stand the situation with you and your father. My half-brother, Frederick. I can't apologise enough for causing you so much distress over the years – I had my reasons, but I see now that they weren't good enough.

So please accept this to assist you in any way you see fit.

With kindness,
David

Touched, Emma looked into the envelope and drew out a small wad of notes. Hurriedly she tucked them into her bag and left the house, walking through streets that were just coming into dawn. All the mill workers were stirring, many on their way to work, most of the women wrapped in shawls as they hurried through the foggy morning. Pulling up her coat collar, Emma waited in the cold, finally catching the tram to Oldham. Calmly she sat in her seat as it stopped and started, crawling its long journey towards the mill town. At last, a while later, she got off at Oldham Mumps, turning her steps towards the rougher side of town.

Only this time she wasn't afraid. Slowly she moved towards Moss Row, hesitating for just a moment before she walked into the passageway. Once inside, she could see the pub sign in the fog, which was beginning to clear, the huge gold acorn catching the light from an upstairs room. Determined, she walked over to the pub, then pushed open the doors.

'We're closed!' a man barked, looking her up and down as a tall, thin woman appeared behind him. 'Remember this one, Marianne?'

The woman nodded, then walked into the back room, closing the door for an instant. Whilst the landlord leaned on the counter and watched her, Emma stood in the middle of the pub, the smell of beer and cigarettes coming stale on the early morning air. After another few moments the door opened again, the thin woman appearing once more and signalling hurriedly for Emma to follow her. She didn't hesitate, walking through the bar into the room she had visited before. Left alone, she had to wait for another few minutes before she heard heavy footsteps coming down the stairs.

He opened the door wearing just his trousers and a vest, his bull neck bare, his ham hands rolling a cigarette.

'Yer back,' he said simply, turning to the woman behind him. 'I want to talk to my granddaughter alone.'

She nodded, then left the room.

Although Emma was wearing a coat, she was cold in the damp room. Ernie Coles moved over to the fireplace and kicked some papers out of the grate. Throwing a bit of kindling on a few pieces of coal, he held his cigarette to a spill of paper and watched the fire catch. It smoked in the small room, then flames slowly began to smoulder.

'What d'yer want?'

Emma shrugged. 'I don't know.'

He laughed, rubbing the back of his neck as he sat down on the windowsill. 'Yer not like yer father and that's a fact. Yer more like me, got some guts.'

'I spoke to my father,' Emma began. 'I told him what you'd told me.'

'What did he say?'

'You were right.'

'So?'

'He won't name his son as the thief.'

'Bye, then,' Ernie Coles said, standing up.

At once, Emma moved towards him. 'Is that it? You can't just brush me off. You've got to do something.'

'I have?'

'You could help my father. I know you could. You know everything that goes on; you must know something that would help him.'

'I've told yer what I know.'

'He's your son!'

'Fucking hell!' Ernie Coles said furiously. 'I get wakened fer this? Yer a bloody nuisance, that's what yer are. I'm getting older, getting to need my sleep more.'

'Your son won't have the chance to get to your age. Not if he stays in that prison.' Emma paused, trying to control her frustration. 'He's not like you. You said it yourself, and you're right. My father can't take it. Is that what you wanted to hear? *He can't take it.* He's not tough. He tried, but he can't do the time.' She stared at her grandfather imploringly. 'And he'll give up now. Now that I know the truth and he can't pretend, can't treat me like a child and jolly me along with talk of appeals and new evidence.'

'He's made his choice.'

'He can't do it!' Emma said, her voice falling. 'I – we – have to get him out of there. You should see him, wasting away.'

'And what can I do about it?'

'You must know something!'

'I'm not a fucking magician!' he snapped, throwing his cigarette stub into the fire.

'You owe him something.'

Her grandfather was shaken by the remark. '*What?*'

'You weren't a good father – to him, or my uncle.' She was afraid, but carried on; it was too late to turn back. 'You didn't give them anything. They were afraid of you, ashamed of you. I'm not saying it was all your fault, but my father is your son. Your son. I know that means something to you, I *know* it does.'

'Get out of here,' he said wearily.

'No,' Emma replied. 'I can't. Your son needed you when he was a child, but you weren't there. He needed you when he was older, but you weren't interested.'

'I weren't good enough for him!' he shouted. 'He made that fucking clear.'

'He wasn't like you! He couldn't live your life, couldn't follow in your footsteps.'

'I gathered that pretty soon,' her grandfather replied, his tone resigned. 'It weren't that good a life anyway. Yer father were probably better off. Look round yer – do I look like I've made a success? I've got a reputation – no one will take me on – but bugger all else.' He spat into the grate, the fire hissing momentarily. 'I can't stop, even if I wanted to. Can't show weakness. I have to be this person, because that's all I am – a hard case. Frankly, I could do with a rest. Do with some peace myself.' He leaned back on the windowsill, folding his brawny arms. 'I don't know what yer want from me. I don't have anything.'

'You have a son,' Emma said quietly.

Laughing, he turned his cold eyes on her. 'I wish I'd had a son like yer. I could have done with a boy like yer.'

'I could have done with a grandfather, and your son could have done with a father.'

'Yer don't care what yer say, do yer?'

'No, not any more,' she admitted bluntly. 'You see, I've ruined everything by trying to make it all work out – when some things *can't* be worked out. I didn't know what the background was, so I just blundered on. And now my father has had to confess to something I'm sure he would rather I hadn't known, and my fiancé has lost his job because of me.' She paused, holding his gaze. 'I have to make it right. And *you* have to make it right.'

Shaking his head, Ernie Coles sighed.

'I don't have a conscience.'

'Yes, you do,' Emma replied. 'You just won't let it catch up with you. But it will, one day. One day you'll have to look at what you are and what you've done. Just as I've had to. You'll have to see yourself as you really are – and then you'll have a conscience, because you'll *remember*.' She turned to the door, then turned back to face him. 'Why are you like this?'

'Because it works fer me,' he said simply.

'People fear you.'

'They do,' he agreed, his tone altering as he turned away from Emma and looked out of the window. 'Yer shouldn't have come. And yer shouldn't have said those things.'

'I'm not going to say sorry.'

'Yer right, yer see. People *are* shit-scared of me. But not yer. And before long, more people will come along who won't find me that frightening. Because I'm getting old, and I can't fight that. Age will have the last laugh on me. I can go to the Black Knight and work out, I can walk around relying on my reputation to keep me going – but I know one day it'll not be enough. Someone will do fer me. Some hard sod like I were – keen to make a reputation.'

Surprised, Emma kept silent as he continued to talk.

'I've a respect fer yer, because of yer nerve. So I'll tell yer something I've told no one else. Seeing as how yer blood and all. I'm ill, not dying, but I've got a wasting disease. Something that affects my muscles.' Incongruously he laughed, turning back to her. 'What I am now – scary, big – I won't be in a while. In a few years, I'll not be able to keep my place at the top of the midden. The old bull will get pulled down by the pack of dogs who've been waiting for a long time to see me show weakness.'

'I'm sorry.'

'I'm tired,' he said bluntly. 'Now, laugh at that. I'm tired, and way past being a good man. I couldn't change if I wanted to.'

'I think you could do anything you wanted to.'

'I could do with a rest . . .'

She kept staring at him.

'Go somewhere out of the way. Off the streets . . .'

There was a moment of understanding between them.

'But what about Adam Hawksworth?' Emma asked, her voice hardly audible. 'He's a thief. He must have known that my father was in jail for what he did.'

'Adam Hawksworth's a bad lot. A craven, sly type. No guts. If he gave it a second's thought, he'd just have been glad that Frederick didn't give him away.'

'And never wondered why?'

Ernie shrugged his thick shoulders. 'How do I bleeding know? Men do worse all the time and live with it.'

It wasn't enough for Emma. 'But why should Adam get away with what he did?'

'Don't worry about him,' her grandfather said, his tone warning. 'I'll have a word with Adam Hawksworth. When I've done that, he won't come back to the north. And he won't dare steal again, because he'll know I'll find out and come after him.' Ernie Coles paused. 'People are very afraid of me.'

'You're a hard man.'

He nodded. 'Yeah.' Slowly he turned back to the window. 'I'm a bleeding miracle. No one's beaten me; no one dared try. I've held on to my power for decades – but that's cost me. Might not mean much to you, or to my son and stepson, but to me it's been everything.' He turned back to Emma, his back straight, his expression formidable. 'I want people to remember me like I am now – a fucking legend. And if I play my cards right, I can *stay* a legend.'

He stared at her, held her gaze, his eyes unreadable, cold as a winter moon. And Emma knew that something momentous was going to happen. Something good was going to come out of the gloomy, sleazy Acorn pub. Something noble from the most ignoble and immoral of men.

FORTY-THREE

'Oh, dear God!' Florence Palmer said, hurrying in and throwing the evening paper at her husband. 'Look at that headline – FREDERICK COLES IS INNOCENT.'

Snatching up the paper, he read it aloud: '*Frederick Coles is to be released from the Moors Prison, having been wrongly convicted of the theft at Oldfield Mill over four years ago. Another man – as yet to be named – has been charged with the crime* . . . Good God, Emma always said he hadn't done it.'

'Of course I always knew Frederick Coles was innocent. I told you the same, Harold, if you remember,' Florence went on. 'How nice for Emma. She can get married now and not feel ashamed of her father. Pity that her fiancé lost his job, but there you are, nothing's perfect.' She dropped her voice conspiratorially. 'Mind you, I'd like to see David Hawksworth's face. Him being so down on his poor brother all these years, he'll have to sing a different tune now.'

David *was* singing a different tune; he was smiling and kissing Irene on the cheek, both of them reading and re-reading the headline. They had known about it before the paper came out, of course, but had kept quiet, not wanting to tempt fate. To jeopardise anything at the last moment. Instead they had kept their counsel, and when Emma had informed them that another man was going to be charged, her uncle had pressed her for his name. When she told him that Ernie Coles was being put on trial for the theft at Oakfield Mill, David had faltered, sitting down heavily and shaking his head.

'*He* did it?' David said, his tone unusually vehement. 'I hope he rots in hell. He deserves it.'

Emma didn't contradict him. She never would – even though she was the only one who knew the truth. Ernie Coles had made a deal with her. He would take the blame for the crime. It would suit him to be thought a bastard, suit his reputation as a hard man. He didn't care what anyone thought of him, just knew that he would be jailed for a very long time. That was fine by Ernie Coles, because in a few years he would be a changed man. His strength would be failing, his reign under threat. And as he grew steadily worse, he would become vulnerable, ready to be picked off by stronger rivals. *But in jail, he would be out of harm's way.* He would still be someone, and live off past glories.

Inside, he was safe. Outside, one day or one night, he would have been torn apart.

Emma knew that after Ernie had talked to Adam, she would never see her half-brother again. He would never steal again either. Because although he would know that Ernie Coles had been jailed, he would also know that Ernie had people on the out-side, watching. Besides, Adam was a coward. Often Emma wondered about that meeting. Wondered how Adam Hawksworth had taken the news that he was related by blood to Ernie Coles . . . She took in a deep breath, thinking of everything she had learned, and knowing that she would never tell her uncle that Adam was not his son.

Never was a long time, Emma knew, but never was short enough for secrets.

When Ernie Coles was arrested and charged, Jim was called back to the Moors Prison, where an acutely embarrassed Governor told him that he would be reinstated, his job secure. After all, the Governor said, Jim had helped to prove that Frederick Coles was innocent. It showed that the justice system worked and that everyone could get a second chance. In fact, he went on, everyone owed Jim a debt of gratitude for his efforts. The Governor smiled, with gritted teeth, and said that the governing body of the prison would like to extend their thanks for his endeavours, above and beyond the call of duty.

He would personally also like to apologise for any misunderstanding.

'Apology accepted, sir.'

'Good,' the Governor said drily. 'Enjoy your time as a hero, Caird, but don't make a habit of it.'

'As if I would, sir,' Jim replied. 'As if I would.'

FORTY-FOUR

She was standing waiting by the Moors Prison. Overhead a few birds flew cawing into the sky, Emma's gaze never leaving the prison gates. From inside she could hear the familiar noises: the clatter of food trays, the slamming of doors and the echoing vastness of tiled walls and iron railings. Then she heard the sound she had been waiting for, the unlocking of the side gate. Holding her breath, she stared at the exit. Slowly, a man came out into the morning light. He was walking unsteadily, as though the fresh air and daylight was overwhelming, but when he saw her, he smiled and held out his arms.

And she ran to him, as she had done so many times before, in childhood, when she was a girl, running down alleyways to meet him when he came home from Oldfield Mill. She ran to him and held him without being told to stand back, to keep her distance, because they were out of the prison now, and Frederick Coles was a free man. His place had been taken by someone else. Someone who was also innocent. Of the robbery at Oldfield Mill, anyway.

Linking arms with her father, Emma walked down

the road towards the bus stop. She wanted to shout out to everyone: *This is my dad, he's a free man. He was never a thief.* But she didn't say anything. Because the sky said it, the air said it, the fact that her father could walk down a road, light a cigarette, buy a paper, *they* said it. Said that Frederick Coles was back in the world. Where he belonged. In the place his daughter had kept safe for him.

I visited my grandfather in the Moors Prison regularly. I know he liked to see me, although he would never admit it. That would have been too much like showing affection. But, God bless him, he proved how tough he really was. It takes a hard man to do time, they say. Well, it takes a harder man to do someone else's time. He got fifteen years, because of the way he had let my father take the blame at first – before Ernie's apparent confession and change of heart. I have to say that my grandfather was very convincing in court. Using his contacts, he made up a plausible story about how he had been waiting for an opportunity to steal the wages at the mill. And with his son working there, he had taken a God-given opportunity – and had a ready-made scapegoat.

With his reputation, he was believed. People around Burnley said that he was a bastard and that he'd got what had been coming to him for years. Fancy, some said, letting your own son take the blame for what you'd done . . . Ernie Coles laughed at that. He was a hard case again, a villain, the worst of the worst. Everyone was talking about him;

everyone was scared of him. Just how he liked it.

My adored Jim: how I loved him then, and love him more as each day passes. He had proved himself and his love, and has never given me reason to doubt it in all the years we have been together. We had two children, both girls, and neither of them a bit like me. Which Jim said was a relief, as he could only take so much. And eventually we took over the jeweller's shop. I ran it, whilst Jim continued at the prison, finally becoming head warder.

I never did see Adam Hawksworth again. No one did.

Bessie and Doug had four girls, and inherited the cobbler's when Mr Letski died, at the age of ninety-seven. Mad as a rat, shooting at the pigeons on the church roof with an air gun. As for Irene and David, they grew closer with every year, my uncle keeping his word and opening his home – and his heart – to Frederick. At one point I thought my father might marry again, but he didn't, and he died only six years after he was released. But it was six years in the open, six years with his good name restored. I hope it was enough.

As I grew older, I remembered Ricky Holmes, who had never aged in my memory, and was always that handsome young man who had rubbed noses with me. I still miss him. And I think of my first husband. Poor Leonard. I had not meant to deceive him, and his death fell like a shade over the early years of my life. But when I had been settled with Jim for a while, and had two girls to replace the baby I lost,

Leonard's memory stopped being so fearful for me. I think he, of all people, would have understood what I did. I was very young, and very traumatised by circumstances and by Ricky's terrible death. I had wanted to be rescued. Leonard was the perfect knight, and I was the perfect lost soul.

But we grow and we learn, and we stand up for ourselves and, if we are wise, for our mistakes. And now, if I had the chance to change anything in my history, I would not. Each one of us goes our own route. Sometimes in the dark, sometimes in sunlight so bright it blinds us. But if we stay with what we believe, we eventually come home.

And if we are lucky, we take those we love with us.